I0637924

The Mad Voyage

of

Prince Malock

Book One in the Prince Malock World

by Timothy L. Cerepaka

An Annulus Publishing Book
Annulus Publishing, Cherokee, Texas, 2014

Published by Annulus Publishing
Copyright © 2014 Timothy L. Cerepaka. All rights reserved.
ISBN-13: 978-0692246146
ISBN-10: 0692246142
Cover by Elaina Lee of For the Muse Design
(http://www.forthemusdesign.com)
Contact: timothy@timothylcerepaka.com
This book, including all its parts, is protected by copyright and must
not be copied, resold or shared without the permission of the author.

Acknowledgments

I want to thank my uncle, James Wilhite, for his help in preparing this manuscript for publication. I would also like to thank the rest of my family for supporting me while I wrote this novel. You guys rock.

Chapter One

EVERY WINTER, FOR ABOUT two or three months, the island of Destan—a small island located south of the much larger Northern Isles, home to a few hundred people, mostly human, with a tiny minority of amphibious aquarians who lived just off the island's shore—was beset by the wrath of Kano. The waves of the Crystal Sea would rise to a height of at least 200 feet (in some cases even larger) and the incessant rain would be enough to drown even an aquarian.

During this time, travel by sea was nigh impossible. Fishermen from the Northern Isles didn't come down to fish and even pirates refused to come down this way during 'murder season,' as it was called, mostly because it seemed like the ocean was trying to murder everyone who dared sail upon its waves.

Most Destanians knew what to do during this time of year. They lashed their boats to their docks or brought them further inland so they wouldn't be swept off into the depths of the ocean, never to be seen again; brought in or tied down any other physical possessions they usually kept outside, and stayed inside their homes almost all day every day. Worship services at the Temple of Kano were often put on hold during this time, which Kinker Dolan, an old fisherman who had spent his entire life on Destan, found rather amusing.

No sane person would ever go out onto the Crystal Sea at this point, especially in a tiny little fishing boat that could be capsized easily. Even large ships rarely strayed into the area at this point. Once, five or six years ago, Kinker remembered seeing an entire fleet of massive battleships from the island of Nikos sink, their entire crews drowning in the terrible ocean. It was a chilling sight, especially the next day, when some of their corpses washed up on shore half-naked and covered in seaweed.

It was an image that stood out in his mind as he rowed his tiny fishing boat, creaking and groaning, out into the darkness of the night. His old bones ached and moaned every time he was splashed with the cold water of the ocean, which was to say they ached and moaned all the time.

Kinker ignored his bones. This was the only chance he had of getting off Destan without the Priestly Guard noticing. It was not ideal weather, to be sure (his beard was soaked through and the rowboat's bottom was already filling with water, which he couldn't scoop out right now), but that was exactly why he had chosen this night to make his great escape. Not even the Priestly Guard, with their magic, would dare set sail on these deadly waters at this time of night, not even to capture someone who knew all their darkest secrets.

The only problem was that Kinker had no idea where he was going. He had forgotten his compass back home and the endless rain, the gigantic waves, and the blackness of the night made it impossible to tell where he was or where he was going. He could not even be certain how far he was from Destan, because the sound of the ocean waves crashing against the island's shores was obscured by the rain and lightning that shook the sky.

In addition, Kinker's stomach kept doing back flips every time the ocean waves raised his tiny boat and tossed it. His boat was tossed around so much that Kinker felt like he was a tiny ball being thrown around by a bunch of young, easily-distracted children who were not careful with their toys. He had faith he would survive, however; because before he left Destan he had made a sacrifice to Kano, the Goddess of the Sea, asking her to protect him and get him to where he needed to go.

Not that he had much time to think or remember what he'd done before he left. He was thrown about once more, this time so violently that both of the oars on his rowboat snapped off and disappeared into the rain and waves. That meant Kinker was totally at the mercy of the sea now.

He gripped the bulwarks of his boat as it rocked back and forth, somehow managing to stay upright despite the weather. His fingers grasped the sides of the boat with a steel grip, but he was all too aware that his capsizing was a when, not an if, and that it would not be long before he found himself sleeping on the bottom of the ocean.

A flash of light disturbed these thoughts, causing Kinker to look up in surprise. He at first thought that his old eyes—which were getting worse every day—were playing tricks on him, but through the wind, rain, and darkness, he spotted what looked like a line of lights not too far from where he was. His first thought was that the lights belonged to the spirits of those who had died at sea, said to travel the Crystal Sea's surface, only appearing to sailors, fishermen, and others when death was at hand.

Then a flash of lightning briefly illuminated the entire area, revealing that the row of lights were not spirits at all but rather lights shining from the side of a large ship.

That wasn't the only thing the lightning revealed, however. It also revealed a gigantic wave—much larger than any that Kinker had ever seen in his entire life—on his port.

Kinker had only a few seconds to register that fact before the wave crashed down on him with the force of thousands of pounds of water, smashing his rowboat into splinters and knocking him out instantly.

Dying at sea was not as painful a death as one might think. Kinker had spent his whole life on or near the Crystal Sea. He had become a fisherman, following in the footsteps of his father and grandfather before him, and had always been aware that the sea was not your friend. Even though he had devoutly worshiped Kano his whole life, Kinker knew better than to let his guard down around the sea. It was an entity, unforgiving and impartial, that would kill you as soon as it would help you.

But now that he thought about it, he wondered if he was really dead at all. Every bone in his body felt like it had been smashed into pieces and he was shivering and cold, which was strange because he had always been taught that death would be feeling-less. As a child, he remembered asking his mother what death would be like and she told him that when he died, he would simply stop feeling because the dead could feel nothing.

In the midst of the pain and coldness, Kinker concluded that he was not yet dead. Somehow, he had survived, but how, he had no idea.

That was when he felt a sharp jolt of pain near his midriff. His eyes flew open as he gasped for air. While he coughed out what felt like the entire Crystal Sea, a chair nearby skitted across the wood floor. Someone with a thick Northern accent said, "He's awake. Quick, get the captain."

Through his waterlogged ears, Kinker heard the sound of another set of feet running, then a door opening and slamming shut. He felt someone put a wet rag on his forehead (that smelled of mold for some reason) and heard the earlier voice say, "How are you, my man? You all right? Feel okay? Can you breathe?"

Kinker blinked several times before his vision became clear enough for him to tell what he was seeing. A man was standing above him, his eyes twinkling. The man had something hanging off his neck, a necklace, which had a set of multicolored beads on it. The man was probably from the North, because his skin was a darker shade of brown than Kinker's.

"Did you hear me?" said the man. "I asked, can you breathe?"

Kinker nodded slowly. His neck felt like it had been ripped off his shoulders and reattached by someone who didn't know what they were doing. He realized he was lying on a bed; furthermore, he was utterly nude, with only a coarse blanket to cover him.

"Good," said the man. "When Vashnas pulled you up from the

sea, we were certain you were dead. But thank the gods, you're alive."

Then the man frowned. "Or perhaps not. Our resources are already stretched thin, and I can't imagine the Captain would be very happy if he found out you are still alive."

Kinker moved his lips, trying to speak, but he only managed a few words because his throat felt like someone had cut it with a long, sharp knife. "Why ... call him ..."

"Hmm?" said the man, leaning down closer. "What'd you say, my friend?"

Kinker didn't think of himself as this man's 'friend,' but he did say, "The Captain ... why call him ... if he doesn't ..."

"Oh, I understand," said the man, nodding as he stood back up. "Well, the Captain gave us orders to summon him if you woke up. Don't worry, though. I doubt he'll toss you overboard, unless you happen to be a murderer or something."

Kinker gulped, which was like swallowing a prickly thorn bush. "Who ... are you?"

"Name's Telka Agos," said the man. "I'm the doctor of this ship. Been keeping you alive, which admittedly has been rather difficult because the medical supplies on this ship are, how should I put it, very bare bones."

"Clothes," said Kinker with a cough, "where ... are ... my clothes?"

"Your clothes?" said Telka with a chuckle. "The sea ripped them off your body. You were brought on board the ship completely naked, my friend. Once you're better, though, I have an extra set of clothes you can borrow."

Despite the pain, Kinker felt extremely embarrassed by the

thought that some people had seen him naked. He changed the subject. "Big ship?"

Before Telka could answer, the door slammed open, causing Kinker to look up from the bed he was lying upon.

Another man entered the room, a tall, strapping young man with dirty hair that looked like it was normally well-kept. His skin was as dark as Telka's. Besides that, the two looked radically different. The man who entered wore a long boat cloak that covered his whole body, except for his head, which made it impossible to tell what else he was wearing underneath.

The man strode into the room with an air of authority and command. At his side was an aquarian, perhaps female based on her figure (although Kinker had never been good at guessing aquarian genders). She had to be an aquarian. Her skin looked like fish skin and her head resembled that of a black fish, narrow and with a row of spines running lengthwise. She had webbed hands and wore a jacket that was completely buttoned up. She looked tired, like she had run a mile.

"Captain Malock," said Telka, saluting the younger man when he saw him, "I see Vashnas told you about the old man awaking."

"Indeed she did, Telka," said Captain Malock, stopping at the foot of Kinker's bed as he adjusted his boat cloak. "I was in the middle of lunch, but I wasted no time in getting here when I heard the news."

"He's breathing," Telka said. "And even starting to talk a little, but it's pretty obvious that he's still in pain. He may not be able to say much."

Malock looked at Kinker and said, "Old man, how does your throat feel?"

Kinker put one hand against his throat and said, "Like it was ripped off and nailed back on."

"But can you still speak?" Malock said.

Kinker swallowed and winced. "A little."

"A little will do," said Malock as he walked over to the left side of Kinker's bed.

The Captain pulled up a nearby chair and sat on it. As Malock did so, Telka took a step back, perhaps to give Malock room. The young female aquarian stood by Malock's side, still not saying anything. Kinker wondered if that was because she was silent or simply couldn't speak Northern Common. Either way, he found himself staring at her a bit too long, mostly because he'd never seen an aquarian up close like this before.

Then Malock snapped his fingers. Kinker looked at the Captain. He leaned forward in his chair, his intense eyes borrowing into Kinker's, like he was trying to read Kinker's mind.

"All right, old man," said Malock. "Let's start with your name. What is it?"

"Why should I tell you?"

"Because if you don't, I won't hesitate to throw you off this ship and into the ocean," Malock said. "I'm a humane captain, but I also do whatever is necessary to keep this ship afloat. And if you don't tell me anything about yourself, then I'm afraid we won't have any room for you here."

Based on the looks that Telka and the female aquarian were giving him, Kinker knew that Malock wasn't joking. Despite his youth, it was clear that the Captain already held the kind of authority over his crew that only the most experienced of captains did. Why, Kinker didn't know, but because he was in no mood for a swim, he decided to talk.

"My name is Kinker Dolan," said Kinker. He spoke slowly because he realized it hurt his throat less to do that. "I am from the island of Destan."

Malock quirked an eyebrow and looked at the female aquarian. "Ever head of it?"

The female aquarian nodded. "Yes. It's a small island, the southernmost of the Northern Isles. Its seas are home to a variety of rare fish, but otherwise is an an insignificant spit of land in the middle of nowhere."

Kinker didn't like hearing his home insulted like that, but he noticed how protective Malock seemed to be of the female aquarian, so he decided not to argue.

Instead, he said, "I've told you my name. Now tell me yours."

Malock brushed some of his dark hair out of his eyes and said, "Fair enough. But I'm surprised you don't already recognize me. My handsome features are renown throughout the Northern Isles, and I am admired by many fine women, even though I have room in my heart for one alone."

"Well, I am not a fine woman," Kinker said, "so forgive me if I fail to recognize you on sight."

Malock sat up straight, puffed out his chest, and said, "My name is Prince Tojas Malock, son of Queen Markinia and King Halock,

Crown Prince of the House of Carnag, Captain of the *Iron Wind*, and the Chosen One of Kano."

He recited all of those titles with the kind of enthusiasm Kinker commonly associated with Priestess Deber, back home, informing the masses of a new message she had received from Kano. Yet none of those titles meant a thing to the old fisherman. Only the last one interested him, but even then, he wasn't sure he wanted to ask because he didn't want to hear Malock drone on about it.

"Well?" said Malock. "Don't you have anything to say?"

Kinker shook his head. "Not really. Most of those titles don't mean a whole lot to me."

Malock looked so shocked that he almost fell off his chair, but he immediately righted himself and said, "Well, if Destan is as obscure an island as Vashnas says it is, then I suppose it makes sense you wouldn't know about me or Carnag. But you've heard of Carnagian boots, haven't you?"

Kinker thought about that for a moment. "My grandfather owned a pair, but he lost them at sea when he was fishing one time. They're supposed to be high quality, aren't they?"

"Indeed they are," said Malock. "My people produce the best boots in all of the Northern Isles. I am wearing a pair right now, in fact. Behold."

Malock raised his right foot high enough for Kinker to see. A large boot made of fine leather covered it, but the boot didn't look nearly as fancy as Kinker expected it to. It looked like it had been exposed to the weather, with water damage obvious at the toe. It was even ripped on one side and had obviously been hastily repaired by someone with no knowledge, training, or skill in boot repair.

Malock rested the boot back on the floor and said, "We produce enough boots to supply the entire Northern Isles. We have buyers from Kiskasa to Nikos and everywhere in between."

"Okay," said Kinker, though he wasn't sure what was so impressive about being the prince of a giant boot factory. "Say, you mentioned something about being the Chosen One of Kano earlier; what does that mean?"

"That is not important at the moment," said Malock in a tone that told Kinker it was actually very important. "What is important is finding out why you were on the sea at that time of night."

Kinker blinked. "That time of night? Don't you mean this time of night?"

"Oh, that's right," said Malock. "You don't know. Well, you were out for, what, three days?"

"Three and a half, actually," said Telka, nodding. "That's why we weren't sure you were alive, Kinker. You were out for so long, why, it's a miracle you woke up at all. Younger men than you have died from the same injuries."

"Three days ..." Kinker repeated, looking at the blanket covering his legs. He couldn't imagine being out cold for three days, yet he had no reason to believe that any of them were lying to him about this.

"So if you were hoping we'd take you back to your home, you are sadly mistaken," said Malock. "We are already well beyond the Northern Isles. There's no going back, no matter how much you beg and plead."

Good, Kinker thought. *I don't want to go back, not after what happened there. Not after what I did.*

"Again, I must ask," said Malock, "what were you doing on the sea in that weather? Our ship was nearly capsized and it's much larger than yours. You must either be very stupid or have a very good reason for risking your life. Were you trying to save someone else?"

Kinker hesitated for a moment. He couldn't tell them the truth. They might kick him off the ship if he told them. He had to come up with a lie quickly.

So he said, "Yes, I was. My granddaughter was out making sure the boats had not been swept away by the sea, but then the ocean waves dragged her out. I suppose she's dead now."

Kinker actually didn't have a granddaughter. He'd never married, never had any children ever. This was mostly because he had been devoted to his work, but also because he had never been interested in women very much. He much preferred men, but even then, marriage had never been a concern of his.

But Malock, Vashnas, and Telka didn't know that. They looked sad at hearing the 'news,' which meant they bought the lie—hook, line, and sinker.

"I am sorry to hear that," said Malock, sounding like he meant it. "Losing a family member is always difficult. I lost my own grandfather to the sea a few years ago, actually. One minute he was there and the next ..."

Malock looked down, breathed in and out rapidly, and then looked back up at Kinker. His face had regained its authoritative, detached look, but Kinker didn't think he'd ever look at it again without seeing the pain in Malock's eyes that was now far too obvious for him to ignore.

"But that has nothing to do with this," said Malock. "The point is, I appreciate you telling us who you are and what you were doing out in the sea on that night. Love makes us do crazy things, whether it's familial, platonic, or romantic, so I won't fault you for doing something so stupid and dangerous."

Vashnas smiled at that, like Malock had just made an in-joke that only she and the Captain understood. A glance at Telka told Kinker that it was indeed an in-joke because the ship doctor didn't react. He simply stood there looking concerned, as if he thought Kinker was going to drop dead if he kept talking like this.

"Now that I've told you my story, it's your turn," said Kinker, pointing at Malock. "What is the Crown Prince of Carnag doing so far from his palace?"

Malock sat up straight and rubbed his hands together, like he couldn't wait to tell Kinker. "Oh, that's a long tale. I'm not sure I can relay the entire thing to you here, right now, but—"

"I have nothing better to do," Kinker said, gesturing at the blanket covering his legs. "Shoot."

"All right, then," said Malock. "You see, Kinker, about two months ago, I was asleep in my royal bedchambers, after a hard day of practicing my fencing techniques and negotiating boot prices with the Shikan military. I was quite exhausted, so when my servants finished dressing me—"

"Your servants dressed you?" Kinker said. "Can't you dress yourself?"

Malock huffed and folded his arms across his chest. "As Crown

Prince of Carnag, I don't have the time to dress myself. It is beneath me; hence why I have servants especially devoted to the task."

Kinker had a hard time imagining that. What was so difficult about slapping on a shirt, a jacket, and pants that you had to hire people to do it for you? It seemed like something that any grown adult could do in less than a minute if necessary. Even a young child could accomplish the task in a short amount of time. When Kinker had been a very young kid, he'd compete with his brother to see who could get dressed for work in the shortest amount of time.

Perhaps royal clothes are more difficult to put on or something, Kinker thought. *Or maybe Malock is just a spoiled brat.*

That last thought seemed likely to Kinker, though of course he did not say it aloud.

"Now as I was saying," Malock said, his tone more than a little miffed now. "When my servants finished dressing me, I fell asleep the minute my head hit the pillow. But I did not get a restful, dreamless sleep. Instead, I was visited in my vision by a beautiful woman, a woman whose beauty exceeds that of nearly every mortal woman I've ever seen in my life."

Vashnas made a face at that, like she was annoyed. At least, Kinker thought she was annoyed. He was not good at deciphering aquarian facial expressions, primarily because he had spent most of his life around humans. The few aquarians that had lived on Destan rarely mingled with the humans, so Kinker had never gotten to know them very well.

Malock didn't seem to notice because he was still talking. "The woman wore robes the color of the sea on a bright summer day, shining beautifully. Looking into her eyes was like staring into the deepest sea; mysterious, dark, yet inviting. And she carried with her a fishing net made entirely of water."

Kinker sat up a little straighter at the description, which had sparked a memory in his head. "Fishing net ... did she have long hair that resembled the ocean waves?"

Malock looked stunned at Kinker's question. "Yes, yes she did. You sound like you've seen her before."

"I think I have," said Kinker. "But go on. I'm still listening."

Malock scratched his chin and said, "Well, as you can probably guess, I was taken aback by her appearance. I was certain she was just a figment of my imagination, but she was far too ... real for that to be a possibility, if you understand what I mean."

Malock looked at Kinker like the old fisherman should, but for the life of him Kinker could not understand. Glancing at Vashnas and Telka didn't help because Vashnas still looked annoyed and Telka looked embarrassed.

"Anyway," Malock continued, "whether you get it or not is unimportant. She then spoke to me."

Kinker tilted his head to the side. "What did she say?"

"I do not remember it all," Malock admitted. "She spoke in an unfamiliar language. Nonetheless, I understood the gist of it: She was summoning me to the edge of the world, to the very last island in creation, an island known as World's End."

"World's End?" said Kinker. "Isn't that just a legend?"

"It's real," Malock said. "I saw it—saw it in my dreams. The woman showed me the most beautiful city imaginable, built on the edge of the world. The Throne of the Gods, as it is also known in the old stories. It was a brief glimpse, true, but somehow I know it was real."

"How can you trust what the woman said, though?" said Kinker. "Maybe it was just a dream."

Malock shook his head rapidly. "No, no, no. I know it was more than just a dream because of the woman's identity."

"And who was the woman, exactly?"

Malock placed his hands on his lap and said, "Kano. Goddess of the Sea, Sand, and Art."

Another memory sparked in Kinker's mind, of when he was a child, seeing the face of a beautiful woman in the ocean surf before it dissipated in the waves. "Kano? I didn't think anyone else worshiped her outside of Destan."

"I do not actually worship her," Malock said. "The Carnagian Royal Family is devoted almost entirely to Grinf, God of Justice, Metal, and Fire, due to the blessings he has bestowed upon us over the years. As a matter of fact, the last member of the Royal Family who tried to worship another god ... well, let's just say that it didn't work out and leave it at that."

The tone in which he spoke made it clear that, if Kinker even asked about it, the old man would find himself back in the Crystal Sea again.

"Anyway," said Malock, his tone brightening, "I didn't even know about Kano until she showed up in my dreams. I actually had to have some of my servants research her in the royal library. We have tons of books on the various gods. Turns out Kano has quite a following among the aquarians but for some reason has never been particularly popular among humans. Wonder why that is."

"Not much of a mystery, if you ask me," Vashnas said. "She controls the whole sea and we live in it. Would be kind of dumb if we didn't honor her."

"Ah," said Malock, "I see. So when I learned that she was an actual goddess, my next choice was not at all difficult to make. I decided I was going to round up a fleet of ships, find the best crew money can buy, and head on down to World's End, which, according to the dream, is at the very end of the southern seas. Simple, yes?"

Kinker scratched the back of his ears. "You mean your parents didn't try to stop you?"

"Oh, at first my parents were against it," said Malock with a snort. "They were convinced I was acting on nothing more than a delusional fantasy. In particular, my mother seemed to treat the suggestion of me going on a voyage to the end of the world as though I had just suggested that I wanted to jump off the tip of Carnag Hall. My father simply thought it was irresponsible, argued that I had to stay here in order to learn more about my future kingly duties and that I couldn't be sure Kano had summoned me at all. Frankly, my parents can be a tad overprotective at times, if I do say so myself."

To Kinker, they didn't sound overprotective at all. They sounded reasonable. But he did not share this opinion, as he was still listening.

"But despite all their faults, my parents are highly respectful of the gods and their wishes," Malock said. "I summoned a dream reader, who confirmed that my dream had indeed been from Kano. When the dream reader confirmed it, my parents dropped all their protests and immediately began helping me put together a fleet and crew that would get me to World's End in one piece. That took about a month total."

"Wow," said Kinker. "So you have an entire fleet of sailing ships, each manned with a complete crew? Just to escort you to World's End?"

Kinker immediately knew that he had said something wrong because Telka shuffled his feet and looked away, Vashnas become interested in her jacket's right sleeve, and Malock's arms dropped to his sides and he suddenly looked as old as Kinker.

"Ah," said Malock, a slight tremble in his voice, "wrong tense, Kinker. We *had* an entire fleet of sailing ships, all manned with a complete crew. Five ships, in fact. Now ... well we only have one. This one, actually."

Kinker could hardly believe his ears. "How did you lose almost an entire fleet of ships?"

"A string of bizarre coincidences and disasters that I doubt even Tinkar, the God of Fate, could have seen coming," Malock said, shaking his head. "I'll tell you about them later. All you need to know is that the current situation is very grim for everyone involved, including you."

Those words seemed to resonate with Kinker in a way he couldn't at first explain. Then it hit him.

He looked around the quarters he was lying in and realized what it was about the place that had bothered him. The room smelled of fish and blood, the walls and floor were stained with bodily fluids he didn't care to identify, and there was a hole in the ceiling that looked to have been created by someone stabbing the ceiling with a sword.

When he looked more closely at Malock, Vashnas, and Telka, he noticed more signs of weariness and damage. Telka's hair was matted and encrusted with dirt, Vashnas stood with all of her weight on her right leg, like her left leg couldn't support her, and Malock himself had several small scratches across his face that messed up his otherwise handsome complexion. All of them shared the same weary, tired look that Kinker had always associated with retired soldiers. He had seen a lot of retired soldiers back on Destan during fishing season, when retirees from the various Northern armies came down south to fish.

Whatever had happened on this voyage, Kinker understood that it was far more serious than he had first thought. And to be honest, he wasn't really eager to find out exactly what had sunk four large sailing ships and killed their entire crews.

Malock shook his head and said, "But enough of that. We have enough sorrow on this ship as is. Let's try to think happy thoughts."

"Happy thoughts?" Kinker said, looking at the Captain in disbelief. "Why haven't you headed back home to Carnag? I mean, you lost four ships and from what you've said this one isn't doing too well, either. Seems irresponsible to risk the lives of everyone on this ship like this."

"I cannot ignore the summons of a goddess," said Malock, as if the very suggestion was insane. "As a Kanonite yourself, surely you have heard stories of what Kano has done to people who ignore or disobey her direct summons?"

Kinker nodded. "Yes, but I'm sure she would understand if you had to go back to get another fleet. She is not an unreasonable goddess."

"I can't risk that," said Malock. "Angering gods is never a wise move, Kinker. Besides, you don't understand. I can't just go back. My very soul is drawn to World's End, like a magnet. I couldn't go back even if I wanted to."

Kinker had to admit that Malock seemed to be genuinely driven. He didn't look away from Kinker as he said that, nor did he tremble or stumble over his words. The Captain of the *Iron Wind* seemed to believe in what he had just said and he wasn't going to apologize for it no matter what. Maybe he was less spoiled than Kinker had thought.

"Fine," said Kinker. "I guess it is too later now to turn this ship around; although I find it strange that Kano didn't protect your fleet from destruction."

"You should direct that inquiry to the other gods," said Malock. "Most of the crews of my fleet were not Kanonites. Perhaps Kano didn't see any reason to protect them or perhaps they just weren't especially pious; either way, that is no reason for me to give up and go home."

"I didn't say you should," said Kinker. "In fact, I said the opposite. By the way, where are we now?"

Malock looked at Vashnas, who said, "We just entered the southern seas a day ago."

Kinker shivered. "The southern seas? Please tell me you're joking."

"Hardly," said Malock. "In order to reach World's End, we have to go through the southern seas."

"But the southern seas are full of danger," Kinker said. "All the old legends say so. Gigantic sea monsters, unpredictable weather, and all kinds of other things are said to exist there. There's a reason Destan is the farthest known southern island, you know."

"So what?" said Malock. "Those are just stories and legends, Kinker. We have so little precious fact to rely upon that I find it silly to be afraid. I mean, so far, the southern seas have been very kind to us, with favorable winds and bright sunshine. You're just worrying for no reason."

"No," Kinker said, shaking his head. "A friend of mine once told me about the giant sea snakes that live in these seas. They have mouths big enough to swallow entire islands whole."

Vashnas laughed. "Giant sea snakes with mouths big enough to swallow whole islands? That's so ridiculous that I can't believe you even thought that was true."

Being laughed at—by an aquarian, of all beings—made Kinker angry, but before he could answer, Malock said, "Fear not, elder. We have the best guide to the southern seas that anyone could ask for. We'll be prepared for whatever these seas have to throw at us, and then some."

"And who is that guide?" said Kinker, looking at Malock.

"Me," said Vashnas, pointing at herself.

Now Kinker shifted his attention to her. "What do you know about the southern seas, young lady? No one who has ever tried to explore them has ever returned alive."

"Except for Vash here," said Malock, reaching over and patting her right arm. "She's been to the southern seas, traveled all the way to World's End, in fact, and can tell us everything there is to know about it."

"Really?" said Kinker. "How do you know that for sure? I would like some proof."

This seemed like a reasonable request to Kinker, so he was shocked when Malock stood up, knocking over his chair, and grabbed Kinker by his beard. The Captain didn't raise his other hand or anything, but he was staring at Kinker with such intense loathing that Kinker felt like he was being held above a fire.

"Don't ... you ... dare ..." Malock said, every word emphasized for impact, "... imply ... that Vashnas is a liar ... or I'll ..."

"Captain, please," said Telka, reaching out and grabbing Malock's arm. "Let go of Kinker right this instant. He's still weak, and any undue shock might harm his still-recovering system."

Malock just shot Telka an even angrier look, but the doctor didn't let go or shift his gaze. That made Kinker respect Telka immensely because his chin was starting to hurt from Malock pulling on his beard.

"Didn't you hear what he said?" Malock said through gritted teeth. "He implied Vashnas is a liar. You think I'm going to stand here and let him get away with it?"

"I understand your anger, Captain, but it's the wrong response," said Telka, his tone even and firm. "He didn't have any malicious intentions. He's understandably skeptical because he obviously believes no one has ever gone to the southern seas and come back alive. Now let go of him or I will be treating your injuries in a moment."

For a moment, Malock didn't let go. If anything, his grip seemed to tighten because his knuckles turned whiter and his normally handsome face became contorted with anger.

Then, to Kinker's relief, Malock let go and stood back. Kinker let out his breath, which he hadn't even realized he'd been holding in, and moved as far away from Malock as he could on his bed. Vashnas put an arm around Malock's shoulders and began speaking to him in low, soothing tones, but that didn't seem to do much to make Malock calm down.

"I'm sorry for implying that Vashnas is a liar," said Kinker. "I wasn't meaning to. You heard Telka. He got it right."

Malock didn't respond. He just kept glaring at Kinker like he was hoping to kill him with his nasty looks alone.

Vashnas looked at Kinker and said, "It's okay. Most people are skeptical when I tell them I've been to the southern seas and survived. Honestly, I don't believe it myself at times, but it's true."

"Could you tell me how?" said Kinker. "Just for curiosity's sake. That's all."

"I received a dream from Kano proving it," said Malock. He seemed calmer now, but Kinker keep up his guard up just the same. "The night before I met Vashnas, Kano sent me a dream in which I saw Vashnas swimming through the southern seas. She explicitly told me that I needed Vashnas if I was going to make it to World's End alive. And the very next day, as I was inspecting the crew of my fleet, I saw Vashnas and immediately summoned her to my court, where I told her about my dream."

"Is that true?" said Kinker, looking at Vashnas.

Vashnas nodded, looking a little embarrassed. "When I first

entered his court, Malock showed me a picture he'd drawn of me, a picture he'd drawn when he woke up. And I know for a fact that he has never seen me before, so there was no way he could have drawn it from memory. There is no other explanation for it. Kano must want me here."

"I see," said Kinker. "I guess that makes sense. The gods surely do work in mysterious ways, do they not?"

"Indeed they do," said Malock, perhaps more harshly than was necessary. "Now if you'll excuse me, I must return to my stateroom. Vashnas and I have to discuss what awaits us in the seas ahead. For now, Telka will take care of you until he deems you fit enough to work on the ship."

Kinker raised a hand. "Hold on. When did I volunteer to join your crew?"

"I suppose you'd like to swim back to Destan naked?" said Malock. "I won't stop you if that's what you want to do, of course, but I doubt you'd make it very far, even if you're a good swimmer."

Kinker cursed under his breath. "You're right. I guess I don't have much of a choice but to work on this ship, do I?"

"No, you do not," said Malock. "When you're better, I'll give you a tour of the ship, introduce you to the crew, and assign you a job. Do you have any useful or productive skills?"

He asked that last question almost too fast for Kinker to catch, but the old man said, "Yes. I'm a fisherman by trade. Been fishing off the coast of Destan for fifty years now."

Malock's scowl disappeared like a cloud on a summer's day, replaced with a giddy smile that took Kinker by surprise. "That's excellent. I hope you recover soon because I already know exactly where I want to put you. Telka, make sure to tell me the minute you think he's ready to start working. I wish to put him to work right away."

"Yes, sir, Captain," said Telka, saluting. "I'll make sure you know as soon as possible."

"I'll pray to Atikos for you, Kinker," said Malock as he and Vashnas left the room, "so that your healing may come quickly."

As soon as Malock and Vashnas left, Telka thrust a bowl of some kind of greenish soup under Kinker's nose and said, "Eat up. You look hungry."

It hadn't even occurred to Kinker to eat, but when he thought about it, his stomach rumbled. He immediately took the bowl and slurped down the greenish soup, even though Telka was about to hand him a spoon. The soup was hot and burned his throat, but he was so hungry that he didn't care.

When the last of the soup entered his mouth, he lowered the bowl and handed it back to Telka. "Thanks, doctor. What was in that soup, anyway?"

Telka took the bowl back, but didn't look at the bowl. He was staring at Kinker in amazement, like he'd never seen him before.

"That was lime fish soup," said Telka. "It's nasty stuff. Fit for human consumption, of course, but still nasty."

"Why are you looking at me like that?" said Kinker. "It was good."

"You're not supposed to slurp it all down like that," said Telka. "It's hard on the stomach, so you have to eat it in small helpings to avoid throwing it all up."

Kinker put his hand on his stomach and said, "My stomach doesn't feel that bad. Are you sure that's what it's supposed to do?"

"Normally," said Telka. "But I guess you're different. What do you Destanians normally eat?"

"Fried fish, zapper stew, and other stuff like that," said Kinker. "Why?"

Telka put the bowl down on a nearby desk and said, "I just find it intriguing that you ate it all so quickly and without any adverse medical—"

The only warning Kinker received was a slight rumble in his stomach. He heaved and managed to avoid hurling all over his bed. Unfortunately for Telka, however, his barf landed on the doctor's trousers and boots, dousing them in lime-green stuff that Kinker didn't try to identify.

Kinker lay back in his bed, shivering and coughing, while Telka looked down at his pants and boots in dismay.

"Well," said Telka, "I guess you Destanians *don't* have stomachs of steel after all. Let me clean this up. I'll get you some water and after that you should take a nap. You need it."

Chapter Two

OVER THE NEXT FEW days, Kinker spent all of his time in bed, being tended to by Telka. He saw no other visitors. None of the other sailors came down to visit or see him, although he often heard them bustling by in the hall outside, going to and fro, perhaps doing chores. He figured Malock had ordered the crew to leave him alone until he was better, but that just made him feel a little depressed because he had no one to talk to except Telka. And Telka was not a very interesting conversationalist.

It wasn't that Telka was an uninteresting man. The doctor had apparently worked on ships his whole life, having been the son of two famous ship's doctors from the island of Shika. He claimed to have been a student of the great doctor Ashef and had an almost encyclopedic knowledge of medicine, magical healing methods, and how the body worked.

That sounded fine and dandy to Kinker, but for whatever reason, Telka refused to answer any of Kinker's questions about the ship, its crew, or anything else relating to the voyage. Every time the conversation turned toward those questions, Telka would immediately shut up and check Kinker's pulse or give him another bowl of that lime fish soup (which Kinker now knew to take in small servings).

Another thing Kinker noticed was how unprepared Telka appeared, despite supposedly being a good doctor. His medical cabinets were either bare or full of bottles and equipment that didn't look like any medical supplies Kinker had ever seen. Once, looking over Telka's shoulder as the doctor searched for some medicine to soothe Kinker's sore throat, he spotted a bottle of red juice with the label 'MEDICINE' on it and its cap missing. Red juice wasn't a medicine, as far as Kinker knew, so he had no idea what it was doing inside a doctor's medical cabinet.

That was when he remembered that the ship had already been through so much on this voyage. Though he had not seen any other patients, Kinker figured that sickness and injuries must be pretty common on board this ship. Maybe Telka had used up most of his medical supplies taking care of them. There was still so much Kinker didn't know and so much Telka refused to tell him that Kinker found himself growing increasingly restless.

That restlessness wasn't the only reason he found it difficult to sleep. The mattress was uncomfortable and rough. The sheets were surprisingly clean, but they still smelled faintly of dried blood, puke, and other bodily fluids, like everything else in the medical room. At night, Kinker didn't get much sleep. Often he'd stay awake, the horrible scents filling his nostrils, listening to the wind and waves that beat against the lee of the ship. He was used to sleeping on ships, but for whatever reason, he just couldn't sleep on this one.

Finally, on the third day after Kinker awoke, Telka declared him ready to work. Kinker knew that already. He had recovered quite speedily the day after speaking with Malock, but until today the doctor had argued for caution and so held him back for two days. That was annoying, but when Kinker remembered that he wasn't looking forward to whatever work Malock had planned for him, it was easier to take.

Telka left to find Malock, returning about five minutes later. The prince looked much the same as he always did, except more frazzled and annoyed, like he hadn't got much sleep himself. He stood near the door, arms folded across his chest, impatiently waiting while Kinker got out of bed and got dressed.

Because Kinker had no clothes of his own, Telka gave Kinker a ratty pea coat, thin white shirt, and rough pants to compensate, as well as some leather boots to cover his feet. The outfit was a tight fit, but as they didn't have anything else for him to wear, Kinker didn't complain.

When Kinker finished buttoning his pea coat, he walked over to Malock, who sighed with relief and said, "Finally. Come along, now. I don't have a lot of time to give you a tour, so I want to make this quick."

When they stepped into the hallway, the first thing Kinker noticed was a middle-aged woman leaning against the opposite wall. She was human and had curly blonde hair that reminded Kinker of his mother's hair, although there was something about this woman that made him tense. She didn't introduce herself when he and

Malock appeared. She just pushed herself off the wall and stood there standing as straight as a board.

"This is Banika Koiro," said Malock, gesturing at the silent woman. "She's the ship's boatswain and my right-hand woman. She is the single most trustworthy sailor on this entire ship. Banika, meet Kinker Dolan, our new fisherman."

Banika said nothing. She merely nodded at him and took up the rear when Malock and Kinker began making their way top deck. Kinker glanced over his shoulder at her as they walked, mostly to be sure that she was still following. It had less to do with his memory and more to do with the way the woman silently moved across the creaking floorboards.

"This is the middle deck," said Malock, waving his arms to indicate the hallway they were in. "Most of the sailors come down here to sleep at night. It's also where we keep a lot of our supplies and equipment that we need but don't want to store in the hold. Like the cannons, for example."

Kinker looked at Malock in surprise. "You have cannons on this ship? I thought this was a sailing ship, not a ship of war."

Malock shrugged. "The southern seas are dangerous. Anyway, so far we haven't had to use them. And I can assure you that the gunpowder is kept under lock and key and is not in any danger of exploding and sinking the ship to the bottom of the sea."

"We learned *that* lesson the hard way," Banika said behind them, her voice so soft that it was almost lost in the sound of their footsteps. "Lost *Our Beloved Lady* because someone didn't handle the gunpowder correctly."

"*Our Beloved Lady* was one of the other ships," Malock said to Kinker offhandedly. "First to sink, actually. But I'll tell you about that later."

Kinker wasn't sure he wanted to hear more about it. He was already starting to feel sick again from the combined odor of seawater, sickness, mildew, and other equally unpleasant scents in the air. He found it difficult to breathe down here, but Malock and Banika showed no problems with breathing at all. Maybe they were used to it.

The smell got worse when they passed by the cracked door of another room. A strong odor that smelled like rotting, burnt fish wafted through the crack in the door and into Kinker's nose, causing him to choke on it. Malock and Banika just stopped and looked at him like he was crazy.

"What's the matter, Kinker?" Malock asked. "Are you not feeling well?"

Between coughs and fits, Kinker pointed at the cracked door and said, "No. It's that smell. It's like a rotting corpse."

"Oh, that means dinner is almost ready," said Malock, like he couldn't wait to eat. "That's the galley, by the way. Head cook is Arisha Frag, but I'll introduce you to her later. She hates to be disturbed when she's cooking, even if it's to meet a new member of the crew."

"What do you eat on this ship?" Kinker asked, moving away from the galley door as far as he could in the cramped hall. "Poison fish stew or something?"

"Fish," Malock said. "We used to have a bigger variety of food, such as ikadori peaches, Frianan cream, and the finest silk tea you can imagine. Alas, the voyage has mostly depleted our stores, but I can assure you that Arisha is an excellent cook nonetheless, very good at making do with what little we have."

If the smell of her cooking was anything to go by, Kinker highly doubted that, but he said nothing more about the matter as he continued following Malock down the hall. He held his hand over his nose the entire time, however, until they climbed the stairs up to the top deck.

As they emerged from the hatch, Malock spread his arms as wide as possible and said, "Welcome to the top deck of the *Iron Wind*, Kinker. Be amazed by its size and magnificence."

The top deck of the *Iron Wind* was indeed large and wide open, much more open than the middle deck was. The awful smells were still present, but they were mixed with the fresh, salty air of the sea. For once, Kinker felt like he could breathe freely on this ship.

But it wasn't quite as magnificent as Malock thought it was; for example, the foremast, the mainmast, and the mizzenmast were in various states of disrepair. In particular, their sails looked like they'd been patched together by someone who didn't know how to sew. The ratlines appeared mostly intact, but he spotted a few snapped ropes here and there that no one had bothered to repair.

And then there were the sailors. This was the first time Kinker had seen the crew of the *Iron Wind*. From what he could see, most were human, but there was definitely a large minority of aquarians present. Having never spent much time around aquarians, Kinker watched in fascination as one aquarian, who had tentacles in place of legs and a head that closely resembled that of a squid's, squashed by, swabbing the deck alongside two humans.

The crew looked like most sailors: tough, rough, and hardworking. There were at least fifty or so present; steering the ship, adjusting the sails, cleaning the deck (although that looked like a losing battle to Kinker), and doing various other things that the crew of a sailing ship generally needed to do. Few of them took notice of Kinker, and those few that did only glanced at him briefly before returning to their work.

Another thing Kinker noticed about the crew was how beaten up many of them looked. Back on Destan, it wasn't uncommon to see sailors who had stitches, scars, and other things to indicate injury, but many of the sailors on board the *Iron Wind* looked like they had been through a war. One human sailor, for example, was missing his entire left arm, while an aquarian sailor who was scrubbing the mainmast had only one foot, the other having been replaced by a block of wood that vaguely resembled a peg leg. Many of them had gaunt faces, like they hadn't had a good meal in a long time.

The ship in general had an air of disrepair about it. True, the crew appeared to have done their best to keep the ship in shape, but if Kinker hadn't seen the crew, he would have thought that the *Iron Wind* was a ghost ship.

Just then, someone behind him said, in a refined voice that took Kinker by surprise, "Could you please move so I can go down the hatch?"

Kinker turned around and was shocked to see a giant of a man standing before him. A long, thick scar ran from his crown down the side of his face to his chin, but besides that he appeared to lack the major wounds that most of his fellow sailors did.

He looked down on the three with the intelligent eyes of a scholar, which contrasted sharply with his massive physical body. In his right hand he carried a short wooden staff, more like a wand really, which he held like a sword.

"There you are, Bifor," said Malock with a smile, patting Kinker on the shoulder. "Bifor, meet Kinker Dolan, our newest fisherman. Kinker, meet Bifor Kamon, our ship's resident—and only—mage."

Bifor nodded at Kinker. "Pleased to meet you, Kinker. I assume you are the man that Vashnas rescued from the sea about a week ago?"

"Yes," said Kinker. He looked at Malock and said, "Wait—it was Vashnas who saved me?"

"Yes, of course she did," said Malock. "Didn't we mention that earlier? She somehow spotted your boat through the storm and wanted to rescue you. Tried to convince her it was too dangerous, but she didn't listen. I almost thought she was going to die with you, but thankfully you both survived."

"I'll have to thank her personally sometime," said Kinker. "Now did you say Bifor is the ship's mage? I've never met a mage before."

Bifor's mouth twitched slightly. "Never?"

"Never," Kinker said, nodding. "On Destan, we don't have any mages. Some of our priests know a little magic, but in comparison to what I've heard mages can do, it's practically nothing."

"Hmph," said Bifor. "Destan must be a very out-of-the-way, obscure little island if it doesn't have even one mage on it."

His tone was disapproving, like Destan's lack of a mage disappointed him greatly.

Defensively, Kinker said, "It's not like it's a choice. It's just that no one wants to live there."

"Oh, I didn't mean to insinuate anything negative about your home," said Bifor. "I was simply observing the unfortunate fact that most mages care more about fame and prestige than in doing good work in places where it is needed—sad, but true."

As if to stave off further conflict, Malock said, "Bifor is a Xocionian. That means he worships Xocion, the God of Ice."

"Yes," said Bifor, nodding. "I studied magic at North Academy, the largest mage school in the Northern Isles."

"Wow," said Kinker, genuinely impressed. "Guess that makes you very well-educated, doesn't it?"

"Yes, it does," said Bifor. "Now if you'll excuse me, I have some work to do below deck. Please let me pass."

Malock, Kinker, and Banika stepped aside, allowing Bifor to pass them and disappear into the hatch that led to the lower decks. Somehow the large mage managed to fit his bulk through the hatch, which Kinker had to assume was magic because he couldn't otherwise see how Bifor managed that.

When Bifor was gone, Kinker immediately turned to Malock and said, "If you have a mage on board, why does the *Iron Wind* look so terrible? Why have you had any troubles at all? Can't magic solve all your problems?"

Malock's reaction was unexpected. He laughed, laughed so hard and so loud that some nearby sailors stopped their work to look for the source of the noise. Even Banika smiled slightly, like she wanted to laugh, but didn't either because she was too polite or Kinker's question had been so silly that she didn't even want to laugh at it.

"What is the problem?" said Kinker, looking between Banika and the still-laughing Malock. "What did I say? What did I do wrong?"

In between gasps for breath, Malock said, "Oh, it's nothing personal, Kinker. It's just ... man, I haven't had a good laugh in a long time, not like that. Haven't had much to laugh about on this voyage."

Still confused, Kinker scratched the back of his head and said, "What's so funny? I wasn't joking."

"You weren't?" said Malock, his laughter quickly replaced with surprise. "Oh. You were serious."

"Yes, I was," said Kinker. "Though if laughter is all I can expect for asking honest questions, maybe I shouldn't speak at all anymore."

Malock chuckled. "Sorry. It's just that magic can't solve all our problems. It is amazing, to be sure, but you gotta understand that there are different kinds of magic and not all of them work the same."

"What does that mean?"

"Take Bifor," said Malock. "He's a pagomancer, which means he's good at ice magic. You know, freezing things, making it snow, stuff like that—very useful in cold weather, you know, when you need someone to break the ice off the ship and keep the sails from becoming frozen solid."

Kinker looked up. The sun was shining and it was quite warm.

"But as you can see," said Malock, gesturing at the ship, "we are not in cold weather; in fact, it's the middle of summer. While all mages, Bifor included, know general magic in addition to whatever they specialize in, most mages are generally useful in their specialties. Therefore, Bifor, for example, could heal someone with a healing spell, but he couldn't cure someone of a deadly disease or heal a fatally-wounded person because he's not a panamancer."

"Then what's he even doing on this ship at all?" Kinker asked. "And why is he the *only* mage? Surely, as the prince of Carnag, you could have hired more?"

"I did," said Malock. "Before we lost the rest of the fleet, each ship had a dozen or so mages, each one specializing in a particular field of magic that are helpful in sailing, such as aquamancy and aeromancy, for example. I personally handpicked every mage to make sure we got the best mages we could."

"What happened to them?" Kinker asked.

Malock sighed. "Weren't you listening? We lost the rest of the fleet, including the mages. A variety of disasters took them all out. It's a miracle Bifor survived because he was on *Our Beloved Lady*, the ship that exploded due to the mishandled gunpowder in its hold. He was, sadly enough, the only survivor of that ship."

"Oh," said Kinker. "Must be hard for him."

"It's hard to tell," said Malock. "He doesn't confide much in other people. Personally I think he was traumatized by it and his ceaseless work ethic is how he deals with it. He's been trying to make himself useful, doing whatever he can do, even if it wipes him out."

"Hmm," said Kinker. "Well, why don't we continue the tour? I want to see the rest of the ship and meet the rest of the crew."

"All right, then," said Malock. "Since you're going to be a fisherman, I should introduce you to the fishing crew. They're at the stern and are in charge of the trawl."

A few minutes later, they reached the stern of the ship, where they found the oddest group of fishermen that Kinker had ever seen.

For one, the only one who looked anything at all like a fisherman was the young man who introduced himself as Deddio Mannon. Even then, Kinker didn't see the usual signs of a fisherman, such as scars from the mishandling of fishing hooks, on him. Malock informed Kinker that Deddio was currently the head of the fishing crew.

The next one was a young woman named Jenur Takren. And by 'young,' Kinker didn't mean early twenties or something. She looked closer to 18, possibly even younger than that. He could tell her age because of her hair, which she had short and dark. Her grip was strong, however, when they shook hands, even stronger than Deddio's, much to his surprise.

Then he was introduced to Gino and Magnisa, an aquarian couple. They both resembled goldfish, with orange skin and large eyes, and were much rounder around the waist than their fellow fishermen. They were friendly, though Kinker felt rather timid around them due to his lack of experience with aquarians.

And finally, there was Daro Loman, an unusually thin man whose eyes always seemed to be somewhere in the distance. At least, that was the most charitable interpretation Kinker chose to give of him because Daro did not look him in the eyes when they were introduced and only barely managed to remember his own name when asked for it.

"All right," said Malock to Deddio, "you show Kinker the ropes.

I'll be back in an hour to finish our tour of the ship."

Kinker looked at Malock in surprise. "Where are you going?"

"Back to my stateroom, of course," said Malock. "I have some things I need to attend to, some very important things, and I cannot put them off any longer. Besides, this is an excellent opportunity for you to get to know your fellow fishermen, as well as the kind of job you are going to be doing from now until we reach World's End. Sounds fun, doesn't it?"

Kinker glanced at the assembled fishermen, feeling uneasy about them for some reason, and said, "Sure. Fun."

After that, Malock departed, leaving Kinker alone with the fishing crew, none of whom had said a word since being introduced.

It was Deddio who broke the silence by stepping forward and saying, "Well, Mr. Dolan, we were told you are a fisherman. Have you ever used a trawl before?"

Kinker scratched the back of his head. "I'm more used to a rod and line, to be frank, though I've worked with trawls before."

"Well, I'm sure you'll catch on," said Deddio. "The rest of us did."

"What do you mean, 'the rest of us did'?"

Deddio's smile never wavered on his sunburned face. "None of us are trained fishermen. Well, I think Daro's father took him fishing for a few summers when he was a kid, but that was years ago; right, Daro?"

Daro, whose eyes were on the sky, nodded. "Yep. Didn't catch a thing, not even once."

"And this is Jenur's first time as a sailor on a ship," said Deddio, gesturing at the young woman. "Gino and Magnisa used to hunt fish underwater, but—"

"But we never enjoyed it," Gino said. His voice, like that of most aquarians Kinker had heard, gurgled, as though he always had water in it. "Always bought our food from the market. We never even learned how to use a fishing rod, much less a trawl."

Kinker ran his hand through his white hair, feeling a little exasperated. "Then why are you five on the fishing crew at all?"

Deddio shrugged. "I don't know if you've been told, but we lost nearly the entire fleet over the last month and with them plenty of experienced fishermen and women. Frankly, Kinker, there are very few people on this ship who are in jobs they are actually trained or qualified for. Probably why the Captain was so eager to dump you here with us."

"How many pounds of fish do you bring in daily?" Kinker said.

"About forty, sometimes fifty if we're lucky," said Jenur, who was leaning against the bulwarks. "Why?"

"How many sailors are on this ship?" Kinker said. "Including aquarians."

"A hundred and twenty," said Jenur, just as promptly as before. "Again, why?"

Kinker did the math in his head and didn't like the answer he got. "Fifty pounds of fish can't possibly be enough to feed one-hundred and twenty hardworking, full-grown sailors, human and aquarian. How have you survived this long with so little food?"

Deddio crossed his arms over his chest and looked out into the sea. "We used to have half a year's worth of food in the hold. Ran out of it pretty quickly, though, which is why we made this trawl."

"How did you run out of so much food so fast?" said Kinker in disbelief. "And what do you mean, you *made* the trawl? Didn't you have one on board already?"

"We didn't store the food correctly, so we had to toss it all out," Deddio said. "As for the trawl, we didn't need one at first. Therefore, we had to make do with what we had."

"And what did you have?" said Kinker.

Deddio glanced over his shoulder at the ropes tied to the railing on the edge of the stern. "You know, we were just about to haul in the noon catch, so we'll just show you. You can watch us and see how we do it."

Kinker did just that, retreating about a dozen feet while the five fishermen grabbed the ropes and began hauling in the trawl with their combined strength. It took them at least half an hour to haul the entire thing onto the poop deck, which did little to improve Kinker's mood. It actually did the opposite; the more he saw of the trawl, the more depressed he became.

When they finally laid the entire trawl on the deck, Kinker got a good look at it. It was at least twice as long as Daro, but instead of being made of fiber web (the best kind of material for trawls), it was made almost entirely of rope, with some netting for good measure. Rather than being cone-shaped, however, it more closely resembled a fishing net, being much wider and open at the mouth than a normal trawl.

Not only that, but it was missing a codend. And he thought that Jenur's estimate of fifty pounds of fish to be very liberal. This catch, at least, was probably only forty pounds, some of which the fishing crew had to throw back into the sea because they were not fit for consumption by anyone, human or aquarian, thus making the actual weight probably closer to thirty-five or maybe even thirty pounds.

"Let me get this straight," said Kinker, watching the others gut and clean the fish. "*That* is your trawl?"

Deddio, who was expertly cleaning the fish he handled, nodded without looking up at Kinker. "Yep. We had to put it to together ourselves when it became clear we needed a way to get a lot of fish fast."

"Had Bifor cast a spell on it to attract fish to it," said Gino, who cleaned his fish with slightly more difficulty than Deddio. "Don't think it really helped, though, because as smart as that man is, he's not much of a fisherman, you know?"

Kinker ran a hand through his hair again. "Is it a bottom trawl or mid-water trawl?"

"Mid-water," Deddio said. "Not long enough to reach the bottom, sadly."

"Okay," said Kinker. "I'm honestly shocked that you've managed to catch anything at all. No wonder the rest of the crew looks so sour. They aren't getting enough to eat."

Jenur stopped gutting a fish and looked at him in annoyance. "Well, Mr. Master Fisherman, if you know how to make a better trawl that will catch us tons of fish, we're all ears."

Her sharp tone surprised Kinker, prompting him to say, "Didn't your parents teach you to show some respect to your elders, young woman?"

"Whatever," said Jenur, as she turned her attention back to the fish in her hand. "Are you just going to stand there and watch or are you going to help us clean these fish? They're going to be lunch."

Kinker wanted to smack her upside the head for her disrespect, but as he doubted that would endear him to the rest of the crew, he simply came over and began helping them clean what little fish they had caught.

This is going to be a very long voyage, Kinker thought as Deddio handed him an extra gutting knife from his pocket. *A very long voyage.*

Malock sat at the desk in his stateroom, looking over a rough map of the southern seas that Vashnas had drawn for him not long after he had hired her. On the opposite side of his desk, Vashnas sat in a rickety old chair that was probably going to fall apart one of these days, scratching the back of her head and yawning every now and then.

"So, assuming we stay our course, the first island we'll run into is this one," said Malock, pointing at a small circle on the map.

Vashnas nodded. "Yes. It doesn't have a name and no one lives on it. I call it Ikadori Island, though, because it has a ton of ikadori peaches along the shore."

"Excellent," said Malock, scribbling a quick note over it. "We'll stop there for a few days and gather as much of those peaches as we can. I'm getting sick of having fish every day for breakfast, lunch, and dinner, to be honest."

"We probably shouldn't stay very long," Vashnas said. "I mean, while there aren't any people on that island, there are animals that live there. Big, ape-like beasts. Pretty protective of their territory."

"So what?" said Malock. "We have a lot of skilled fighters and hunters on board this ship. Besides, we're not going very deep into the island. You yourself just said the ikadori trees were along the shore, after all."

"True" said Vashnas. "There are so many ikadori peach trees that you could probably get enough to feed the entire crew for the next three months just from the ones lining the shore."

"Then we won't have to fight the beasts that live there," said Malock. "Vash, I just wanted to thank you again for being so helpful. I would be far less confident about our chances of survival if it wasn't for you."

Vashnas looked a bit embarrassed, which made her look really cute to Malock. "Oh, it's nothing, Mal. I'm just happy I can be of service."

"No, I'm serious," said Malock. He reached across the desk and grabbed her hand. "This voyage has been extremely stressful for me and we've only been in the southern seas for a little less than a week. You've proved even more faithful to me than Banika. Without you, I would be lost."

Their eyes met. She had such beautiful eyes, dark and round as they were. They did not break eye contact until Vashnas slipped her hand out of his, stood up, and walked around the desk. Malock turned in his chair, skidding it across the floorboards of his stateroom, and held out his arms, which Vashnas gently lowered herself into.

For a moment, the two just stared into each other's eyes. Then she kissed him on the lips; a deep, firm kiss. Her mouth tasted like fish, but rather than being an off-putting sensation, it was delicious. He pulled her in closer, as close as he could, almost causing his chair to fall over, but he righted it before they fell.

After several seconds of kissing, Vashnas pulled away, but only a few inches. The taste of her mouth lingered on Malock's lips, a taste he hoped he would never forget.

"What's the matter?" Malock muttered, stroking her back. "There's no one watching. No one to judge."

Vashnas didn't break eye contact with him. "It's not that. It's just ... I'm not sure."

Malock kissed her briefly. "Didn't we already talk about this? I love you, Vash, and you know that. There's no need to hesitate."

Vashnas pushed herself a little away from him, but she was still in his arms. "I know. It's just that we've spent a lot of time doing this together and I'm wondering if maybe I'm distracting you from your actual duties."

"You're hardly a distraction, Vash," said Malock, once again looking into her eyes. "Do you regret that we can't really tell the rest of the crew about our relationship?"

"No," said Vashnas, shaking her head. "They already know, anyway. They gossip about us behind our backs all the time."

"And?" said Malock. "If anyone gives you any trouble about it, the Captain will punish that person severely."

"That's not what I mean," said Vashnas. "And you don't have to refer to yourself in third person, you know."

"Then what do you mean?" said Malock. "Just come out and say it. I can handle it."

45

Vashnas actually pushed herself entirely out of his arms now and stood up.

"It's just this entire voyage has put a strain on all of us," said Vashnas. "There are times where I've wondered if we should just go back."

Malock stood up, pushing his chair back as he did so. "Just go back? But we've just reached the southern seas. We can't go back."

"I know," said Vashnas. "What I'm really trying to say is ... well, I guess I'm just scared. Scared of what awaits us further on."

"Oh, I doubt there's anything we can't handle," said Malock. "Kano wouldn't have summoned me if she didn't think I could make it. And with your firsthand knowledge of the southern seas, I'd say we're going to be just fine."

"Just because I know about the southern seas doesn't make them any less dangerous," said Vashnas. "And I don't know *everything* about them. Last time I was here, I took a pretty straight line from the north to the south. I stopped for a rest every now and then, but otherwise I didn't do much exploring."

"We're taking the same route as you, so I don't understand what your problem is," said Malock. "I mean, when did you do that? Five years ago, was it? I doubt the southern seas have changed drastically in that time."

"Maybe not," said Vashnas. "But often, it's not the major things that sink ships. It's the small things, like the tiny holes in the hull that no one notices until the entire ship is halfway underwater. It's the small things I'm afraid of."

Malock pulled Vashnas into a hug again. "Don't worry, Vash. I will do everything in my power to keep you safe. I swear this on Kano's name."

Vashnas looked at him in surprise. "That's a pretty serious thing to swear by, Mal. You know what that means, don't you?"

"Yes," said Malock. "Which is why I did it. I love you more than anyone else in the world, regardless of what any narrow-minded fool thinks about our relationship, and I will defend you no matter what."

Vashnas smiled, which made her look even more beautiful. "Thanks. I really appreciate it."

Malock returned the smile, but it disappeared when he felt her grab his behind. He looked at her in surprise and saw that she was smiling seductively.

"Now why don't we ... play a little?" said Vashnas. "I'm in the mood now, if you know what I mean."

"I would love to," said Malock. "But unfortunately, I must leave very soon because I have not yet finished showing Kinker around the ship."

"Aw," said Vashnas. "Well, all right. But maybe later you and I can play, when you don't have anything else to do, of course."

Malock smiled. "Of course."

Chapter Three

KINKER HAD BEEN SO busy teaching the other fishermen about the inadequacy of their trawl that he hadn't realized that an hour had passed until Malock came up behind him and tapped him on the shoulder. Kinker turned to face the Captain, who looked slightly bemused for some reason.

"I see you are getting along with your fellow fishermen," said Malock. "But what are you doing with the trawl?"

Kinker looked down at his hands. He had been showing the others how to make a codend (he didn't have the right materials to make an entirely new trawl), but that had been difficult because the ship's trawl had been designed without a codend in mind. So far he had only managed to make a tiny codend, not big enough to catch anything but the smallest of fish, and it didn't look very good.

"He's 'improving' the trawl," said Jenur, making air quotes with her fingers.

"I tried to stop him, sir," said Deddio, scratching the back of his head. "But he insisted that the trawl needed a codend right away if we were to catch anything."

"Is that right?" said Malock, looking with more interest at Kinker's work. "You know, we threw that trawl together without knowing a thing about making trawls."

Kinker glanced at the mangled mess of slimy wet ropes in his hands and grimaced. "Yes, I can tell."

"But I must ask you to leave it here," said Malock. "Our tour of the ship is not yet complete, after all. When it is, then you can come back here and play with the trawl to your heart's content."

Kinker reluctantly dropped the trawl to his feet and followed Malock across the stern back to the center of the ship. He couldn't help but glance over his shoulder, however, at the fishing crew, who were now lugging the trawl back into the sea. None of them looked happy about it, making Kinker wonder if he had left a bad first impression.

Considering I am going to be working with them for the next several weeks or months or however long it will take for us to reach World's End, that's not good, Kinker thought. *At least they don't know about what I did on Destan. Then they* really *wouldn't like me.*

Malock led Kinker across the deck of the *Iron Wind*, occasionally pointing out something or introducing him to another member of the crew. Kinker tried his best to pay attention, to learn as much as he could, but it was difficult because his mind kept returning to that bundle of ropes and netting that they called, with sincerity, a trawl.

When they reached the bow, Malock pointed at the bowsprit and said, "That's the bowsprit, which I'm sure you already know. Take a good look at it."

Kinker walked as close to it as he could get. He at first thought that the bowsprit was a simple one, a long wood pole sticking out in the front of the ship, but the more he looked, the more he noticed that it actually was in the shape of a woman. From his current position it was impossible to see the woman's front, but he could tell that she had long, cascading hair, holding her arms above her head in a point.

"Our figurehead is a statue of Kano, naturally enough," said Malock, though he didn't sound very proud of it. "Or at least, an artist's representation of Kano and it's a very inaccurate one at that. It makes her look like a mermaid when I know for a fact that she resembles a woman made of water. All I can figure is that the artist must have never seen Kano before."

Kinker was about to say that most people probably hadn't seen Kano before when two loud, arguing voices floated on the wind from the center of the ship.

"Watch where you're going," one of the voices, which sounded human, snapped.

"You first, sinker," said another, colored with the distinctive gurgle of an aquarian. "Besides, I was just cleaning the deck, as I am supposed to. Are you lazing off again?"

"I was just heading below deck to grab some extra rope," said the human. "If anything, I think *you're* the lazy one around here. Look at how slowly you're scrubbing the deck. It's ridiculous. A human could do it faster."

"Then why don't you do it?" said the aquarian.

Malock immediately wheeled around and made his way back to

the deck without saying anything. Kinker hurried after him, trying to keep up with the younger man's long, quick strides.

The source of the commotion soon became obvious. Two sailors were arguing with each other, one human and one aquarian, as Kinker had suspected. The human was a burly man with pale skin, his fists as big as rocks, who wore only a jacket without a shirt. The aquarian had an octopus-like head and was holding a scrubber in his hand, although it took Kinker a moment to realize that the aquarian was holding the scrubber using the suction cups on its fingers and palm without actually gripping it like a human would.

Both of the sailors looked close to blows. The human sailor was red in the face and was holding his fists up in a way that suggested he knew how to use them, while the aquarian sailor held his scrubber like a knife. A handful of other sailors had stopped to watch the argument, but immediately went back to work as soon as Malock approached.

Kinker didn't blame them. Malock walked with heavy feet, his every step echoing loudly off the floorboards of the deck. He stood straight and tall and somehow seemed larger than he was. He gave off such an aura of anger and authority that Kinker felt compelled to trail a few feet behind him, rather than walk beside him, even though he knew that the Captain was not angry with him.

The two arguing sailors either didn't see their Captain approaching or didn't care. The human was now cussing so hard that even Kinker, who was not above swearing himself, felt embarrassed. The aquarian kept switching between a language he didn't understand (perhaps the aquarian tongue) and Divina, the language of the gods used by humans and aquarians to communicate. Nonetheless, the aquarian's meaning was clear even to Kinker.

Malock didn't wait for them to stop. He just walked up between them, saying, "All right, break it up, break it up you two," and shoved them apart. He almost slipped, however, because the deck beneath his feet was wet from the aquarian's scrubbing, but he caught himself quickly and looked at the two sailors with anger.

"All right," said Malock, folding his arms. "What happened?"

"This ..." the aquarian seemed to struggle to come up with a less-than-nasty word to describe his fellow sailor. "This *human* almost tripped over me while I was scrubbing the deck. I'm almost certain he did it on purpose."

"Captain, that's a damned lie from the mouth of a damned fish," said the human, folding his arms across his chest. "He tried to trip me up. I was minding my own business, making my way to the hold, when he got in my way and tripped me. Fell flat on my face and almost broke my nose."

"I didn't do that," said the aquarian. "As I said, you should have seen where you were walking, you ..." he glanced at Malock as he spoke, "... uh, you *human*."

He said that as if that was the worst insult he could think of, although Kinker knew there were worse.

"All I see is an aquarian playing the victim card," said the human sailor. "For the one hundredth time. Sometimes I wonder if you aquarians ever take responsibility for your actions."

The aquarian made an odd shrill sound that Kinker realized was a laugh. "How rich. The *human* is asking the *aquarian* to take responsibility for his actions. The irony is so thick that I'm surprised you can still see me."

Before the human could respond, Malock held up a hand and said, "Enough arguing. I don't know or care who started it. There shall be no fighting among the crew on this ship while I am Captain. Banika?"

Almost as if by magic, Banika appeared at Malock's side. Her sudden appearance made Kinker jump. She didn't comment on that. Instead, she stood at attention as usual, her arms at her sides and her face blank.

"I want you to take these two below deck and lash them," said Malock. "Ten times each. That should be enough to teach them not to fight, but not enough to cripple them or make them unable to work."

The two sailors' expressions changed from anger to fear in one instant.

"Sir, Captain, please," said the human, putting his hands together as if in prayer. "I just realized that I actually did trip over him. It was an honest mistake on my part and I don't care if he tried to do it. Honest."

"No, no, I'm the one who should be apologizing here," said the aquarian, his words becoming harder to understand through the fear clouding his accent. "I really should have paid more attention to where I was scrubbing. I've learned my lesson."

Malock shook his head. "As Captain, I have every right to discipline you for your failure to get along. Follow Banika down into the hold. Now."

Banika was already on her way to the hatch and the two sailors followed her without question. It was clear that they didn't want to, but they evidently did not dare question their Captain's orders.

Malock watched them disappear under the hatch and then he turned to Kinker and said, "Kinker, I'm sorry you had to see that. Occasionally fights break out and I have to break them up and punish the two fighters."

"But they weren't even exchanging blows," said Kinker. "Ten lashes each seems like a harsh punishment to me."

"I see you don't understand, despite your age," said Malock. "Very well. I suppose, since you've never been the captain of a ship before, you don't understand the necessity of swift and painful punishment."

"Perhaps I do not," said Kinker, "but still—"

Malock took a step closer to Kinker and leaned in closer. "You may not have noticed yet, having only been on the ship for less than a week and having spent much of that time in one room, but everyone here is on edge. Losing the rest of the fleet, plus hundreds of sailors, has harmed my crew in myriad ways, physically, mentally, and emotionally. I've been doing everything in my power to prevent a mutiny and maintain order, but it's been very difficult, mostly due to the distrust that the human sailors and aquarian sailors have for each other."

"Ah," said Kinker. "I was wondering about that. Why do you have a mixed race ship? Seems to me like that's asking for trouble. Why not just humans?"

Malock looked offended. "Because aquarians are some of the best sailors around. They have an instinctive understanding of currents and weather conditions at sea. And I know that you came from a small backwards island in the middle of nowhere and you probably have never actually met any real aquarians, but come on, Kinker. That's just offensive."

Kinker tilted his head. "How often do fights break out between the human sailors and aquarian sailors?"

"Ever since we lost the fleet, about once a week," said Malock. "Even though I make sure to punish both participants, someone always says or does something that angers or offends someone of another species, and they get into a fight. The rest of the crew hasn't been much help because they like to stand by and watch, sometimes even goading the fighters into being more violent."

"How many of the fights are started by humans and how many by aquarians?" asked Kinker.

"That's none of your business," said Malock. "Why does it matter?"

Kinker shrugged. "I just know that aquarians are by nature much more aggressive than humans. Maybe what you need to do is minimize the contact between sailors of different species."

"Aquarians aren't any more aggressive than humans," Malock said. "And anyway, there is no way to minimize contact. The *Iron Wind* may be a large ship, but she isn't that big. What I am trying to do is promote unity among the sailors, not separate them by species."

"Then perhaps you shouldn't have hired both human and aquarian sailors," Kinker said. "I have heard that the aquarians are less respectful of the gods than we humans are. Perhaps that's another source of conflict."

Malock looked like he was about to explode with anger and when he next spoke, it was in a forced calm voice. "Kinker, because you're new here, I'm not going to punish you for your extremely bigoted, wrongheaded opinions. I'm just going to give you a warning, if I catch you fighting an aquarian or saying something intentionally offensive I *will* punish you same as anyone else. Do you understand?"

"Perfectly," said Kinker. "I don't see why you're so offended, by the way. You're not an aquarian."

"And you don't know anything about actual aquarians," Malock said. "So why don't you keep your mouth shut on this issue until you've actually interacted with real aquarians? Maybe have your preconceived biases challenged?"

Kinker sighed. "All right, I'm sorry for being offensive. Can we continue the tour now?"

Malock turned away from him and said, "No. You're going back to the stern. I'll have someone else show you the rest of the ship later. Right now, I've got better things to do than listen to your ignorant opinions."

With that, Malock stomped off, leaving Kinker standing alone and slightly confused, near the mainmast. He didn't call Malock back, however, because frankly he was starting to dislike the Captain, primarily for his attitude toward his elders.

Then again, Kinker thought, as he began making his way back to the stern, having nowhere else to go, *he probably thinks that his status as royalty gives him the right to treat me however he wants. Very much like how Priestess Deber treated me back home, actually.*

Then he stopped dead and tried not to think about Deber, but just remembering her like that cause a memory to flash in his head. A young boy lying at the altar, as cold as stone ... Deber standing over him, holding a knife in hand, smiling like a madwoman ... the blood, so much blood ...

Kinker shook his head. He did not want to remember that. He had escaped Destan specifically so he could forget.

But though he managed to shove that memory out of his head, as he resumed walking back to the stern, it was all he could do to blink back the tears that the memory had invoked.

Chapter Four

THE NEXT FIVE DAYS were surprisingly uneventful, despite the southern seas' reputations for sinking any ships that sailed them. After hearing about the dangers of the southern seas for his entire life, Kinker thought they would be attacked by sea monsters daily, yet all they ever saw were the fish they caught in the trawl (which Kinker had failed to improve on in any significant way).

The weather was beautiful as well; clear skies, a warm sun, and water so blue it looked like paint on a canvas. Legend said that Kano had painted the ocean blue because she wanted it to look like the sky; but true or not, it was a wonderful sight to behold nonetheless.

A routine became apparent to Kinker. Every day, he and the fishing crew would get up at the crack of dawn and haul in the trawl. They would then spend about an hour going through the morning's catch, tossing out the fish unfit for human and aquarian consumption, keeping those that were, and then tossing the trawl back into the sea.

After that, they spent another hour or two cleaning the fish. This was probably the easiest part of the job because Kinker had had a lot of experience cleaning fish, but it sometimes took longer than expected because he kept trying to correct the others' methods, which were often clumsy and ineffective. This did not endear him to the others.

When they'd cleaned all the fish, they would haul the bits of fish to the galley, where the ship's cook, Arisha Frag—an older woman who was probably a few years younger than Kinker—would begin making breakfast. Often Kinker and the other fishermen would help, as Arisha could not make enough meals for a hundred and twenty sailors by herself.

By this time, the rest of the crew would be up, doing their daily chores and checking on the things they had left the night before. While Malock never came to breakfast, Kinker often saw Banika going around making sure that everyone was doing what they were supposed to do. He never asked her about the punishment she had inflicted on the two fighting sailors from the day before, mostly because when he saw those two sailors himself at breakfast the day after they were punished, they looked as docile as puppies.

Breakfast was always a noisy, messy affair. Due to the low food supply, each sailor, whether human or aquarian, was only allowed one fish. This was very clearly not enough for the fully-grown men and women who made up the crew, but they all seemed resigned to it, probably because it was the only way to make sure that every sailor got at least something to eat.

After breakfast, the crew would return to their normal duties.

The fishing crew usually took this time to sit around and rest after a long morning of hard work. Often the fishermen began talking about various things, such as how awful the food was (even though they helped prepare it), what the weather was going to be like that day, and whether Malock and Vashnas actually were sleeping together, among other topics. Kinker rarely participated in this conversations, partly because they did not interest him but primarily because the rest of the fishing crew didn't really like him that much.

The routine was repeated at lunch and dinner time. The fishing crew would haul the trawl out of the water, pick out the good fish and toss away the bad, clean the fish, deliver them to the kitchen, help prepare the food, and then eat with the rest of the crew.

Then after dinner they'd toss the trawl back into the sea one last time, make sure it was firmly attached to the bulwarks, and then go to sleep below deck. Kinker always slept well, despite the cramped conditions and lack of proper bedding, because by the end of each day he was always drop-dead exhausted. It was usually a good exhausted, the kind you get after a good day of hard work, which was probably the only reason he managed to sleep through the combined unwashed body odor of four humans and two aquarians sharing a cramped room together in an even smellier ship.

Because Kinker had direct access to the food supply, he noticed that Malock often got more food—not a whole lot more, but enough that Kinker noticed—than the rest of the crew. Not only that, but the Captain's face was fuller than the faces of his sailors, which were mostly due to a lack of food. Of course, Kinker didn't see Malock very often due to his busy schedule, but every time he saw the young

Captain, he was always struck by how well-fed he seemed to be.

On the fifth day, shortly after lunch, Kinker shared this observation with Jenur Takren, as they and the rest of the fishing crew rested at the stern, near the trawl. Despite her earlier attitude toward him, she was the only member of the fishing crew who didn't actively avoid or exclude Kinker from their conversations; if anything, she seemed to like him (despite her wisecracks) which Kinker was thankful for because he felt very alone on this ship. Having someone who he could talk to, even if that someone was old enough to be his granddaughter, made him feel a lot better.

"Yeah, I noticed," said Jenur as she tossed the remains of her fish overside, which was the usual disposal method for the sailors. "He's got his own supply of food in his stateroom. It's been that way for a while."

She sounded more than a little bitter, prompting Kinker to say, "So he's keeping a lot of food for himself? Why?"

Jenur rolled her eyes. "Isn't it obvious? He's the Captain and he's a Prince. He thinks he's the most important, special person ever. Thinks he's chosen by Kano, remember?"

Kinker looked around uneasily, but the other fishermen were having a spirited conversation about when the next fight would break out and there was no one else nearby who might eavesdrop on them. "I don't know if I'd talk that way about our Captain, Jenur."

Jenur stared at Kinker. "Why do you think I care about what Malock hears? He knows what we think about him. He just doesn't care."

"He doesn't?"

"Of course," said Jenur. "The boatswain, Banika, she doesn't just make sure the ship doesn't fall apart. She spies on us and reports everything she hears directly to the Captain. There are no such things as secrets on this ship, at least to Malock."

Kinker disagreed with that (after all, he had plenty of his own secrets that he was determined to take to the grave), but he kept his disagreement to himself.

"As long as we don't try to mutiny, Malock doesn't care what we think about him," said Jenur. "All he cares about is getting to World's End."

"That's not exactly true," said Kinker. "There was a fight five days ago between a human sailor and an aquarian sailor. He broke that up and punished both of them."

"Oh, right," said Jenur, rolling her eyes. "Yeah, human-aquarian relations are a big pet issue of his. That's why he's sleeping with Vashnas, you know."

Kinker could not help but shudder at the thought. "But that's so ... disgusting. Why would any human do that?"

"Who knows?" said Jenur, who Kinker was pleased to see was equally disgusted by it. "All I know is that he's royalty and so he thinks he can do whatever the hell he likes."

Kinker leaned against the bulwarks and nodded. "That is true. It still boggles my mind, though, and probably always will."

Jenur looked like she had a lot more to say about that, but at that moment, a loud voice roared from the crow's nest: "Land ho!"

Those two simple words acted like a spark to dried wood on the ship. Sailors dropped what they were doing and ran to port, starboard, and bow, leaning over the bulwarks, trying their best to see the land that the lookout had announced. Kinker didn't try, mostly because his eyes were not that good, but he nonetheless walked over to the starboard side, where the rest of the fishing crew had gathered in order to see the island.

It seemed like the entire crew had gathered on the top deck, straining to see the first island of the southern seas. There was a lot of pushing and shoving to get the best spots, but no fights broke out. A few of the smarter sailors climbed the ratlines, putting themselves well above the others, and put their hands over their eyes in order to catch a glimpse of the island.

"Where is it? I don't see it."

"Vinji! Did you really see an island or did you make another false call?"

A head poked over the side of the crow's nest above, too far up for Kinker to make out any details, and shouted, "I sure as hell see an island. Just because I made a false call *once*—"

A loud whistle suddenly blew, its sound so loud that it drowned out almost every other noise on the deck. All of the sailors immediately turned to see Malock and Banika standing near the mainmast, Banika holding a boatswain's call in her hand, the obvious source of the whistle.

Malock himself stood on a box, as though trying to make sure that everyone could see him. He waited until all of the sailors were paying attention to him before saying, "I am glad to see that you are all excited to see the first island of the southern seas. It has been many weeks since we last set foot on solid ground and I can confirm that we will definitely be anchoring off the shore of this new island, which Vashnas informs me is called Ikadori Island."

Excited murmurs swept through the assembled sailors. Jenur had her arms crossed across her chest, but even she looked a bit happy at the thought they were going to be back on land again. Kinker didn't care, as he had only been on the ship for a week or two, but it was hard not to feel the same excitement as everyone else.

Malock raised a hand and all of the sailors fell silent. "We will land on Ikadori Island to pick ikadori peaches from its trees. According to Vashnas, the island has hundreds of ikadori peach trees, all fit for human and aquarian consumption. We will spend three days picking and packing the fruit into the hold and then we'll continue this voyage."

"You mean we'll *finally* have something else to eat other than fish and crap?" one sailor yelled from the crew.

Malock nodded, looking as pleased as the yelling sailor. "Yes. We'll pick so many peaches that we'll never have to worry about food again, maybe not even have to use the trawl anymore."

"Uh oh," Jenur said in a low voice that only Kinker could hear. "Guess we'll be out of a job if that happens."

Kinker wasn't sure if she was joking or not, so he simply continued listening to Malock, who said, "For this first expedition, which will begin as soon as the ship is anchored off the island's coast, I am only going to take ten sailors with me onto the shore."

"Only ten?" another sailor shouted, sounding angry. "But we've been on this ship for so long—"

"We will be a scouting party," said Malock, not even bothering to apologize for interrupting. "Though Vashnas assures us that we will be safe as long as we do not go beyond the ikadori treeline, we must scout it out anyway just to be sure there haven't been any changes since Vashnas last set foot on the island herself. Therefore I will only take along those who I believe are good hunters, trackers, or fighters."

There was even more grumbling about that, though a handful of the sailors looked hopeful, as if they thought they had a better chance of being picked than the others.

"I know everyone here really wants to get onto dry land again, but the southern seas are still dangerous," said Malock. "We've been lucky that we've had sunny skies and calm seas so far, but I don't want any of us letting our guard down around here, not when we've made it this far. So I don't want to hear even one word of complaint from any of you because all of you will get a chance to go on land at some point during the next three days. Got it?"

He said that last sentence with such authority that the sailors stopped grumbling immediately. Even Jenur stopped rolling her eyes.

"Now," said Malock, looking down on them all like children. "All of you, get back to your stations. Tomorrow morning, I will have Banika put up the list of the members of the first expedition on the mainmast, where everyone can read it. Until then, the wind is still blowing and the sea is still flowing, so get back to work."

The crowd of sailors dispersed immediately, every sailor going back to his or her station. Kinker did not hear even one word of complaint from any of the sailors, which meant they took Malock's orders very seriously.

What he heard instead, for the rest of the day, was constant speculation about who would be on the first expedition. Gino, for example, seemed convinced that he was going to be picked because he had earned a reputation as a skilled hunter back in his home, while Jenur seemed equally convinced that Malock wasn't going to choose one of the fishermen because they still were the main providers of food and he wasn't stupid enough to risk one of his fishermen until they had a more stable food supply.

The speculations went on for the rest of the day. Kinker did not partake in them much, mostly because they seemed pointless to him. He had no control over Malock's choices and he didn't see how speculating about who would be part of the first expedition would help anything. He just listened to the fishing crew as they worked and to the rest of the sailors at mealtimes endlessly speculate over who would and who wouldn't be picked.

The next morning, at the crack of dawn, Kinker was surprised to see so many sailors already up and about. Usually only the fishing crew was up this early, but as he and the other fishermen emerged from the hatch, the reason became obvious: There was a piece of paper nailed to the mainmast at eye height, which was undoubtedly the list of Malock's picks for the first expedition. That explained why some sailors were walking away with their heads down while others were high-fiving their friends as they returned to work.

"Want to see who's on the list, Kinks?" said Jenur.

"I suppose it wouldn't hurt," said Kinker with a shrug.

The entire fishing crew came along with them, even though they were supposed to be hauling in the trawl at this time. They quickly reached the mainmast, but due to the large amount of sailors still standing around it, it was impossible for them all to get close enough to read the list.

So Jenur slipped through the crowd and returned a few seconds later. "None of us are on the list."

"What?" said Gino. "You must be mistaken. Surely there's at least one of us on the list?"

"None," said Jenur. "Not you, not me, not Kinks, not any of us. Guess I was right when I said that Malock wasn't dumb enough to risk one of us. We're just too special."

"Besides, Gino, the Captain did say that everyone would get a chance to go onto the island eventually," Deddio said, slapping the aquarian on the back in his usual upbeat manner. "So maybe you won't get to go there on the first expedition, but perhaps on the next ones you will."

Gino didn't look at all happy about it, but he nodded and said, "Eh, well, maybe you're right, Ded. Still, that means another couple of days, at the most, on this god-forsaken wreck of a ship. I'm gonna go crazy if I have to stay on here any longer than that."

Kinker shrugged. "Perhaps we should get back to work, now that we know who isn't going to be on the expedition. The trawl isn't going to pull itself out of the water, after all."

So the rest of the day went by as normal, although the sailors who were part of the expedition seemed to take great pride in being chosen. In particular, a woman named Kocas Iknor bragged about how she had obviously been chosen for her great skills as a hunter, skills that she had developed back on her home island in the Friana

67

Archipelago. She seemed to think this endeared the others to her, but whenever she wasn't around, the other sailors cracked a lot of inappropriate jokes about her. Kinker should know because he cracked a few himself.

As the *Iron Wind* continued to sail south, Ikadori Island gradually came into view until eventually everyone could see it. By the time they could, however, it was early evening and getting colder, forcing Kinker to pull his pea coat more tightly around his body. He didn't actually get to see the island, not even when they anchored, because by the time they reached it, the sun had set and night came on like a thief (or so it seemed to him). He wondered if the God of the Sun had decided to end the day early for some reason.

It was only in the morning that Kinker saw Ikadori Island for the first time. After breakfast, he and Jenur joined another group of sailors to the port, which was the side facing the island. Jenur leaned against, almost over, the bulwarks, while Kinker stood by her, trying not to get in the way of the other sailors who were also trying to see the island.

From what Kinker could see of it, Ikadori Island was large. The shore stretched around the island like a ring, while a thick, dark jungle covered almost every inch of available space. The only space on the island that had not been conquered by the jungle was the white, sandy beach. Big, hand-shaped fruit hung off the trees near the shore, which Kinker instantly recognized as ikadori peaches.

No sounds came from the island. Nor was there any movement among the trees. Ikadori Island looked totally uninhabited. There was no sign of civilization, nor any sign of animals either. Of course, if there were any animals, most of them were probably deep inside the jungle. Still, the island seemed unnaturally silent to Kinker, making him grateful that he was not part of the initial expedition.

Malock soon emerged from his stateroom, now wearing a hunting jacket instead of his boat cloak, and gathered the ten sailors he was taking with him to the shore. They stood near the davit, but they weren't the only ones there. Malock had summoned the rest of the crew, too, in order to give some last orders before the expedition departed.

"All right," said Malock, once the rest of the crew had assembled before him. "While I and my expedition pick fruit and explore Ikadori Island, Banika Koiro will act as captain of the ship. Obey her every word as if it were my own. And if something happens and the expedition is killed, you must weight anchor and depart right away. There is no reason for you to go any further south if I am dead."

That was a surprisingly humane thing for Malock to say. Kinker supposed he shouldn't be too surprised. Malock did have a human side to him, despite being stern to his crew. Kinker had seen it a few times, but he still thought this was awfully generous of Malock.

After that, it took only a few minutes for the members of the expedition to hop into the rowboats, which were then lowered into the sea. Kinker stood at the port with the rest of the crew that was staying behind, watching as the expedition rowed to the shore of the island and hoping they would be all right.

When the expedition got within a couple dozen yards of Ikadori Island's shore, the rowboats got stuck in the shallow waters, forcing the members of the expedition to get out of their boats and haul them the rest of the way. The water was warm, thankfully, but Malock still didn't like getting water in his boots.

As soon as they hauled their boats safely up the shoreline, Malock was glad he had chosen to wear his hunting jacket, rather than his boat cloak. Sand clung to his boots and pants and the dark jungle ahead of them looked like it would snag and tear the clothes of anyone who tried to enter. It was not an inviting-looking place.

Nonetheless, actually setting foot on the sand was wonderful. He had not realized how used he was to the constant motion of the *Iron Wind* until he found himself unable to stand straight for more than a few seconds on the sand. The other sailors also had a hard time adjusting to the stability, one of them even falling flat on his bum, like he was dizzy.

Despite that, Malock felt far more at home on the sandy beach of the island than he did on the deck of the *Iron Wind*. Unlike the rest of his crew, Malock wasn't a sea dog. He had never been much interested in the sea until he received his vision from Kano. A part of him wondered if that was why he had lost the entire fleet besides the *Iron Wind*, but he ignored that and put it down to bad luck instead.

Malock unsheathed his sword and said to his men, "All right, men, we're going to mostly skim the treeline and shore. Don't let your guard down and if anything attacks you, shoot or stab it."

The sailors all checked their guns and swords. Malock wasn't sure how well the guns would work, as this was the first time they had ever needed to use them on the voyage, but he had taken special care to make sure that the gunpowder and the guns themselves stayed dry. So he figured they would at least shoot, which was all he needed them to be able to do.

Of course, Malock didn't have a gun himself. Guns were the common man's weapon, after all, and Malock was certainly no common man. Instead, he had brought along a Carnagian sword, a special one of a kind blade designed by the best Grinfian blacksmiths in all of the Northern Isles. Having received extensive sword training as part of his education back home, Malock knew he could defend himself if necessary.

To conquer the beach more quickly, Malock split the party into two groups of five (not counting himself). One would go to the left end of the beach, the other to the right. They would then meet back in the middle, right where the rowboats were landed, and report what they found there. Malock stressed to the left party (he was in charge of the right) not to go beyond the treeline, even if they saw something, because they knew very little about what lurked within the jungle.

In case of emergencies, Malock gave the leader of the left party, an aquarian named Danaf, a loud whistle he could blow. The whistle was rather ordinary, aside from the fact that it had been enchanted by a mage to increase its sound, which would ensure that even the sailors aboard the *Iron Wind* would hear it. So the expedition split up, agreeing to regroup in the center of the beach in half an hour.

Malock was at the head of the right party, his sword unsheathed. He sensed the eyes of the men behind him, searching the trees, the sand, the waves, the ikadori peaches; anything that could possibly hide a threat. It was all so quiet and so still that not even the wind was blowing, which only made Malock and his party ever more anxious.

The sun continued its slow, lazy ascent in the sky behind them, its rays reflecting off the white sand. One ray caused something in the sand to glint, causing Malock to raise his sword, signaling to his men to halt.

Without saying a word, Malock approached the glinting object and knelt over it. The object in question was a diamond, similar to the kind that decorated the Temple of Grinf back on Carnag, except much smaller and duller, like it had been there for a while. Malock was surprised that a treasure crab or some other animal attracted to shiny objects had not yet taken it; after all, it was right there for the taking.

"What is it, sir?" said one of Malock's men, a human named Forl Mas. "Is it dangerous?"

Malock reached down and wrapped his fingers around the tiny rock. "It's just a diamond. Possibly Grinfian, by the look—"

He stopped talking when he noticed how the diamond refused to budge, even when he pulled, as if it were attached to something deep beneath the sand. That didn't stop Malock, though. He put his sword aside and, using both hands, tugged at the diamond with all of his might.

A loud *pop* preceded Malock staggering backwards. Forl caught him before he could fall and said, "Sir, what ... happened ..."

Forl's words trailed off when he spotted the very bony, very human remains of a hand sticking out of the sand, its middle finger now missing.

When Malock saw it, he looked at the diamond in his hand. It was actually a diamond ring that he had pulled out of the sand, a ring with the skeletal hand's missing middle finger still stuck through it. This caused Malock to gasp and, without thinking, hurl the detached finger into the bay. The finger landed in the water with a small splash and sank out of sight.

"You desecrated a grave, Captain," said another sailor, a female aquarian whose name Malock could not recall at the moment. "Do you know what that means, sir?"

Malock shook his head, trying not to look afraid, even though the sight of the skeletal hand still sent shivers down his spine. "I don't care what that means, sailor. Dig the rest of it up. I want to see if there's a whole skeleton under there."

The female aquarian stepped back. Her face resembled that of a guppy, thus making the fear in her eyes evident. "No way, Captain sir. I'm a follower of Diog, God of the Grave, and we Diogians aren't supposed to desecrate the graves of any dead being, human, aquarian, or whatever. Part of the Diogian Creed, you see."

Malock sighed. "Fine. Does anyone else here have objections to 'desecrating' the grave of a dead person?"

The other four did not look thrilled at the idea of digging up a grave, but they nonetheless complied while the female aquarian stood back, looking even more disgusted than they did. Malock was annoyed at her refusal to dig, but he respected her commitment to her god nonetheless.

The party lacked shovels, so they mostly used their hands to dig. Forl showed some creativity by stripping off a large layer of bark from a nearby ikadori tree and using it as a shovel, but it still took them ten minutes to dig the entire skeleton up.

Or, rather, skeleton*s*. As they cleared each layer of sand, they found more and more scattered body parts. Some were obviously human, such as a complete lower torso, while others, like the bony fins, were just as obviously from aquarians. Some of the bones were mixed together so thoroughly it was impossible to tell where the human began and aquarian ended or vice versa. Some of the bones had bits of clothing attached to them or some sort of jewelry, but the vast majority were bare.

Malock became so interested in this mystery that he actually got down on his hands and knees and started helping his men. He immediately wished he hadn't, however, because he immediately came upon a dreadful skeleton: That of a human baby, missing the upper half of its head, its tiny arms and legs with teeth marks in them.

It was so horrible that he stood up and, being careful not to look at the skeletons, ordered his men to stop and take a step back so they could see what they'd dug up.

When they did, it became clear what it was they had found: A mass grave made up of dozens of beings, humans and aquarians alike. It had obviously been there for a while, but how long, Malock couldn't say for sure.

"This is bad," said Forl, wiping the sweat off his forehead. "Bad, bad, bad. There's gotta be at least three dozen skeletons, maybe more, and I wouldn't be surprised if this was just the top layer."

"But what killed them all?" said the female aquarian, whose name Malock now remembered was Crina. "Maybe there's a tribe of cannibals on this island. I've heard tales of cannibals living on the southern islands."

"Doubt its anything human," said another sailor. "Look at the teeth marks on all the bones. Maybe a shark aquarian ate 'em or something."

"Those aren't shark teeth marks," Crina said. "These almost look like human teeth."

"Impossible," said Malock, shaking his head. "Human teeth aren't strong enough to bite through bone or even leave a mark."

But he had to admit that her description wasn't entirely inaccurate. When he glanced at the baby again, he noticed that the upper half of its skull appeared to have been bitten straight off, the way a person might bite off a large chunk of steak. The thought was so horrible that he immediately rejected it from his mind and vowed never to think it again.

"Whatever it is, we need to return to the center," said Malock. "It's been nearly twenty minutes and I'm sure that the others will want to—"

A loud, shrill sound struck their ears, a sound that Malock recognized immediately:

The whistle was being blown.

Chapter Five

MALOCK AND HIS PARTY didn't waste any time abandoning the mass grave. Soon they returned to the center of the beach, where they found the left party gathered near the boats. As soon as Malock's party came within shouting distance, Danaf looked up and immediately ran to meet them.

The aquarian looked terrible. His face was bloody and cut in several places. His jacket sleeves were torn off completely, revealing a long, bloody wound that made Malock's stomach churn. His webbed hands were torn in a few places. He looked so terrible that Malock was surprised he could walk at all, much less run to them.

"Captain!" said Danaf, skidding to a halt in the sand as they stopped. "My brother ... taken into the jungle ... couldn't save him ... please, help ..."

Before anyone could respond, Danaf collapsed face first onto the sand, the blood from his wounds staining the white beach.

Alarmed, Malock bent over and held Danaf in his arms, trying to wake the wounded aquarian. By the time Danaf regained consciousness, the rest of the left party had joined them, but when Malock did a quick head count, he realized that one of the sailors was missing.

"Danaf," said Malock. "Where is Sumsa? Your brother?"

Danaf's face was partially crusted with sand, but he managed to say, "Took him ... the jungle took him ..."

Malock looked up at the rest of Danaf's party and said, "What's he talking about? What does he mean, 'the jungle took him'?"

"It is exactly as he said, sir," said one of the other sailors, a human. "We was searching the left side of the shore, like you ordered us to, when Sumsa saw something moving in the trees. Sumsa's an impulsive lad, I reckon, because he went to investigate it even when we told him to stay back. When he got close to the treeline, a bunch of vines snatched him right in front of our eyes."

"Vines?" Malock repeated. "That's impossible."

"'Tis true, though," said the sailor. "The others can confirm my story. Right, guys?"

The other two members of the left party nodded fervently. They looked a little better than Danaf, though not by much.

"What happened to Danaf, then?" said Malock.

"Ran after the lad, he did," said the sailor. "A good big brother he is. Almost got killed, though, because it's as dark as night in that jungle. We went in after him and just barely managed to drag him out."

"You couldn't find Sumsa?" said Malock as he gently lowered Danaf (who had fallen unconscious again) back onto the sand.

"Nope," said the sailor. "Far as we can tell, the jungle took Sumsa and isn't going to give him back anytime soon."

Malock cursed and looked at the treeline. The jungle had always looked dark to him, but now it looked downright sinister. "All right, men. Half of you, go back to the *Iron Wind* and tell everyone what happened."

"Sorry to burst your bubble, sir, but I think they already saw," said the sailor. "We were in plain sight of the ship the entire time. Bet the whole crew saw it happen. Wouldn't be surprised if they were already assembling a team to come here."

Malock stood up and unsheathed his sword. "I still want half of you to go back. Take Danaf with you and get him to Telka immediately. The rest of us will go into the jungle and try to find Sumsa."

"Sir?" said Forl, glancing into the jungle. "Are you sure that's a wise move? I mean, you saw what happened to the left party. Maybe we should all go back."

Malock whirled and pointed the tip of his sword under Forl's chin. Forl shrank back, looking quite timid despite his buff arms.

"Are you questioning my orders, Forl?" said Malock, in his most authoritative voice. "Or do you just not care about your fellow sailors all that much?"

"I'm not questioning you at all, Captain, sir," said Forl, holding his hands up in a submissive position. "It's just ... well, I didn't think you'd risk your own life like this. Th-that's all."

Malock lowered his sword and looked at the jungle. "As Captain of the *Iron Wind*, I will not unnecessarily sacrifice the lives of any of my sailors. Besides, as Kano's chosen, I will probably be okay."

It didn't take Malock long to divide the expedition into two teams. To avoid losing his best men, Malock sent Danaf, Kocas, Forl, and the other two injured sailors back to the *Iron Wind* on one of the rowboats. The other half, consisting of Crina, the human sailor, and the other two who weren't badly injured, were going with him into the jungle.

Right before the second party left, Malock took Forl aside and said, "When you get back to the ship, tell Banika to refrain from sending a rescue party for the next six hours."

"Six hours, sir?" said Forl. "Do you think your party will find Sumsa in six hours?"

"Possibly," said Malock, though privately he doubted that. "I just don't want to risk the lives of anyone else on the crew." *Especially Vashnas,* he thought.

Forl saluted and said, "And if you don't return in six hours, what do we do then?"

Malock looked at the *Iron Wind* anchored just off the shore and said, "Turn the ship back north and head home. Because if we don't return by then ... then we will probably be dead."

The jungle of Ikadori Island was as silent as the beach. There were no insects buzzing, no birds chirping in the trees, not even the screeching of monkeys to break the stillness. It was like walking into an audimancer's study, except far muggier and much less friendly.

Every member of Malock's party had their weapons drawn. Though Malock didn't think that anything was following them, he had ordered his men to keep quiet at all times so they could hear anything coming up behind them. They consented readily, perhaps because the stillness of the jungle made talking seem inappropriate.

It seemed like the ikadori trees were mostly found along the shore because the farther in they went, the fewer ikadori peaches they found on the ground. Eventually, the ikadori trees disappeared entirely, replaced by odd-looking trees with black bark, wrapped in red and green vines, with great white leaves that shrouded them in darkness.

Not even the wind blew in the jungle; the leaves on the trees were perfectly still. Vines hung from the branches, reminding Malock of the hanger snakes from Carnag, a species of snake that hang from tree branches like a vine and killed whatever grabbed them. These vines were clearly not snakes, but every time Malock's arm brushed against one, he jumped and his men would aim their guns at it only to discover that it was nothing more than a mere vine.

And it was dark, almost like night time, as the sailor from the left party had said earlier. The leaves and branches above their heads crisscrossed so tightly that little light shone through, despite the bright mid-morning sun. Malock wished he'd brought along a lamp because he was certain that, if there was something stalking them right now, it would have no trouble picking them off one by one, if it wanted to.

Because the sun was obscured, it was impossible to tell how many hours had passed. Malock supposed it had probably only been one hour, maybe two, but his sense of time was off and he didn't want to ask the others how much time they thought had passed because he didn't want to create any unnecessary sound.

Then Crina's voice whispered through the darkness suddenly.

"Hey ... did you guys hear that?"

The rescue party stopped and listened. At first, Malock heard nothing, but then he heard something swishing through the air and the next moment something hard slammed into his face. Seeing stars in his eyes, Malock fell over backward amid the noises of gun shots, shouts, and what sounded like slapping ropes twirling through the air.

Confused and scared, Malock rolled away from the scene, got to his feet, and ran. Something hot whizzed by his ear, almost taking it clean off, and he felt a vine try to snag his foot but he slapped it away with his sword and kept running, never looking back, never slowing down even slightly.

He had no idea how many hours he ran. He crashed through the bushes, cut down vines and branches that got in his way, and didn't even try to be quiet. There was no point in being silent now, not when his location was known and the *thing*—whatever it was—could get him if he wasn't careful.

Then his foot met empty air and he went falling. He landed flat on his back in the bottom of a pit, causing pain to shoot up his spine like he'd never felt before. This time he bit back his scream, even biting his own tongue to keep silent. He had no idea what was chasing him, no idea what had attacked (and probably killed) his men, but he was betting that the thing relied on sound more than sight, so if he kept quiet then it might not find him.

'Might' was the operative word because above him he could hear movement. It sounded like a hundred snakes were slithering across the ground at once, like the branches of trees were creaking, like the entire jungle was coming alive. A loud, long scream pierced the air, making his heart skip a beat, and then the scream abruptly ceased and the entire jungle went silent once again.

For the next several hours, Malock didn't move a muscle. He just silently prayed to Kano, to Grinf, and to every other deity he had ever paid homage to in his short life (which, he realized, wasn't very much). It was all he could do.

"I'm going after him and there's no way any of you are going to stop me."

Vashnas stood near the davit on the port, her fingers clenched tightly around a gun in her hands that she obviously didn't know how to hold correctly. Before her, Banika guarded the rowboat, leaning against it with her arms folded across her chest. Though Banika's face was as inscrutable as ever, she was clearly ready to tumble if necessary.

Kinker observed this scene from a safe distance, several dozen yards down from them. Normally, at this time of day, he and the other fishermen would have been hauling in the trawl for lunch, but because the *Iron Wind* had been stationary all day, the fishing crew pretty much had nothing to do until Malock returned. Kinker had decided to spend his time looking at Ikadori Island, as he had never seen a jungle before.

Frankly, he was surprised Vashnas had waited so long to try this. When Forl and the other sailors returned with the news of Malock's decision to rescue Sumsa from the jungle five hours ago, Kinker had been certain that Vashnas would immediately go after him. Instead, she had disappeared below deck, missed out on lunch, and only emerged a few minutes ago, armed to the teeth with knives, guns, and hunting gear that Kinker hadn't even known were in the hold.

In spite of Vashnas's impressive array of weapons, Banika hardly looked terrified. The boatswain was always a difficult read, but if Kinker had to describe her attitude right now, it was confidence. It was an amused kind of confidence, as if Banika was thinking, *Oh, so you think you can get past me with all of those toys of yours? Think again.*

"You heard what Forl said the Captain told him," said Banika, her tone even and calm. "If he doesn't return in six hours—and it's only been five so far—then we're supposed to turn this ship back north and return home. We're not supposed to send anyone after him."

"I'm not asking for your permission," Vashnas said. "I want to go, and I'll fight you if I have to."

Banika didn't even move. "That would be an unwise move on your part, Vashnas. Very unwise."

Vashnas flashed a confident smile. "Says the middle-aged woman. As much as I respect Malock, I've often wondered why he chose someone so ... *old* to be his first mate. You might still have some moves, but I doubt that aging body of yours is as fast as it was when you were younger."

Now Kinker didn't have the best eyes in the world, but he was pretty sure that his vision didn't mess up when Vashnas dropped her gun and grabbed her right wrist while Banika actually smirked ever-so-slightly. It took Kinker a moment to spot the knife Banika held in her hand. Where she had gotten it from, he wasn't sure. Nor was he sure that he wanted to know.

"True, I may not be as young as I used to be," said Banika, "but you forget that with age comes experience. And I have plenty of that."

"When Malock returns, I'll tell him you hurt me," Vashnas grumbled. "He won't like that."

"And I'll tell him that I was keeping you from getting yourself killed," said Banika. "Which do you think he'll respond to better?"

Kinker thought Vashnas was going to give up, but much to his surprised, she ripped off a portion of her right sleeve and tied it around her bleeding wrist as a makeshift bandage. Then she looked Banika straight in the eye.

"I think he'd respond better to me making a rescue attempt, personally," said Vashnas. "And that was a neat trick you pulled back there, with that knife. Too bad it's not enough to make me give up."

Banika opened her mouth to say something, but then her eyes rolled into the back of her head and she fell face forward. She would have hit the deck face first if Vashnas had not caught her instead.

"What did you do?" said Kinker, abandoning his spot by the bulwarks and walking over to her. "Did you hit her?"

"No," said Vashnas as she gently lowered the boatswain onto the deck. "I—"

"I thought Banika needed a nap," said a deep voice behind them.

Kinker and Vashnas turned around to see Bifor standing not far behind them. He held his short wand up, pointing it directly at Banika, his expression cool and unreadable.

"You didn't put her in a coma or anything, did you?" said Vashnas, glancing over her shoulder at the unconscious Banika.

Bifor shook his head. "Just cast a basic sleep spell on her, that's all.

She'll wake up refreshed in a few hours, so I'd say this actually benefits her quite well."

"But why did you do that?" said Kinker, looking up at the large mage. "She didn't do anything to you."

"Because I wish to save the Captain, too, of course," said Bifor. "Mostly because I am convinced that he is the only thing keeping this crew together. If he died, do you think we would be organized enough to mount a return voyage home, even under Banika's leadership? I doubt it, myself."

Vashnas smiled. "Then come along, Bifor, because I'm going to Ikadori Island right now and I need all the help I can get. Kinker, do you want to come, too?"

Kinker felt torn. On one hand, he didn't want to face whatever was lurking in the jungle, especially after seeing what happened to Danaf. Even with Bifor and Vashnas, he wasn't sure they would survive.

On the other hand, he realized Bifor was right. Without Malock's strong leadership, the racial tensions bubbling just beneath the surface would burst out and the entire crew would likely fall into chaos. True, they would still have Banika to lead them, but as strong as she was, he wasn't so sure she would make for the best replacement Captain.

So he said, "All right. But we should get a few others first. Three people might not be enough to rescue Malock."

Vashnas sighed, but said, "All right. Grab three others. Quickly. Doesn't matter who. We've got to go before it's too late."

Malock didn't realize it, but he must have dozed off sometime in the last hour because he jerked awake when he felt something crawl over his legs. He raised head high enough just in time to see the tail of a snake slither somewhere into the darkness.

The sight of the snake made him start. The sudden movement sent a jolt of pain up his spine, forcing him to groan louder than he would have liked. When nothing attacked him, he allowed himself to sit up, but slowly because his back still ached from the fall. He looked around the bottom of the pit to observe his surroundings, hoping to distract his mind from his aching back.

It was still dark, but not quite as dark as before. A gap in the trees above allowed a little sunlight to shine through, showing him that he had landed in a bed of old vines, fallen leaves, and bushes. The pit smelled much like the rest of the jungle, although a whiff of blood told him that he was bleeding and a quick check of his body showed that a small cut in the back of his head was the source of the bleeding (though it was thankfully not very much).

Standing up, Malock looked at the walls of the pit. They were tall and covered in vines, so he figured he could climb out of the pit if he tried. His back and head still ached and there was still the possibility of a monster above, but he didn't want to stay down in this pit forever, so he decided he would take his chances. He sheathed his sword and walked over to the nearest wall.

The first vine he grabbed snapped straight off, but the second vine held his weight and he began climbing it. It was hard work. The walls were much taller than he had first supposed and his aching back and head made him feel like he was lugging a hundred swords lodged into his spine. Nonetheless, he had to get out of there, find the shore, and try to return to the *Iron Wind*. Nothing else mattered.

It wasn't until after he reached the top of the pit and pulled himself over, his body and clothes drenched with sweat and his back almost literally screaming with pain, that he realized six hours must have already passed. If they did, then that meant that the crew of the *Iron Wind* were probably already on their way home, abandoning him on this strange island, just as he had ordered them to.

It seemed like such a noble idea at the time, Malock thought, lying flat on his stomach near the lip of the pit. *The selfless Captain, putting the interest of his crew first by giving them the opportunity to leave even if he is not dead. Now I can't help but think it was the stupidest decision I've made yet on this voyage.*

There was the small chance that maybe they disobeyed or perhaps ran into some kind of trouble that prevented them from leaving. That seemed unlikely to Malock until he remembered the jungle attacking and probably killing his team. Maybe the waters around the island were as violent and unpredictable as the jungle.

After a few minutes of resting, Malock sat up. His back didn't hurt quite so bad anymore, but it was still bad enough that he had to sit still for several minutes, practicing a form of meditation that a Grinfian monk had taught him in his teenage years. It was a simple technique in which Malock tried to focus on something else to distract his mind from the pain. Supposedly, masters of this technique could wipe away even chronic pain, but Malock had never bothered to master it because it seemed unnecessary.

Now Malock wished he'd been a better student as a teenager

because he found it almost impossible to focus on anything but the pain. He decided to give up and just start walking to the shore. He wasn't sure what direction the shore was, but he reasoned that he would reach it no matter what direction he walked in; after all, Ikadori Island was not a continent. So long as he kept walking, he would eventually reach the beach.

Carefully, Malock rose to his feet, leaning against a tree for support. This simple movement made his back ache, but he bit his lower lip to keep from crying out, remembering that the monster in the jungle was probably still out there, perhaps searching for him even now.

Just as Malock decided to test walking, a loud voice, like the rustling of leaves, came from above, saying, "How was your nap, mortal?"

The unexpected voice caused Malock to jump, almost causing him to fall back into the pit. But he caught himself and stumbled back away from the pit. His sudden movement caused his back to flare in pain again, making him curse the Powers and the world they created.

"Back pain?" said the voice above, sounding amused. "You might want to think about going to a doctor for that ... if there were any doctors on this island, of course."

Rubbing his back gingerly, Malock looked up and spotted a tiny, overweight man sitting on the branch of a nearby tree. He almost missed him at first because the man's skin was a green as the trees' leaves and he had vines wrapped around his arms and legs like muscle bands.

Malock had never seen a man quite like him before. He was

completely naked, his genitals being covered only by a small leaf that left little to the imagination. His hair was long and flat, like grass, and his eyes resembled that of a cat's, glowing red through the strands of hair that covered his face. He swung his feet back and forth, feet that looked less like real feet and more like wooden replicas, like the work of a master carpenter.

"Who are you?" said Malock, reaching for his sword. "Are you a native of this island?"

The man chuckled. "I am the ruler of this island, actually. And you and your friends have trespassed upon my domain."

Malock's eyes widened. "Are you the one responsible for the vines that attacked me and my men earlier?"

The man snapped his fingers and a vine immediately shot out of the the trees and wrapped tightly around Malock's waist. Before the prince could react, the vine zoomed back up, taking him with it, and then jerked to a stop, making him level with the green man. The sudden stop made his back burn with pain, but he forgot about it quickly when the green man's smell—a mixture of leaves and mud—entered his nostrils and made him gag.

Up close, the green man was even less pretty. His chest was splattered with mud, his teeth looked like crude wooden replicas of the actual things, and his lips were stained with what looked like blood. The green man also held a femur in his hand, a femur with teeth marks in it, but that was perhaps the least strange thing about his appearance.

The green man smiled and said, "Of course I did. I control all the plants on this island. I don't really like visitors, which is why I live all alone here and why I ate every one of your men."

Malock ceased struggling against the thick vine upon hearing that. "Eat? By the gods, Crina was right. There *are* cannibals on this island and you're one of them."

The green man looked offended. "Me? A cannibal? Hardly. I am neither human nor aquarian and I eat both. That makes me a predator and you the prey. Not a cannibal."

"But ..." Malock realized what the red stains on the green man's lips were. "If you're not human, why do you look kind of like a human?"

"Because I like this form," said the green man, patting his big, round belly. "Besides, it's easier to speak in your filthy language with this body. I'd rather not do it at all, but I've been getting bored of quick kills recently and so want to draw this one out as long as I can."

"If you're not human or aquarian, then what are you?" said Malock. "A katabans? Perhaps some kind of demonic spirit attached to the jungle of this island so you can't spread your evil ways elsewhere?"

The green man laughed at that. "Demons are the things of nightmares and ghost stories, mortal. I am one hundred percent real. I can even offer objective, verifiable proof, if you want."

Without warning, the green man slapped Malock in the face. He slapped Malock so hard that the prince briefly lost consciousness before he came to. The green man still stood there, looking quite pleased with himself.

"I like to beat up my lunch a bit before I eat it," the green man said, licking his lips, smearing the blood that stained them. "I've always been criticized for my methods, even by my siblings, but I say you can't have a good mortal meal unless the meal in question has been thoroughly beaten. Wouldn't you agree?"

Malock wanted to say, *No, I wouldn't,* but realized it was a rhetorical question.

Instead, he said, "Who are you? I've never heard of you. Not even Vashnas mentioned you to me."

"I like to keep to myself," said the green man. "After all, I am the Loner God, God of Solitude, the Jungle, and Animals."

Malock frowned. "You can't be Kitos, the God of Loners. He looks nothing like you."

"I didn't say I was that mortal-loving idiot," said the green man. "Your mortal tongue is incapable of pronouncing my real name. Therefore, I had to use the closest translation I could find, which unfortunately makes me sound like my less-than-intelligent younger brother. It is inconvenient, but I blame that on you mortals and your stupid language."

Malock tried to recall the entire Northern Isles pantheon, which was difficult because there were so many deities in it. "I don't remember there being a god like you. Are you a minor god?"

The Loner God slapped Malock again and said, "I'm not minor. Gods aren't minor. You're lucky I didn't rip your head off for that remark."

His head spinning, Malock decided to be more careful about what he said to this deity. "I still don't remember you in any of the pantheon lists, though."

"That's because I shun the worship and attention of mortals," said the Loner God. "Unlike my northern siblings, whose fragile egos require that they receive constant praise and adoration from you cattle nearly every day. Frankly, it astounds me that they haven't started farming you for food. Your mortals are so delicious, despite being as dull as rocks and far less useful."

"But all gods have cults and religions," Malock said. "Sure, some cults are small and obscure, but all gods are worshiped by mortals and all gods want to be worshiped. My parents always taught me that the gods needed our praise, love, and respect."

"Your parents sound like a couple of pathetic little mortals who are trying not to invoke the wrath of my northern siblings," said the Loner God with a snort. "Hearing that just makes me all the more grateful for my decision to stay in the south with my other brothers and sisters."

"You mean ... there are more of you southern gods?" said Malock with a gulp.

The Loner God flashed his wooden teeth and said, "Yep. At least as many as our northern siblings. And, like me, they all see mortals as useful only for a good meal."

Until now, Malock hadn't realized just how much he had not feared the southern seas. Before, he had supposed that he and his crew would only have to fight bad weather and perhaps a few hungry sea monsters. But if the Loner God was telling the truth, then there was an entire pantheon of deities that had no problem with killing and eating mortals, human and aquarian alike.

The Loner God must have sensed his fear because he said, "Until today, you didn't really think you and your crew on that pathetic raft you call a ship were in any real danger. The arrogance and ignorance of mortals astounds me, almost as much as my northern siblings demanding your praise and worship. Almost."

Malock quickly realized he had little time before the Loner God decided to dig in, so to stall, he asked, "I don't understand. Up north, we know nothing about you southern gods. Until today, I had no idea you or your siblings even existed. Why have we not known about you?"

The Loner God took a bite out of the femur, crunched on it thoughtfully for a second, and then swallowed and said, "I imagine my northern siblings wanted to keep your mortals safe. I imagine they believed that you mortals would live in perpetual fear if you knew that we southern gods existed. Or perhaps they are afraid you mortals would demand that they fight us for your own safety. Of course, it is equally possible they may see we southern gods as a threat to their worship and so keep you mortals in ignorance so you think they are the only deities in this world. There are myriad reasons why they may have kept you ignorant and I don't care about any of them."

"I see," said Malock. "But when did this happen? Why do some of you gods stay in the north and some in the south? I bet it's a fascinating story, no doubt spellbinding, especially coming from the mouth of a god as powerful and respectable as you."

"Flattery will get you nowhere among us southern gods, mortal," said the Loner God. "But I suppose I could tell you. I'm still digesting your men, so I imagine that, by the time I end the tale, I will be hungry enough to eat you."

Malock nodded. He thought about reaching for his sword while the Loner God talked, but he realized the could not do that without the hungry god noticing. He would have to think of another way to free himself, and quickly, because he didn't know how long this tale was going to be.

"It started in the beginning," said the Loner God. "Literally. When the Powers first crafted this world, they made us gods first of all. Our job was to maintain the various domains and realms of this world, both the concrete and the abstract. We were the first of all creation, older than the stars, older than the earth, even older than the sea. The sun was young in those days and there was not an imperfection to be found anywhere."

A hint of longing colored every word that came from the Loner God's mouth. The story utterly contradicted the creation story that Malock had been told, however, which said humans were created first and gods second, but somehow he didn't think the Loner God would appreciate hearing that version very much.

"Then the Powers created you mortals," said the Loner God, his tone turning to annoyance. "Humans and aquarians. Smarter than animals, but not quite as powerful as we gods. We were told you mortals served a special purpose in the world, but to be frank, the Powers never told us what that purpose was. I imagine they thought that would be enough to keep us from actively trying to kill you all."

Malock, too, wondered what that 'special purpose' might be. He gave it little thought, though, because he was too busy trying to come up with a way to get out of this situation alive.

"So the Powers left the world, putting us in charge of it," the Loner God said. "We gods quickly became divided over the matter of you mortals. Half of us wanted you to worship us, to shower us with adoration and respect, to build temples in our honor and to sing hymns in our name. The other half saw you as little more than cattle and rather tasty cattle at that. Guess which group I was a part of."

Malock knew, but did not say.

"Those of us who saw you mortals as food came up with the sport of mortal-hunting," said the Loner God. "Several of us gods would get together and hunt down mortals. They were not much of a challenge, mostly because you mortals are weak and slow, but my, oh, my, were they fun. The dumb mortals were especially fun to hunt because they tried to fight us and always failed spectacularly."

He spoke of the sport the way Malock's father had always spoken of drafna-hunting, like humans and aquarians were mere animals or something.

"But you see, the mortal-lovers didn't like that," said the Loner God. "Didn't like that one bit. They argued and debated with us about the ethics of it, often sabotaged our hunts, took certain tribes or races of mortals under their protection, and occasionally even traded blows with us over it. But nothing serious came of it until dearest sister Mica, then the Goddess of Earth, slew the Ink God when he tried to hunt some of her followers."

Malock had to interrupt here. "But gods can't be killed. That's impossible."

"Impossible for you mortals, maybe, but we gods are certainly capable of taking each other's lives," said the Loner God. "Anyway, that was the last straw for both sides. The mortal-lovers were angry that the Ink God had tried to kill mortals under their protection, while we mortal-hunters were angry that Mica had killed one of our own and taken his domain under hers. This started a terrible war between us, the first and only war between the gods."

"War?" said Malock. "It couldn't have been that bad, could it?"

"Oh, it was terrible," said the Loner God. "Think of the absolute worst war you mortals have ever fought among yourselves. Then imagine the sea at war with the sky, the clouds at war with the trees, love at war with hate, countless mortal and godly lives dying wherever battles are fought, and you will get a dim idea of what the Godly War was like."

The Loner God spoke of the War as if it had happened yesterday. And he didn't sound happy about it, either, as if he regretted partaking in it. Or maybe he was sad about not winning.

"I imagine the War would have destroyed the entire world if the Powers had not stepped in and forced us all to stand down," said the Loner God. "They were quite angry ... or at least, as angry as they can ever be. It is hard to tell with them sometimes."

Malock breathed in sharply. "You mean ... you've met the Powers?"

"Of course I have," said the Loner God. "But that's not important. When they stopped us, they forced us to clean up the mess we'd made. Couldn't get us to reconcile, though, because the wounds were just too deep. So they came up with the Treaty."

"The Treaty?"

"Yes, the Treaty," said the Loner God. "The Treaty forbid any and all warfare among the gods. Doesn't mean we gods always get along. It's just that we can't declare war on each other anymore, even if we wanted to. That was the very first clause on the Treaty, which I think is a bit extreme, but I suppose the Powers had their reasons for doing what they did."

Forbidding war between gods didn't seem 'a bit extreme' to Malock, though he said aloud, "Is that all the Treaty said?"

"Oh, the Treaty says a lot more than that," said the Loner God. "It divides us gods into northern and southern. My northern siblings —who you know as Kano, Tinkar, Grinf, and all the others—got the northern half of Martir, while we got the southern half. You mortals are not restricted to any one area of the planet; however, there is a reason why you mortals mostly live up north and why the southern seas have so many dangerous myths surrounding them."

"So how many of those myths are true and how many are false?" Malock asked.

The Loner God either didn't hear him or, more likely, simply ignored him because he continued speaking. "We southern gods are not allowed to hunt mortals in the north. Any mortals that come south are fair game, but we are not allowed to hunt you mortals beyond the Dividing Line, the area that denotes where the north ends and where the south begins. I wish it were different, as this clause has severely limited mortal-hunting, but alas, it was written in stone by the Powers and therefore cannot be disobeyed."

That must be why the southern gods haven't killed us all, Malock thought, more than a little bit relieved.

"There is a lot more to the Treaty, but I believe that that is all that is relevant to you and all that your puny mortal mind can understand anyway," said the Loner God. "That is how things have stood for thousands of years. Very boring, wouldn't you say?"

Malock could sense the Loner God was almost finished telling his tale, so the prince said, "If you say so. But may I ask why you southern gods like to hunt mortals? That doesn't seem right to me."

"Why do you mortals hunt animals less intelligent than you?" said the Loner God. "It's fun. And it is the way of nature. The powerful have the right to slaughter the weak. We are the powerful and you are the weak. Even an idiotic mortal like yourself should be able to grasp that simple concept. Plus, you mortals are just so tasty."

Malock gulped. "But the northern gods don't hunt us. Clearly, it is not necessarily the way of nature."

The Loner God laughed. "They still dominate you, don't they? My northern siblings love to pontificate about their greatness, but I know that they get as much of a thrill punishing you fools for disobeying or disrespecting them as we southern gods get whenever we're hunting you. You are nothing more than animals in our eyes."

"I ..." Malock struggled to think of a response but could think of nothing. "Well, are you going to let me down now?"

"Why would I ever do that?" said the Loner God. "Weren't you listening? I know your language is awkward and clumsy, but I thought I made it clear that I am going to eat you. Telling you that story made me hungry again, so—"

"Wait!" said Malock, holding up a hand. "If you kill me, my men will come into the jungle after me and take you down. They're a group of professional god-killers who will do anything to save me, up to and including killing a god like yourself."

The Loner God shook his head. "That's a nice lie, but very

unconvincing. No such thing as a god-killer and your crew especially is so pathetic that I doubt they could even so much as scratch me. Besides, some of your men are already in the jungle searching for you even as we speak."

Malock perked up at that. "They are?"

"Yes," said the Loner God. "I've left them alone because they're not much of a threat, but I think, once I'm done with you, I'll eat them, too. It's been a long time since I last feasted on so many mortals. By the time I am done, I'll be the fullest I've been in five centuries. Who knows? Maybe I'll even feast on the rest of your crew, if I'm feeling up to it."

The Loner God was licking his lips and the more he licked his lips the faster Malock's mind raced for a solution—*any* solution—to this predicament.

Then an idea came to mind and Malock said, "Oh, I wouldn't touch me if I were you, God of Solitude."

"Oh, and why wouldn't I do that?" said the Loner God.

Malock cross his arms, trying to look as authoritative as possible, and said, "Because I am Prince Tojas Malock, son of King Halock and Queen Markinia, Crown Prince to the Throne of Carnag, Captain of the *Iron Wind*, and Chosen One of Kano."

The Loner God's expression went from amused, if a bit hungry, to pale in less than a second. "What was that last one?"

"Chosen One of Kano," said Malock. "Kano summoned me to World's End. I am under her complete and total protection, you know."

The Loner God looked down at his feet, muttering quickly,

"Can't believe I almost broke the Treaty ... came this close ... must be lying ... no, he's telling the truth all right ..."

"Excuse me," said Malock, "but what are you muttering about?"

The Loner God looked up. For the first time, Malock saw fear in the god's eyes. "I can't kill you. Part of the Treaty, you understand."

"No, I don't," said Malock. "I mean, I don't want you to kill me, of course, but I don't understand what you mean about the Treaty."

"It's my least favorite clause," said the Loner God with a grunt. "See, we gods can place individual mortals under our protection. So long as you are under Kano's protection, then I can't kill you and neither can any other god, whether northern or southern. Even if you stumble into the domain of a southern god, we still can't touch you."

"Oh," said Malock. "Well, that sounds pretty good to me."

"It does work out rather well for you mortals, doesn't it?" said the Loner God. "You smell like Kano. Thought at first it was just the sea, but I can smell her all over you like a blanket. You got lucky, mortal."

Malock smirked. "So the high and mighty Loner God is stopped by a mere Treaty. Being a southern god must not be all its cracked up to be, eh?"

"Shut up," the Loner God snapped. Then he paused, as if thinking, and said, "Interesting," in a tone that Malock didn't like.

"What's interesting?" said Malock. "Me?"

"Not you," the Loner God said. "I just did a quick sweep of the island and the seas around it and discovered that you aren't the only one under the protection of another god. Some members of your crew have that same protection."

"What?" said Malock in surprise. "Who? Which gods? Why?"

"That's what I'm trying to figure out," said the Loner God. "Why would my brothers and sisters place their agents on your ship without you knowing unless ... oh, I see. Politics as usual."

"What does that mean?" said Malock.

The Loner God chuckled, like he was sharing a private in-joke. "Unlike we southern gods, the northern gods are prone to infighting and politics. I imagine they must have learned it from you mortals. Personally I tend to stay out of these conflicts, which is why I am going to spare you and the members of the rescue party that are currently in the jungle."

"Wow," said Malock. "But will you please tell me who is chosen and what gods chose them?"

"No," said the Loner God. "That would help you and frankly I don't like helping mortals. I may not be able to kill you myself, but I can make your voyage that much more difficult for you. Besides, if I outed your fellow chosen ones, then my siblings would get angry at me and I'd get drawn into it. Already cutting it close by killing your men and attacking you, so I'm gonna give up while I'm ahead and let you go."

The Loner God snapped his fingers and the vine began lowering itself. When Malock was a few feet above the ground, the vine let go of him and he landed on his feet, jolting his spine and making him curse the Powers again.

When Malock looked up, he saw that he stood in front of a pathway that he was sure hadn't been there before. And when he looked up at the trees, he could no longer see the Loner God.

"Take this path, Chosen One of Kano," said the Loner God's

voice, which seemed to come from everywhere at once. "If you follow it, you will eventually reunite with your party and find the beach. Then you may continue your quest, but if I were you, mortal, I would get onto your ship, head back north, and never look back. Mortals rarely prosper from the politics of the gods."

Malock didn't respond. He simply began walking down the path, feeling more lost and confused than he had wandering around in the dark.

"Mal!" Vashnas called out, slashing through the thick underbrush of the jungle. "Tojas! Where are you?"

As Kinker ducked underneath the remains of a vine that Vashnas had chopped down, he wondered why she had allowed him, Bifor, and three other sailors (among them Magnisa, Gino, and Forl) to tag along at all. She could probably have stormed the island all by herself, found Malock, and returned to the ship just in time for dinner. Did she honestly think she needed backup or did she just let them tag along because she didn't want to waste time forcing them to stay on the ship?

Whatever the reason, Kinker was beginning to regret agreeing to go along. The underbrush was thick and his pants constantly snagged on bushes. His beard had little twigs and leaves stuck in it, which he did not even try to remove, knowing as he did the fruitlessness of that task. The air was hot and muggy, too, and more than once he had to slap an insect off his exposed neck.

Bifor was in the back, waving his wand and muttering incantations under his breath all the while. Exactly what he was doing,

Kinker didn't know. Bifor had been acting that way as soon as they landed on the island's shore and when Kinker asked him what he was doing, the mage made an incoherent comment about the 'magic levels' of the jungle being 'off the charts.' It made no sense to Kinker, though he supposed that was because he was not trained in the magic arts.

So far, the trio had not found any sign of Malock or any of the sailors that had gone with him into the jungle. Of course, the jungle was very dark, even though it was the afternoon and the sun was out, but Kinker thought that at some point they would have to find pieces of clothing or discarded weapons or even bodies. He didn't see any wild animals; in fact, there were so few animals that he wondered if there was any life on this island at all, aside from the insects that kept trying to bite his neck.

That was when a drop of some kind of liquid fell on Kinker's nose. He blinked and wiped the liquid off his nose with his finger and looked at it closely. In the dark, it was impossible to tell what it was, so he licked it. It tasted like blood.

"Guys," said Kinker, not daring to look up, knowing what he would see. "I think I've found a clue."

Vashnas immediately stopped calling out Malock's name and turned to face Kinker, her face alight with eagerness. "What did you find?"

"Blood," said Kinker. "A drop of it fell on my nose."

"Blood?" Bifor said. "Fell from where?"

Kinker pointed up. "From the trees, presumably. That's all that's above us."

Bifor spun his wand around twice and it suddenly flared,

illuminating the area they were in quite well. He then raised his wand above their heads, allowing them to see what was in the trees. When they did, Kinker wished he had kept his mouth shut.

Wrapped tightly among the vines and branches of the trees were the sailors who had gone with Malock to search for Sumsa. They were nothing but bones now; in fact, the only reason Kinker recognized them was due to the bits of cloth hanging off their bodies, which looked like the sailor uniforms that the crew of the *Iron Wind* commonly wore. Little droplets of blood dripped from the ribcage of one unfortunate sailor, an aquarian by the look of it.

"Oh my god," said Vashnas. "Do you think any of those are—"

"Vash?" said a familiar voice nearby. "Is that you?"

Bifor turned his wand in the direction of the voice, revealing Malock, who stood on a path several dozen yards away from them, a path that Kinker hadn't even noticed until Bifor's light showed it. For some reason, Malock didn't look surprised to see them.

Vashnas shoved her sword into Kinker's hands and ran at Malock. She scooped him up in a big hug, causing Malock to gasp for air, saying as she did so, "Oh, Mal, I thought ... for a moment I thought you were ... oh, I'm just so glad you're alive and well."

"I won't be if you keep hugging me like this," Malock said, his voice strained. "I'm happy to see you and all, Vash, but if you could let up just a little, then I could breathe again."

Vashnas let go, looking sheepish, as Kinker, Bifor, and the others approached.

"We are pleased to see you are alive, Captain," said Bifor, inclining his head in Malock's direction. "Please don't be angry with us. We know you told us to go home if you didn't return in six hours, but Vashnas here simply couldn't stand the idea of abandoning you, at least not without knowing if you were alive or not."

Malock rubbed his back as he said, "Oh, it's not a problem. Really, I'm actually glad you disobeyed my orders for once. This was the one time where I really needed you guys to do that."

"What happened?" said Kinker, glancing back at the skeletons of the sailors in the trees. "We found the rest of your team in the trees and we thought you were dead. Were you attacked by some animal?"

Malock looked at Kinker with an odd look in his eyes for a moment, almost as if he didn't trust Kinker, and said, "It's a long story. Did you say you found the rest of my team's bodies?"

"Yes," said Vashnas. "They're little more than skeletons, their skin stripped off by ... well, we don't know what. We thought you'd know."

Even by the dim light of Bifor's wand, Kinker could tell, based solely on Malock's expression, that the Captain knew exactly what had happened to his crew and he didn't want to talk about it.

"I've had a long day," said Malock, running a hand through his hair. "A long, long day. We're going back to the *Iron Wind* and when we do, we're continuing our quest south."

"But sir," said Bifor. "We haven't picked any ikadori peaches yet. Shouldn't we fill at least a few crates full before we leave?"

Malock shook his head so rapidly that Kinker thought it might go flying off his shoulders. "No. We will make do with fish. So long as we still have the trawl, we'll be fine."

His voice trembled as he said that and he looked around, as if afraid someone might be eavesdropping, listening to make sure that Malock was doing exactly what he should be doing and nothing more. It was a silly thought, so Kinker dismissed it.

"This path will take us directly back to the beach," said Malock. "I'll lead the way. As soon we are safely back on the ship, we're heading south again. Got it?"

The trio nodded, but that did little to stifle Kinker's curiosity. What did Malock run into that made him seem so frightened? Why did he insist on them leaving before they picked even one ikadori fruit?

All of these questions and more filled Kinker's mind as he followed Malock, Vashnas, Bifor, and the others down the surprisingly flat path that led to the beach. He doubted Malock would answer them, however, because the prince's jaw was closed so tightly that it seemed unlikely to open ever again.

Chapter Six

WHEN THEY RETURNED TO the *Iron Wind*, Malock wasn't even angry that they'd knocked out Banika in their attempt to rescue him. He just woke her up, gave her orders to get the ship ready to depart, and went to his stateroom with Vashnas by his side, without speaking a word to anyone else except Bifor. He asked the mage to heal a small wound on the back of his head, which Bifor succeeded in doing despite his lack of training in healing magic.

When the crew heard the order to weigh anchor already, there was quite a commotion. Many of the sailors wanted to go on land and pick ikadori peaches. A few of them even began muttering about mutiny, but when the members of the rescue party told everyone about the skeletons they saw, the sailors immediately began to weigh anchor, prepare the sails, and check the compass to make sure they were headed in the right direction.

Because of their speed and work ethic, the entire ship was ready to set sail within an hour and soon they were heading south once more. Kinker watched the island slowly grow smaller the further they sailed away from it, he still wondering what had happened there and why Malock refused to talk about it.

Because Malock spent all of his time in his stateroom, the rest of the crew came to Kinker, Bifor, and the others for answers. Unfortunately, Kinker and the others were not able to provide much information, as Malock had said nothing to them about whatever had killed the others back on Ikadori Island. Kinker had no doubt that stories would soon begin circulating among the crew, though, because in his experience that was what sailors generally did when confronted with a lack of facts.

Though all of the sailors mourned the lack of ikadori peaches to some extent, the fishing crew seemed to complain about it more than anyone else. Perhaps that was because Kinker spent most of his time with the other fishermen, but he figured it was also because the fishing crew was in charge of providing food for the rest of the crew. Deddio expressed their collective disappointment by saying that they would have had to catch much less fish if they had gotten the peaches, like they had originally planned.

Nonetheless, things eventually returned to normal after a while. According to Vashnas, it would be quite sometime before they reached the next island, which made her unpopular with the rest of the crew for the next few days.

A day after they left Ikadori Island, the crew held a collective funeral for the sailors who died on the island. This surprised Kinker, as he had not thought the crew was close enough to do that. It was a highly informal funeral, however, in part because none of them were priests and in part because they did not have the bodies of the fallen sailors. That all of the dead sailors had all worshiped different deities made preparing funeral rites exceptionally difficult, so the funeral was kept short and generic. They tossed a few of the prized possessions of their fallen brethren, said a few prayers to help their spirits find solace in whatever afterlife they found themselves in, and then returned to work. Danaf almost broke down when he gave a eulogy for his brother, but aside from that, the rest of the crew seemed more concerned with their own wellbeing than in the deaths of five of their fellow sailors.

The next few days after the funeral were mostly quiet. The most exciting thing that happened was an illness that spread through the whole ship, making everyone sick and causing most of them to throw up. Kinker got so ill that he almost thought he was going to die, but luckily he recovered, thanks to the combined efforts of Telka and his medical expertise and Bifor and what little healing magic he knew. No one else died, either, thankfully.

Yet the sickness did nothing to halt their progress. Kinker even began to think it might be smooth sailing from here on out. That is, until about a week after leaving Ikadori Island, when the fishing crew hauled in something very different from the fish they usually caught.

It was right before dinner, when the fishing crew was hauling the trawl out of the ocean for the final time that day. It was heavier than usual, however, so heavy in fact that they had to call in help from a few other sailors to get it on the ship. Kinker assumed that meant they had caught more fish than usual, so he was more than a little surprised when he saw, lying among the usual thirty pounds or so fish they caught, a full-grown, adult male aquarian.

The aquarian looked like an eel, with a long, thin, smooth body and a head to match. His limbs were equally as thin and he had a tattoo on his chest that resembled a rose with an arrow sticking out of it. He didn't look like any of the aquarians aboard the crew and was so still that for a moment everyone thought he was dead.

Then his eyes opened, an odd gurgling noise came from his throat, and he leaped to his feet. The fishing crew and the other sailors who helped haul in dinner stepped back because the aquarian looked crazy. His eyes were crossed and his body was shaking and jittery, like he was high on sugar. Kinker believed they could defend themselves if they had to, but that didn't mean he wasn't afraid of the crazy aquarian.

And then, without warning, the eel-like aquarian turned, ran over to the railing, and launched himself back into the ocean. The sailors rushed to the railing and looked over the side, but he was no longer visible in the water and seemed to have disappeared entirely.

"What was that all about?" said Jenur, pushing away from the railing and looking at the others in confusion. "Seriously, the guy didn't even try to attack us."

"I don't know," said Kinker. "Gino? Magnisa? Do you know him?"

Gino shook his head. "Why would we? We've never seen anyone like him before; right, Maggy?"

"Right," said Magnisa. "Maybe there was another ship around here that he fell off of. Doesn't explain why he jumped off when he saw us, though."

"I bet he was scared," said Deddio. "We don't look much better than pirates, after all. Sadly, I doubt he'll last very long out there on his own, considering how dangerous these seas are."

"The southern seas aren't that dangerous," said Jenur, folding her arms. "At least not so far. I'd say the northern seas are more dangerous, when you consider that we lost most of the fleet back there. So far, we've lost what, four or five sailors? Not much compared to what we lost up north."

"It will get worse before this is all over," Deddio insisted. "I don't know what awaits us ahead, but it will be even worse than mysterious jungles."

"You're a bundle of joy, Ded," said Jenur. "You know that?"

Before Deddio could respond, Kinker turned away from the stern and said, "Enough arguing, you two. Whoever that aquarian was, we still have to prepare dinner for the rest of the crew. I'm sure everyone is starving for the same old crap we serve day in and day out."

Back on Carnag, Malock never liked wine or beer or any sort of alcoholic drink. Yes, he often drank in accordance with the expectations of royalty, but even the best wine always left a bad taste in his mouth. He was not one to judge people who enjoyed it. He simply didn't like it, which was why he had refused to take even one sip of wine from any of his personal store during the entire voyage.

As to why he brought along alcohol in the first place, well, much of it was used for medical purposes. Doctor Telka often used the alcohol to treat wounds. Malock was careful to let Telka use only as much as the doctor needed, however, because he didn't want to run out of it. He wanted to keep a little on hand in case he ever needed it.

TIMOTHY L. CEREPAKA

Despite Malock's dislike of wine, not for the first time since departing Ikadori Island, he poured himself a tall glass of wine from one of his wine bottles. He was not sure what brand the wine was, as the bottle's label had been ripped off at some point and he wasn't enough of a wine connoisseur to tell purely from taste. All he knew was that he needed it.

He wasn't sure how many glasses he had poured himself over the last week. He lost count every time he lost consciousness from drink, which was often, and so had decided not to keep track anymore. He suspected that the number, whatever it was, would depress him even more than he already was.

Not depressed, Malock thought. *Confused.*

His mind was still reeling from his encounter with the Loner God. Northern and southern gods, the Treaty, the Godly War ... thinking about all of this made his head hurt. It contradicted everything he had ever been taught about the gods, about the history of the world, and so it caused him conflict in his heart as well as his head.

That was why he had spent almost all week in his stateroom. He was still processing everything he had been told, trying to decide what was true and what wasn't. He had even told Vashnas to stay away. He knew he needed her more than ever, but at the same time he didn't want her anywhere near him at the moment.

In particular, Malock worried incessantly over the identity of the other chosen one among his group. Who was it? Why were they keeping their chosen status a secret? Which god had placed them on the ship? Why had the god done that? And what did the Loner God mean when he said, 'Politics as usual'? Were Malock and his crew simple pawns in a game played by the gods? Was there something deeper going on than any of them realized?

To drown out these unpleasant thoughts, Malock had taken to drinking, and drinking hard. He was aware of the dangers of drinking, especially aboard a ship like the *Iron Wind*. Nonetheless, he knew of no other way to calm his nerves and to clear away the doubts and questions in his mind. All he wanted now was bliss ... pure, ignorant bliss, like the kind enjoyed by the imbeciles that roamed the streets just outside of the Hall of Carnag, the ones Malock had often seen and pitied growing up.

A sharp knock at the door to his stateroom snapped him out of his stupor. Malock looked up and shouted, in a slurred voice, "Go away. I'm busy making plans to invade the Kingdom of ... of, um, somewhere."

The door opened anyway and Vashnas entered, looking concerned. Malock pointed at her with his wineglass, accidentally sloshing some wine onto the map on his desk, and said, "This is a secret meeting. I'm the only one allowed. Go away."

Vashnas shook her head. "No way, Mal. You've been in here by yourself for too long. I want to know what happened to you back on Ikadori Island. Whatever happened shook you up."

Malock lay his head on the table because it hurt and he was tired. "You don't want to know what I learned, what I saw. Can't understand it."

He heard her approach and then felt the cool touch of her hand on the side of his face.

"You can tell me," said Vashnas. "I won't judge you, if you did something you regret. I won't even ask any questions. You can tell me the entire story from start to finish without any interruptions from me."

Malock looked up at her through drunken eyes. It occurred to him that she was a member of the crew. And the Loner God did say that it had been one of Malock's crew who was a Chosen One as well ...

He rejected the implications immediately. No. Vashnas would never betray him or hold secrets from him. She was a true friend and lover, through and through. His skeptical side did ask why she forgot to mention the Loner God living on Ikadori Island, but he swiftly rejected that thought when he remembered Vashnas saying that she had not explored the island very much the last time she was there.

Malock sat up, slowly, and leaned back in his rickety chair. His head pounding, he told Vashnas everything that he had seen, heard, and experienced back on Ikadori Island— from the Loner God's appearance to the origin of the gods. Vashnas listened, as she promised, without word or interruption, which made it easier for Malock to tell her all about it. It was still difficult, however, because his drunken lips constantly slurred words, and more than once he lost his train of thought, only to find it again with Vashnas's help. The only fact he omitted was the Loner God mentioning that there were multiple Chosen Ones in the crew, mostly because a small part of him, for some reason, didn't trust Vashnas. He did, however, mention a spy among the crew, but only one and he didn't know the spy's identity.

When he finished, Vashnas looked thoughtful, but not surprised. Malock didn't know whether that meant she believed the story or not. All he knew was that his headache was starting to go away, albeit very slowly.

"How very strange," said Vashnas. "A god living by himself on an island; moreover a god who eats mortals. I am surprised you got away alive at all."

Malock remembered the Loner God's wooden teeth, his lips streaked with blood, and shuddered. "The only reason ... only reason he let me live is because he thought this whole voyage was doomed. Didn't see the point in killing us when he could let everything play out to its gruesome end."

"That's not good," said Vashnas. "That's not good at all. We'll have to remain vigilant. If there is a spy in the crew, then we need to find them and root them out right away."

Malock rubbed the back of his head, which no longer bled, thanks to a healing spell by Bifor. "Only problem is, I don't know who the ... uh ... who the spy is."

"Do you have any ideas at all?" said Vashnas, taking a seat in the chair on the opposite side of his desk. "Any?"

Malock's first impulse was to say, *Yes. You,* but he didn't want to scare her off and was horrifed at himself for thinking that.

He simply said, "Like I said, no. Could be anyone. Maybe even me."

Vashnas gently tried to take away the wine bottle. "Mal, I think the drink is starting to affect your thinking. I'll put this away and you can take a nap until you feel better. We won't reach the next island for another few days, so you have plenty of time to recover."

Malock didn't let go of the bottle. "I don't ... no. You don't understand."

Now Vashnas's gentle expression faltered slightly. "What don't I understand?"

"All of it," said Malock, waving his free hand. "The southern gods, politics as usual, the spy, the Treaty, the War ... all of it. Aren't you the least bit, uh, concerned? It's all so paradigm-shattering. I don't know how I can ... how I can go on knowing this."

Vashnas began to undo his grip on the bottle, finger by finger. "It's okay, Mal. You're strong. You can do this. You've made it this far after facing countless tragedy. We still have a long way to go before we reach World's End. You don't need to get yourself drunk out of your mind to finish the voyage."

Malock was completely unconvinced by that argument and was going to have another go at it when the door swung open and Banika entered. Her hands twitched when she spotted Vashnas, perhaps because she still remembered being knocked out, but that was the only sign of emotion in the otherwise unreadable boatswain.

"Banika?" said Malock, briefly forgetting his argument with Vashnas. "What are you doing? Is there a problem?"

Banika nodded. "Yes, sir. We have completely stopped."

Malock blinked. "Say that again."

"We have completely stopped," said Banika, this time slightly slower. "We aren't moving forward, backward, or in any direction at all. I guess you haven't noticed the stillness of the ship."

Now that Banika mentioned it, the floor was awfully still. The world still spun for Malock, but he figured that was the drink's fault more than anything else.

"Who dropped the anchor?" Malock demanded in his most authoritative voice, although the effect was ruined by his slurring of the word *anchor* at the end of the sentence.

Banika shook her head. "The anchor is still weighed. We were stopped by ... well, I think it would be better if you saw for yourself. It's hard to explain."

Malock stood up, letting go of the wine bottle as he did so, causing Vashnas to snatch it and stash it in a drawer in the desk. "Take me to it, then."

Malock managed to make his way out of the stateroom without falling down too much, thanks to Banika's help. When he did, he noticed that the sails were no longer blowing in the wind and nearly the entire crew was assembled on both sides of the ship, looking down into the water and talking in an incoherent mess that Malock doubted he'd have understood even in his sober mind.

Banika led Malock over to starboard and pointed at the sea below. "There's the obstruction, Captain. That is why it was hard for me to explain."

Malock leaned over the railing, remembering to grip them tightly so he wouldn't fall overside in his drunkenness, and peered into the water.

A thick, green moss covered the area around the *Iron Wind* for several feet in all directions. The moss ran up the body of the ship, so thick that it looked like solid ground. It was like two large, mossy hands had grown from the sea and grasped the ship, making Malock wonder if the Loner God's influence extended well beyond the borders of Ikadori Island.

"When did this happen?" said Malock, pulling back (with some difficulty) from the railing to look at Banika.

"Ten minutes ago," said Banika. "It spontaneously grew out of nowhere. We're not sure where it came from."

"Probably just a freak accident of nature or something," said Malock. "Okay, send some of the aquarians to rip it off."

"Already tried that, sir," said Banika. "It just grew back."

Malock swore loudly and said, "Then get Bifor on it. He's a freaking mage. He should be able to wave his wand and make the moss go poof."

"It's not that easy," said Bifor, appearing seemingly out of nowhere, twirling his wand in his hand. "Watch."

Bifor pointed his wand at the moss scaling the side of the ship. The moss froze, but immediately was covered by another layer of moss, melting the ice.

"As best as I can tell, this is magic at work," said Bifor. "That means someone is trying to stop us. Or rather, has succeeded in stopping us."

"You mean like a ... like a ..." Malock struggled to think of the word. "Like a mage?"

Bifor nodded. "Yes. Though who it could be, I can't say."

Malock was just about to tell Bifor to find out who it is when a loud shout made everyone jump. Another shout, followed by a loud *thump*, followed, and Malock realized it was coming from the center of the ship. He quickly made his way down the steps to the main deck, with Banika, Vashnas, and Bifor following, and stopped as soon as he spotted the source of the sound.

Lying face down on the deck, with a knife sticking out of his back, was Forl Mas, one of the sailors who had gone with Malock to Ikadori Island. His stillness, combined with the blood leaking out from the wound, told Malock all he needed to know about the sailor's fate.

Standing above Forl's corpse was someone Malock had never seen before but who he knew was not a member of the crew. She was an aquarian, clearly, her face resembling that of a crab's and she had two large crab claws in place of hands. A thick, cracked gray shell covered her body. A red bandanna was wrapped around her right arm, which was the only piece of clothing on her entire body.

By now nearly the entire crew was looking at her. Many of them looked ready to fight, although something about the confidence with which the crab aquarian stood in the midst of so many hostile faces kept Malock from ordering them to attack.

"Glad I got your attention," said the aquarian. Her voice was very human-like, though the words were occasionally obscured by the odd chittering sound her teeth made. "Murder is always a good way to get attention from other people, though I will admit that it's not always *good* attention."

Malock stepped forward, trying not to look drunk, and said, "Who are you and where did you come from?"

The aquarian looked offended. "You mean you don't recognize Garnal Gray, Captain of the Gray Pirates? I am wanted all over the Northern Isles for my daring exploits and thefts. My bounty is about a million coins right now, which is a paltry sum in comparison to all of the loot that I and my gang have stolen over the years."

Malock could not, for the life of him, recognize the name, so he leaned toward Banika to his left and muttered, "Is she telling the truth?"

Banika nodded. "Garnal Gray is indeed the notorious pirate leader of the Gray Pirates, the most infamous and longest-lasting pirate group in the history of piracy. Practically every member of her crew is wanted for some crime or another. Their collective bounty is ten million coins, last I checked."

"As it should be," said Garnal. "My crew and I have worked hard to earn our place as the best pirates in the history of Martir. Not even the legendary Varew the Black evaded capture as long as I have."

"Still didn't answer how you got here," said Malock. "Getting onto our ship without any of us noticing is quite the accomplishment."

Garnal chuckled. "'Twas easy, my precious prince. I am an initiate of the Thief's Way, one of the best in all the Northern Isles. Even your mage didn't notice me sneak aboard."

"Okay, now what's the Thief's Way?" said Malock, looking at Banika.

It was Bifor who answered. "The Thief's Way is a magical path that followers of Hollech, the God of Deception, Thieves, and Horses, often pursue. Initiates of the Thief's Way learn how to use magic to increase their stealth and, while not all initiates of that path are thieves, it has always been popular among the members of that morally dubious profession. Hence why it is called the Thief's Way."

"They teach that at magic school?" said Malock in disbelief.

"Sort of," said Bifor with a shrug. "When I was in the Academy, there was only one teacher of the Thief's Way, and he was constantly on the verge of being fired because everyone kept accusing him of stealing their things. He only ever had a handful of students at any one time and many of them dropped out before they graduated from his program because they couldn't handle the hate from everyone else."

Malock returned his attention to Garnal and said, "So you're a graduate of the Academy, too?"

The pirate snapped her claws open and shut, as if amused. "Of course not. I met a practitioner of the Thief's Way some twenty years back who agreed to teach me how to do it. I had to kill him, however, because he was planning to hand me over to the authorities the entire time so he could get my bounty and never have to work another day in his life. Quite the lazy thief, he was."

"Wait," said Malock, putting a hand on the back of his head. "If you're from the Northern Isles, then what the hell are you doing down here in the southern seas? Trying to expand your territory?"

"I was about to ask you the same question, actually," said Garnal. "I know who you are, Prince Tojas Malock of Carnag, though I am surprised, because I always thought you royals were too delicate to go on a dangerous voyage into unknown waters."

"My reasons for being here are none of your concern, pirate."

"And my reasons for being here are mine, prince," Garnal said. "But I can tell you why I am on this ship, specifically: I am going to take it."

Malock laughed, which he immediately regretted because it made his head hurt. "Oh, really? You may be tough, Garnal, but there's over a hundred sailors on this ship, all of whom are even tougher than you. Maybe you ought to rethink your plan."

"You assume I am alone," said Garnal. "If that were so, I would not have been able to stop your ship cold."

"So you summoned the moss," said Bifor. "I had no idea you were a botamancer."

"Not me specifically, mage," said Garnal. "Rather, a certain member of my crew did that."

Malock looked around and said, "Your crew? I don't see anyone but yourself. If you're trying to intimidate us, it's really not working."

"You will be intimidated soon enough, gold blood," said Garnal.

Without warning, the ship lurched to the port; this caused most of the crew to fall over. Malock just barely managed to retain his balance, while Garnal looked completely unaffected by it.

"What was that?" said Malock, looking around in surprise.

"My men making a point," said Garnal. "If you refuse to stand down and let me have the ship, I will have my crew sink it to the bottom of the ocean and kill the whole lot of you. Seems like a reasonable deal to me."

"Don't you have a ship of your own?" Malock said.

Garnal's expression turned to fury very quickly. "Don't change the subject. Give us the ship or you go down with it, like a real captain would."

"Doesn't seem to be a way out of this, Captain," said Bifor, who was one of the few sailors not to lose his balance when the ship lurched. "Even if we take out Garnal, her men will probably rip a hole in the ship's hull and we'll sink anyway."

"Not helping," Malock growled.

His mind raced, trying to think of a way out of this. This was far more difficult than it should have been because his mind was still heavy with drunkenness. His mind felt like mud and more than once he found himself distracted by something not immediately relevant to their current situation, like Vashnas's jacket or that odd discoloration halfway up the mainmast.

Garnal didn't look like she was in a hurry at all. She was whistling a tune he didn't recognize, rocking back and forth, and occasionally looking up at the sky as if concerned about the weather, even though the sky was clear. She almost looked harmless.

Malock looked at the rest of his crew. Banika and Vashnas had fallen when the ship lurched and had not yet gotten back to their feet. None of the other sailors seemed likely to do anything. The only thing Malock figured they needed to do (this thought came slowly) was figure out how to stop Garnal's crew that were under the ship. If they could just do that ... but they couldn't.

Malock's arms dropped to his sides. "All right, Garnal. You win. I'm not going to sacrifice the ship and the crew just to stop you."

Garnal's feet skittered across the deck happily as she said, "Excellent, quite excellent. I expected your royal arrogance to get the better of you, my precious prince, but for once you listen to reason."

Without warning, the ship lurched back into an upright position, knocking over the few sailors who had remained standing from before. Malock himself almost fell before being caught by Bifor, who helped him up.

"Men!" Garnal yelled at the top of her voice. "Climb aboard! The ship is ours!"

Malock wasn't sure how her men were supposed to hear her, but a moment later, he heard people climbing the sides of the ship and then a dozen pirates climbed over the bulwarks. A quick glance told Malock that all of the pirates were aquarians, just like Garnal, though not all of them were crab-like in appearance. They had rusty, sharp-edged swords tied to belts or their backs and they looked like they knew how to use them. Their hungry eyes and gaunt bodies added to their terrifying appearances.

"All right," Garnal called out, her voice loud enough for the entire crew to hear her. "You heard your former Captain. I am now in charge of this vessel. You are all my slaves and will do whatever I or any of my men tell you to do."

A large commotion started, but Garnal shouted, "Or would you rather sleep in the bottom of the ocean tonight? It's your choice."

That silenced the entire crew quickly.

"Good," said Garnal. "My first order, as Captain of this pathetic ship, is to turn this ship around. We are heading north, back home, where the Gray Pirates will rise again more powerful than before. Anyone who hesitates or tries to sabotage this voyage home will be immediately executed on the spot by whichever member of my crew is closest. Understood?"

Malock's hands balled into fists, but he knew he couldn't order his men to attack Garnal or her men. He sensed how betrayed and angry the rest of his crew felt, but there was nothing any of them could do without jeopardizing the entire voyage.

"Good," said Garnal. "Then prepare the sails and turn the rudder. We are going home."

Chapter Seven

THE NEXT THREE DAYS were the worst Kinker had experienced on this voyage so far. By all appearances, the basic schedule of the *Iron Wind* had not changed. The fishing crew still hauled in the trawl at breakfast, lunch, and dinner; the cleaning crew scrubbed the deck; Vinji remained in the crow's nest, and the rest of the crew continued their various duties around the ship.

But in reality, a thick atmosphere of fear and tension filled every nook of the ship. The Gray Pirates monitored every activity, which might not have been so bad if they were not drunk and violent all the time. The Pirates seemed to have discovered Malock's secret store of wine because they were constantly seen with the drink, gulping it down, carousing loudly, and partying well into the night.

This might not have seemed so bad, but the drink made the Pirates even more violent and volatile than usual. Often they beat sailors for no reason at all, except perhaps because they could. Kinker had so far avoided a beating, but poor Gino got beat upside the head by a lug of a Pirate who got angry when Gino accidentally dropped a fish instead of giving it to him.

In addition, the Pirates often ate more than their fair share. At mealtimes, they'd gobble down the fish that Arisha prepared, leaving only bones and scraps for the rest of the crew. As a result, hunger, which was always a problem on the ship, became even worse than before. It was quite common for Kinker to have only a few pieces of fish a day, if even that, because the scraps they did get were not distributed evenly among the crew, turning every mealtime into an every-man-for-himself brawl, which Kinker refused to participate in, knowing that he could not beat the younger sailors even if he wanted to.

As for Malock, he was kept locked up in his stateroom. Banika, Vashnas, and Bifor had been taken to the hold, where they were kept under lock and key all day every day. As far as Kinker knew, none of them got even scraps, causing him to realize that the Pirates were slowly starving those three. He didn't know why the Pirates didn't kill those three right away, but as he never understood pirates in the first place, it perhaps wasn't as shocking as it could have been.

In particular, Daryh, Garnal's first mate, was bad. He was a botamancer, the one behind the moss from earlier, and had apparently at one point been a accomplished academic before being fired for reasons Kinker didn't know. The only reason Kinker knew any of that was because Daryh usually monitored the fishing crew and spent long periods of time ranting about the idiocy of the Academy and how he would love to slit the throat of every one of his former colleagues if given the chance.

TIMOTHY L. CEREPAKA

Not only that, but Daryh showed a creepy interest in Jenur, despite he being aquarian and her being human. More than once he would try to run his slimy hands up her behind or grab her breasts, but to Kinker's relief Jenur would always glare at him and make him back down. Well, it didn't *always* work. The first time she slapped his hands away, he hit her and threatened to rape her right there before being summoned by Garnal to discuss something. He never followed up with that threat, but it did make Kinker worry for Jenur more than he already did.

The uncertainty of it all was the worst for Kinker. It was almost impossible to tell what pleased the Gray Pirates and what didn't. Kinker suspected, too, that once they returned north, the Gray Pirates would simply slaughter them all, as the crew of the *Iron Wind* would no doubt be more of a liability than help then. Perhaps they would keep Malock to use as a bargaining chip, but the rest of the crew had no worth in their eyes, which was why Kinker knew they had to overthrow the Pirates somehow.

Kinker was no hero, which was why he kept his head down. He doubted there was anything he could do to defeat these Pirates. He thought it best to let them have their way, at least for now. Without Bifor or Malock, Kinker didn't see how they could possibly beat the Pirates. Not to mention he could not plan a mutiny with the fishing crew while Daryh constantly watched them. He heard every conversation because once, when Deddio whispered to Kinker about doing something to defeat the Pirates, Daryh jumped to his feet and kicked Deddio in the crotch.

So the entire situation seemed unlikely to change, unless a miracle happened. Kinker went to bed every night praying fervently more than ever for Kano to intercede, to provide them with a miracle, but so far the goddess had yet to answer his prayers. At this point, he doubted she would.

On the third day, not long after lunch, Daryh was summoned by Garnal to the stateroom. At first Kinker thought this meant they would be free to plan in secret, but then Daryh called one of the other Pirates to take his place, an octopus-like aquarian named Hino. Unlike Daryh, Hino seemed more attached to his drink because all he did was sit back against the mizzenmast, downing a bottle of wine while occasionally hurling drunken insults at the fishing crew, though because he spoke in the aquarian tongue, Kinker never understood them.

Having just tossed the trawl back into the water, the fishing crew were hard at work cleaning the fish. It was not difficult work, but due to Kinker's deep hunger he had a hard time concentrating. That was why it took him a moment to notice Jenur subtly tugging at his shirt sleeve in a way that Hino wouldn't notice (although considering how drunk the Pirate seemed to be, Kinker doubted he would have noticed even if she'd been blatant).

"What?" said Kinker in a low voice. "What do you want?"

"Your permission for what I am about to do to you," Jenur replied in an even lower voice. "It's going to be painful, but I think it will be just what we need to kick these Pirates off our ship and save Malock and the others."

Kinker looked over his shoulder at Hino. The Pirate was still sitting against the stateroom's back wall, swinging his now-empty bottle of wine through the air like a bird.

"What do you mean, it's going to be painful?" Kinker said, looking back at Jenur. "How painful, exactly?"

"Not very painful," said Jenur. "But painful enough that you might feel it for a few days."

"A few days? Jenur, whatever you're planning to do—"

Kinker had always known Jenur was stronger than she looked, but until her fist smashed into the side of his face, he hadn't really understood it. The blow knocked him flat off his feet, causing him to crash to the deck and let out a sharp intake of breath. This was then followed by a kick to the gut from Jenur's booted foot, the blow hitting him so hard that he thought he saw stars in his eyes.

The rest of the crew gasped in response and Deddio even said, "Jenur, what the hell are you doing?" but no one tried to stop her, perhaps because they were afraid of her.

At the same time, Hino was perhaps not as drunk as he looked because he was there almost instantly, his tentacles flailing as he shouted, in a heavily accented voice, "Break it up, you two, break it up. What's the deal here? Daryh said no fighting!"

Through watering eyes, Kinker saw Jenur take on a completely innocent expression as she turned to Hino. "Oh, this old perv just tried to touch me in a way I didn't like. I was just defending myself, you see."

Hino glanced at Kinker and said, "Doesn't change a thing. Daryh told me to keep the peace until we get to—"

Kinker wasn't sure what happened next. All he saw was a knife slip out of Jenur's sleeve into her hand, her arm jerk upward, and

Hino fall to the deck silently. The Pirate lay in a pool of ever-expanding blood, which Kinker moved away from to avoid getting stained with it.

Jenur held out a hand to Kinker, which Kinker reluctantly accepted. He glanced over his shoulder at Hino and noticed a cut in the Pirate's throat from which blood was leaking. The rest of the fishing crew just stood there, looking on in disbelief and confusion, which was exactly how Kinker felt right now.

"Sorry about hitting you so hard," said Jenur. "I needed to make it look real enough so the big lug would decide he needed to do something about it."

"You killed him," said Deddio, his eyes on the Pirate's corpse. "And expertly so, too. How did you know that slitting his throat right there would kill him instantly?"

Jenur wiped the blood off her knife on Hino's jacket, not looking at any of them as she said, "Doesn't matter. What does matter is rallying the rest of the crew to get Hino's friends."

"But how do we do that?" said Kinker, rubbing his face, which still hurt from Jenur's fist. "There's still a dozen or so murderous Pirates who have Malock in their custody. Not to mention Bifor, Vashnas, and Banika are also in the hold, which is guarded."

"I know," said Jenur. "I already figured out how we're gonna save everyone. Kinker, you and I will make our way down to the hold, where we'll kill the guard and free the prisoners."

"But they took Bifor's wand," said Deddio. "Even if we freed him, I doubt he would be able to do much against them. Mages need wands to use their magic, don't they?"

Jenur shook her head. "Wands are helpful, but they only channel magic. A mage's real power lies in their devotion to their gods. But we probably do need to get Bifor's wand. He obviously needs it; otherwise, he would have escaped by now."

"How do you know that?" said Kinker. "You're not a mage."

Jenur, once again, ignored the question. "Last I saw, Garnal had taken it. She probably has it on her person, so if we want to get it back we'll need to steal it from her."

"Steal it from her?" said Gino with a gulp. "Isn't that like trying to steal from an oversized crab that knows how to chop you into a million pieces?"

"That's why I've decided upon a change of plans," said Jenur. "We don't have much time until Daryh returns, so we need to act as natural as possible. Attacking now would only give the Pirates time to kill Malock or sink the ship. We need our attack to be so sudden that they don't have time to do either."

"Then what's the plan?" said Gino. "I'm all ears."

"Firstly, only one of us will be going below deck to free the prisoners," said Jenur. "And that will be Kinker."

"Hold on," said Kinker, holding up a hand. "I'm not a fighter. What if the guard tries to attack me? I'd be toast."

Jenur immediately held out another knife, similar to her own, and said, "Act as natural as possible. When he raises his neck, stab him directly in the throat. Do it right and he'll die without making a sound."

Kinker took the knife uncertainly and turned it in his hands. "I'm not very fast."

"You just need to be fast enough," said Jenur. "Anyway, I'm going to sneak around and find Garnal. I'll try to snatch the wand from her; if I can't, I'll slit her throat and then take it from her. The rest of you should stay here and act like nothing is out of the ordinary until I or Kinker return."

"What about the corpse?" said Gino, gesturing at Hino's body. "Do we—"

"Toss it overside," said Jenur. "No one will notice and by the time any of the Pirates do, they'll all be dead. Let's go."

Malock wasn't used to feeling hungry. Back on Carnag, he had always had three meals a day, and they were big meals, too; roasted black fish, fried calamari, strawberry pudding, Friana chocolate cookies, the freshest of Carnagian bread, and so much more.

Even after running out of their food stores, Malock had remained well-fed, in contrast to the rest of the crew. True, he didn't have the same variety and richness of meals that he had had back in the Hall of Carnag, but he did have three meals a day; this he accomplished by hoarding what little food that hadn't gone bad and making sure he got more food than the rest of the crew at mealtimes. As Captain of the ship, he felt that he needed to remain well-fed more than the rest of the crew did, so he often ate as much as he pleased.

Now, however, Malock's stomach grumbled with hunger. In the three days since the Gray Pirates had somehow managed to take over his ship (he was still wondering how that happened, to be honest), his meals had dropped from three to one a day, sometimes even less than that. Whenever he was fed, he was spoon-fed by Garnal, which was always an awkward experience in part because her claws made it almost impossible to grip the spoon correctly, and even when she succeeded in gripping it, she always spilled more food on his shirt and lap than in his mouth.

There was a reason he couldn't feed himself. When the Gray Pirates took over the ship, Garnal had taken Malock to his stateroom and tied him up to his chair behind his desk. Despite her clawed hands, Garnal was extremely good at tying knots, so good that Malock could barely even feel his arms and legs anymore. The chair itself was not nailed down or anything; however, that was a useless fact because every time he tried to move, his chair would tip over and he would remain that way for hours until Garnal decided to check up on him.

Malock had not yet eaten today because Garnal had gone to discuss something with her first mate, Daryh. They were standing just outside the stateroom, but all he could hear were their muffled voices. He had no idea what they were talking about. All he knew was that it probably wasn't ways in which they could improve their treatment of the crew of the *Iron Wind*.

A few minutes later, Garnal returned. She walked up to Malock's desk and took a seat opposite him, on the chair that Vashnas usually sat on. It reminded Malock that Vashnas was in even worse conditions than him, being locked up in the hold with no food or water at all. It made him angry, so angry he wanted to spit on Garnal (although he didn't, knowing from experience how she would react to that).

On the table between them was a bowl of cold lime fish soup. It was the only thing Malock had been allowed to eat day in and day out and he was getting sick of the taste. He now understood why the rest of his crew despised the dish so much.

"My precious prince looks hungry today," said Garnal, as if she were speaking about a child. "Want mommy to feed you?"

"I'd rather starve than accept food from you," Malock said, snarling.

Garnal shook her head. "That's a nice sentiment, but I'm afraid we still need you alive until we get north. You dying on us would ruin our plans, and frankly I dislike it when my plans are ruined."

Malock gave her the most skeptical, scathing look he could muster. "Oh? And may I ask what your plans are?"

"Sure," said Garnal. "Won't hurt to tell you, since you can't do a thing about 'em and you'll find out what they are soon enough anyway. I was just discussing them with Daryh, actually, so they're fresh on my mind."

Garnal leaned back in her chair, folding her claws across her chest and looking quite pleased with herself. "You see, my precious prince, we Gray Pirates are not in a particularly good situation. I won't tell you the specifics, but we are in desperate need of men, money, and a good ship."

Malock raised an eyebrow. "So you're going to take the *Iron Wind* and turn it's crew into pirates?"

Garnal laughed. "Ha! As if. Not even I could whip these wimps into pirates. They're hardly better than plankton, if that. No, I will kill them all eventually."

"And the ship?"

135

"This chunk of flotsam and jetsam?" said Garnal. "We'll sink it and get another. This lady is clearly on her last legs and it would be far more merciful to let her die in peace rather than try to fix her up."

"I don't understand," said Malock. "How are you going to get men, money, and a good ship if you're going to kill my whole crew?"

"That's where you come in," said Garnal. "You're the Prince of Carnag. That makes you worth a lot of money, thousands of coins, perhaps even millions. I imagine your parents are probably worried sick about you right now, praying to Grinf that you will have a safe voyage and that you will return alive and whole."

"Hold on," said Malock. "Are you going to hold me for ransom?"

"Looks like you royals aren't so dumb after all," said Garnal. "Yes, indeed. Once we return north, we'll offer your parents a deal. We'll return you, alive and whole, in exchange for a million coins. Seems like a reasonable deal to me, especially if your parents care about you even half as much as I think they do."

"A million coins?" said Malock. "That would bankrupt Carnag. It would make Carnag look like Ruwa."

"And what's so wrong about Ruwa?" said Garnal. "Lawlessness, poverty, perpetual hunger, and constant strife. Sounds like a pirate's paradise to me."

"You'll never get away with this," said Malock. "Kano is on my side. She'll drag you to the bottom of the ocean and torture your broken soul if you even so much as touch me."

Garnal's expression changed from amused to angry in a flash. "Don't you dare mention that divine bitch to me, gold blood. Why, if she were here right now, I'd throttle her, chop her into pieces, ground those into fine power, and scatter it across the entirety of the Crystal Sea personally. After what she did to us—"

"What did she do to you?" Malock said, not caring if he was interrupting. "Is she the reason you don't have a ship and only have a dozen men left on your crew?"

"Shut up," said Garnal. "You may be a prince, but that doesn't mean you are entitled to know everything about everybody. All you need to know is that Kano will not save you; if she wanted to, she would have already done that by now."

Malock opened her mouth to correct her, but before he could say anything, the door slammed open and Daryh walked in. Garnal looked over her shoulder in irritation and said, "Daryh, what are you doing here? I thought I told you to—"

Daryh let out a long, shuddering gasp and then fell face first to the floor. Blood leaked out of his back like a spring, but that wasn't what caught Malock's attention. What caught Malock's attention was the young woman standing just behind the now-dead Pirate, the woman who held a long, deadly-looking knife like she did this sort of thing every day.

Garnal rose to her feet, knocking her chair over in the process, and said, "Who in the Crystal Sea are you?"

The woman smiled. "Jenur Takren. And I'm here to take you out."

Five minutes earlier ...

With the knife hidden up his sleeve (Jenur had shown Kinker how to hide it so he could easily draw it when he needed it), Kinker made his way from the stern to the main deck. He tried to look as casual as he could, hoping against hope that he would not be stopped and searched by one of the Pirates, that he could make it to the hatch without being noticed. If any of the Pirates stopped him, the entire plan would probably fall apart.

To calm himself, he recited the story in his head again and again, the exact reason he was going down to the hold.

I am going to the hold to retrieve some supplies to repair the trawl, Kinker thought, climbing down the steps from the poop deck to the main deck. *I am going to the hold to retrieve some supplies to repair the trawl. I am going to the hold to retrieve some supplies to repair the trawl. I am—*

"Hey, you!" said a voice, causing Kinker to freeze. "Where are you going?"

Kinker turned and saw Daryh above him, standing just outside the stateroom, near the helm, where a couple of sailors were steering the ship. The eel-like aquarian's eyes almost burned him, but Kinker tried to look as innocent as he could.

"I am going to the hold to retrieve some supplies to repair the trawl," Kinker said. "I'll be back in a few minutes."

Daryh didn't look convinced. "Did Hino give you permission to go wandering about the ship like this?"

"Yes," said Kinker. "He threatened to beat me to death if I didn't return in ten minutes, so I must be going, if you'd let me."

Daryh shook his head. "No way. I know exactly what you're trying to do. You can't fool—"

Jenur appeared behind Daryh just then and stabbed him in the back. The first mate let out a loud scream, causing the rest of the crew —Pirates and sailors alike—to turn and look at him in surprise. Even Kinker was too stunned to move for a moment.

Still driving her knife into his back, Jenur shouted, "Everyone! The time has come to kick these Pirates off of our ship! Fight for your freedom!"

Everyone was still too surprised to react, but Kinker realized that he had a rare opportunity here to go below deck before the Pirates recovered from shock. He ran as fast as he could to the hatch, pulled it open, and climbed down the ladder below deck even as the sounds of battle and cries of pain began to fill his ears.

As he made his way down the hall, he passed several sailors, telling them as he did, "Go top deck and help the others fight the Pirates," but didn't stop long enough to tell them the whole story. Not that he needed to. When the sailors he passed heard that, they let out big whoops and dashed in the opposite direction that he was going. Kinker would have joined them, but he had his own job to complete right now.

As he climbed down the ladder that led to the hold, he realized just how stupid he'd been. In his rush to get to the hold, he had forgotten to get help from some of the other sailors. He was so focused on the original plan, which involved him discreetly killing the guard and freeing the prisoners, that he had forgotten that things had changed, which meant the plan had changed, too.

But Kinker kept climbing down anyway. He didn't have time to go back up and find someone. All of the sailors in the lower decks were probably already on their way to the surface. Right now, the guard probably didn't know about the fighting and if he saw Kinker climbing down with three or four other armed sailors, he would probably realize what was happening and attack them. Kinker hoped that Jenur's earlier advice to him would work.

The lowest deck, where the hold was located, was much darker than the middle deck. Kinker had never been down here before, never having a reason to, and he now wished he didn't have to. While light would stream through the ceiling of the middle deck, down here, the only light was a lamp at the end of the hall, in front of the door to the hold, leaving the rest of the deck in darkness.

Not only that, but Kinker could feel the ocean currents better down here, too. The ship lurched slightly, sending him staggering to the right. He leaned against a wall and realized it was wet. He realized that he was technically underwater and that, if a hole was busted open down, he would undoubtedly drown. It was not a pleasant thought.

Doing his best to retain his balance and hide his fear, Kinker made his way down the hall. Through the walls of the lowest deck, the slightly muffled sounds of the ocean currents drowned out most of the other sounds, which certainly worked in Kinker's favor because that meant that the guard would not hear the noises from the fighting above. And with luck, the guard would never learn about the battle at all.

Kinker reached the end of the hall sooner than he wanted, stopping a few feet away from the guard. The guard looked to be asleep at first, his eyes closed and his shark-like head lowered onto his chest. He was sitting on a chair, which was leaning against the door to the hold, a key ring tied to his belt. Kinker wanted to reach out and take those keys, but he refrained from doing so. It was not yet time.

Then the guard's eyes opened and he looked up. Kinker wished that the guard's eyes would look more human and less shark-like because right now the old man felt like he was being scrutinized for lunch.

"What are you doing down here?" said the guard. His arms, Kinker noticed, were quite large, probably thicker than Kinker's entire body. "Garnal said no one was allowed down here except for Gray Pirates."

"Yes, well, you see, I am in desperate need of supplies to repair the trawl with," Kinker said, his voice accidentally trembling over the word 'trawl.' "Daryh sent me down here to retrieve some rope we could use to fix it. It's in the hold, so if you will just let me in—"

"I smell fear," said the guard. He raised his head to sniff the air, exposing his neck. "I don't think you'd be afraid if you were telling me the—"

Kinker didn't let him finish. Just as Jenur showed him, Kinker let the knife slip out of his sleeve and into his hand. And then, again as Jenur had showed him, Kinker leaped forward and rammed the knife straight into the Pirate's exposed throat.

The Pirate lashed out with a kick, hitting Kinker in the knee and sending the fisherman falling to the ground. Yet a moment later, the Pirate slumped in his seat, blood pouring from his neck onto his shirt, staining it and making it look even uglier than usual.

Rubbing his knee, Kinker stood up and looked at his knife, which was covered in blood. He was surprised at how easily the guard had died. It made him wonder how Jenur knew the right place to kill someone instantly, but he decided that was a question for another day. Right now, he had to free the prisoners.

The shark Pirate was as heavy as a log, but Kinker eventually pushed the Pirate's body onto the floor and pushed the chair aside. He fished the key ring from the Pirate's body and fiddled with several different keys until he found one that fit the hold's lock. He turned the key and opened the door.

As soon as he opened it, a terrible smell of unwashed bodies, rotting food, and seawater entered his nostrils, making him gag. He had little time to recover, however, because Banika appeared in the doorway, holding a chunk of wood, and brought it down on his head even as he held up a hand and said, "Wait! Its me, Kinker! Stop!"

His words did little to stop her. The chunk of wood slammed into the top of his head and he crashed to the floor, losing consciousness instantly.

Currently ...

Now Malock didn't know Jenur very well, but he was so glad to see her that he could have kissed her. The sounds of battle raged behind her, but that didn't matter right now because he was certain he was going to be saved now.

"You're going to take me down?" said Garnal, her back to Malock. "That's a funny joke, young girl. You may have killed Daryh, but he was always an idiot despite his academic credentials."

"I didn't just kill Daryh," said Jenur. "Killed Hino, too. Oh, and the rest of your band of dirty thieves is currently fighting for their lives. I imagine the rest of the crew is showing them no mercy at the moment."

For the first time, Garnal's claws shook. "Impossible. You sailors are too scrawny and weak to defeat my men."

"True, we haven't had a good meal in a long time," said Jenur. "But we still out number you— two to one—and all of us are incredibly pissed off, which is a pretty good combination in any fight. We might suffer a few losses ourselves, but it'll be nothing compared to the losses you will suffer."

"Big words for such a small girl," Garnal said. "Besides, if knives are the best you got, I'm afraid you'll be losing your head tonight. My armor, if you haven't noticed, is extremely thick. Not even Grinfian knives can pierce this hide."

Garnal tapped her shell as she spoke, a hollow ringing sound echoing as she did that.

Jenur shrugged. "My knives have pierced things much thicker than a crab shell before. Like the skulls of idiots."

Garnal immediately moved behind the desk. With her claws, she snapped the ropes tying down Malock as easily as string and then forced the prince to stand. Malock struggled to escape her grasp, but he felt one of her claws close around his throat, causing him to cease struggling.

Jenur took one step forward, but Garnal tightened her claw around Malock's neck, making her stop. Malock felt the nails of her claw pierce his neck slightly, enough to make it bleed but not enough to cause any serious damage.

"Take just one more step forward, girl, one more step, I dare you, and your Captain will lose his head," said Garnal. "Quite literally, in this case."

Jenur gave her a hard look. "You wouldn't dare."

"Many people have said similar things to me in the past, girl, but every one of them has been wrong," said Garnal. "I wouldn't be the most wanted pirate in the Northern Isles if I didn't dare to do things that lesser pirates would never even dream of. And let me tell you that I have dreamed of killing royalty before."

Malock met Jenur's eyes. He tried to look as in command and confident as he could. But frankly, in this situation, he didn't feel confident that he or Jenur could get out of this with his head still attached to his shoulders.

"Drop your knife, and I'll spare your precious prince's pampered life," said Garnal. "If you don't, then we'll see if the color of the blood of princes really is gold, as the old song says."

Jenur looked torn. For a long moment, Malock thought Jenur would attack anyway.

Then Jenur tossed her knife to the floor. "Fine. I'm unarmed."

Garnal chuckled. "Now tell your fellow mates to stop slaughtering my men. I can still hear them fighting outside. And if I don't hear them stop in five minutes ..."

Her claw tightened around his neck again. It was getting harder and harder for Malock to breathe, not in the least because Garnal smelled exactly like a crab that had spent too much time lying under a rock.

"What?" said Jenur. "That wasn't the deal, Garnal. You said—"

"So long as I hold Malock's life in my claws, I decide what the 'deal' is, girl," said Garnal. "Now call off your mates. Tell 'em this little mutiny of yours is over. For good."

"Don't," said Malock to Jenur, daring to speak for the first time. "Don't let this lowlife Pirate—"

"Shut your trap," Garnal said, tightening her grip once more and forcing him to stop speaking. "Stop trying to play the hero. We know what you royals are really like. You care only about saving your own skin. You'd step over this naïve girl's corpse if you thought it would save your own life."

Malock didn't dare speak. He had a feeling that if he spoke even one more word, Garnal would drop any pretense of making a fair deal and behead him in one swift stroke.

"All right, then," said Garnal. "Now, girl, remember the deal. You step outside, call off the mutiny, and I won't kill this spoiled brat. Deal?"

Jenur looked defeated. Her shoulders slumped and she turned to leave when Malock remembered something very important. Saying it might get him killed, but it was the only opportunity he had.

So Malock said, in a strained voice, "Jenur, stay where you are. You don't need to deal with lowlife scum like this Pirate."

Jenur stopped and looked over her shoulder. "What? But if I don't, she'll—"

"She wouldn't dare touch a hair on my head," said Malock. "Right, Garnal?"

"What are you babbling about?" said Garnal. "This isn't Poetry Day, gold blood. You don't win prizes for spouting nonsensical gibberish."

"I know that," said Malock. "I also know that you need me alive so you can ransom me off to my parents back on Carnag. If you kill me, then you won't get the million coins you want so badly."

"Don't tempt me, gold blood," said Garnal, though there was a hint of doubt in her voice. "I've killed people more important than you for much less."

"But you wouldn't kill me now," said Malock. "Consider your situation, Pirate. By now, my men have probably made short work of what little of your crew remains. You don't have a ship, not even a small rowboat to call your own. Your own funds are obviously depleted. And even if you kill me, my men will slaughter you and bury your corpse with the rest of your sorry crew. I'm the only bargaining chip you have left and I know you're too smart to kill me that easily."

Malock didn't know if talking her down would work. Garnal was a bloodthirsty pirate and bloodthirsty pirates rarely listened to reason. Still, he also knew that she was a coward who would do whatever she needed to preserve her own life, even if it meant losing. It was the only chance of survival that he had.

The seconds ticked by slowly. Malock didn't know what to expect and based on Jenur's expression, she didn't, either. What either of them did next relied entirely upon what Garnal did next.

Then, without warning, Garnal's claw let go of his neck entirely. Her other claw let go of his right arm and he staggered forward against the desk. He turned around to see Garnal still standing there, her arms at her sides, looking far more defeated than Jenur had.

"I'll give you this, gold blood," said Garnal. "If you were a pirate, I'd fear for my very life on these sorry seas."

At that moment, the sounds of feet beating against the wood floor reached Malock's ears and then a dozen or so sailors spilled into the stateroom. They all looked like they had been through a war, with torn clothing, bleeding wounds, broken noses, and their weapons at the ready. Those who had guns, about half, aimed them directly at Garnal, while those with swords moved to apprehend her.

"Don't kill her," Malock told the sailors who were approaching the desk. "Tie her up and lock her up in the hold. I want to talk to her."

To Garnal's credit, she didn't fight back. She allowed the six sailors to bind her with some of the rope that had bound Malock and allowed them to lead her out of the stateroom. She held her head high the entire time, however, much like Malock's mother did whenever she was walking about the capital. The other sailors, the ones with the guns, moved Daryh's corpse out of the doorway to let the others through easier.

Jenur had stepped aside to allow the other sailors to enter, but when they took Garnal out of the room, she went over to Malock and sliced the few ropes still binding his hands together. The ropes left marks around his wrists, but other than that they were fine.

"Thank you, Jenur," said Malock, looking at her with appreciation as he rubbed his wrists. "There are not enough words in the language of the gods to describe my thankfulness to you."

"It's nothing," said Jenur, sheathing her knife. "I have a special hatred for pirates, so the pleasure of killing so many is all the reward I need."

"But you deserve far more," Malock said. "When we return to

Carnag, I'll ask my parents to make you royalty. How does Duchess Jenur sound?"

"Seriously, you don't need to do anything," said Jenur, shaking her head. "Like I said, killing pirates is reward enough."

"But I insist," said Malock. "At the very least, please let me praise you in front of the entire crew. You are an example to them all, a true sailor to your Captain."

Jenur shrugged. "Whatever. I'm going to go find Kinker. He was supposed to free the prisoners from the hold. Should be done by now."

"I will go with you," said Malock. "I want to make sure Vashnas is okay. I also need to see Banika and get her back to work overseeing the clean up and disposal of the Pirates' corpses."

"Okay," said Jenur, already making her way to the door. "Try to keep up."

Chapter Eight

KINKER AWOKE A FEW hours later, his head still pounding, to discover that Banika had stayed behind to take care of him while Bifor and Vashnas went to join the rest of the crew in mutiny. Banika apologized to Kinker when she saw he was awake, explaining that she, Bifor, and Vashnas had been planning to jump any Pirates that came to check on them. She had mistaken Kinker for one of them and had only realized her mistake a moment too late.

Kinker forgave her for that, even though he had a feeling that, between being beaten by Jenur and getting thwacked on the head by Banika, his head was going to be pounding for the rest of the voyage. So he and Banika made their way to the top deck, where they discovered that the mutiny had been successful and that all of the Pirates were now dead, except for Garnal, who was taken to the hold for further questioning.

It wasn't without some losses, however. During the mutiny, a few sailors had been lost, among them Daro Loman and Magnisa. These losses hit Kinker and the surviving members of the fishing crew hard, but Gino seemed to be hit the hardest of them all. He and Magnisa had been married for fifty years, which surprised Kinker until he remembered that aquarians had a longer lifespan than the average human.

As with the sailors they lost on Ikadori Island, a mass funeral was held for those who lives were lost. They lost about five sailors overall, so on that day, five bodies, wrapped in some extra sail cloth that Vashnas had found in the hold while being held prisoner down there, were dropped into the sea. Gino gave the eulogy for them. He was fine for the first three sailors, got emotional when talking about Daro, and broke down so completely when he got to Magnisa that Malock himself had to finish the eulogy for the widower.

No one broke down for the Pirates. Their bodies were looted for clothes, weapons, and anything else useful they might have on them, and then frozen together by Bifor's pagomancy. The block of ice was dumped into the sea without much fanfare or ritual and was lost from view as the *Iron Wind* continued its voyage.

Regarding the injured, most of the crew suffered minor injuries during the mutiny, though nothing worse than a cut or some bruises, surprisingly enough. Those few who had suffered broken limbs were healed by Telka and Bifor with little trouble.

The ship itself had suffered some damage. Bullet holes riddled the deck and the middle sail, which they had to take down for a few hours to patch. The top deck reeked of blood and death, even with the wind blowing in the cool sea air. The *Iron Wind* already smelled awful, but it was even worse now.

All things considered, however, Kinker was surprised at how

smoothly the mutiny went. His heart ached every time he thought about Daro and Magnisa, of course, and their food supply was even lower than before, but it seemed like the Gray Pirates had done little lasting damage to the ship itself. They had lost a few days, true, but the wind was blowing unusually hard recently and the ship had been turned around back south, so Kinker figured they would make up that pretty quickly.

When he mentioned that to Jenur, as they sat together at the stern during breakfast two days after the mutiny, Jenur nodded.

"Yeah," she said. "Though really, it's not that surprising. There were only a dozen of them and half of them were mostly drunk most of the time and the other half were completely drunk all the time. I'm surprised they had control over the ship as long as they did, to be honest."

Kinker took a bite from his fish, grateful to be to eating even this much, and said, "Makes me wonder what happened to their ship. The Gray Pirates are supposed to have had over a hundred members, right?"

"Right," said Jenur. "And did you see how hungry they were? They looked even worse than us. Something on these seas must have got 'em good. Don't you agree, Gino?"

Gino was sitting near them, quietly eating his fish. He had been quieter since Magnisa's death, at least during the day. At night, Kinker heard the aquarian fisherman singing a song in the aquarian language. Kinker didn't understand the words, but the tone was always sad, so sad in fact that Kinker himself had a hard time not shedding a few tears as he slept.

When Jenur spoke to him, Gino looked at her and said, "I wish that whatever had gotten them had gotten all of those bastards. And I wish Malock would let me have a go at Garnal. I just want to beat that scum to a pulp. Is that such an unreasonable thing to ask for?"

"You know Malock," said Jenur. "Seems to think Garnal might know something about the seas that could help us."

Gino looked at her with flagrantly unsympathetic eyes. "You're just defending him because he praised you for rescuing him."

Jenur blushed. "I already said, I don't care. I don't care if Malock thinks I'm the best sailor ever or if he hates my guts. I'm just saying that I agree with Malock that beating Garnal to a pulp isn't going to help us avoid whatever decimated the Gray Pirates."

Kinker smiled. After the collective funeral for the fallen Pirates, Malock had praised Jenur in front of the entire crew for her bravery and courage in the face of the Gray Pirates. He had even offered her a promotion to third mate (Banika was first and Vashnas was second), but Jenur had declined because, in her own words, she "would rather play with fish guts than boss around a bunch of surly sailors." Despite that, Kinker noticed that her opinion of Malock had improved dramatically since that day.

"If it's any consolation, Gino, Malock might let you beat up Garnal when she tells him what he wants," said Kinker. "I've heard Malock is starting to lose his temper. Been interrogating her for two days now and she still hasn't told him anything."

"I doubt she ever will," Gino said, looking disgusted. "I know her kind. Their mouths can close even tighter than their claws. Malock could shove a burning iron rod up her ass and she still wouldn't tell him anything if she doesn't want to."

"She'll have to talk eventually," said Deddio, sitting down next to them, his meager breakfast of one fish in his hands. "I heard that Malock is starting to starve her. Even a tough pirate like her needs to eat occasionally, right?"

"I doubt it," said Gino, taking a bite out of his cooked circle fish. "Lowlife like her feed off the thrill they get from murdering innocent people. She probably got enough of that from us to last her a lifetime."

"That reminds me," said Kinker. "We need to find replacements for Daro and Magnisa."

Gino almost dropped his fish. "What?"

"New members of the fishing crew," said Kinker. "Preparing food for the whole crew is a six person job. We're down to four now."

"Oh," said Gino, looking down at his lap. "Right. Well, who do you think we should choose?"

"Not sure," Kinker admitted. "Malock is usually in charge of assigning sailors to specific jobs. Deddio, have you spoken with Malock about it?"

"No," said Deddio. "Been so busy over the past couple of days that it's slipped my mind. Besides, Malock's been so busy. He spends almost all of his time in the hold, interrogating Garnal. Sometimes I wonder if he sleeps down there all night, just in case Garnal mutters something in her sleep."

"He's interrogating her right now, isn't he?" said Kinker. "I wonder how that's going."

"Probably not very well," said Gino. "I'm sure we would have heard by now if he was making any progress."

The air in the hold was dull, damp, and heavy. The walls creaked and groaned, threatening to break apart and sink the entire ship, yet they held as they always had, reinforced by a basic repair spell Bifor had cast on it a few weeks back before the *Iron Wind* had entered the southern seas. Boxes and crates of various sizes—many of them empty, though several were full of things like ammunition, fishing equipment, and a couple of other odd objects—were scattered everywhere.

Malock sat on a stool, his boat cloak traded in for a much cooler white long-sleeved shirt that breathed better, eating some lime fish soup that Banika had brought down for him. Banika sat on a nearby crate, eating her own bowl of the foul-tasting soup, though far more discreetly than he was.

Sitting opposite Malock, with her arms and legs bound so tightly together that she probably couldn't even feel them anymore, was Garnal. She watched with hungry eyes as Malock slurped his soup, burped, and generally made noises that indicated he was enjoying his meal immensely (even though it actually wasn't that good). He saw saliva dripping from the corners of her mouth, but pretended not to notice.

Putting his bowl down on his lap, Malock wiped the remains from his lips and said, "Hungry, Garnal?"

The Pirate scowled and looked away. "Of course not. Crustaceans like me can go weeks without eating. Your sloppy table manners hardly tempt me."

Malock smirked. "Are you sure? I'd be willing to share if you'd just tell me about the thing that completely decimated your entire crew and ship."

Garnal made an angry chittering sound with her teeth. "You don't want to know about it. If you are lucky, you will never have to face it. I'd rather die than give you information you could use to save yourself, knowledge that I could have used to save my own crew if I'd had it."

"And by withholding this information, you are surely not dooming yourself to death if that happens to us," said Malock. "For such a big-time pirate, you sure are stupid."

"You don't want to know it," said Garnal. "If I tell you about it, it will haunt your dreams and you will never be able to sleep peacefully again."

"I didn't know you cared about my wellbeing," said Malock. "Maybe you aren't such a bad person after all, Gar."

"Shut up, gold blood," Garnal said. She shuddered. "That thing ... telling you about it would force me to relive it. And trust me when I say that you only want to experience that kind of thing once."

Malock leaned forward, being careful not to drop his bowl, and said, "Here's the deal. You tell me all about the thing, as much as you can remember, and I'll let you go. You will be free to terrorize the seas again. Doesn't that sound like the kind of thing a pirate like you would want?"

Garnal inclined her head, as if thinking about the offer.

Then she said slowly, "Fine. I am getting tired of being tied up and forced to sleep in this hold like a cabin boy. I'll tell you what you need to know. You promise to let me go when I do?"

"Of course," said Malock. "In case you forgot, I am not a pirate. I actually keep to my word."

Garnal snorted. "The last time I heard a royal say that ... oh, never mind. I will just begin. The quicker I tell you this story, the quicker I get my freedom."

"Just don't skimp on any details," Malock told her. "Banika here is a telemancer who specializes in truth-detecting. If you leave out even one detail, she'll know."

Of course that was a lie. Banika didn't know any magic (at least, as far as Malock knew, she didn't). She didn't know anything about telemancy, a field of mind magic that covered subjects like telepathy, telekinesis, and so on.

But Garnal didn't know that. She just glanced at Banika uneasily, who was still eating her soup as if Malock had said nothing, and then looked back at Malock.

"Fine," said Garnal. "I'm sure you know that we, the Gray Pirates, are the longest-lasting and most successful pirating group in the history of Martir. We have stolen the Golden Scepter of Nargode, a priceless historical artifact valued by all humans; defeated the Shikan Navy; and successfully raided the treasury of the aquarian city of Nemo, among our many other fine exploits."

Malock nodded. He remembered hearing about all of those tales growing up. His own island, Carnag, had once lost an entire shipment of their finest boots to the Gray Pirates, which was what caused his father to pledge ten thousand coins to anyone who could bring Garnal's head to his throne.

"But haven't you ever wondered what we did with all of that?" said Garnal. "None of the money or objects we stole ever ended up on the black market. Countless bounty hunters, government officials, treasure hunters, and others have tried to find our loot and failed."

That was also true. It was also why the Gray Pirates were so feared. It seemed like every time they stole something, it disappeared forever, never to be seen again. Malock had privately assumed they simply destroyed everything they stole, though now that he thought about that, it was a silly assumption to make.

"We hid it all on a tiny island in the southern seas," said Garnal. "We discovered the island when we fled from our first successful theft. I won't tell you where the island is located, but I will say that it is not far from our current position."

Good old pirate greed. Malock had no intention whatsoever of taking Garnal's loot or visiting her island, but she apparently believed he did.

"There is a large underground cave there," said Garnal. "Very thick walls with an entrance so well-hidden that even a topomancer would have a difficult time finding it. Because no one lived on the island and it was unknown to everyone else, we turned the cave into our treasure vault. We'd dump our loot in the cave after a successful theft and hide on the island itself if the Northern Isles became too hot for us. It is how we managed to avoid capture and disappear whenever we needed to."

That was another thing about the Gray Pirates that no one had ever understood. Every time a bunch of bounty hunters or government navies got together to hunt them down, the Pirates would always disappear as if they were ghosts. Malock remembered the speculations, most of them centering on an aoramancer cloaking the ship in an obscure part of the Northern Isles. Hiding in the southern seas made so much sense that Malock felt stupid for not thinking of it himself.

"We thought our little island base was the safest place in the world," said Garnal. "For years, we were the only ones who ever set foot there. We never even saw any other ships come, probably because it was located in the southern seas. We even began to believe that the legends about the southern seas, all of those tales about monsters and dangerous weather and mysterious beings, were just scary tales made up by cowards who didn't understand anything. We felt we ruled the southern seas and that that little island of ours was our throne. How foolish were we."

They must not have met the Loner God, then, Malock thought.

"Then, about a week before we discovered you guys, everything changed," said Garnal. "We were celebrating another successful raid, having recently stolen the crown of your mother, Queen Markinia, and—"

"Hold on," said Malock. "You stole my mother's crown? When did this happen?"

"While you were out on this stupid quest of yours, of course," said Garnal. "Anyway, we just evaded the Carnagian navy and decided to lay low on our island for a while. We decided to throw a party because it had been a few days since the last one and we'd managed to acquire some fine black beer from a dealer on Carnag. It was a great party. You should have been there."

"I don't party with pirates," said Malock. "Are you getting somewhere with this story?"

"Don't worry, gold blood, I am," said Garnal. "I am just trying to remember the good times me and my crew used to have before all hell broke loose. Besides, I enjoy watching you get impatient because it confirms what I've always believed about you royals: you're nothing more than impatient spoiled brats who can't wait for anything."

Malock ignored the insult. "Continue, please."

"Anyway," Garnal said, sounding more than a bit pleased that she had managed to anger Malock, "we were partying on the deck of our ship, a fine schooner called the *Gray Ghost*, when a storm suddenly came out of nowhere. This took us by surprise, partly because we were drunk as hell, partly because the night sky had been very clear and none of us had been expecting it to rain. The more sober of us managed to horde the rest of us into the cave to wait out the storm."

"And then what happened?"

"As I said, I am getting to it," said Garnal. "So we continued the party in our treasure cave, dancing and drinking and fornicating and all that good stuff. I don't remember even half the stuff I did that night, I was so drunk, but I can assure you that most of it would probably offend your royal sensibilities.

"Then ... it happened."

"What happened?" said Malock.

Garnal looked away, as if the very thought of it shook her to the core. "The roof of the cave was ripped straight off. The rain fell on us and then I looked up and saw the Verch."

"Verch?" said Malock. "What is the Verch?"

"You mean you haven't heard?" said Garnal. "And here I thought you were supposed to be a lover of all things aquarian. Well, the Verch is a figure from the mythology of my people. According to the old legends, it is a powerful being, weaker than the gods but stronger than we mortals, who brings swift and terrible punishment down on those who have angered the gods. The word 'Verch' roughly translates to 'Punishment' in your human tongue, I believe."

"Interesting," said Malock. "So you think this 'Punishment' attacked you?"

"Think? I know so," said Garnal. "Saw it with my own eyes. Standing there, hefting the roof of the cave above its head, its big red eyes glaring at us, smoke and smog shooting out from its ears, slime dripping everywhere ... it was the most horrible thing I have ever seen in my entire life and let me tell you that I have seen many horrible things in my life."

Malock leaned back in his chair, his arms crossed across his chest and a smirk on his lips. "How appropriate that thieves and murderers were punished by a servant of the gods. It is poetic justice at its finest."

"You wouldn't be saying that if you actually saw the Verch yourself," said Garnal. "Anyway, to finish the story, the Verch killed almost all of my men, save for those dozen who managed to escape with me, destroyed all of our loot, and then smashed our ship into tiny little pieces. I believe the only reason we managed to escape, despite being drunk out of our minds, is because we got caught in a current that pulled us away."

"And you've been on the run since."

"More or less," said Garnal. "Daryh got snapped up in your pathetic excuse for a trawl, which is how we found out about you. We were desperate, which is why we attacked you, even though we knew the chances of us succeeding were slim at best."

Malock scratched his chin thoughtfully. "Well, if your story is true, I don't see any reason to fear for my life. I've done nothing to anger the gods. I understand why you were punished, though. You had it coming."

"Perhaps," said Garnal. "But I and my men looted, pillaged, raped, murdered, and plundered for years without any of the gods lifting so much as one finger to stop us. Why did they wait until just recently to punish us?"

"The gods' ways are mysterious," Malock said. "We do not always understand why they do what they do. I'm sure they had a good reason for it."

Garnal snorted. "If you say so. Now, if I remember correctly, you promised to let me free if I told you my story. You promised."

Malock grinned and looked at Banika. "So? Did she tell the truth?"

Banika looked up and, without changing her expression even slightly, nodded. Garnal let out an audible sigh of relief.

"All right," said Malock. "As I said, I am a man of my word. But if you ever try to come back, I will kill you. Got it?"

Garnal nodded. "I would not expect anything less from my new worst enemy."

"Good," said Malock as he stood up, holding his soup bowl in his hands. "Banika, let's get this Pirate out of here and back into the sea, where she belongs. She's wasted enough of our time as is."

Chapter Nine

GARNAL WAS MADE TO walk the plank. Literally. A few of the sailors found an old board lying around and nailed it down to the scuppers. Garnal walked onto the plank with the crew yelling obscenities at her, jeering at her, and in general treating her with the level of disdain that only a pirate of her caliber deserved.

Not that Garnal seemed to care. When she got to the end of the plank, she didn't look back or even acknowledge that she'd heard them. She simply jumped off and fell into the water with a splash and disappeared instantly. Some of the rowdier sailors got their guns out and fired into the water after her, but she was gone before they could shoot her.

After that, Malock assigned two other sailors to the fishing crew: one was a human woman named Kocas Iknor, who seemed incapable of shutting up about her great hunting skills; The other was an aquarian named Byki, who resembled a squid in the face. Neither of them were trained fishermen or even just hobbyists, so Kinker spent the next few days teaching them how to haul in the trawl, how to clean and cook fish, and anything else about fishing that they needed to know.

That was one thing Kinker noticed more and more as the days progressed. Since joining the fishing crew, Kinker had been doing much of the things that Deddio, the head fisherman, was supposed to do. In practice, Kinker felt like he was in charge of the group, spending much of his time telling the others, even Deddio, the proper ways to haul in the trawl and clean the fish.

That wasn't very surprising. Kinker was the only professional fisherman on the entire ship. None of them understood fishing quite the same way he did. The others were definitely learning and improving, but they still deferred to his wisdom and experience whenever they had to make a difficult decision.

But Kinker was not interested in leading. He wasn't a leader. He had never held a leadership position back on Destan or on any of the dozens of fishing ships he'd worked on over the years. He had nothing against leadership or leaders in general, but he did not feel that he was suited for the job. He was especially worried about gaining prominence because it might force him to reveal his secret, a secret he had done his very best to hide so far.

Kinker tried not to worry about his secret most of the time. None of the sailors aboard the *Iron Wind* had any connection to Destan or to its priests, as far as he knew. Yet he was still determined to take the secret with him to the grave. Even though he knew he didn't do it on purpose, he doubted the others would believe him. They would probably despise him more than he despised himself if they found out what he did.

The only question was how long Kinker could keep this a secret. That was a long-term question and he didn't like to think long-term. That meant thinking about what he would do if they returned to the Northern Isles. He couldn't go back to Destan, not after his escape. He thought about staying with Jenur, but every time he asked her about her past or where she came from, she changed the subject so naturally that it wasn't until hours later that Kinker realized what she had done.

What secrets does she have to hide? Kinker thought. *She doesn't want to talk about her past, just like me. I wonder why.*

Then again, it seemed like everyone on the *Iron Wind* had secrets. Malock still hadn't talked about his experiences on Ikadori Island or what Garnal had told him in the hold. Jenur had a strange knowledge of magic and ways to kill people but refused to explain where she got that knowledge from. And it wouldn't surprise Kinker one bit if it turned out that Vashnas had some secrets of her own. With so much secrecy, he was surprised that anyone trusted anyone on this ship.

Then again, he thought on the second day after Garnal's departure, glancing into the sea as he and the others hauled in the trawl for the day's lunch, *when the only other option is try to survive in a sea that cares for you even less than your mother sea, I suppose learning to live with secrets is how one gets by.*

It was a week after Garnal departed from the ship, shortly after breakfast, that a large storm blew in from the east. The rain fell hard, the waves rose and fell, and the sky rumbled, but compared to murder season up north, it was bearable. Its sudden appearance was surprising, true (the sky had been clear), but Kinker didn't see any reason to freak out.

Malock, on the other hand, seemed to be in full-on panic mode now. He was running around the ship, ordering sailors to tie down whatever they couldn't take below deck and to stay away from the bulwarks so they wouldn't get swept overboard by the waves. That Malock was personally ordering them himself and not Banika, made Kinker so worried that he actually decided to talk to Malock himself.

He got his chance when Malock came to check on the trawl. The Captain's hair was being blown around by the wind as he demanded the fishing crew to haul in the trawl and take it below deck until the storm passed.

"What?" said Kinker, raising his voice over the howling wind. "But we just tossed it back in."

"I don't care!" said Malock, raising his voice as he pulled the hood of his boat cloak over his head. "I don't like the look of this storm, not one bit, and I don't want us losing anything we might need just because we didn't take this storm seriously!"

"Yes, sir, Captain," said Deddio, saluting Malock. He turned to the others and said, "Men! Let's haul in the trawl! And then take it down to the hold!"

While they did that, Kinker turned to Malock and asked, "What are you so worried about? It's just a storm."

Malock shook his head. "I didn't ask for your opinion, Kinker. Just help your fellow fishermen haul the trawl in and take it to the hold. That is an order."

Before Kinker could ask any more questions, Malock was gone, already making his way to the bow, shouting orders to the nearest sailors to furl the sails. Kinker looked up at the sky, seeing the dark, rumbling clouds and bright lightning, and decided that, whatever Malock's real reason for being so worried about the storm, it did make sense to haul in the trawl, just so the ocean wouldn't rip it off the stern.

By the time the fishing crew managed to get the trawl onto the deck, the storm was in full swing. The wind whipped their clothes and hair about, the raindrops fell like bullets, the *Iron Wind* rocked back and forth like a cradle, and the ocean waves splashed against the ship's side, dousing anyone who happened to be near the bulwarks. By the time the fishing crew—dragging the trawl behind them— reached the hatch that led to the lower decks, their clothes were soaked through and through and the only ones who seemed to enjoy it were Byki and Gino, although even they looked a bit disgruntled at the iciness of the water.

In some ways, though, Kinker would have preferred to be outside in the rain than inside the lower decks. Despite the *Iron Wind's* large size, there simply wasn't enough space to give each sailor—all 109 of them—their own room or space to stand in. The fishing crew spent several minutes dragging the trawl through the crowded decks and it took them even longer to find a spot in the hold to put it because quite a few sailors, having nowhere else to go, had decided to ride out the storm there.

Once they did, they took up a space near the back of the hold. The hold was an unpleasant place to be, mostly due to the smell and lack of clean air, but at least they weren't being pounded with rain. The walls of the hold creaked and groaned, however, which made

Kinker feel skittish.

"This is a pretty violent storm, isn't it?" said Jenur to Kinker, her hands gripping the crate she sat on. "Worst one we've been through so far, not counting the one we found you in."

"Yeah," said Kinker with a shudder. "Where's Malock?"

"No idea," said Jenur.

"He's top deck, in his stateroom," said a familiar voice not too far away.

Kinker looked to his right and saw Bifor striding toward them, his wand attached with a rope to his wrist. Ever since getting his wand back from Garnal, Bifor had kept his wand tied to him at all times. It seemed like an unnecessary precaution to Kinker, because he didn't think anyone on the crew would try to steal it, but he supposed it was none of his business.

"Top deck? In this storm?" Jenur repeated. "Look, I know Malock can be a bit thickheaded sometimes, but come on. He made such a big deal about getting the rest of us below deck and now he's risking his own life for no reason?"

Bifor sat down on the floor near Kinker and Jenur, but even sitting down he was at least a head taller than either of them. "I've learned that you don't usually question the Captain's decisions in times of crisis. I'm sure he has a good reason for doing what he's doing."

Jenur looked up at the ceiling, from which water dripped occasionally. "If you say so."

Malock sat in his stateroom, on his favorite chair, gripping the sides of his desk hard. The rocking of the ship had tossed about nearly everything in his room. The books on his shelf were scattered across the floor. The maps and papers and quills on his desk were everywhere, and even the sofa had been knocked over. Through the window, Malock occasionally caught a glimpse of a huge ocean wave or of a lightning bolt striking somewhere, often nearby.

He was not alone. Banika sat on the floor nearby, her legs folded underneath her, her hands placed in front of her like prayer. It seemed an odd thing to do in a storm like this, but she had explained to Malock that this form of meditation—which she called 'calming meditation'—was useful for keeping one's balance in this kind of situation. He supposed it was true because, despite the constant rocking of the ship, Banika had not budged an inch from her spot on the floor.

If only Vashnas had been as lucky. She had tried to sit on a chair, but that had resulted in her falling to the floor. Now she just lay on her belly on the floor, her hands on her head, wincing every time a particularly loud clap of thunder burst overhead. Malock wished there was something he could do to comfort her, but right now he wasn't particularly comforted himself, so he didn't think there was anything he could do to help her.

Besides, if this storm was indeed the herald of the Verch ... well, then Malock figured being comforted was the least of their worries.

Now Malock was hardly a superstitious man. Yes, he respected the gods and yes he understood that they were mysterious and worked in ways that mortals rarely understood, but that didn't mean he believed every myth, legend, or plain old story about them. In particular, Malock had always disbelieved the story about the god Grinf becoming a sheep and mating with a willing human woman, their union producing a monstrous half-sheep/half-human hybrid known as the Sheep Child that, according to legend, was killed by its own mother who was horrified by its appearance.

But Malock remembered the fear he had seen in Garnal's eyes. Even though all pirates were liars and deceivers who always looked out for number one, Malock could tell that Garnal's tale about the Verch had not been a lie. Something had indeed attacked and destroyed Garnal's crew, something preceded by a storm on the ocean, and considering that this storm had come out of nowhere just like in Garnal's story, Malock felt justified in taking the precautions that he did.

Of course, it could just be a normal storm, Malock thought. *Just like how Ikadori Island could have been just a normal uninhabited island that wasn't home to a mortal-eating god. Best not to take chances on these seas.*

A particularly violent lurch almost tossed Malock off his chair, but he held on tightly to the desk and managed to remain upright. Banika was as calm and still as usual, while Vashnas had now placed one of the discarded books over her head. He had told them both about his suspicions of the Verch; in fact, that was why he had brought them both here. If the Verch was indeed coming, then he wanted to have two of his most trusted friends by his side to face it.

The ship stopped rocking and swaying. The sudden stop made Malock's stomach lurch, but he held down his lunch as he looked around tentatively.

Vashnas took the book off her head and also looked around. "Why ... why did the ship stop?"

Banika's eyes opened. "Captain, do you hear that?"

Malock shook his head. "Hear what?"

"Listen," said Banika, holding up a finger for silence. "It's outside."

Malock and Vashnas both became as quiet as they could be. Then Malock heard it. Above the roar of thunder and the swaying waves, he heard something walking through the water. That was the best way he could put it. The swish-swish of the water was the same sound it made whenever someone walked through it, but that made no sense. Who could be out in this weather? Unless ...

Malock stood up and gestured for Banika and Vashnas to do the same. "We're going outside. Be prepared for anything, and I mean anything."

Stepping out onto the top deck was much more terrifying than it should have been. Malock fully expected to be instantly killed by whatever was waiting for them, but when he, Banika, and Vashnas passed through the doorway of his stateroom and onto the main deck of the ship, they were greeted by a very bizarre sight.

All around them on every side, rain poured heavily from the clouds, but the *Iron Wind* was completely dry. Not a drop of rain fell onto their ship and even the waves around the ship were avoiding it. When Malock peered over the side of the ship, he saw that the water in which the *Iron Wind* rested was as still as could be. It hadn't frozen over or anything. It just stopped. It looked especially weird because the rest of the sea was still flowing around them normally.

"What is going on?" said Vashnas, wringing her hands. "What kind of magic is this?"

"Divine magic," Malock said. "Only the magic of the gods could do something like this."

Vashnas gulped. "Does that mean that a god is trying to get us?"

Malock looked out over the sea, trying to locate the source of the sound of the being walking through the water, and said, "I think something worse—*much* worse—than a god is after us."

As soon as the words left his lips, it appeared. Its appearance was sudden. One moment, it was not there; the next, it walked out of the water and waves as if borne from the water. It towered over the tallest mast of the *Iron Wind* and strode through the water like it wasn't there. Every step it took sent vibrations up the *Iron Wind*, shaking the ship far worse than the storm did.

It was perhaps the strangest thing Malock had ever seen in his life. Though humanoid in build, the giant resembled neither human or aquarian. A green slime that smelled strongly of rotten eggs dripped off its body, almost like sweat, its reptilian skin glistening underneath. Large, sharp claws protruded from the tips of the dozen or so tentacles that flailed from its sides, claws that looked at least as sharp a Grinfian sword, if not sharper.

Its face was impossible to see. A cloud of smoke and smog covered it, the only features visible being its eyes. And what eyes they were, huge and red and glowing. Simply looking into the eyes was enough to strike fear into Malock's heart, the kind of fear that paralyzes you where you stand and makes all hope lost.

The giant, the Verch, stopped about a dozen yards from starboard. Up close, it was even bigger, standing so tall that Malock, Vashnas, and Banika had to crane their necks to see its head. It did not do or say anything, didn't even make a noise. It simply stared at them, perhaps trying to decide the best way to smash the *Iron Wind* into a million pieces.

Then a strange sucking sound emanated from the Verch's head and the next moment a large blob of slime shot out of the cloud. The blob landed on the deck with a splat, causing some of the foul-smelling slime to land on Malock and Vashnas, but not Banika, who due to her position behind them managed to avoid it.

"Ew," said Vashnas, wiping the slime off her face. "If this really is the Verch, I'd say this is punishment enough."

Malock tried to wipe the slime off his boat cloak, but then the blob started moving and he stopped, anxious to see what was happening.

Part of the blob extended upward, a long, thin pole, before two arms sprouted out of the sides. Then, at the top of the thin pole, two red eyes blinked open, followed by a mouth that had no teeth or tongue. The entire thing looked like a crude approximation of a human, as if an artist had drawn a human using a vague description provided by someone who had only seen a picture of a human once years ago.

The blob creature resembled the Verch in miniature. Its red eyes swept across the entire ship before fixing on Malock, Vashnas, and Banika. The intensity with which it stared at them caused the three to step back collectively, Malock reaching for his sword.

Then the blob held up a crude hand that constantly dripped slime. "Don't hit."

The blob's voice was strange. It did not sound either masculine or feminine. If anything, it always sounded like how Malock had imagined a wasp's voice would sound if it could speak: halting, jerky, and with a slight buzz, too.

"It can talk?" said Vashnas. "I know the gods are strange, but talking blobs?"

"Quiet," said Malock under his breath. "You want to get that thing angry?"

"Come in peace," said the blob. Its voice was very uncertain, like it was not used to speaking Divina. "Not bad. Here to aid Chosen One."

Surprised, Malock said, "I'm the Chosen One. You're here to help me? Not punish me?"

The blob creature tilted its head to the side. "Why punish? No. No punish. No wrong you did. Spy on crew did, however."

"Sorry, but what's wrong with your voice?" said Vashnas, who Malock was beginning to feel less kindly to right now. "You sound weird."

"Mortal language," the blob said, grimacing as though it had just spat out a large wad of spit. "Clumsy. Awkward. Useless."

"What was that you said about a spy?" said Malock. "And if I may ask, who are you? Are you the Verch of legend?"

"Verch? Don't know," said the blob. "In filthy mortal tongue, name is Messenger-and-Punisher. Come to bring message from Kano."

"A message from Kano?" said Malock. "Well, why didn't she just send me another vision? Surely that would have been more practical than sending, uh, you."

Messenger-and-Punisher—who Malock decided to call 'Messenger' for short—frowned. "Other job, too. Get spy. Take away to be punished."

"So you're here to deliver a message and take away this so-called spy," said Malock. "Okay, what is it?"

"First, message," said Messenger. "Kano says not to worry, you be safe from harm. Says she still awaits you on World's End. Says you trust me, I help you get the spy, help you get World's End safely."

"Ah," said Malock. "That's nice to hear."

"So you're not going to destroy our ship?" said Vashnas. "Like you did with the Pirates?"

Messenger's face was hard to read, but it looked confused. "Destroy ship? Pirates? Not sure what you talk about. Is confused."

"What Vash meant is that you destroyed the hideout and ship of a group of pirates about a week ago," said Malock. "Their leader told us that you ripped off the top of their hideout."

Realization dawned on Messenger's face at that moment. "Remember now. Just Grinf told me go and kill them for their crimes. Tired of tolerating their crimes. Did good job."

"That's ... strange," said Malock. "I didn't know Grinf used you to dish out judgment on criminals."

"Do work for all gods," said Messenger. "North and south. Kept busy all day. Don't remember always what I do. Hence name. Messenger-and-Punisher."

"Of course," said Malock. "But back to the subject of the spy. What do you mean?"

Messenger made a face very similar to that of the Loner God. "Godly politics. Member of crew trying to cause trouble, trying to stop you from getting World's End. Servant of Tinkar."

"Tinkar?" said Malock. "You mean the God of Fate?"

"One and only," said Messenger. "Go below deck and I fetch spy."

Malock raised his hands. "Wait, wait. You don't need to do that, really. No need to waste your time looking for the spy among the crew. You don't want to tire yourself out, do you?"

In actuality, Malock was only trying to keep Messenger above deck because he was certain that the blob's appearance below deck would cause a panic among the sailors. Even he wanted to run and he was not in any sort of trouble. He didn't want to think about what Messenger's sudden appearance below deck would cause for the rest of the crew.

Messenger frowned. "Not big deal. Just go below, grab spy, and leave."

"But I could do it for you," said Malock. "Just tell me the name of the spy and I'll fetch him myself."

"Don't know name," said Messenger. "Just know that spy is on board. Wish to make this quick. Have other jobs to do. Gods very impatient."

Messenger started sliding toward the hatch, but Malock stepped in its way. He knew it was risky, but he reasoned that a servant of the gods wouldn't dare harm him, even if he annoyed it.

"Look, Messenger," said Malock in his most pacifistic tone. "You're obviously a very hardworking servant of the gods. No need to spend hours searching my crew looking for the spy when I could do it much more easily."

Messenger stopped and actually looked angry now. "Don't be wall. Get out of way."

"I'm hardly a wall," said Malock. "It's just that I—"

"Don't be wall," Messenger repeated. "You safe, perhaps, but does not mean I must respect. Move or else."

Malock stood his ground. "Give me one day, just one day, to find the spy. Just one day. That's not such an unreasonable thing to ask for, is it?"

Messenger looked unconvinced. "How find spy if you don't know who it is?"

"I know a way to do it," Malock said. "A way that is much quicker than going through each sailor one by one. I can assure you that by the end of the day, I will have the spy."

Messenger grunted. "Fine. Do as you wish. I leave, but I return tomorrow same time. I do other thing in meantime. Do not disappoint."

With that, Messenger collapsed back into a gooey, formless blob, and slunk back to the bulwarks. It jumped over the bulwarks and landed on the giant's body, crawling into one of the open pores on its body. The ugly sight made Malock feel ill.

Then the giant stood back up its to full height, turned around, and marched back into the storm raging all around the ship. As soon as it stepped outside of the range of the still water, it vanished, like it had been dissolved by the rain and wind.

As soon as it vanished, the storm disappeared as well. The clouds evaporated, the sea grew calmer, and the sun appeared once again, making everything feel quite humid. It also made the trail of slime left by Messenger smell even worse, but Malock didn't pay attention to that. He was just glad Messenger was gone because despite its assurances that it was on his side, it had still freaked him out.

"That was the weirdest thing I've ever seen," said Vashnas as she and Banika approached Malock. "And I've seen plenty of weird things in my life, trust me."

Malock wiped the slime off his boat cloak as he said, "We don't have time to waste talking about it. Banika, gather the rest of the crew. They have to know about what Messenger told us, as well as what I am about to do."

Banika nodded, but didn't leave. "If I may ask, sir, how are you going to find out who the spy is? Not even Messenger knew and he was sent here to capture whoever it is."

Malock smiled. "Don't worry, Banika. I've got it all figured out. Just get everyone top deck in twenty minutes and then everyone will know about it."

Chapter Ten

EVERYONE BELOW DECK FELT the ship stop, which led to a lot of speculation as to what caused it. Due to the lack of windows in the lower decks, it was impossible to tell what was going on outside, which was why everyone was so eager to come top deck when Banika appeared with orders from Malock to bring everyone to the surface.

The ship didn't look much different than it had before the storm, except for the large splotches of a foul-smelling green slime on the starboard. Kinker didn't know where that stuff had come from or what it was, but he nonetheless avoided it because it smelled even worse than the hold did.

Malock stood above them all on the quarter deck, his hands gripping the railing. His eyes scanned the crowd of sailors, like he was looking for any suspicious behavior. It made Kinker feel uncomfortable, even though he knew for a fact that he was not guilty of anything except for what he had done back on Destan and as far as he knew Malock didn't know about that.

He, Jenur, and Bifor took up a spot at the back of the crowd, near the bow. Despite the entire crew being present on the deck, it felt far less cramped up here than it did down in the lower decks, probably because it was wide open.

As soon as the sailors spotted Malock they started directing their questions to him all at once in such a muddled confusion of noise that Kinker couldn't even hear himself think. A loud whistle blew just then, the boatswain's call, which immediately silenced the entire crew.

"My loyal crew," said Malock, looking around at them with searching eyes that did not match his reassuring tone, "I see you all want to know exactly what happened. I heard some of you asking if we were attacked, while others think Garnal has returned. Let me assure you that none of us are in any trouble ... save for one whose identity is unknown."

Kinker exchanged a look with Jenur as the sailors exploded with even more questions. "What does that mean?"

Jenur shrugged as Malock continued, "Earlier, a messenger of the gods appeared on the deck of this ship to deliver me an urgent message. He revealed to me that there is a spy on this ship, a follower of Tinkar, who has been attempting to sabotage the entire voyage right off from the start."

"Who's the bastard?" one of the sailors shouted. "Tell me and I'll rip his—"

"That is the point," said Malock, interrupting the angry sailor. "I do not know who the spy is. Not even the messenger knew. The messenger wished to search the crew for the spy himself; however, I convinced him that we could do it on our own."

"Why should we believe him?" said another sailor near the front, shouting loud enough for everyone to hear. "Where's the proof? I ain't seen no spies on this ship of ours."

"You would dare question the authenticity of a divine messenger of the gods?" said Malock. "Besides, the messenger's message has confirmed my own suspicions. This voyage has been one large disaster from the start and I've long suspected that a member of this very crew is doing everything in his or her own power to make it that way. Until today, however, they have only been suspicions and nothing more."

"Still sound like suspicions to me," Bifor said, in a low voice that only Kinker and Jenur could hear. "He still hasn't offered any proof."

"I'm sure the Captain has good reasons for suspecting that," said Jenur. "I mean, this voyage has been pretty disastrous. And I can't see any reason why this divine messenger would lie to us."

Bifor looked like he disagreed, but he didn't get to voice these disagreements because Malock continued speaking:

"As it is unlikely that the spy will out him- or herself, I have therefore devised a method to weed him or her out," said Malock.

He reached into the folds of his boat cloak and pulled out something too small for Kinker to see. He held it up for everyone to see, but even then, all Kinker could make out was that it was just big enough to fit in Malock's hand.

"I hope everyone can see this deck of cards in my hand," said Malock. "These are divination cards, commonly used by Tinkarians to determine the future and fate of other beings. I myself carry this particular pack of cards for this reason, even though I am not personally a follower of Tinkar."

"That's odd," said Kinker. "He carries a pack of those cards but isn't a Tinkarian himself?"

"That's actually not very strange," said Bifor. "Royalty commonly carry divination cards and use them regularly to determine their own future and the future of their kingdoms. Even those who openly scorn fortune-telling and divination still keep some on them."

"Oh," said Kinker. "Do they really work, then?"

Bifor folded his arms. "Depends. I've always been skeptical of their use. Most divination card decks are fakes, anyway, manufactured by scam artists who see a way to make easy money off gullible royals. I wouldn't be surprised if the Captain's own deck is a fake."

"So do real ones work, then?"

Bifor opened his mouth to answer, but Jenur swatted his arm and hissed, "Malock's speaking. You two, talk about this later. I'm trying to hear him."

Bifor shot her a rather angry look before returning his attention to Malock, who was now explaining his method to out the spy.

"You are all probably wondering how these cards will tell us who the spy is," said Malock as he shuffled the cards. "It's quite simple. There are one hundred and nine cards in this deck, the exact same number as the crew. Banika has set up a table here, which I will sit behind. You sailors will then organize into a line, coming up to the table one by one. You will then take the top card on the deck and show its face to me."

Malock held up the face of one of the cards, but again it was too far for Kinker to see properly.

"Each card has a picture of a god or goddess on its face," said Malock. "In divination, they normally are used to determine the individual's fate; in this case, however, the one who draws the Tinkar card will be the spy."

The crowd went into an uproar. Even though it was difficult to hear their individual voices, Kinker knew exactly why they were upset.

Malock raised his hands to quiet down the crowd. "Quiet, all of you! This is a time-honored technique used by Carnagian royalty for generations to root out spies and traitors. Not only that, but I have shuffled the deck so thoroughly that not even I know the order in which the cards lay. My belief is that fate will out the spy for us, which is ironic, really, when you consider that the spy is a Tinkarian."

"That doesn't sound very reliable to me," said Kinker as the rest of the sailors continued to yell obscenities at their Captain.

"Same here," said Jenur. "What if someone innocent picks up the Tinkar card? Is he going to hand over the wrong person to the messenger?"

"He's right about one thing, though," said Bifor. "Carnagian royalty has used this exact method in the past to discover spies among their servants."

"Has it really worked as well as Malock says it does?" said Kinker.

Bifor shrugged. "Sometimes. Sometimes, they got the wrong man. And some cases are still being debated by Carnagian historians today. Depends on who you listen to."

"There must surely be a more reliable way to out the spy," said Kinker. "What about you, Bifor? Can't you use your magic to read everyone's minds or something?"

Bifor folded his arms across his massive chest and shook his head. "I'm not a telemancer. I know enough telemancy to perform telekinesis, but I can't read peoples' minds. Telepathy is an extremely difficult to learn technique that requires years of commitment to Hamin, Goddess of the Mind. Being a follower of Xocion, I've never had the opportunity to learn it."

The crowd kept yelling at Malock and one sailor near the front even tossed a boot at him. The Captain dodged the boot and yelled, "I am your Captain and what I say goes! Besides, there is only one spy. There is a low chance any of you will draw the Tinkar card, so what do you have to worry about if you know you aren't the spy? I want everyone to get organized into a line right now or else I will have Banika flog you. Got it?"

Despite their continued grumbling, the sailors began to organize into a line that started at the table at the front and twisted and turned from the quarter deck to the bow. Banika and Vashnas helped organization, going up and down the line to make sure that everyone was where they were supposed to be. Kinker found himself four from the back, with Jenur, Deddio, an aquarian sailor whose name he didn't know, and Bifor behind him.

Once the line settled down, it slowly but tensely began to advance. Every time a sailor picked up a card to reveal that it was a god or goddess other than Tinkar, the line grew tenser. Even Kinker, who knew for a fact that he was not a spy, felt the tension fill his bones, making it difficult if not impossible to remain calm. He just hoped that Malock knew what he was doing.

"So who do you think the spy is?" Jenur said to Kinker as they both watched Arisha Frag pass them, looking quite relieved as she went to join the others that had already picked a card.

Kinker looked ahead and behind him quickly. "No idea. I didn't even know there was a spy on this ship until today. It could be anybody."

"Do you think it's me?" Jenur asked.

Kinker shook his head immediately. "No. Why would I ever think that?"

"Just wanted to be sure," said Jenur. "When you said it could be *anybody* ... well ..."

Kinker patted her on the shoulder. "Jenur, I'd never suspect you of being a spy. I know you well enough to trust that you would never intentionally sabotage this voyage. You're a better person than that."

Jenur smiled and even looked a little embarrassed. "Thanks, Kinks. I mean it."

"What about me?" said Deddio, who was behind Jenur. "Am I on your list of suspects?"

"I don't believe anyone on the fishing crew could possibly be a spy," said Kinker. "So you don't have to worry about that, Deddio."

Deddio sighed in relief as the lined moved forward. "Of course, I suppose it doesn't really matter if you think I'm a spy or not. Only what the cards say matters."

Kinker nodded. "Unfortunately."

Perhaps it was the tension that permeated the air, but the line seemed to take forever to go forward. Some sailors wept with joy when they drew a card and it turned out to be a deity other than Tinkar. Others simply got on their hands and knees and praised whatever deity whose card they had drawn, some even pledging their lives to that particular deity right there and then if they hadn't before.

Kinker prayed a quick prayer to Kano that he wouldn't be the one who drew the Tinkar card.

Finally, after what seemed like hours (though it was probably only an hour and a half, if even that), Kinker's turn finally came. Malock was sitting in front of his stateroom on a rickety old chair on the other side of the wooden table, his hands folded. Vashnas stood by his side, a hand on his shoulder, while Banika stood on the table's right, probably ready to grab whoever drew the Tinkar card.

There were now only five cards left, making the deck small and flat. A large pile of cards lay scattered to the deck's right, all of the cards that the other sailors had drawn, all of them not Tinkar. The backs of the cards were emblazoned with a shooting star, while the faces featured stylized depictions of each god or goddess.

Before Kinker drew his, he glanced between Vashnas and Banika and said, "Have they drawn theirs yet?"

"Yep," said Malock. "Vashnas got Hollech. Banika got Yaona. They're both safe."

Kinker gulped. "Okay, then. Good to know."

"Don't be so worried," said Malock. "I don't suspect you of being the spy at all. Just want to be thorough and fair. No need to take it personally."

Kinker didn't know how to respond to that, so he simply reached down with a shaking hand, grabbed the top card of the deck, and flipped it over onto its face.

He let out a sigh of relief when he saw that it was Kano, not Tinkar, on the card's face.

Malock smiled. "Knew it couldn't be you. All right. You can go now and let the next person come forward."

"Y-Yes," said Kinker, who hadn't realized until now just how tense he had been. "Of course."

Kinker walked a few feet away from the table and then stopped to watch. Only Jenur, Deddio, the aquarian sailor, and Bifor were left, which meant that one of them had to be the spy. Kinker didn't think any of them could be the spy. Well, okay, the aquarian sailor (who he was pretty sure was a member of the cleaning crew, though he couldn't be sure) was suspicious, but he doubted that Jenur, Deddio, or Bifor were the spy. It just didn't seem possible.

Jenur came up next. She strode up to the table without hesitation, threw a confident smile in Kinker's direction, and, without saying a word, flipped over the top card of the deck.

A loud *gasp* came from Malock and Vashnas and the next moment, Jenur was pinned to the deck by Banika. The boatswain had twisted Jenur's arms behind her back and was putting a pair of large, rusted shackles around her wrists.

"Hey!" Jenur shouted, struggling against Banika's hold on her. "It was a mistake! I'm innocent!"

Kinker stepped forward, a hand held out, but then Malock noticed him and said, "Don't, Kinker. Otherwise, Banika will have to arrest you, too."

"But ... why?" said Kinker, though he already knew the answer. "Why is Banika arresting her?"

Malock held up the card Jenur had drawn. On it was a picture of an elderly man, his skin as pale as the sandy beaches of Ikadori Island, covered in robes with clocks etched in them, a large sundial topping his staff.

"She drew the right card," said Malock, sounding triumphant. "Tinkar, the God of Fate. Now take her to my stateroom, Banika, and make sure she can't get free. I don't want that spy causing any more problems for us ever again."

Chapter Eleven

I T WAS AMAZING HOW quickly the tide of opinion turned against Jenur. Not an hour earlier most of the crew had thought that Jenur was just like the rest of them: hardworking, loyal to the ship and Captain, and willing to do whatever necessary to get Malock to World's End. Among the fishing crew, Jenur had been almost like family. At the very least, she had been liked and respected and no one had ever thought there was anything suspicious about her.

Now, however, wherever Kinker went, he heard sailors bashing Jenur. Some said they should have seen it all along. After all, she rarely, if ever, talked about her past to anyone, had not even told anyone which God she worshiped. Her badmouthing of Malock was well-known and a few of the older sailors (not including Kinker) pointed out how youngsters nowadays weren't as respectful of authority nowadays.

All of these attacks on Jenur's character made Kinker mad. He got so mad, in fact, that he actually punched out the aquarian sailor who had been behind Jenur. The sailor, whose name was

Ranof and who resembled a starfish, was saying that he'd once overheard Jenur planning to kill Malock in his sleep, a lie so wrong that Kinker didn't regret punching him at all.

Unfortunately, Ranof was a lot younger than Kinker and as a result a lot stronger. He soundly knocked Kinker off his feet in one blow and probably would have wailed on the old man if Malock—who had been walking around ordering the sailors back to work—had not stepped in and broke up the fight. He sent Ranof below deck to clean out the hold and helped Kinker to his feet.

"What was that all about, Kinker?" said Malock, watching as Ranof stomped toward the hatch. "I've never seen you get into a fight with anybody before. What made you attack Ranof?"

Kinker pulled his arm out of Malock's hands and glared at the captain. "He said that Jenur was planning to assassinate you. I was merely correcting him."

"Correcting him?" said Malock. "Is that what you Destanians call punching someone out?"

"Don't play dumb with me, young man," said Kinker. "You know Jenur is innocent. She saved you from Garnal and led the rebellion that saved the whole ship from the Gray Pirates. That is proof enough of her innocence."

Malock looked out over bulwarks. They were standing on the starboard side of the ship, which was where Ranof had been entertaining some friends with that horrible lie of his. Ranof's friends had fled the minute Kinker had punched him, however, so it was just Malock and Kinker now.

"Well, I admit that is one point in her favor," said Malock. "But you know, I didn't choose her. The cards did. And the cards are never wrong."

"Never?" said Kinker. "Bifor told me that they don't always work."

"What does Bifor know?" said Malock. "He's a pagomancer. He doesn't know anything about fate or the future."

"But you must still recognize that this is wrong," said Kinker. "Jenur has always proved herself an innocent friend, ally, and fisherman. Sure, she's always been blunt about her opinions, but in all the time I've known her, I have never heard her utter even one word against this voyage."

"Obviously," said Malock. "She doesn't want anyone to know who she really is. If you were a spy bent on stopping this voyage, would you tell anyone?"

Kinker bent his lower lip. "But there is no evidence against her, besides some questionable cards. You're making a huge mistake."

"Actually, I'd say there's plenty of evidence against her, looking back," said Malock. "Consider, for example, how secretive she is about her past. She has never told anyone where she came from, what gods she worships, or anything of the sort. Has she ever told you any of that?"

Kinker's hands balled into fists. "Well, no, but—"

"See, she hasn't even told you and you're supposed to be friends," said Malock, smirking in satisfaction. "And you know why she saved me from Garnal? Because she wanted to kill me herself. Wouldn't be surprised if she's actually a ship saboteur in disguise. She's young enough."

"What's a ship saboteur?" said Kinker. "Never heard of 'em."

"The lowest breed of sailor in the entire Crystal Sea," said Malock, leaning against the bulwarks. "They sink or sabotage ships for pay. It's very common for Northern royalty to hire ship saboteurs to sink the ships of rival royals for political reasons."

Kinker raised an eyebrow. "Sounds like you have some experience in the matter."

"Of course not," said Malock, a little too quickly. "The Carnagian Royal Family has always treated its rivals and enemies fairly. We would never stoop so low as to hire a ship saboteur to harm our enemies. That would make us less than scum."

"Right," said Kinker. "But how can you be sure Jenur is a ship saboteur?"

"They're usually quite young," said Malock. "And they tend to be young women. They use their youthful charms to fool everyone into thinking they're naïve kids who don't know what they're doing. In reality, these 'kids' are doing everything within their power to sabotage a ship's voyage, doing things like ripping sails, destroy rudders, or even poisoning captains. Most of them are self-taught, but a few of the older ones have taken to teaching new ship saboteurs even better ways to sabotage voyages."

Kinker shook his head. "Jenur's young, true, but she hasn't done a thing to sabotage this ship. Your voyage has simply had a run of incredibly bad luck, coupled with some bad decisions on your part."

Malock stood to his full height. "Are you insinuating that I am a bad Captain?"

"I am just saying that you can't trace every bad thing that's happened on this voyage to one woman," said Kinker, not backing down. "Paranoia never helps anyone."

"It's not paranoia," said Malock. "It's simply logic. We have a mysterious young woman who fits all the right criteria for a ship saboteur who picked up the Tinkar card, singling her out as a Tinkarian, which is what the messenger said the spy was."

"Are you saying that a god hired a human to sabotage this voyage?" said Kinker. "You do realize how crazy that sounds, don't you?"

"It's not that crazy," said Malock. "On Ikadori Island—"

He stopped speaking, like he was about to say something that he wasn't supposed to.

"Yes?" said Kinker. "What happened on Ikadori Island?"

"Nothing," said Malock abruptly. "Absolutely nothing. It doesn't concern you. Now if you will excuse me, I see a couple of sailors over there lazing off when they clearly should be working."

Malock tried to leave, but Kinker grabbed his arm and said, "Hold on, Malock. I want to make one more request of you."

Malock threw an irritable look over his shoulder at Kinker. "What is it?"

"I want to speak to Jenur one last time before you hand her over to the messenger," said Kinker. "I won't try to help her escape or anything. I just want to talk to her one last time in private."

Kinker worried Malock would say no, but to his relief the Captain nodded and said, "All right, Kinker. Banika is currently interrogating Jenur right now, just to find out what other things she may have been up to, but you can go and tell her Malock sent you. She'll know."

"Thank you," said Kinker, letting go of Malock's arm. "I appreciate it."

"But just so you know, talking to her won't change anything," said Malock. "All it does is provide some closure for you. Don't expect me to soften up and let her go or anything."

"Of course," said Kinker, with more than a hint of sarcasm. "Why would I ever think that?"

When Kinker came to the stateroom, knocked on the door, and told Banika that the Captain had sent him, Banika let him inside. She stepped outside when he asked her to give them some privacy, but even when he closed the door, he had a feeling that Banika had her eyes on him, like she could see through walls.

Kinker had never been in Malock's stateroom before, but he marveled at how messy it was. Books, maps, and writing utensils were scattered across the floor, the sofa was upturned, and the curtains on the window were ripped and smelled of mildew. He supposed he shouldn't have been surprised, considering the state of the rest of the ship, but he thought Malock at least would have tried to keep his personal quarters nice.

At the end of the room was a large wood desk and in front of that desk, on the same rickety chair that Malock had sat on earlier, was Jenur. She was tied down to the chair, her arms at her sides and her legs tied to the chair's legs. She didn't look injured or harmed in any way, but she did look resigned to her fate.

"Kinks?" said Jenur, raising her head to look at him. "The old witch decided to let you in?"

Kinker approached her and stopped a few feet from her. "Malock gave me permission to speak to you one last time before ... well, you know."

"Ah," said Jenur. "You know what? Forget what I said earlier, about Malock having good reasons for what he does. He's just a bastard, plain and simple. Like all royalty, actually."

The bitterness in her tone was so sharp that Kinker was not sure what to say at first.

"So what do you want to talk about?" said Jenur. "This isn't really the best time for casual conversations about fishing, you know."

"That's not what I came here to talk with you about," said Kinker. "I just came to talk to you about you. Your past, where you came from, what you believe, things like that. I figure, since this is going to be the last time I ever see you, we should get to know each other better."

Jenur looked away. "I'm not sure you want to know my past. If you do, you'll just think that I deserve to be tied up and handed over to the gods for punishment."

"It can't have been that bad," said Kinker. "You're not a bad person."

Jenur chuckled. "Yeah. You say that *after* I murdered two Pirates in cold blood. Excellent sense of morals there, Kinks."

Kinker scratched the back of his head irritably. "I still don't believe you're the spy. I think Malock and his deck of cards are completely wrong."

"They are," said Jenur, slumping in her chair. "I've tried explaining that to him and Banika, but when those two idiots get an

195

idea in their heads you just can't convince them it's wrong. I'm just waiting until that messenger guy comes by to take me away."

"Even so, we have an entire day before that happens," said Kinker. "Surely, you and I could have one last conversation? Why is that so hard for you?"

"Because there is a good reason I've kept my past a secret," said Jenur. "I revealed too much when I took down those two Pirates. I'd rather you remember me for who you met me as, rather than who I am."

She spoke like a much older woman, even though she was only eighteen or so. It reminded Kinker of his own secrets, which sparked an idea in his head to get her talking.

"Let's make a deal, then," said Kinker. "A trade, so to speak."

Jenur frowned. "Kinks, you do realize I don't have anything to give you, right? I've only got the clothes on my back now and I'm pretty certain you're not a young woman, so they'd probably look really awkward on you."

"Not that kind of deal," said Kinker, shaking his head. "I mean, let's trade stories. I tell you my past and you tell me your past."

Jenur raised an eyebrow. "I doubt your past is anywhere near as bad as mine. Doesn't seem like a fair trade to me."

Kinker's legs were starting to get tired, so he pulled up a nearby stool and sat on it. "Let me tell you, Jenur, that I haven't been entirely honest about my past, either. There's a secret I've been keeping from everyone. I don't know if it's as bad as yours, but as you said, I've my reasons for keeping quiet about it."

Jenur looked thoughtful for a moment. "Never would have

pegged you for the guy with the mysterious past, Kinks. You just never seemed that mysterious to me. No offense."

"None taken," said Kinker. "Like you, I've been careful about the information I give to people about my past. Have you never wondered why I fled Destan in the first place? Especially in that terrible storm?"

"Never really thought about it, actually," said Jenur. "I just thought that as an old man you had lost some of your marbles and were looking for them in the sea. I know you better now, though, so that's probably not likely."

Kinker laughed. "So do you agree to the deal? I'll even go first, if you want."

Jenur shifted in her seat as best as she could. "All right. Sounds like a fair deal. And yeah, you can go first, if you want. I'll listen."

"All right," Kinker said. He hesitated, then began. "My home is an island called Destan, the southernmost island in the Northern Isles, located right before the southern seas. I was born there to my parents, both accomplished fishermen. I was practically raised on fishing boats and ships and probably learned to swim before I learned to walk."

"What were your parents like?" said Jenur.

Kinker looked at her in surprise. He hadn't expected her to start asking questions so soon. "My father was a great man. Always laughing. Very kind. He could be a bit forgetful at times, but he was the best fisherman I ever knew and he taught me everything I know about the sport. My mother was a bit like you, actually. She sometimes acted a bit sarcastic, but she had a loyal heart. I suppose that's how their marriage worked out."

"Oh," said Jenur. "Are they still alive?"

"No," said Kinker. "Father died while fishing. Got knocked overboard by a wave. He unfortunately drowned because he was too far from shore and no one was close enough to help. As for mother, she died of old age ten years ago. Hit me really hard, but I've moved on, taking what they taught me and living my life."

"Your hands are shaking."

Kinker looked down at his hands and saw that they were indeed shaking. "I must be cold."

"Right," said Jenur. "Continue. I'm listening."

"All right," said Kinker. "Let's see ... I never married. Not very interested in women, to be honest. Always preferred men."

"Same here," said Jenur. "I knew there was a reason I liked you."

Kinker chuckled. "Yes, well, I was too busy with my work to get into romance or relationships. Between fishing and worshiping at the Temple, I barely had time for anything else. Destan's a pretty small, slow island, so I kept up this routine of fishing and worshiping for decades."

"And you never got bored?" said Jenur. "Never wanted to do something different?"

Kinker shrugged. "It never occurred to me to do anything differently. My life was good. Everyone around me seemed happy with their lives, and the priests often told us that we pleased Kano with our behavior. It really wasn't until a month ago, when I joined the crew of this ship, that I started to doubt."

"Doubt?" said Jenur. "What do you mean?"

Kinker leaned forward, putting his hands together and said, "You see, there are six tribes on Destan, united by our common belief in Kano. Each tribe has a different job, such as fishing or governing. My tribe was the Hook tribe, made up of fishermen, sailors, and other people who worked on or near the seas. That's why I became a fisherman."

"You mean you never had a choice in your career?" said Jenur. "Ever?"

Kinker blinked. "Choice? I don't think you understand, Jenur. When you're born into a tribe on Destan, that's where you will be for the rest of your life. The tribe is your family and friends. The tribe is where you get a job, learn skills, and contribute to the community. Granted, not every Hook enjoys fishing, but in all of my years on Destan, I've never heard anyone of any tribe wish they could belong to another tribe."

"Hmm," said Jenur. "Doesn't sound like a very good way to live. No offense, Kinks."

"It's all right," said Kinker. "Outsiders who came from the north never really understood. At least when we explained it to them. Most visitors only came for the abundant zappers and black fish that can be found in the seas around Destan. Few were interested enough in our culture to ask any questions."

"So what made you leave home?" said Jenur. "Sounds like to me you had it going. A good job, a stable community, plenty of food, water, clothes, and everything else. Can't imagine why anyone would want to leave that."

Kinker frowned and looked at his feet. "For a while there, it did seem idyllic. You see, one of the tribes is the Priest tribe. It is the smallest tribe, but it is the tribe that rules all the other tribes and leads worship of Kano. I'm not sure how the Priest tribe gained that kind of power. It probably happened a long, long time ago. That's all I know.

"The head priestess is a woman named Deber Sinrod. She's around my age, perhaps a year or two older, and only became head priestess a couple of years ago when her predecessor passed away in his sleep. In many ways, she was like a queen to us. No one ever questioned her or said anything bad about her. And those that did ... well, they often disappeared, their bodies washing up on shore days later. We just assumed they drowned, which is a common way to die on Destan, especially among us Hooks."

"Let me guess," said Jenur. "That's not what happened, is it?"

Kinker shook his head. He tried to focus on Jenur and not think about what he saw. Because if he did, he doubted he would be able to finish the story.

"Deber even established a group known as the Priestly Guard. Their job, supposedly, was to act as bodyguards for the priests, but I know firsthand that they often carried out Deber's dirty work, the kind of work she would never do herself. I bet they were behind some of those 'accidental' deaths, but I don't have any proof for that."

"Reminds me of Ruwa," said Jenur. "But continue."

Kinker put a hand on his forehead. The memories were coming back swiftly now. The temple's inner sanctum. Deber standing with a knife. An innocent young boy. The more Kinker talked, the more vivid these memories became, but he couldn't stop. He had made a deal with Jenur and he intended to be true to his word, no matter how hard it may be. Even if it made her hate him.

"About a month before I tried to leave Destan, I was in the Temple of Kano after services were over," said Kinker. "I wasn't there because I wanted to be. I had somehow lost my lucky lure, a genuine shiner—"

"I don't know what that is," said Jenur.

"A really rare lure," said Kinker. "Given to me by my father before he drowned. Anyway, I'd somehow lost it and thought I might have left it in the Temple's main worship area because I often brought it with me to worship. The Temple's doors are usually open during the day for anyone seeking guidance from Kano, but on that day no one was there but me while I searched the seats for my lure. I eventually gave up and was going to leave when I heard a sound."

"What sound?"

His memory flared again. Walking to the door. Opening it. And wishing he hadn't.

"It sounded like a little boy crying," said Kinker. The words came out broken, but he tried to keep them as coherent as he could. "Very faint, but I knew I wasn't hearing things, even though I couldn't see the little boy anywhere. It's unusual for little children to be in the Temple by themselves, so I searched for him so I could bring him back to his parents."

As he spoke, the story played out before him like a play. Saw Deber, smiling, as she handed him the knife.

"That's when I noticed a door behind the altar," said Kinker. "I mean, I had always seen the door, of course, but it was never opened and I never saw anyone go in or out of it. Always assumed it led to the head priestess's chambers. On that day, though, it was cracked, like someone had forgotten to close it all the way. The sound of the crying boy was coming from it."

He no longer saw Jenur now. All he saw was the little boy, his brown hair unkempt, staring up at him, the tears streaming down his round young face.

"And I found the boy," said Kinker. "He was tied down in front of an old stone altar, one covered in blood. The room was dark and small. It looked like nothing like the rest of the Temple; in fact, it felt evil. I remember the little boy seeing me, begging me to free him, asking me to make the pain stop."

He raised the knife high. He could still feel Deber watching him, her eyes showing no sympathy or kindness in them at all.

"So I tried to untie the boy," said Kinker. "But the knots were too tight and my hands were too weak. I tried to leave, telling the boy I'd be back with a knife or some help, but before I could leave, Deber appeared in the doorway with two of her Priestly Guard. She was shocked to see me and ordered her two guards to pin me down. She closed the door behind her, plunging the room into darkness, lit only by a small candle she had brought with her."

He hesitated. Felt the darkness around him. He didn't want to do it, but he knew what they would do to him if he did.

"'What are you doing here?' she demanded. 'Were you trying to rescue this little boy? How did you know he was here?'

"I said I didn't know, that I just found him. That seemed to calm her somewhat, but she still was angry at me. For a moment, I thought she was going to kill me. Her Priestly Guards were both strong enough that they could have taken my life with little effort if they wanted to. She had a long knife in her hand that I'd never seen before and I could just imagine it piercing my heart or slitting my throat. It was terrifying."

The little boy was still crying, still asking him not to do it. He wanted to tell the boy that he didn't want to do it, but he didn't have a choice. Deber stood nearby, looking quite impatient, and Kinker hated her for it.

"Instead, Deber handed me the knife and told me to drive it into the young boy's heart. When I asked her why, she told me it was because that was what Kano wanted. 'Kano desires human sacrifice,' she said to me. 'In order to continue gaining her blessing, we must sacrifice this little boy's life. It is our only option.'

"That didn't sound right to me at all. I had never been taught Kano wanted human sacrifices. I mean, I had been taught that Kano could be a harsh goddess and that she sometimes required great sacrifices from her followers, but this went against everything I knew. So I told her no.

"But she said, 'If you don't, I will kill you and the boy.'

"I asked her what was to stop me from telling the other people about this. I knew that most of the Destanians wouldn't stand for this."

Kinker looked over his shoulder at Deber one last time, her eyes glinting maliciously in the glow of her candle.

"And she said, 'Because, fisherman, you will never want to tell anyone that you killed an innocent boy. I will make sure everyone knows you were willing and eager to do it. Your reputation will be tarnished, especially when I mention how you tried to kill me, too.'

"And I realized she said the truth. The only way I could get out of that situation alive was to kill the boy. But if I did that and told everyone about what Deber was really doing, then everyone would know that I murdered a child. I could see no way out of it that ended well for me."

He turned to the boy and, the tears streaming down his own face, praying for forgiveness, brought the knife down.

"I was a coward," said Kinker. "An idiotic coward. I ... I spilled the boy's blood on that altar. Deber offered praise to Kano. They let me wash my hands and then moved me out of the Temple. I didn't tell anyone else what I did. There was no way I could, no way anyone would believe me."

He was now being hurried out of the secret room, staring at his clean hands. There was still a small bloodstain on his shirt, but no doubt it would be easily washed out.

"I decided to flee Destan after that," said Kinker. "Couldn't handle it. I wanted to leave, but the Priestly Guard kept an eye on me, thwarting my every attempt to leave. I think Deber was afraid her secret would get out if I left. I finally got my chance a month ago, during murder season. The weather was so bad that not even the Priestly Guard dared patrol the shores like they usually do, so I got on my rowboat, rowed out to sea, and ended up here. You know the rest."

"That's ... awful," said Jenur.

Her voice broke through his memory and he suddenly saw her

again. She still sat in her chair, tied down, looking rather uncomfortable.

"I get why you didn't want to talk about it before," said Jenur. "That's just ... I can't even put that into words. Horrible. Evil. Monstrous."

"I know," said Kinker. "I know."

The two were quiet for a while.

Then Jenur said, "Kinks? If somehow I survive all of this and we end up going back north, I'd like to go up to Deber's front door and knock that old witch out. As a favor to you."

"You mean you don't think I'm horrible for killing a little boy?" said Kinker.

Jenur shrugged, which looked awkward due to the ropes binding her. "I don't know what to think, to be honest. What you did wasn't right, but on the other hand, you were forced to do it. It's all very confusing."

"Agreed," said Kinker. "Sometimes I think I fled when I did because I was trying to kill myself. I am certain that's what Deber thought and still thinks. She probably thinks I'm dead."

"Bet if you showed up on her doorstep, she'd have a heart attack," said Jenur with a smirk. "She'd probably think you're a ghost coming back to get her."

Kinker chuckled. "That would be rather amusing, but I don't think I'll ever return to Destan. There's just too much pain, too much sorrow, for me there."

Jenur nodded. "Well, a deal's a deal. You told me your story. I'll tell you mine. Mine's pretty bad, but after hearing yours, it doesn't really seem as bad as yours for some reason, even though I've killed loads more people."

Kinker blinked. "What?"

"I'm getting ahead of myself," said Jenur. "I should start at the beginning, like you did. But I still don't think you want to hear it. You've got enough sadness on your mind that I don't think you really need more."

"A deal's a deal, like you said," said Kinker. "I will listen. Just as you did to mine."

Jenur's grim expression didn't change. "If you insist ... well, I'm from Ruwa. Know where that is?"

Kinker shook his head. "No, I don't."

"It's on the eastern side of the Northern Isles," said Jenur. "Right in the center of the Friana Archipelago. It's not as small as Destan, but it's still a small island. Had a royal family that ruled for centuries. Never a big player in international politics; actually, from what I've gathered about its history, Ruwa's always been doing its best to avoid being crushed by the bigger powers, like the Red Empire or the Aquarian Federation."

She didn't sound enthusiastic about it, but Kinker said nothing.

"In recent years, though, Ruwa has been wracked by a variety of natural and economic disasters," said Jenur. "There's little food or water and most people live in poverty. Crime is rampant and even the king isn't safe. Not sure how it got that way, to be honest, because it happened before I was born. I was told that the last king incited the wrath of the gods onto Ruwa; if so, fuck the gods."

Kinker's eyes widened. "Jenur, watch your language. Do you want the gods to hear you saying stuff like that?"

"I've been saying stuff like that for years," said Jenur. "And not a single god has given me any shit about it. I'm thinking they either don't care or have bigger fish to fry. Either way, I don't care."

"Hey," said Kinker, snapping his fingers. "You don't care about the gods, which means you don't worship Tinkar. Doesn't that count as—"

"Kinks, you know Malock won't listen to reason," said Jenur. "He's already decided I'm guilty and the cards just confirmed that. Anyway, you're supposed to be listening to my story, not trying to think of ways to prove my innocence."

Kinker sat back on the stool, feeling disappointed. "You're right. Continue."

Jenur looked a little irritated now, like she didn't appreciate the interruption. "So those are the conditions I grew up in. I don't know who my parents were. They probably abandoned me when I was a baby, maybe couldn't feed me. That's actually rather common on Ruwa. Parents who can't feed their children often leave them to fend for themselves in the wilderness. Most don't survive."

"That's horrible," said Kinker. "But how did you survive?"

"I got lucky," said Jenur. "An aquarian named Quro found and raised me. He was basically my father."

"You were raised by an ... aquarian?" said Kinker, wrinkling his nose.

"Yes," sand Jenur. "Have a problem with that?"

Kinker shook his head. "No. Just wanted to be sure."

"Anyway," said Jenur, "Quro was a member of the Dark Tigers.

Ever heard of 'em?"

"I think so," said Kinker. "They're an assassin's guild, correct?"

"The best in the Northern Isles," said Jenur. "Our—their—headquarters is on Ruwa, deep in the Swamp of Light. It's treacherous terrain, easy to get lost in and even easier to die in. In all of my years as a member, I don't remember any non-Dark-Tiger getting through the Swamp on their own. So I never spent a lot of time around other children, mostly because the other Dark Tigers didn't have children and didn't want any."

"Yet they still let Quro raise you?" said Kinker.

"Quro was a pretty well-respected member," said Jenur. "He promised his fellow Tigers that I would be a Dark Tiger when I grew up. So as you can imagine, my childhood was a little, um, unconventional. You know how you said you were swimming before you learned how to walk? Well, I learned how to slit the throats of rodents before I could walk."

"Why did he want to raise you?" said Kinker. "If the other Dark Tigers didn't want children, what made him so different?"

"Easy," said Jenur. "Quro had a daughter who he lost to the death plague, a disease that occasionally crops up on Ruwa and when it does, it always kills. Think he might have seen me as his second chance, even though I'm human and he's aquarian."

Kinker shook his head. "So you're not a ship saboteur after all."

"Why would I be?" said Jenur. "Is that what Malock told you? I'd never sink that low. Yeah, we Dark Tigers may have been assassins, maybe even unpopular assassins, but in all of my time with the Guild, I never heard or saw anyone take on a ship saboteur job. We're not scum."

Jenur looked so annoyed at being conflated with the ship saboteurs that Kinker regretted saying that. He was happy, though, that she wasn't one, even though there was no way of proving that to Malock or anyone else.

"Anyway, as you can guess, I had to grow up fast. The Dark Tigers were a rough group and you have to be tough if you're going to make it. I didn't actually leave the Swamp of Light, though, until I was sixteen, which is the youngest age at which a person can join the Guild. That was when I was given my first job, a simple job that involved assassinating a priest of Ghatmos who was pissing off a few royals. Did it and came home in three days, which is pretty good for a newbie like I was."

She spoke rather casually of assassinating another person. It was almost like she didn't regret doing it at all.

"Don't get me wrong," said Jenur suddenly. "At the time, I didn't know any different. The way I was raised, killing someone for money was just something you did. And in my defense, I never really enjoyed it nor was I ever pressured to. We just treated it as a job and nothing more."

"What gods did you worship?" said Kinker. "I mean, surely you believed that a god was telling you to do this, right? Maybe the God of Assassins?"

Jenur shrugged. "A good chunk of our membership was aquarian and aquarians in general are less likely to honor and revere the gods as we humans. And those of us who were human, well, we came from backgrounds where we faced a lot of hate and prejudice from our more religious fellows. We never paid the gods much homage or respect. That's one thing I've carried over from my time as a Dark Tiger, which is why I've always avoided telling anyone what deity I worship."

Kinker could scarcely wrap his mind around the idea. Not respecting the gods? It seemed so strange. Then again, when he considered how Deber had justified her human sacrifices to Kano, it made a bit more sense.

"So for two years, I took whatever jobs they gave me," said Jenur. "And I did them to the best of my ability. I went all over the Northern Isles, so gradually my view of the world became larger. I also trained with many of the older Dark Tigers, who taught me the best ways to kill humans and aquarians instantly. Once I even went to the aquarian city of Nemo, which was probably the toughest job I ever took on because it was underwater and I was not used to performing undersea assassinations."

"You don't sound like you regret it," said Kinker. "You almost sound like you missed it."

Jenur frowned. "Of course I miss it. The Dark Tigers were my family. Even those who didn't want anything to do with me when I was a kid treated me like one of them. But I'm getting ahead of myself. I haven't told you why I left the Dark Tigers yet."

"I'm listening."

"So like I said, I was officially a member of the Dark Tigers for two years," said Jenur. "During that time, I traveled far and wide, saw and met and—yeah—killed a variety of people. Now I never made any friends outside of the Tigers. I was good at faking it because I sometimes needed to win the favor of certain individuals in order to get close to my targets, but I always cut off the relationships before they could get real or interfere with my work."

"Must have been tough," said Kinker.

"Wasn't, really," said Jenur. "Not at first. After all, I had the rest of the Dark Tigers as friends and family. I didn't think I needed anyone else. Still, I did learn more about how other people lived their lives and was surprised at what I learned. Many people lived their entire lives without taking the life of another being. I learned that, though the Dark Tigers were always well-paid and popular among royals, assassins were looked down upon among most people, even among simple people. This led to a lot of self-doubt and confusion on my part, making me question everything I'd ever been taught."

"You mean the other Dark Tigers never told you?" said Kinker. "Did they really present their lifestyle as normal and acceptable?"

"No one ever saw the need to tell me about the wider world," said Jenur. "Hell, even Quro didn't tell me much. I tried to talk with him about what I learned about how other people lived, but he was never interested in that stuff. I think he made his peace with the fact that he was in an unpopular profession, so when I questioned him about it, he got angry. Didn't hit me, but he did get angry and I didn't want to make him angry.

"So I stopped asking others about it, but I never stopped thinking about it. On my off-days, I'd spend a lot of time thinking about why I was doing what I was doing. I realized I didn't really enjoy it. I mean, I enjoyed the security of having friends who would be there for me, but I didn't enjoy the killing. Even though I was one of the best killers in the Guild, I became so sick with it that I started intentionally fudging missions and jobs I was given."

"That doesn't sound very good," said Kinker. "Bet your boss wasn't happy with that."

Jenur shuddered. "Yeah. The Grand Tiger, Nijok Wirm, started noticing. At first he just credited it to my youth, but then it became far too frequent, so he took me aside and beat the hell out of me. You can't see it now because the Guild's panamancer put my face back together, but when he was done I looked like I'd been run over by this ship. The Grand Tiger didn't like slackers, as you can tell."

"And Quro let him do that?" said Kinker. "What kind of father would let another man beat his own daughter?"

"Quro may have been my dad, but he was also a Dark Tiger and a loyal subordinate to the Grand Tiger," said Jenur. "He respected the Grand Tiger's authority too much to openly disagree with him or stop him. He did pull me aside after that and asked me why I was slipping up, but I didn't tell him about my doubts because I didn't think he'd understand."

"Crazy," said Kinker. "Is that what caused you to leave the Dark Tigers?"

"Pretty much," said Jenur. "I didn't intend to go back to my old efficiency, not after that. So one night, while everyone was asleep, I slipped out of the Guild base, made my way through the Swamp, reached the coast, and took the first ship off Ruwa that would take me. Turned out it was a pirate ship heading to Carnag. Only reason I didn't get raped and killed (not necessarily in that order) is because I showed them my Dark Tiger mark, which scared 'em senseless.

Threatened to knife 'em in their sleep if they so much as looked at me funny."

She smiled like she was remembering the good old days. "Kinks, you've never seen funny until you see a bunch of big, burly, full-grown men cowering before a teenage girl armed only with a knife. Anyway, I got to Carnag and immediately got a job on Malock's fleet, on this very ship in fact. I was originally a deckhand, but got promoted to fishing crew when we started losing ships like marbles in a pond. You know the rest."

Kinker stroked his beard. "That is one wild story, but I think you're telling the truth. I suppose telling it to Malock is out of the question."

Jenur let out a long sigh of frustration. "Look, Kinks, I appreciate your desire to want to help me. Really, I do. It's just that I don't think there's anything you can do to convince Malock to change his mind. He's already convinced that I'm the spy. Arguing with him is like arguing with a wall."

Kinker stood up. His feet had almost fallen asleep he had been sitting for so long. "Okay. I guess I should leave now. I appreciated having this conversation with you, Jenur. I'll always remember it."

"Same here," said Jenur. "Though I doubt I'll live that much longer, honestly."

Kinker reached out and brushed her cheek with his rough hand. "If we make it back to the north, I'll try to find Quro and tell him about what happened to you. I'm sure he's still proud of you, even if you did run away without telling him. It's the least I can do."

Jenur smirked. "Actually, Quro already knows I'm gone. He saw me leave, but didn't try to stop me. Of course, he doesn't know where I am, but ... well, I'll just say he's a lot cooler than I thought."

"I'll still find him and tell him," said Kinker. "So good bye, Jenur. I hope that your spirit finds peace in the afterlife."

Jenur snorted. "Considering all the lives I've taken over the years, I'll be surprised if I don't get sentenced to Grinf's chamber pot."

Kinker didn't know what to say to that. He just nodded and left, not glancing over his shoulder as he opened the door and left the stateroom. He didn't want her to see the tears already starting to stream down his face.

Chapter Twelve

THE DAY COULD NOT go by fast enough for Malock. He hadn't expected to find the Tinkarian spy so quickly, but now that he did, he wished he had some way to contact Messenger to get it to come early. Malock spent the rest of the day mostly wandering the ship, getting onto lazy sailors, looking at the sea, talking with Vashnas, and making note of parts of the ship that required repair. He kept glancing at the sky as he did these things, watching as the sun made its lazy journey across the sky.

He didn't go to his stateroom. He had no interest in interrogating Jenur. He had delegated that particular task to Banika, who was a lot better at it than he was. So far she had not succeeded in getting Jenur to talk, even after the spy poured her heart out to Kinker.

For that matter, Kinker had not told Malock what he and Jenur had talked about. When Kinker emerged from Malock's stateroom, the Captain tried to speak with Kinker, but the old fisherman brushed off his questions and made his way to the stern where the rest of the fishing crew was. That annoyed Malock, but he dropped the issue, as he doubted Kinker had learned anything to cast doubt on Jenur's identity as the spy. If he had, he surely would have mentioned it.

So the hours rolled by agonizingly slow. Even when the sun finally set and darkness set upon the entire sea, time still seemed to move too slowly to Malock. He could barely sleep, primarily because he slept on the *Iron Wind*'s top deck that night, rather than in his stateroom, because he didn't want to give Jenur an opportunity to get him in his sleep. Vashnas slept by his side, but she seemed to be less concerned than Malock was because she didn't make a noise all night until the first rays of the sun streamed over the eastern horizon.

But even then, no matter how hard Malock strained at the sky, he could not spot any clouds or any hint of a storm. If anything, the weather was quite nice right now and already most of the crew was milling about, working and talking and eating breakfast.

It wasn't until after breakfast that the familiar storm came in again and Malock ordered all of his men below deck. Many of the sailors expressed a desire to see Messenger, but Malock said they would not be able to sleep for the rest of their lives if they saw it, so they obliged and went down into the lower decks.

Thus, the only remaining members of the crew top deck were Malock, Vashnas, Banika, and Jenur. Jenur's hands and feet were tied together, with Banika gripping her arm tightly to help her balance. It started to rain just outside the ship's diameter when Malock glanced at Jenur. So far, she had not tried to run away or do anything except refuse to tell Banika anything about her past. Malock was starting to regret not asking Kinker about his conversation with her, as he had surely learned a lot about her that everyone else didn't know.

While the wind rose and lightning shook the sky, Malock turned to Jenur and smirked. "Didn't expect this to happen, did you, spy? I'm sure you thought you'd never be caught or found out. I bet you fantasized often about sticking that large knife of yours into my neck while I slept. Well, you didn't get a chance to do that, now did you?"

Jenur rolled her eyes, but said nothing. She obviously had no witty comebacks or sarcastic remarks, like she usually did. Her resistance appeared to be broken entirely, which pleased Malock greatly.

The sloshing of water that usually heralded Messenger's arrival met Malock's ears, and only a few seconds later, the giant appeared from out of the wind and rain. Jenur started when she saw it, almost falling over, but Banika must have had a grip of steel because she kept Jenur upright the entire time that the giant strode toward them.

As before, its face was covered by a thick dark cloud, only its glowing red eyes visible. It looked down on them, made a loud sucking sound, and then spat out a green blob. The blob landed in front of them, but this time Malock was prepared. He had made sure to put Jenur in front, meaning she got the full brunt of the blob's ooze all over her shirt and pants, while he, Vashnas, and Banika were mostly safe.

The blob once again took on a vaguely humanoid shape. It peered at the four mortals with red eyes, as though it was not sure what it was seeing.

"Well?" said Messenger. "Where spy?"

Malock relieved Banika of Jenur and dragged the foul-smelling spy forward. He then pushed her forward, causing her to fall face-first to the deck.

Messenger took a closer look at Jenur as Malock folded his arms across his chest and smiled triumphantly.

"There you go," said Malock. "The Tinkarian spy. Just as you—"

"Not spy," said Messenger, looking up at Malock suddenly.

Malock faltered. "What do you mean, not spy? Of course she is. I used the most foolproof method I know to root out spies to pick her. You must be mistaken."

Messenger shook its head. "Not spy. Doesn't smell like Tinkar." Then it added in a mutter, "Must do everything meself?"

"But ... but I ..." said Malock, struggling to think of what to say.

"No mind," said Messenger as it straightened up. "I do. Wait moments, please."

Without wasting another moment, Messenger collapsed into its gooey form, which then seeped through the cracks in the floorboards. Malock reached out a hand to stop it, but it was too late. It was soon gone completely, leaving behind only a thin layer of ooze on the deck.

Malock looked between Vashnas and Banika helplessly. "I thought ... but I was so sure ..."

"Yeah, about surety," said Jenur, who had rolled onto her back. "It doesn't always mean you're right."

Malock fell to his knees and put his face in his hands. "What was I doing? I almost gave up an innocent girl—"

"Woman," Jenur grumbled.

"—whatever, to be punished by the gods," said Malock. "How could I have been so ... so stupid?"

"It's all right," said Vashnas, patting him on the shoulder. "You just made a mistake, that's all."

Malock looked up at Vashnas and said, "A mistake? It was more than a mistake. I was so eager to catch the spy that I didn't think about what I was doing."

"That's nice," said Jenur. "So could someone untie me now? 'Cause I think—not sure, but I *think*—that I'm not the spy."

"Yes, yes, of course," said Malock. "Banika, free her, would you? No, wait. Give me your knife. I'll do it myself."

Banika handed her knife to the prince, who quickly cut off Jenur's ropes. Jenur was on her feet immediately, rubbing the spots where the ropes had dug into her wrists and ankles. She didn't thank Malock or look very happy.

"I am so sorry," said Malock as he handed Banika her knife back. "I didn't know what I was doing. I ... I guess I was just so caught up in the moment that I didn't think. I mean, how was I supposed to know?"

"I dunno," said Jenur. "Maybe you could have, y'know, used a more reliable way of figuring out who the spy is than a deck of cards? Just a suggestion."

"I will definitely have to repay you now," said Malock. "Somehow. I don't know how, but I'm sure that something will occur to me eventually."

Jenur stepped away from him. "That's nice and all, Captain, but I'm not sure I really want anything from you. You apologizing is enough, thank you very much."

Malock looked at her seriously. "Are you absolutely sure? I wish to make it up for you. I practically destroyed your reputation. Not only that, but you could have been taken to the gods to be punished. And if the legends of the place of punishment are at all accurate ... well, you understand why I would like to make reparations."

"And like I said, I don't want anything from you," said Jenur. "Just don't do this again, okay? Otherwise I might have to slap you around a little."

"I would deserve that," said Malock, looking down at his feet. "I *do* deserve that, actually."

"So if Jenur isn't the spy, then who is?" said Vashnas.

"Well, that's what we're about to find out, isn't it?" said Jenur. "That blob messenger thing is going to come back pretty soon, I bet, so this mystery—"

Her sentence was interrupted by the slimy ooze of the blob arising from the cracks in the deck, right where it had been a moment before. Just a few seconds later, Messenger returned, looking much the same as it always had. The difference, however, was the human man now lying inside of its body, his eye closed like he was asleep.

Malock gasped. "Telka? I don't understand. How can he be the spy? I thought he was a follower of Atikos."

"Is spy," Messenger confirmed. "Tried to fight back, but beat him soundly. Will take. Gods punish."

"Okay," said Jenur. "I admit that I didn't see *that* coming. Out of all the people who could have been the spy—"

"I leave," said Messenger. "Must go. Have urgent errands to run. Farewell, mortals. Keep going south. Kano is awaiting you."

Messenger's upper half collapsed back into the rest of its form and then snaked across the deck back to the bulwarks, Telka bobbing soundlessly around inside. The blob climbed onto the bulwarks and then launched itself onto the giant's body, once again sneaking into its open pores.

Then the giant turned around and walked back into the rain and wind. And as before, it disappeared into the storm like it had never been there at all.

Malock didn't need to tell anyone that Telka was the spy because Messenger had taken the doctor away in front of several other sailors. The news spread quickly and within the next hour everyone on the ship knew who the traitor was.

The entire crew was shocked by Telka's true identity. It was especially shocking because Telka had always been a highly respected member of the crew due to his skills as a doctor. Almost every member of the crew had suffered from an injury of some kind on this voyage and the only reason any of them had survived was thanks to Telka's excellent medical skills.

Replacing Telka was difficult. Telka had been the only certified doctor on the ship, after all. In the end, Malock chose the aquarian Ranof, who claimed to have studied medicine back up north several years ago. True, Ranof was not a professional doctor, but he was the only other sailor who seemed to know anything about medicine and Malock couldn't afford to be picky.

With Messenger's departure, the *Iron Wind* could once again sail south. Over the next few days, Banika reported to Malock that a lot of sailors were skeptical that Messenger had made the right a choice. A few even speculated that Jenur had somehow tricked Messenger into taking Telka over her, though as far as Malock could tell, most of the crew no longer harassed Jenur. That was good. After all he had put her through, he didn't want the rest of the crew to give her more grief.

Malock didn't quite relax just yet, however. He remembered what the Loner God had told him, about some of the northern gods placing their agents—plural, not singular—on his ship. Telka had apparently been one of those agents, but who were the rest? What were they trying to do? How come they had not revealed themselves yet? And why did Messenger only take Telka and not any of the others?

For that matter, Malock wondered why Tinkar, out of all of the many gods in the world, would place a spy on his ship. It was true that Malock was not a big fan of Tinkar, but he had never gone out of his way to blasphemy or insult the God of Fate. What would Tinkar have to gain by killing Malock or sabotaging his voyage? Did Tinkar have a grudge against Kano or something? Or was there something bigger going on than any of them knew?

All Malock knew for certain was that they still had quite a ways to go before they reached World's End. He also knew that their food and water supplies were running dangerously low, thanks in no small part to the Gray Pirates' gorging on their resources earlier. The fishing crew was bringing in a lot of fish every day, true, but the fish always went quickly and it never seemed to be enough. Water was another difficult thing, as they couldn't drink the saltwater of the ocean. They had Bifor desalinate the water by freezing and melting it, but it was a time-consuming process and the water always had a tinge of salt to it no matter how thoroughly Bifor desalinated it.

According to Vashnas, in just a few more days they would reach another island. She claimed it was going to be an island of snow and ice and that they would feel the cold weather coming in very soon. Hence why she advised Malock and the rest of the crew to bundle up as best as they could so that when the cold weather came they would be prepared.

And not a day after she told Malock about that, a strong gust of cold wind blew through the ship. It was icy cold, made even worse by the waves of the ocean splashing against the sides of the ship. Malock managed to keep warm, thanks to his thick boat cloak, but when he checked on the rest of the crew, he saw that they were not doing nearly as well as he was.

For one, almost all of them worked above deck in the cold wind, with little to protect them from the chilliness. For another, they did not have thick or warm clothes to wear. The aquarians in particular seemed to be taking the cold hardest, shivering and shaking hard. More than once Malock spotted Bifor walking around the ship, waving his wand and leaving a trail of blurred air wherever he waved it, perhaps casting a heat spell. Malock wished he had thought to pack some warm clothes for the crew before departing Carnag.

The weather grew colder the further south they traveled. Ice began forming on the bulwarks, sails, and even over the surface of the main deck. The *Iron Wind* became even more dangerous than it usually was, with the possibility now of slipping and falling flat on one's back a real danger now. Malock was glad that he didn't have to work outside, even though his stateroom wasn't much warmer than the rest of the ship.

He and Vashnas spent a lot of time cuddled up together in his stateroom, his boat cloak spread out wide enough to cover them both. This was primarily how he kept warm, as he had no way to start a fire and wasn't even sure a fire would be a good idea on a wooden ship anyway.

In fact, for the next few days, that was almost all he did, lie on the sofa in his stateroom with Vashnas by his side. Banika would come in at mealtimes to bring food and updates about the crew and ship, but other than that, Malock and Vashnas didn't move much. Vashnas confessed that the next island they were going to was one she wasn't very familiar with because she didn't spend a lot of time there when she first went through the southern seas, due to the coldness of the water.

Malock merely nodded when she told him that, like he understood. And he did. Aquarians had colder blood than humans and so had even less tolerance for icy temperatures than they did.

What he didn't understand, however, was why Vashnas didn't tell him about the Loner God, back on Ikadori Island. Yes, she had said she hadn't fully explored the island the last time she was there, but he had a hard time believing that she had not known about a god.

And if what the Loner God said was true, then he was not the only god on the southern seas. There were more, hundreds, maybe even thousands more, and yet Vashnas had not mentioned a single one of them in all of her talks with Malock about the southern seas and the dangers they held. Shouldn't she have run into at least one of these gods? They hunted mortals, after all, and Vashnas was a mortal herself, wasn't she?

Malock tried to ignore these thoughts. After all, Vashnas was his partner, his lover. He couldn't suspect her of being up to no good or withholding important information from him for her own selfish reasons. So far, she had been a loyal and steadfast friend to him, defending him and supporting him even when no one else did.

And if she did have secrets of her own? Well, didn't everyone have secrets? Malock certainly had secrets that he had not revealed to anybody, not even to Vashnas. Not dark secrets, per se, but mostly embarrassing ones he preferred to keep to himself. He couldn't honestly expect Vashnas to know everything about the southern seas anyway, as it was a large area that held dozens if not hundreds of islands.

Of course, Malock didn't spend literally all of his time in his stateroom. Occasionally, about once a day, he'd go out to stretch his legs and see how the rest of the crew was doing. Most of them were cold, damp, and miserable, but Malock saw no way to relieve them of their misery. They had little extra clothing to pass around, after all, and they had no way of heating the ship (aside from Bifor's minor heat spell). He hoped they would pass through the cold quickly, before any of them died or got frostbite from the gelid water.

It was on one of these trips, about four days after Messenger's departure, that Stalf (which what Vashnas called the next island) came into view. It was actually spotted by Gormas Okina, a sailor who worked as part of the cleaning crew near the bow. That made Malock send Banika up to the crow's nest to find out why Vinji, the lookout, didn't report, which led to a depressing discovery: Vinji was dead, his body frozen and stiff.

This was disheartening, but not surprising. Vinji had always been a private aquarian, which was why Malock had chosen him to be the lookout in the first place. Banika theorized that Vinji had fallen asleep during the night at some point and passed away in his sleep due to a lack of sufficient clothing and heat, probably without ever realizing it himself.

They held a quick funeral for Vinji, but due to his private nature, no one was sure what kind of funeral was appropriate for him. Malock let the aquarians lead the services, as he figured that they would know the best way to prepare his body. They said a quick prayer to Kano and then dumped Vinji's body in the sea. It had to be quick because the wind and waves were cold and standing around made everyone even colder and more miserable than they already were.

Afterward, Malock decided to not assign a new lookout to the crow's nest, at least not right away. Going up there was a death sentence in this weather and considering how low the crew was on sailors, Malock didn't want to risk anyone's life unnecessarily. Besides, Stalf was already within sight, and in just a few hours they would reach it.

Now Malock had a tough decision to make: either keep on going past Stalf until they eventually reached warmer waters or stop by the island briefly to hunt for food. Vashnas said she thought there might be some edible animals on the island, as she had once spotted some seal-like creatures lying on the Stalf's shore, but she wasn't sure if those animals were native to the place or were simply resting there from a long journey.

Malock really wanted to keep going south; however, they were low on food. The food that they did have was barely edible even after Arisha cooked it, and everyone was getting tired of fish. Not to mention that Stalf might also be home to some fresh water, which was another thing they were low on. That most of the crew had not set foot on land in over two months was another good reason for landing there.

But then he remembered the Loner God and Ikadori Island. There could very well be another god on Stalf, perhaps one that liked to eat mortals, a god who may not be very fond of visitors. Or maybe it wasn't a god, but perhaps wild animals that killed whatever invaded their territory. Or perhaps the flora was violent and unpredictable, ready to eat or poison or stab anyone who walked into it.

In the end, Malock decided they would land at Stalf. Not very long, of course, and if they saw the slightest hint of trouble, they would leave without hesitation. When he shared this with Vashnas, she didn't seem happy about it at all, but she agreed to it regardless.

After making this decision, Malock went out and announced to the crew that they were going to land at Stalf for a few days. Many of the crew (at least those whose mouths hadn't been frozen shut by the cold) cheered the decision and quite a few asked who was going on the expedition. Malock explained that he would have a list in another few hours or so but that in the meantime, the crew would have to keep working.

This the crew did cheerily, much more so than they had since Vinji's death. And so Malock returned to his stateroom, where he began drawing up a list of people to go with him onto Stalf when they landed there.

Kinker was quite glad that Jenur was not taken away by Messenger. He had to admit he was shocked when he heard about Telka being taken away, but he didn't grieve for the doctor much. True, Telka had saved his life when he first joined the crew, but the two had never been close and after all of the stuff he had been through over the last few days, he didn't have much room in his heart to be broken about this betrayal.

Yet, as glad as he was that Jenur was not taken away, he found the time they spent around each other to be quite awkward now. Even when they were just hauling in the trawl or preparing the fish for Arisha to cook, the fact was they both still knew their deepest, darkest secrets. Kinker's conversation with Jenur back in the stateroom had been done under the impression that he and Jenur would never see each other again, but now—unless one of them got killed somehow— it seemed like they were stuck together.

The two made a silent agreement never to talk about the things they shared with each other, either among themselves or with anyone else. After everything they talked about, there wasn't much else to say on the matter.

When the cold weather came in, life on the *Iron Wind* became far less bearable than before. Especially for the fishing crew, who spent most of their days getting splashed by icy cold water, hauling in the freezing trawl, and doing their best to skin the fish, which were becoming far less common now, thanks to the cold weather. Kinker managed to scrounge up some old blankets and coats from the hold, but those did little to keep him and the others warm.

It became even harder when Vinji died, if only because his death came as a genuine surprise to most of the crew. As with Telka, Kinker did not shed any tears over the lookout's death, not because he disliked Vinji but because he didn't know the aquarian. That, and he was an aquarian, which made it even harder for Kinker to feel sad about Vinji's death.

The most immediate danger that met Kinker every day was the frozen surface of the deck. Though Kinker had had years of experience working on boats and ships, he had to be extra careful when walking across the frozen desk of the *Iron Wind*. More than once, his old feet nearly caused him to slip and fall on his behind, often only catching himself at the last minute. He wished the trawl was located on one of the lower decks, which had not yet frozen over, but because that was impossible to do, he had to make the climb up the stairs from the hatch to the top deck, with the knowledge that at any moment he could slip and crack his head wide open.

Yet even that wasn't too terrible until the snow started falling. The snow began falling not more than a couple of hours after Stalf came into view. It was not heavy snow by any means, but there was enough snow to cover the entire ship in a thin layer of it from stern to bow. Beautiful flakes fell gently from the sky, covering the ship in a gentle blanket of the white stuff.

While Kinker wasn't too fond of the snow, Jenur was ecstatic. She'd pack snow together into large balls and throw them at some of the other sailors, who retaliated with snowballs of their own. Not only that, but she also somehow built a snowman that vaguely resembled Malock, which she cheerfully knocked over when she got bored of it.

"Why are you so energetic?" Kinker asked at lunchtime, shivering as he ate his fish (which thankfully was still warm from the oven). "It's just snow."

Jenur stopped kicking the remains of the Malock snowman around and looked at Kinker with enthusiasm shining in her eyes. "Just snow? Kinks, back where I come from, you'd be lucky to see even some sleet once a year. But I've always loved snow and always loved islands that have regular snowfall. It just makes everything look so different, magical even."

Kinker looked around. The other members of the fishing crew were in various states of displeasure at the snow, from Deddio dusting snow off his jacket to Gino shivering so hard that he looked like he was about to fall apart. The snow that had melted so far had created yet another layer of ice, which Kocas discovered when she slipped and fell on her bum trying to stand up.

"Magical," said Kinker. "If you say so."

"You just need to learn how to have some fun," said Jenur. "Take it easy for once."

Kinker wished his fish was a little hotter. "I'll take it easy once we're back in saner seas."

Jenur rolled her eyes. "Whatever. Say, what's that?"

Jenur pointed toward the oncoming island. Kinker had to rise to his feet to see what she was talking about, but carefully, as the spot where he sat was covered with ice like the rest of the ship and he didn't want to trip and fall.

Once he succeeded in that endeavor, he looked out at Stalf and squinted. The island wasn't very far away at all now; in fact, they would probably make landfall in an hour or so. Despite that, Kinker could not make out as many details about the island as he'd like. The entire thing looked like a big white splotch, probably because it was completely covered in snow, but soon Kinker spotted what appeared to be rounded white walls (whether of ice or snow, he couldn't say) in the interior, surrounded at its base by a ring of trees.

"Huh," said Kinker. "I have no idea what that is."

"Looks like someone built it," said Jenur. "At least, I doubt nature could have made something like that. Only question is, who?"

Kinker didn't have the answer to that, nor did he try to think of an answer. His brain was too frozen for anything like that.

After lunch, Malock nailed up the list of people who would be going on the expedition with him to Stalf. As usual, Kinker had to rely on Jenur to read it for him. She informed him that only five sailors were going on the expedition with Malock this time and that, surprisingly enough, she was one of them.

"You're going on the expedition?" said Kinker as he and Jenur walked back to the poop deck, away from the gathering crowd of sailors who were trying to read the list. "Why would Malock pick you? Especially after, well, you know."

"I don't know," said Jenur with a shrug. "Maybe he thinks I'm a good hunter or maybe he is trying to make up for being a dick. Either way, I'm not complaining."

"Why not?" said Kinker. "You remember what happened on

Ikadori Island, don't you?"

"Yeah, but look at all of the snow," said Jenur, gesturing back over her shoulder. "Looks like there are layers and layers of it, completely undisturbed by anyone. I've never seen so much snow in my life."

At that moment, Kocas appeared out of nowhere, her dreadlocks frosty, and got right up next to Jenur. She glared at Jenur, being so close to her as to make even Kinker feel uncomfortable.

"How did you do it?" said Kocas.

Jenur looked at Kocas, frowning. "What do you mean?"

Kocas brushed her dreadlocks out of her eyes and said, "Don't play dumb with me. How did you convince Malock to make you part of the hunting expedition that's going to Stalf?"

"Excuse me?" said Jenur as she, Kocas, and Kinker climbed the steps from the main deck to the poop. "I didn't do anything."

"No, I'm pretty sure you did," said Kocas as she and Jenur stopped at the top of the stairs. "Malock would never have chosen you and you know it. Even now that we know you aren't the spy, everyone knows about Malock's paranoia and I know for a fact that he wouldn't want to be anywhere near you under ordinary circumstances."

"Yeah, Malock can be paranoid, but he's also about as threatening as a puppy dog sometimes," said Jenur. "He was really broken when he found out that I wasn't the spy. He apologized so much. You should have seen him. If you did, you wouldn't be saying this crap."

"Did you sleep with him?" said Kocas. "I mean, everyone knows that he's sleeping with Vashnas, obviously, but I could see him sleeping around with female members of the crew."

Jenur's face quickly turned into a grimace. "Sleep? With Malock? That's disgusting. Besides, unlike a certain dirty-minded somebody who is talking to me, I'd never consider sleeping with someone in order to gain their favor. I value my body too much."

"I'm not dirty-minded," said Kocas. "Just realistic. I know how horny royals are and I know how much Malock likes younger women. So maybe—"

"I did not do anything to get Malock to put me on the hunting party," said Jenur in her firmest voice. "He chose me entirely on his own. Kinker can back me up. Right, Kinks?"

While those two talked, Kinker had spent the last few minutes doing his best to mount the stairs leading up to the quarterdeck. This was normally not a difficult task, but with the steps as icy as they were, Kinker had to exercise extreme caution. He had just made it about halfway up when Jenur appealed to him, causing him to look up and say, "What?"

Unfortunately for Kinker, all of his attention had been focused on making the climb and so when he looked up at Jenur, he accidentally missed the next step and went sliding down the stairs back to the bottom. It wasn't a particularly long fall and he didn't break any bones, but the fall was so painful that all he could do was groan.

"Kinker doesn't look like he's in any condition to give us his opinion," said Kocas. "Doesn't matter. I'm going to go talk to Malock and convince him to let me go instead of you."

"A little help?" Kinker called from the bottom of the stairs. "Just an old man here, with a back that is possibly broken, needing some help from you youngsters. That's all."

Unfortunately, neither Jenur nor Kocas seemed to hear him, so Kinker was forced to think of thinking of another way to get back up. Or perhaps he could just lay there, trying not to get stepped on, waiting until one of the other sailors noticed him and decided to help him up. He could not decide.

"Why do you want to go to Stalf so badly, anyway?" said Jenur. "Getting a little sick of the sea?"

"Because at heart, I am a hunter," said Kocas, putting one fist over her heart. "I am, after all, a follower of Ghatmos, the God of Hunting and the Woods."

"And?" said Jenur, sounding a bit bored. "What does that have to do with anything?"

"This expedition is going to be a hunting expedition," Kocas said. "Captain Malock is hoping to gather some food and fur from the native animals on the island. Before becoming a sailor, I hunted for years in the dark forests of Natachan. I am the most logical choice for this party."

"I guess Malock didn't think so, otherwise he would have chosen you instead of me," said Jenur. "But sure, you can go and talk to him. See if you can convince him to let you go. You might have to sleep with him first, though."

Kocas threw such an evil glare at Jenur that she seemed to be trying to kill her with it. Then Kocas stomped down the slippery stairs, somehow making it to the bottom without falling over, and walking over Kinker without stopping to help him.

"Geez," said Jenur, leaning against the stairs' railing. "That girl sure has some issues, doesn't she?"

"Yes, she does," said Kinker. "Now, Jenur, could you please help me up? Contrary to popular belief, the deck of the ship is not a soft place to land on. Especially when it is covered in ice like it is now."

Chapter Thirteen

THE *IRON WIND* WAS incapable of landing close to the shoreline of Stalf, not due to to the depth of the bay, but rather because of a thick ice ring that surrounded the entire island. Malock considered ramming the ice ring, but then he remembered that the *Iron Wind* was not a cutter and any attempt to break the ice ring would probably do more damage to the ship's hull than to the ring.

So instead, Malock directed the ship to be anchored right next to the outer edge of the ice ring. Then he gathered his hunting party together, which consisted of Jenur, Gormas Okina, and three others who he had picked based on their skills as hunters. One of them was Kocas Iknor, a Natachan woman who had not been one of his original choices but who had managed to convince him of her capability as a hunter a few hours ago.

All of them were armed with guns and swords, with one of each per hunter. The guns were partly frozen, but a quick test revealed that they all still worked. At the very least, a frozen gun could always be improvised as a heavy bat of some sort, which didn't make them entirely useless.

They then gathered near the davit, where Malock gave Banika orders to keep the ship under control while he was away. Here he said his good byes to Vashnas, while also asking for any last minute knowledge she may have had about Stalf. Unfortunately, she had nothing new to give him, so Malock and his hunting party got into the remaining rowboat and Banika lowered it to the ice ring from the davit.

As soon as the bottom of the rowboat hit the ice ring, Malock and his hunting party climbed out and dragged the rowboat the rest of the way across the ice ring. The rowboat was heavy, even with all six of them working together, but they managed it and soon they were in Stalf Bay, rowing across the freezing water to the island's shore.

As they drew nearer to the shore, however, Malock spotted some strange animals crawling out of the water onto the beach. He waved at the rowers to stop, which they did, and then pointed at the animals. The hunting party watched in silence as the creatures, about a dozen in all, rested on the beach, like they were taking a nap.

The animals looked like walruses, but they had to be at least as big as bears. Their sleek skin was completely black, contrasting sharply with the long white teeth that jutted out from their upper lips. Some of the lay on their backs, while a few lay on their stomachs. Their fins looked as sharp as swords, but thankfully the walrus-like creatures didn't seem to notice Malock and his crew at all. They looked like they were taking a nap.

Jenur gulped. "Anyone know what those are?"

"Vashnas told me about them," said Malock. "She always called them 'baba raga,' which is an aquarian phrase meaning 'big animal.'"

"That's helpful," said Jenur. "But what do they do? Can they fly and shoot lasers from their eyes?"

"Vash just said they're tough, but usually don't go around picking fights," said Malock. "So I imagine, if we don't try to fight them, that they'll just leave us alone."

Kocas, who was one of the rowers, leaned forward on her seat, licking her lips as she looked at the resting baba raga. "I think the more important question is, how edible are they? Because I think even one of those things could provide enough meat to feed a small family for a couple of days at least."

"Not sure," said Malock. His stomach growled. "But let's find out. Once we get to shore, of course."

The hunting party quickly crossed the rest of the bay. They landed near a cove, where they stashed the rowboat so they wouldn't lose it when the tide came in. They then made their way across the snowy beach, slowly and carefully, trying not to draw the attention of the baba raga to them.

Despite their best attempts at stealth, the baba raga noticed them. One of them raised its head lazily, blinking its small eyes in their direction, as if wondering who they were and what they were going to do. It looked rather innocent, but when Malock's stomach growled again, he didn't feel any regret in aiming his gun, pulling the trigger, and putting a bullet through its head.

The rest of his party followed, aiming and firing their guns at all of the baba raga. Instead of fighting back, as Malock expected them to do, the remaining baba raga slid down the sand into the ocean and disappeared beneath the waves, where no one could see them. Not that Malock was complaining, as their initial attack had bagged them three baba raga and they were big ones, too.

Malock left the task of gutting the baba raga to his hunters, as it was a messy task that was beneath his station. He watched Kocas and Jenur use their gutting knives to pierce the skin of the baba raga.

Or rather, watched as they tried to. As it turned out, baba raga skin was far thicker than they had first supposed. Although the bullet holes were as visible as day, their knives just glanced off the sides of the creatures' hides, almost like they were made of rock. The hunters tried to pierce the baba ragas' hides for about an hour, but all they succeeded in doing was to damage their knives and waste time, prompting Malock to say, "All right, men. Looks like we can't skin 'em. Just leave them here. I'm sure there're more edible animals further inland."

Jenur sheathed her knife and pointed at the giant white walls in the center of the island. "Maybe we should figure out what are behind those walls. Maybe someone lives there who might be willing to give us food."

Kocas laughed as she stood up, adjusting the belt of her pants. "Please. I know you're young, Jenur, but naïve, too? Or weren't you paying attention to what happened the last time we went too far inland on an island?"

"Kocas is right," said Malock. "Whatever is behind those walls probably doesn't want anything to do with us and we probably don't want anything to do with it. We'll stick to hunting in the forest around it."

Jenur frowned and looked at the dead baba raga before her. "If you say so, Captain."

The party of six walked through the snow into the thin forest. It was rough going, however, not because of the snow on the ground, but because their feet and boots were already wet from the water. Now that they were slogging through the snow, even with their thick Carnagian boots on, it was pure torture, but Malock ignored it and encouraged his men to do the same.

Unlike the jungle on Ikadori Island, the forest of Stalf was sparse, so spare that it could barely be called a forest. The branches above them were thin enough that light could shine through, although it was a weak light, not strong enough to warm them or melt the snow. Even the trees thick with leaves did not have as many leaves as the thinnest tree on Ikadori Island; nonetheless, Malock kept looking over his shoulder, up at the treetops, and to both sides.

None of his hunters commented on his odd behavior. That was partly because the group needed to keep silent in order to prevent prey from hearing them and running away, but it was also because they likely already knew why he was doing that. True, none of them knew about the Loner God, but they all knew that something bad had happened on Ikadori Island and that whatever it was had shaken Malock badly.

Not that Malock would ever actually admit that. As Captain of the crew and head of the hunting party, Malock believed that any sign of weakness on his part was unacceptable. He needed to make the rest of his crew think he was confident and in charge and he couldn't do that if he admitted he was afraid. It was how his father, the king, ruled

Carnag and it was how Malock had lead his crew so far.

One thing that made Stalf better than Ikadori Island was the abundance of animals. Of course, none of them were very big—a few white rabbits, some snow squirrels, a pale deer or two—but it was refreshing to finally see animals they recognized for once and so they shot with pure abandon. The animals of Stalf didn't seem to know what humans were, but by the end of the hour, Malock and his hunters had already shot two snow squirrels and a pale deer. The rest of their prey ran away, but Malock was confident that his hunters would have no trouble at all tracking them down if they needed to. The tracks in the snow the fleeing beasts made were obvious.

Over the next couple of hours, things went extremely well for the hunters. They shot and skinned animals, storing away the tastiest bits in their hunting bags, and despite the cold were all having a good time. Things were going so well for them that Malock actually let his guard down, feeling that perhaps Stalf wasn't home to a crazy god that wanted to kill them and that his hunters could take down whatever this island threw at them.

In fact, Malock himself actually managed to shoot some game. His best shot so far was the large pale deer he spotted a dozen yards or so from where they stood. The pale deer darted off faster than any they had seen before, but with a steady hand and quick aim Malock put a bullet through its head and killed it in one hit. He even skinned it himself; well, after Jenur taught him how, of course.

For the first time since Ikadori Island, Malock felt on top of the world. Sure, he was cold and tired and figured they'd have to head back to the ship within the next hour unless they wanted to get frostbite, but honestly none of that seemed nearly as bad as what he had been through on this voyage so far. He kept imagining the scent of cooked pale deer meat wafting from the galley, a scent he hadn't smelled since the day he left Carnag Hall.

Things were going so well, in fact, that Malock was genuinely surprised (and horrified) when Gormas Okina dropped dead in the snow suddenly and without warning.

The hunters had just caught a particularly fat snow rabbit, thanks to Kocas's superb aim with a gun, when Okina touched his neck, said, "What the—" and then fell face forward onto the not-yet-skinned snow rabbit, which he had been kneeling over while Kocas skinned it.

This caused all of the hunters to step back, but Malock moved in and crept down next to Okina's body. He placed a hand on Okina's neck and felt no pulse.

"What happened?" said Jenur, her eyes darting back and forth. "Is he unconscious?"

Malock shook his head. "Dead, by the look of it. Died instantly."

"How?" said another hunter, a male human named Aseth. "That makes no sense. I know Okina was always joking about how he was just going to drop dead from old age one of these days, but I didn't think he was being literal about it."

Malock felt along Okina's cold neck and found something sticking out of it. He plucked the thin thing and held it up for all to see.

"It's a dart," said Kocas, sounding impressed. "Very aerodynamic, too, by the look of it. And the needle looks even sharper than my mother's knitting needles. I think we're dealing with a professional here."

"But who shot it?" said Aseth, looking around nervously. "And where are they? Are you sure Vashnas didn't mention anything about other people living on Stalf, sir?"

Malock nodded. "She said she didn't explore Stalf very fully when she first came here. So we were basically going in blind."

Kocas took the dart from Malock's hand and turned it over, going over it with a critical eye. "Look at it. This thing had enough poison in it to kill a full-grown zinyu in a second. Poor Okina probably didn't even feel it reach his heart."

"That means we're dealing with someone who knows what they're doing here," said Malock. "Jenur, will— hey, where's Jenur?"

The young woman was missing from the group, even after they did a quick check of the area. They called out her name for several minutes, but in all that time the only answer they received was the howling of the wind, which picked up rather suddenly.

Malock stood up, dusting off his hunting jacket, as he said, "Okay, we're getting out of here. Whoever killed Okina is clearly not interested in entertaining guests, so—"

Without warning, something large and heavy fell out of a tree and into a clump of bushes at its base. This caused the group to jump and they jumped again when Jenur leaped down from the same tree. Her knife was out and stained slightly with blood, which she was wiping off on her pant leg as she approached the group.

"Found him," said Jenur, gesturing with her head in the direction of the thing that had fallen from the tree. "He was just loading his blowgun with another one of those killer darts when I came up behind him and slit his throat. He probably didn't even know I was there."

"Who didn't even know you were there?" said Malock. "And how the hell did you sneak away without any of us even hearing you leave?"

Jenur shrugged. "The guy who killed Okina. As for how I sneaked off, well, that's not really any of your business, now is it?"

"Excuse me?" said Malock, taking a step forward. "I don't like that tone."

"And I don't like the fact that you falsely accused me of being a spy and almost sold me off to a weird blob thingy," said Jenur. "But you don't see me whining about that, now do you?"

Malock's hands shook with anger, but he said, "Whatever. Let's get a better look at our silent assassin, shall we?"

They had to clear away the bushes in order to see him clearly, but when they did, Malock wasn't quite sure what he was looking at. The being had skin as rough as rock, with a lopsided, jagged mouth that revealed a row of uneven teeth. His entire body was covered in a large fur coat, so white that it faded in with the snow extremely well. Aside from his face, only his hands and feet were exposed, covered in thick black fur, with four fingers and four toes on each. In his left hand, he had what had probably been his blowgun, which was now broken in two, possibly because of the fall.

"Is it human?" said Aseth, tilting his head to one side like the being's appearance might make more sense from another angle. "Or something else?"

"He died like a human," said Jenur. "I'll admit, though, that he didn't make any human-like noises. Just sort of made a weird gurgling noise when I slit his throat."

"Let's check his body," said Kocas. "Maybe there will be a clue on it that will tell us about his identity."

"Way ahead of you," said Jenur as she fished something out of her pocket. "He didn't have much on him, except a dozen darts, his blowgun, and this."

Jenur held out a oval-shaped stone in her hand. It was colored bright red, almost like fire; in fact, unless Malock was mistaken, the stone radiated heat, although it wasn't very much. The stone was covered in markings, but they were in a language that Malock couldn't read.

"Wait," said Malock, looking at Jenur. "So you climbed up the trees, slit this guy's throat, looted his corpse, and then pushed it down?"

"Yep," said Jenur. "Why? Is there something wrong?"

"No," said Malock, shaking his head quickly. "Nothing wrong. Just ... curious about how the sequence of events played out. That's all."

"So then what's that?" said Kocas, pointing at the stone Jenur held. "Anyone seen anything like it before?"

"No," said Aseth. "But if I had to compare it to something, I'd say it resembles the kind of stones that lithomancers carry around in order to channel their stone magic better. My sister is a lithomancer and she has one like that."

"Too bad none of us are lithomancers," said Malock. "We'll keep it anyway. It might be useful later."

Malock took the stone from Jenur's hand and dropped it in his left pocket. He could feel its warmth against his thigh, even through his pants, but all that did was remind him of how cold the island was and how much he wanted to get off it.

"So ..." said Aseth. "Should we leave now? I mean, what if there are more guys like him hiding in the treetops?"

"Unlikely," said Jenur. "I didn't see any in the trees. Most likely this guy was alone."

"Still, Aseth has a point," said Malock. "This ... whatever he is, probably didn't live alone, unless his ship happened to crash off the shore of this island and he's the only survivor. He probably had some friends and when they realize he's been gone for too long, I bet they'll send some people to go find him."

"Are we going to run away, then?" said Kocas. "Just head back to the ship? Even though there's plenty more game to be caught and skinned?"

"Of course not," said Malock. "We're going to go to the most likely place that these people are located on this island."

"Why?" said Jenur. "I'm not afraid of 'em, per se, but it sounds like we're going to be causing a lot of trouble for no reason."

"Because I want to know what secrets this island has to hide from us," said Malock. "I'm tired of being afraid of the unknown. I would at least like to know what is going on here, if nowhere else."

"You're the boss," said Jenur, shrugging again. "But where *would* this guy's friends be, anyway? There don't seem to be any villages or towns on this island and I doubt, based on his coat and equipment, that the guy just lives in the wilderness like a wild man."

Malock turned and pointed in the direction of the ice walls. "That way. If his friends are anywhere on this island, then they are probably behind those walls. Now let's go."

Chapter Fourteen

THE STILLNESS OF THE *Iron Wind* had not done anything to make the ship warmer; if anything, Kinker thought the ship actually was colder, although that may have just been his imagination. Of course, he also spent a lot of time by the port, near the davit, where he could see Stalf. He had seen the hunters attack the walrus-like creatures and heard several gunshots go off in the forest, but he didn't know if they were okay now. He knew better than to worry about Jenur, as she could take care of herself, but he still found his thoughts straying to her every now and then.

A cold wind blew off the port just then, causing him to shiver and bring his jacket up more tightly around his body. Not much help. The wind from Stalf was so fiercely cold that Kinker thought he would become an icicle before a refreshing warm breeze fell over him, like the first day of summer. He closed his eyes and took in the heat, enjoying it as one might enjoy a fresh-cooked meal, before hearing something moving behind him.

Kinker opened his eyes and turned around to see Bifor

standing above him. The mage was moving his wand back and forth, the heat shimmering in the air.

"Thanks, Bifor," said Kinker, loosening his jacket a little. "I was wondering where the heat came from."

"No problem," said Bifor, his voice etched with tiredness. "Can I rest here for a bit? I've been working all day and got maybe only three hours of sleep that night, if that much."

"Sure," said Kinker, gesturing at his right. "Sit where you please. I don't mind the company."

Bifor gave him a grateful smile and plopped down on Kinker's right, with his back against the bulwarks. The mage lowered his wand and closed his eyes, as though he were asleep. Nonetheless, the air remained warm and comfortable, even causing the icicles hanging off the bulwarks to drip.

"I thought you were a pagomancer," said Kinker, looking at Bifor. "But you can also control heat."

Bifor didn't open his eyes, but he replied, "Part of basic mage training. All mages have a basic grounding in the most important magical fields. So yes, I do know some pyromancy, but I'm hardly a master."

"Ah," said Kinker. "I see. Just like how you know repair magic and such?"

Bifor nodded. "Yes."

"Okay," said Kinker. "But if you're a pagomancer, why haven't you used your magic to get the ice off the ship? Surely you could do that?"

"That's the problem," said Bifor. "This ice works very differently from ice back up north. I am not quite sure what the problem is, but for whatever reason, the coldness around Stalf does not feel like magic or nature. It feels artificial."

"Artificial," said Kinker. "What do you mean?"

"Like something is generating it," said Bifor. "That may just be me, though."

Kinker shrugged. "I don't know a thing about magic, to be honest, so I don't think I can help you here. At least your fire magic still works, though, eh?"

"True," said Bifor. "And for that I am grateful. Why are you standing here, anyway, Kinker? Waiting for the hunters to come home?"

"Mostly," said Kinker. "There's not much for me or the rest of the fishing crew to do until the ship starts moving again. Can't do any fishing or anything."

"I see," said Bifor. "Well, you got it lucky. Banika has been ordering me about all day. Only managed to get away from her because she finally decided to give me a break."

Kinker glanced over his shoulder. Banika was standing near the mainmast, overseeing a group of sailors who were attempting to clear the ice and snow off the stays. Though she spoke in a low tone, the sailors appeared to have no trouble following or understanding her orders.

"I've never understood Banika," said Kinker, returning his attention to Stalf. "Why is she Malock's first mate? Why does he trust her so much, perhaps only second to Vashnas?"

"I have no idea," said Bifor. "Heard some rumors she was in the

Carnagian Navy. Worked as a captain of the *Grinf's Justice*."

"The *Grinf's Justice*?" said Kinker. "What's that?"

Bifor opened his eyes and looked at Kinker. "Oh, that's right. I keep forgetting you're from Destan. Well, the *Grinf's Justice* was the flagship of the Carnagian Navy, also doubling as a pleasure ship for the royal family. Biggest and best ship ever constructed in the Northern Isles, or so the announcement said when she was finished. Had a hundred guns and could hold a crew up to about five hundred, not counting the extra three hundred or so passengers she could hold. Was a beauty."

"You're talking about it in the past tense," said Kinker. "Do you mean to say that it's no longer around anymore?"

"More or less," said Bifor with a shrug. "She sailed fine for five years, but sank off the coast of Carnag when on a return voyage. The exact cause of the sinking is still not known, but it is believed that a ship saboteur hired by some rival nation had sunk her in an attempt to kill the entire royal family of Carnag, who were aboard the ship at the time. No one found any proof, though, not even after a team of aquamancers hired by Carnag investigated the wreckage."

"Did anyone die in the sinking?" Kinker asked.

"The entire royal family made it out alive," said Bifor. "But a good chunk of the crew and passengers all died. Most of their bodies were recovered from the wreckage, but they were mostly unrecognizable, so they were all given a mass burial at sea, sort of like the ones we do here, in fact."

"Hmm," said Kinker, turning to face Bifor, leaning against the bulwarks with one elbow. "Sure seems like Carnagian ships have a habit of sinking, don't it?"

"If you are referring to the rest of the fleet on this voyage, then yes, it is a disturbing trend," said Bifor. "But we've only lost so many ships thanks to freak accidents no one could have predicted, such as the mishandling of the gunpowder in the hold of *Our Beloved Lady*, or when a previously dormant volcano exploded and sunk the Cat's Hook—things no one expects to happen but do anyway."

"Are you sure that those aren't the result of some ship saboteurs on board, trying to make this voyage a failure?" said Kinker.

Bifor sat up straighter and looked Kinker straight in the eye. "No, I do not believe so. Why?"

Kinker shrugged. "Admittedly, my understanding of international politics is very limited and probably incorrect, but it seems to me that Carnag must have some political rivals who for whatever reason would not want to see this voyage completed."

Bifor snorted. "As if. It's true that Carnag has some enemies, but in recent years Carnag has been making peace with many of its former enemies in an attempt to prevent another war from breaking out. And so far, all of the peace negotiations have gone smoothly, even with such hated enemies as the Shikans."

"But you said that Carnag still has some enemies," said Kinker. "Who might these be?"

"Off the top of my head, I'd say that the Shikans are still our worst enemies," said Bifor. "Despite the recent advances in peace negotiations we've made, they still have a rather negative opinion of us. And we, too, have a rather negative opinion of those boot-haters."

"Why?" said Kinker. "What caused this hate between you

Carnagians and the Shikans?"

Bifor sighed. "That's a rather long story I don't really want to get into right now."

"I'm listening," said Kinker. "Don't have anything else to do at the moment, anyway."

"All right," said Bifor. "It started back in—"

Bifor was interrupted when, without warning, a massive water spout burst out of Stalf Bay. The water shot high into the air, well above the highest mast of the *Iron Wind*, and fell back into the ocean with a loud splash.

Kinker and Bifor looked out into Stalf Bay, surprised.

"What was that?" said Kinker. "A giant whale or something?"

Bifor got to his feet and peered over the bulwarks into the part where the water spout had blown up. "No. The Bay is too shallow for a whale to get there."

"Then what—"

A low rumbling in the Bay caused the entire ship to shake. Kinker and Bifor grabbed onto the railings to avoid falling over, while a few nearby sailors fell over onto their behinds as a result. The surface of the water was bubbling, huge bubbles that instantly popped in the air, and then a large, round black object began to arise from the bubbles. Water cascaded down its large shoulders as the creature rose to its full height.

The monster looked similar to the baba raga that had been lying on Stalf's shores a few hours ago, except as big as the ship. Not only that, but its huge eyes gleamed with intelligence ... intelligence, and hunger. Its large front tusks looked large enough to rip straight through the hull of the *Iron Wind*, while its snout sniffed the air as though trying to determine where it was.

"What in Kano's name is that?" said Kinker, pointing at the giant monster in fear.

The giant baba raga let out a low growl, prompting Kinker to take a step back. Bifor, however, didn't seem frightened by the noise.

"It's calling someone," said Bifor. "Or multiple someones, perhaps."

By now, the rest of the crew had gathered nearby to see the giant monster, but Kinker paid them no attention. "How do you know that it's calling others?"

"Because back in the North Academy, I had to take a course on the behavioral patterns of baba raga before I could graduate," Bifor said, his eyes fixated on the giant before them. "When a baba raga is angry, it lets out a low growl that other baba raga nearby will immediately understand to be a cry for help."

"A cry for help?" said Kinker. "What does that thing need help for? Looks strong enough to kill us on its own."

"Maybe it's not a cry for help at all," said Bifor, his voice full of dawning realization. "Maybe it's actually an order to attack."

Without warning, the *Iron Wind* rocked again, not as badly as last time, but still enough to force Kinker's knuckles to turn white over the tops of the bulwarks. When it steadied again, Kinker looked overside and saw a dozen or so baba raga rapidly climbing the side of the ship, moving faster than their bulk should have let them, their flippers clinging to the sides thanks to the suction cups underneath them.

In fact, the baba raga moved so fast that Kinker had to step back, again almost slipping over the icy deck, just as the first beast stuck its head over the side and let out a terrifying roar. It was followed by eleven of its brothers, their flippers slapping against the frozen deck and their tusks slicing through the air. Forced to retreat, Kinker and Bifor found themselves at the mainmast, where the rest of the crew had backed up. Behind them, another dozen or so baba raga had climbed over the starboard, effectively trapping the crew between them.

The baba raga did not yet go in for the kill. They circled the sailors, making deep growling noises, baring their teeth and enormous tusks, and generally acting threatening. The sailors were mostly unarmed, but even if they had been armed, Kinker doubted they would have been able to do much against these beasts.

Then the giant baba raga's tongue—long, pink, and slimy—shot out of its mouth and wrapped tightly around the *Iron Wind*'s mizzenmast. Like snapping a twig off a tree, the monster tore the mainmast, beam and all, off its foundations, sending bits of wood and metal flying through the air and causing the entire crew to duck to avoid being hit.

The giant baba raga rolled the mainmast up to its mouth and then threw it over the ship. The mainmast fell into the ocean with a loud splash, sending ice cold water splashing onto the second group of baba raga, which didn't seem to bother them at all.

"Now my subjects," said the giant baba raga, its voice difficult to understand due to its snorts and grunts, "wreak vengeance on these pathetic mortals who dared to harm my people. For I, the Tusked

God, the God of Baba Ragas, demand it."

The gigantic ice walls radiated so much cold air that it was almost impossible to draw near to the walls. Malock and his party had to stay a certain distance away from the walls to prevent being frozen, which meant they couldn't investigate as closely as they would have liked.

As far as Malock could tell, the ice walls had no entrances or exits. They were completely solid, covered in a light layer of snow that made them look completely white. He considered the possibility that there could be an entrance on the other side; however, the walls were too wide for him and his crew to walk around without wasting a lot of time in the cold snow. Besides, he strongly suspected that the walls had no openings at all, not even a roughly carved one, which meant that he and the others were going to need to figure out how to make their own way in.

"I wish Bifor were here," said Jenur, after the hunters spent the last half hour unsuccessfully trying to look for an entrance to let them in. "He could just use his magic, I bet, and make an opening for us."

"I doubt even a pagomancer could make a hole in this thing," said Kocas, shaking her head. "Look at it. It's gotta be at least a dozen feet thick, maybe two dozen. I bet Bifor would just get himself frozen."

"Be that as it may, we cannot give up," said Malock. "Not until we get our answers."

Another half hour of attempts to find a door failed. So the party regrouped near the spot they had started at and began thinking again.

"Hey," said Aseth. "What if that stone is the key?"

"Key?" said Jenur, glancing at the walls. "I don't see any

keyholes."

"Not a literal key," said Aseth. "But like, maybe it has a secret that will help us get inside."

Malock fished the stone out of his pocket and turned it over a couple of times. "What kind of secret, exactly?"

"I don't know," said Aseth. "We're all out of ideas and I am sure that that assassin from earlier must have had a good reason for carrying that around. Maybe it's a signal to let someone on the other side know he's a friend or something."

"It's the best idea I've heard all day," said Malock. "Guess it wouldn't hurt to try. Let's see what we can do."

Malock walked as close to the ice walls as he could without getting frozen, which was difficult to do because he did not know the exact distance to stand. When he saw frost forming around the edges of his jacket, however, that's when he knew he had reached it.

The red stone continued to burn warmly in his hand. Not knowing what else to do, Malock raised the stone until he was pointing it directly at the walls. He didn't expect anything to happen at first and indeed for a moment the stone just sat in his gloved hand, which was beginning to frost over due to the cold emitted from the walls.

Then the stone flew out of his hand, like it had been yanked out by a powerful sucking force, and slammed into the ice walls. As soon as it did, its temperature must have rose because it immediately began melting a large hole in the walls, a hole big enough for Malock and the other hunters to walk through.

In just a few seconds, the stone had melted through the walls completely, creating a tunnel that led to the other side. The stone itself hung in midair, as though suspended by an invisible string, its heat radiating so powerfully that Malock could feel it even from where he stood.

"Damn," said Jenur. "Guess it worked after all."

Malock turned to the others and gestured at the tunnel. "Well? What are you waiting for? I doubt this tunnel will remain open forever. Follow me."

Kinker wasn't much of a fighter. True, in his youth, he had participated in the wrestling tournaments held in the courtyard of the Temple at the end of every spring and had even done pretty well in them, but when he got older he put more and more of his attention on fishing, a task which was far less physically-demanding than wrestling.

As a result, Kinker became less and less fit over the years. Joining the crew of the *Iron Wind* forced him to be more physically active than usual, true, but the lack of good food and water had taken a toll on his body, which he soon learned when he found himself cornered by one of the baba raga that was currently attacking the ship.

When the Tusked God ordered its minions to attack, Kinker had immediately tried to flee to the lower decks. It was less due to Kinker's cowardice and more to do with trying to get a weapon—a gun, a sword, heck, even a kitchen knife—that he could use to defend himself.

Unfortunately, one of the baba raga, a particularly fat one with a scar across its forehead, jumped on top of the hatch, keeping him from getting inside. It growled at him, the sound intimidating enough to make Kinker back off.

Kinker looked around at the rest of the crew. Despite the immense size difference between the crew and the baba raga (a hundred sailors versus a little less than twenty-five beasts), the crew was clearly not winning. Already Kinker spied a few dead sailors (although he couldn't tell who they were), but the vast majority, thankfully enough, were simply wounded in many places. Only one baba raga lay dead on the deck, its skull cracked, but the rest of its brothers were fighting ferociously, even when they got smacked in the face by chunks of wood that a few sailors had picked up as improvised weapons.

Kinker returned his attention to the baba raga. It had not yet moved from the hatch, which meant that this one was simply trying to keep him away. Kinker took a step forward, but as soon as he did, the baba raga's tongue shot out and wrapped around his wrist. Its tongue burned like fire, causing Kinker to cry out and stagger backwards, but the baba raga held on tight to his wrist, looking quite pleased at his pain.

He tried to grab and squeeze the tongue with his other hand, but he could not get a firm grip on it and every time he touched it, the palm of his hand burned. When he glanced at his free hand, it was covered in sores and burn marks, like he'd stuck it on top of a burning stove top.

"Let go of me, you dumb beast," Kinker growled, his voice lost in the commotion all around him. "Let go, damn it."

The baba raga simply looked at him triumphantly, like it was thinking, *I enjoy your suffering, human. Why would I ever let go?*

Its smug look immediately disappeared, however, when Banika appeared out of nowhere and slashed at its exposed tongue with her knife. The knife cut through the tongue cleanly, causing blood to pour out as the rest of the tongue retreated back into the baba raga's mouth. Kinker immediately shook off the bit of it that had been wrapped around his wrist and grimaced at the bruises and burns on his wrist.

Then he looked up and saw the baba raga staggering off the hatch. It hacked and coughed loudly, trying to breathe with only half its tongue, and then Banika kicked it over and drove her knife directly into its eyes. The baba raga screeched in terror and then stopped immediately, making it the second baba raga to die so far.

Banika pulled her knife out of the baba raga's eye sockets as Kinker ran up to her and said, "Thanks for saving me. I thought I was a—"

Banika immediately pushed Kinker to the side, making him fall to the deck. The next moment, a baba raga barreled through, almost crushing his legs. Kinker recovered from the fall quickly and looked up in time to see Banika in battle with the other baba raga, its tongue lashing out at her while she expertly dodged or blocked it with her knife.

Then Kinker looked toward the hatch, which was now entirely unguarded. He got to his feet and immediately climbed down into the hatch, hoping against hope that he would be able to get to the harpooning tools that he knew were down there, even though he was starting to doubt they would be of any practical use.

Chapter Fifteen

WHEN MALOCK EMERGED FROM the tunnel into the interior of the ice walls, he was not sure what he had been expecting to see. Perhaps he had been expecting to see an icy forest, similar to the one outside the walls, or at least scattered trees dotting here and there. He supposed he had been expecting to see some hills (though why, he couldn't tell) and maybe a small, cozy house that the assassin would have called home. At worst, he expected to see a whole group of assassins, just heading out to find out what was taking their deceased friend so long to return.

What Malock found instead, however, was a wide-open, snowy field, with streams crisscrossing here and there, streams of cool clear water that sparkled in the sun. Trout danced in the water, which seemed to be coming from underground springs, as there were no mountains for the stream water to be coming down from.

Scattered across the snowy field were a couple dozen small wooden huts. It was difficult to judge their exact size from where

Malock stood, but if he had to guess, he'd say that they were big enough for a small family of two parents and a young child. They had a very simple, bland design and all looked exactly the same, like the boots that came off the factory conveyor lines back on Carnag. A cobblestone road connected the houses to one another, occasionally going over small bridges that stood over the streams.

In the center of it all was a large, imposing palace. Its turrets—about four or five, by the look of it—were stunted and blunt at the ends, with no spires at the top at all. The outer walls appeared to be made of an ugly black metal, while the palace itself was made of an old gray metal that reminded Malock of the color of his grandfather's skin in his last days. The palace appeared to have been designed purely for practical purposes, rather than aesthetic, as though the palace's occupant cared more about practicality than looks.

Jenur stood by his side, taking in the entire scenery like she couldn't believe her eyes. "Huh. An entire village, complete with castle, protected by gigantic ice walls, on an island that is supposedly uninhabited. I can't be the only one who sees something wrong with this picture."

"You're not," said Kocas, cocking her gun. "We should be cautious."

"I wonder if anyone lives in those huts," said Malock, looking down at them curiously. "I don't hear any noises. Perhaps the people are all asleep."

"Sir, if I may suggest something," said Aseth, who was actually sweating in the cold, "could we go back to the ship? I have a very bad feeling about this and we really should have given Okina a proper burial or at least a better burial than covering him with snow, at any rate."

Malock shook his head. "Sorry, Aseth, but we didn't come this far just to turn back. I came in order to find out who sent that assassin and who lives here. And now that I've actually seen the place, I have even more questions I would like answered."

Jenur looked at the cobblestone road they stood upon. "Think they're booby-trapped?"

"I doubt it," said Malock. He gestured at the scene and said, "Look at all of these peaceful huts. They probably never expected anyone to get past the ice walls, which means they probably aren't very good fighters. I imagine we could take the whole place ourselves, if we wanted to."

"Conquest isn't our goal, though, is it?" said Aseth, scratching the back of his neck nervously. "We're just here to get info, right?"

"Of course," said Malock. "And who knows, maybe the people who live here will be willing to give us food and furs that we could take back to the ship."

"If they're as friendly as that guy from earlier, I can't imagine anything going wrong here," said Jenur. "Lead the way, Captain."

Malock walked down the cobblestone road, his hand on the hilt of his sword. The others followed, but even though none of them spoke, Malock could feel their unease and worry. He understood it, but once again saw no reason to pay heed to it. Besides, the ice wall had already sealed the tunnel back up and the stone with it, so they had no choice but to go forward now and hope for the best.

They reached the first hut quickly. The windows were closed and covered with brown curtains that were too thick to see through. Because there was no one outside, Malock decided he would simply knock on the door and see if anyone would answer.

He walked up to the door and knocked on it a few times.

No one answered.

Malock sighed and knocked again, this time more insistently.

Once again, no one answered.

He looked for a knocker or doorbell of some sort, but as far as he could tell, outside of knocking, there was no way you could let the hut's inhabitants know you were there.

"No one's home," said Malock with a sigh, turning to face his men. "We might as well go onto the palace. We'll probably find people there."

"Hold on," said Jenur, striding forward. "You didn't knock very loudly, you know. Let me try."

Jenur pushed Malock out of the way (much to his displeasure) and then knocked rapidly and loudly on the solid wood door three times. She stepped back and waited a moment while Malock said, "That didn't work at—"

Then the door swung open, revealing the strangest little being standing in the doorway that Malock had seen so far (although not as strange as the Loner God, perhaps)).

The being was as small as a child, perhaps just a few inches taller, with metallic skin that covered its body completely. It wore no clothes and had no genitals, which perhaps was why it didn't wear any clothes. It looked up at them with emotionless orange eyes, one hand grasping the doorknob, like it was ready to slam the door shut on them at any moment.

"Hello," said Malock, recovering from the shock before any of the others could. "My name is Prince Tojas Malock, Crown Prince of Carnag, Captain of the—"

The little being immediately slammed the door shut in his face.

"Guess he wasn't impressed by your list of titles," Jenur muttered.

Malock let out a frustrated growl, but instead of getting angry, he knocked on the door like Jenur did, saying as he did so, in a forced calm voice, "Hey, I'm sorry. I didn't mean to scare you. I was just trying to let you know who I am so you could—"

The door swung open again, causing Malock to take a step back. Not because of the door but because of the five or six metallic-skinned beings that now stood there, aiming sharp-pointed metal spears at Malock and the others. These other ones were much taller than the first one, but they had the same glowing orange eyes and similar humanoid structure.

Malock's men immediately raised their guns, but as soon as they did, the little metallic being in the front waved its hands and the barrels of their guns bent up at an odd angle. Jenur immediately discarded her now-useless gun in favor of her knife, but the little metallic being simply waved his hand and the knife launched out of her hand into its. The hunters drew their swords, but another wave of the small metallic being's hands and the blade flew out of their hands and into the roof of the hut before them.

"Okay," said Malock, holding up his hands in a nonthreatening manner. "You disarmed us. Not that that was necessary, but you did it and now you know for sure we're not a threat. If you could just point our way out of here, we'd really appreciate it."

The group of metallic-skinned beings marched out of the hut, like an army unit, forcing Malock and the others to back up. The beings formed a loose circle around the hunters and began herding them down the path to the palace. None of the hunters tried to fight back or argue, mostly because they were unarmed and the metallic-skinned beings were not.

Climbing down the hatch ladder into the lower decks was not as easy as it usually was. Kinker was in such a hurry that he missed a step and went tumbling all the way down to the floor, landing flat on his back and knocking his head on the steps as he did so. It didn't help that the ship itself was shaking, probably from the waves that the Tusked God was stirring up outside. His wrist still burned, too, but the pain had died down enough to where he could ignore it.

His back had taken the brunt of the fall and he felt it. It was like his entire body had broken in half, even though he thought his back was still in one piece. The smell of blood and water and bodily fluids entered his nostrils, making it difficult to concentrate long enough to figure out what he needed to do. All he wanted to do was lie there for a while, let his back recover.

But somewhere, deep inside himself, he felt a force pushing him. True, he might not be able to defeat the Tusked God or save his friends, but goddammit if he was going to go down without a fight. If he could at least get to the hold, at least get to the harpoon down there, he would be able to fight back, if nothing else.

Kinker's hands reached out for anything to grab, anything he could use to pull himself back to his feet. At first, he succeeded in grabbing nothing, as there were no side railings on the hallway's walls and he was still lying on his back, his arms and legs weak from the fall. He just about gave up hope until his right hand wrapped around the second to bottom step of the ladder, which he firmly grabbed hold of.

Just sitting up was like climbing a mountain. His back screamed in protest. All he wanted to do was lie down, maybe curl into a ball, and never get back up ever again. He wanted to wait until his back stopped acting up, but by the time that happened, he had a feeling that the *Iron Wind* would be at the bottom of the sea.

So Kinker somehow succeeded into sitting upright. It felt like someone was running a knife down his back now, carving out huge chunks of flesh, but he didn't give a damn about that. He grabbed onto a higher step and began pulling himself up to his feet.

In many ways, this was even worse than trying to sit upright. Whereas sitting upright allowed him to rest his legs, here he was asking his legs to support the rest of his body. This was a difficult enough task when his back didn't feel like it had been smashed into pieces like a fragile brick wall, but now it was almost impossible. He realized he must have hurt his legs in the fall, too, because his knees and ankles ached.

Nonetheless, Kinker succeeded in standing up. He immediately leaned against the right bulkhead, his head spinning. He attempted to take a step forward and almost managed it before the ship suddenly tilted to port, causing him to slam against the left bulkhead. That caused him to gasp in pain, but he didn't fall down again.

Instead, he began making his way down the hall, slowly but

deliberately, toward the ladder that would take him to the hold. He ignored the sounds of battle overhead, although once a chunk of wood was knocked from its place in the ceiling above and almost hit him on the head. It only grazed his shoulder, but he didn't let that stop him. He just kept going.

Finally, Kinker reached the next ladder. He peered down into the darkness of the lowest deck. He wished he had brought along a candle or something. He needed to be able to see what was down there if he was going to find the harpoon, but sadly it looked like he was going to have to rely on his other senses to find what he needed.

Bracing himself, Kinker climbed onto the ladder. His back had not recovered since the fall and now it was worse than ever, the pain so bad that he almost fell off the ladder before he readjusted his grip on the rungs. He took this ladder easy, one rung at a time, trying to maintain his balance even as the ship unexpectedly lurched every now and then.

You should be back up there, his mind told him as he climbed down further. *Fighting like the rest of them. What do you think Jenur would say if she saw you in this position, running away like a coward?*

Kinker ignored his mind. He knew it was just guilt, good old guilt, playing tricks on him again. He had no time for such nonsense, especially with his back hurting like hell and not knowing what the current state of the battle outside was.

Just like on Destan, Guilt said. *You were too cowardly to tell the people about Deber's true colors. You didn't want to be arrested or lead a revolution or do any of that. How many young boys do you think Deber has killed since then? Five? Ten? Maybe even fifteen? And how many do you think you could have saved if you had stayed?*

For the first time in his life, Kinker was quite happy about his old back. It hurt so badly that he had a difficult time paying attention to Guilt. Of course, the pain made it difficult to grip the ladder's rungs, so it wasn't all good.

How many of your friends have died in this assault so far, do you think? Guilt asked. *I can't see Deddio lasting very long. For that matter, what about Jenur and the others on Stalf? Haven't heard from them in a few hours. Maybe the Tusked God killed them first and then came after you, just to be neat and tidy.*

Kinker felt his foot finally touch the floor, prompting him to let go of the ladder. It was still far too dark down here for his taste, but having been down this far once before, he knew that it was just a straight line from where he stood to reach the door to the hold. So he began walking straight ahead, once again using the wall for support.

It's too dark, Guilt complained. *Dark and cold. It's like an ice chamber down here.*

For once, Guilt had a point. The narrow hallway that lead to the hold was much colder than the top deck, even though there was no ice. That was probably because the lower half of the ship was submerged in the icy water around Stalf. Kinker tried to draw his coat tighter around his body, but even that simple gesture caused his back to flare with pain, forcing him to stop that.

Eventually, he reached the end of the hallway, where he felt in the darkness for the door handle. He soon found it and, with a grin, tried to turn it.

It was locked.

Well, that was a complete waste of time, Guilt said. *I imagine Gino was probably the first to die. He was so overcome with grief over Magnisa's death, that I doubt he even saw it coming. And you could have saved him.*

Kinker didn't have the keys on hand and couldn't go to Banika to get them. He considered breaking the lock, but just the thought of the physical exertion that would require made his back tingle. That meant he would have to go back up and join the fight, even though he was fairly certain that the battle was lost.

Then an idea occurred to him. It was a crazy idea, one he wasn't so sure would work, mostly because it involved using the cannons, which were weapons that he had zero experience working with. Nonetheless, he was desperate enough to try it, because as far as he knew, the cannon room was always unlocked and there was no one else in there at the moment.

So, turning around, Kinker made his way to the ladder that would take him back to the middle deck. Guilt seemed to have shut up now or at least was a lot quieter, perhaps because, if Kinker's plan worked, he might just succeed in saving his friends and the rest of the crew.

The most disturbing thing about the metallic beings, in Malock's opinion, was not their silence or their glowing eyes or their apparent ability to manipulate and bend metal to their will. Nor was it their stubborn refusal to show even the slightest hint of life in their movements. It wasn't even the loud creaking sounds their joints made, like the noises made by the conveyor belts in the boot factories back on Carnag.

What disturbed Malock more than anything else was their utter indifference to his many titles. In spite of the fact that he had revealed himself to be a prince and a Captain, the metallic beings showed no sign that they thought either of those two titles to be worthy of respect or reverence. They barely even showed any interest in him, unless he slackened, in which case one of the rear guard would poke him with one of the metal spears and force him to speed up.

Not that the walk was unpleasant, mind. The cobblestone path was devoid of snow, which Malock found odd because it was currently snowing, albeit very lightly. The source of its clearness became obvious to him, however, when he saw the snow literally bounce off the cobblestone onto the ditches on either side. He figured it was probably magic at work, which meant that either a mage or a god ruled this island; he hoped it was the former.

The rest of the hunters seemed as disgruntled as he was by this whole arrangement. Jenur had even attempted to make a break for it, but the metallic beings were as quick as they were tough and caught her easily. Now she had a set of thick manacles around her wrists and ankles that she complained were too tight. None of the metallic beings seemed to care.

The path to the palace took them away from the other huts, although occasionally Malock caught a glimpse of glowing orange eyes peering at them through the windows. They passed over one of the clear streams, which Malock stole a glimpse at, but he saw nothing in the water except smooth stones and weird-looking metallic fish.

Soon, the group reached the palace's front gates. The front gates opened almost immediately, without any of the metallic beings uttering so much as a word, and the hunters were shepherded through. Half of the metallic beings stayed behind on the other side, while the other half went through the front gates with Malock and the others.

The palace's courtyard was quite different from the rest of the area behind the ice walls. There was no snow on it at all; rather, there was a bright green lawn, with rows upon rows of exotic flowers that Malock had never seen before. One in particular caught his interest, a tall blue flower with a dozen bubs that glowed slightly in the sunlight.

They weren't alone, however. Bending over one of the flowers was a young woman who couldn't have been older than Jenur. The young woman immediately noticed the group and stood up, causing Malock to look at her again just to make sure he wasn't seeing things.

Yes, she really was dressed in a giant flower. Or at least, her dress was designed in such a way that it looked like she was wearing a giant yellow blooming flower upside down over her body, the hem of which went to her knees. Her hair was long and green, the same shade as the grass actually. She looked almost human, but something about the way she walked and held herself told Malock otherwise.

"What's this?" said the woman as she walked over to them, speaking perfect Divina. "Did my brother invite some guests over?"

The lead metallic being, the small, childlike one from before, walked up to her and spoke in a strange language Malock couldn't understand. It also made a variety of movements with its hands and fingers, which appeared to be part of the language, though Malock couldn't be sure.

The woman seemed to understand the metallic being completely.

She tapped her chin, nodding occasionally, and saying, "Interesting ... yes ... of course ... I see ..."

For the life of him, Malock just hoped that the woman was as kind as she was beautiful. If she was a goddess, though, like the Loner God ... well, he had a feeling that his hunters' luck had just run out.

The metallic being stopped speaking and then turned to its brethren and spoke again. The other metallic beings immediately lowered their spears and stepped away from the hunters, causing Malock and his men to look around in surprise.

"So sorry about that," said the woman, gesturing at the metallic beings. "These automatons can be so reactionary sometimes. My apologies."

Malock regained his composure quickly and said, "No offense taken, Miss ...?"

"Hanarova," said the woman, curtsying him. "You can call me Hana for short."

"Miss Hana," said Malock. "I am Prince Tojas Malock, Crown Prince of Carnag, Captain of the—"

"Yes, yes, I know all of that already," said Hana, interrupting him with a wave of her hands. "Little Jingus here already told me. That, and everyone on the southern seas already knows who you are. I did not believe I'd ever get to meet you, to be honest, but I suppose Tinkar decided it would be funny to see what would happen if we met."

Malock immediately reached for his sword's hilt before remembering that the automatons had taken it from him earlier. "Are you a goddess, then? Like the Loner God?"

"The who?" said Jenur, but neither Malock nor Hana bothered paid her attention.

Hana chuckled. "Wouldn't that be something? No. I'm a katabans."

"A what?" said Jenur. "Are you guys just throwing around words now to confuse us or something?"

"Ugh," said Hana, rolling her eyes. "It's your awkward tongue. Doesn't have an exact equivalent. If I had to describe it using your mortal terms, it means I'm a minor spirit. Surely you mortals have heard of minor spirits before?"

"Vaguely," said Malock. "In my education, I was taught about the different creatures that live in the world. I remember something about katabans. I think it was a footnote in a textbook or something that mentioned katabans sometimes working for gods."

"Bingo," said Hana, though there was a touch of sarcasm to her voice. "Yes, we katabans serve the gods and goddesses of Martir, both north and south. I am currently the servant of the Mechanical Goddess, who is the ruler and patroness of this island upon which you have landed."

"Mechanical Goddess?" said Jenur. "You mean Asix, God of Mechanics, right?"

Hana laughed. "No, no, no. The Mechanical Goddess and Asix are siblings, true, like all of the gods are, but the two are as different as night is from day. Don't confuse the two when you are in her presence, please."

Damn it, Malock thought. *We just had to run into another southern deity, didn't we?*

Aloud, he said, "Okay. So your mistress rules this island. I suppose we'll be on our way, then, as that's all we wanted to know."

Hana's smiled immediately disappeared from her lips. "Sorry, but you five aren't going anywhere, I'm afraid. Not until I find out which of you killed Bet."

"Who?" said Malock, trying not to show the fear rising in his chest. "We have no idea who you are talking about, Miss Hana."

"Bet," said Hana. "My brother. There's no way you could have gotten beyond the ice walls unless you killed Bet and took his entry stone. I don't know where his body is or how you managed to kill a katabans, but until I do, you five are staying put here."

The front gates slammed shut and Malock saw no other way out of the courtyard. The walls were too high to climb or jump and he doubted that he and his unarmed men could fight the automatons and Hana, whose true power was still a mystery to them all.

"Are you going to kill us?" said Jenur.

"It would only be fair," said Hana. "As big of a lug as my brother was, he was still my brother. I honestly didn't expect him to get killed by mortals, but mortals have killed katabans before, so perhaps it's not as shocking as it could have been."

"I don't get it," said Malock. "If you're a spirit, how come you have a physical body? How can we kill you? Aren't you stronger than us mortals?"

"We katabans can take on physical forms in order to perform certain tasks that are beyond our spiritual forms," said Hana. She gestured at hers and said, "This one I've had for a while, as I and my brother have been serving the Mechanical Goddess for many years.

It's rather ugly in comparison to how I really look, but it gets the job done."

"'Ugly' is a bit of an overstatement, wouldn't you say?" said Malock. "I mean, you are almost as beautiful as Kano herself."

Hana shot him a irritated look. "Did you kill Bet? Because I'm starting to think you did."

Malock, without thinking, immediately pointed at Jenur. "She did it."

"Hey!" said Jenur. "What the hell, Malock? I thought you weren't going to betray me again."

"So you didn't kill Bet, either?" said Hana.

"Well, I did," Jenur said. "But only because he killed one of our guys first. And that's not the point, anyway. If you knew about what we've already been through—"

"I do not care," said Hana. "I'll kill all of you equally and then dump your bodies into the sea. The cold will probably preserve you, though, so you don't need to be afraid of losing your good looks."

Hana snapped her fingers and the automatons immediately began walking toward them. Malock and the others prepared to fight for their lives, but just then, a series of tremors shook the ground beneath their feet. The first was barely noticeable, but soon the tremors became more and more obvious, until all of the automatons stopped cold as if obeying an unheard command. Hana turned to look at the center of the courtyard, which seemed to be the source of the tremors.

"What's going on?" said Jenur. "An earthquake?"

Hana gulped. "Not an earthquake, murderer. A goddess."

The top of the courtyard's center slid away like a panel and from within it arose a large machine that towered over everyone in the vicinity, human, automaton, and katabans alike.

When the machine rose to its full height, the ground ceased shaking. The machine looked like a shrunken lighthouse, with a small red light at the top whose rays swept across the entire courtyard in seconds. Whistles and snaps and other mechanical noises emitted from its black-armored body so loudly that Malock could barely even hear himself think.

Immediately, the automatons fell to their knees, but they weren't bowing at Malock. They were bowing at the black lighthouse, which continued to make loud noises. It sounded like a toddler that had been awakened from its nap too early or maybe that was just Malock's imagination.

Hana hadn't bowed, but the expression of reverence on her face meant she knew what it was. "Mechanical Goddess! What a surprise. I didn't know you were awake."

"*That's* a goddess?" said Jenur, not even bothering to keep her voice down.

"Shh!" Malock said to her in a low voice. "Don't do, say, or even think anything that will get her on your bad side."

"Sir, you sound like you've met her before," said Aseth, raising his voice a little to be heard over the sounds of the Mechanical Goddess. "Have you?"

"No," said Malock, shaking his head, all the while keeping his eyes on the Mechanical Goddess. "But I know exactly what her kind thinks of us mortals and we don't need to give her an excuse to want to eat us even more than she already does."

"*Eat* us?" Kocas repeated, her face turning pale. "What does—"

The whirring and creaking noises of the Mechanical Goddess became louder, cutting off Kocas's question. Hana cringed at the noise, looking much like how disobedient servants looked whenever Malock or one of his parents yelled at them back home on Carnag.

"Yes, I'm sorry," said Hana, looking more and more subdued the further the Goddess raged. "I was going to get around to telling you about the visitors eventually. It's just—"

Though Malock could not understand the Mechanical Goddess's language, somehow he knew that she wasn't at all pleased, especially when a burst of steam exploded from the top of her head.

"Okay, okay, I know," said Hana, holding up her hands, like she was afraid she was going to be hit. "I won't do it again. Sorry. I'll call off the automatons."

More whirring and creaking, this time punctuated with a rather violent-sounding beep.

"Oh, you still want the automatons around?" said Hana. "Oh. Must have misheard you. Won't happen again. I'm sorry."

The Mechanical Goddess became quiet. Then Malock remembered where he had heard those noises before: from the automatons, who he realized must have been constructed by the Mechanical Goddess herself.

Hana sighed and turned around to face Malock and the hunters again. "You lucked out. The Mechanical Goddess doesn't want any of you dead yet. She was very angry that I didn't inform her of your arrival right away, as I should have."

"So we gathered," said Malock, though he didn't let his guard down one bit. "Listen, if it's going to be a problem, we'll just head back to our ship. The only reason we came here was to find out who killed one of ours and you know what? We did. We really don't have any reason to be here."

Hana smiled. "The Mechanical Goddess doesn't want you leaving just yet. She would like to invite you to dinner in her palace. She is sure you are all very hungry. You look like little more than skin and bones."

Malock looked at the rest of his party. Sure enough, they all looked as hungry as a baba raga. Malock's own stomach betrayed him by rumbling loudly at that exact moment.

"That's a very generous offer and I am not normally one to turn down a generous offer made by a goddess," said Malock as he took a step back. "But we have plenty of food on our ship, you see, and we just caught some fresh pale deer. Really, we wouldn't want to intrude."

"Oh, it's not a problem at all," Hana said, folding her hands behind her back. "The Mechanical Goddess has not had visitors in quite some time."

"You mean she isn't pissed that we killed one of her servants?" said Jenur.

Hana's left eye twitched at the mention of her brother, but she said in her normal voice, "Not really. She never really liked Bet all that much, mostly because he was never particularly bright or clean, unlike me. She was actually quite happy to be rid of him, if you can't tell."

It was impossible to judge the Mechanical Goddess's mood right now, due to her complete lack of body language and facial expression, but Malock nodded anyway like he understood completely.

"Now follow me," said Hana, turning around to face the palace. "And by the way, you have to come whether you want to or not."

Malock balled his hands into fists, but Hana was right. The doors were shut closed, the automatons were still at the ready, and the Mechanical Goddess probably wouldn't take very kindly to having her invitation declined.

So Malock nodded his head and said, "All right. We'll come, but that doesn't mean we have to like it."

Hana was already halfway to the front steps. "Don't worry. She doesn't expect you to."

Chapter Sixteen

MIRACULOUSLY, KINKER MANAGED TO climb the ladder up from the lowest deck, where the hold was located, to the middle deck, where the cannons were located. Not that it had been easy. The ship still swayed, his back was still giving him grief, and now his head was starting to hurt from the fall he'd taken earlier. Either that or he was just starting to notice the pain throbbing in the back of his head, but he figured it didn't really matter when he noticed the pain or when it started hurting because the result was the same.

But the climb had taken a lot out of him. Kinker lay sprawled on the floor near the ladder, sweating despite the coldness. He panted hard, wiping the sweat off his brow and wishing that he was younger. In his younger days, his back had been much stronger, much better able to take falls and hits. More than once he had prayed to Kano to grant him his youth again, even though she wasn't Senva, and now he found himself once again praying to Kano, this time asking her for his back to be healed.

She didn't answer. He'd noticed her silence over this voyage, which disturbed him greatly. True, Kano hadn't always answered all of his prayers even back on Destan, but he had always had the feeling she was at least listening if nothing else. Now, though, he doubted she was doing even that much.

She must think we'll get to World's End quickly, Kinker thought. *Without any trouble at all. That either makes her insane or extremely optimistic. I am willing to consider the former.*

Kinker rolled onto his stomach and started crawling up the hallway, as he had no way to pull himself to his feet to walk. He managed a few feet before stopping, panting and biting his lower lip and trying to ignore the pain. The sounds of battle above sounded more ferocious than ever, but he paid them little attention. His pain was the more immediate problem and if he didn't come up with a way to get rid of it soon, he was unlikely to get anywhere.

But he was no doctor or mage. He could not simply wave a magic wand and heal his back instantly. The only choice he had, as far as he could see, was to keep going, even if his back didn't want to. He'd simply have to tough it, like his father had always taught him. There was no avoiding that fact.

So Kinker pulled himself forward again and let out a loud moan of pain. Ignoring it, he kept pulling himself forward and kept moaning, but he once again only managed a few feet because the pain paralyzed him. So he just lay there, face-first, feeling his beard cling to the grime of the floor, listening to the battle above grow louder and more violent, wondering if this was the end.

The interior of the Mechanical Goddess's palace was different from every other palace or castle Malock had ever been to. There were no paintings of famous ancestors or heroes or gods, no sculptures representing any of the aforementioned famous people, not even a special vase on a pedestal that could be broken at any moment.

The halls were not wide and open, either, but cramped and confining. Complicated systems of gears, belts, and pipes, all clinking and clanking and steaming, covered the walls, ceiling, and even the floor, which made walking difficult. It was like walking through a large machine, the parts intertwined so exactly that it was impossible to tell where one part began and the other ended. Small, bright lights flickered on the ceiling and walls, barely illuminating the floor.

Malock and his party stuck close together, not sure what parts of the palace were friendly and what weren't, while Hana made her way through the complicated mess of machinery like she was taking a stroll through the park. It was clear that she knew her way around this place, probably because she had served the Mechanical Goddess for so long, but Malock had a feeling that even if he were to live here for years, he wouldn't be able to make his way through without tripping a few times.

The constant sound and motion of the gears, belts, and pipes made conversation impossible. The gears creaked and cranked, the belts whoomped and whomped, and the pipes hissed and shook. The hallways smelled strongly of oil, causing Malock to cover his mouth and nose with a handkerchief he had brought along, but that did little to make the air more breathable for him.

While walking through the palace, they passed a group of automatons building something on a conveyor belt. What they were building, Malock wasn't sure, as the group walked by too quickly for him to stay and watch, but he thought they must have been building more automatons because he saw bits and pieces of other automatons lying on the belt.

Finally, after walking for what felt like hours, they arrived in front of a surprisingly normal-looking wooden door. Hana walked over to a control panel next to it and input a complicated code that Malock couldn't follow; the next moment, the door swung open inwards and Hana bowed.

"After you," said Hana, gesturing at the open door.

Malock exchanged a look with the other hunters before he stepped through the door. The others followed and soon they were all standing inside a plain dining room. It was less claustrophobic than the rest of the palace, but the terrible scent of oil was still present.

A long dining table, covered with a variety of exotic dishes that Malock couldn't identify, was in the center of the room, with about six chairs on either side and one at each end. A white table cloth lay on top of it, which caught and reflected the light from the chandelier hanging from the ceiling. A single window stood open near the ceiling, well above their heads, and there was no other entrance or exit aside from the door behind them.

The door closed behind them as Hana entered last, spreading her arms wide as she did so. "Welcome to the dining room of the Mechanical Goddess. Please feel free to sit down and enjoy some delicious food, courtesy of yours truly."

Malock whirled around and pointed a finger at Hana. "All right. What's the catch?"

"Catch?" said Hana, folding her arms behind her back. "I have no idea what you're talking about."

Malock walked straight up to her and poked her in the chest. "You know what I mean. The Mechanical Goddess has gathered us all here for a reason. Is she going to eat us? I know the southern gods love to eat mortals."

Hana pushed Malock's finger away, looking disgusted as she did so. "Eat you? Hardly. Unlike the rest of her siblings, my mistress has lost her taste for mortal flesh. Nowadays, it's oil and steam for her. She says it tastes better than flesh and blood."

"Still confused here," said Jenur. "Why would she ever want to eat us? Gods don't eat mortals. That much I know."

Malock ignored Jenur's confusion, still looking at Hana. "So ... you're saying that she really does just want to have us over for dinner?"

Hana nodded. "Yes. As I said, my mistress is a gracious host. She knows how hungry you are, and can't stand to see you all looking so thin and sick."

"That food does smell awfully good," said Aseth, rubbing his stomach as he looked over at it, "even though I don't even know what most of it is."

"It's the finest food you will ever find on the entire southern seas," Hana assured him, looking over Malock's shoulder as she did so. "Please feel free to eat. I can assure you that it is all mortal-friendly."

"Don't change the subject," said Malock. "I don't get what's going on here and neither I nor any of my crew are going to touch even one chicken leg until we find out what is."

Hana pouted. "What do you want to know? You know the Mechanical Goddess rules this island, know she is friendly to mortals, and know that she's offering you the best meal you've probably had in a few months. There's really nothing else to say."

"Nothing else to say?" said Malock. "I doubt it. The ice walls, the mechanical palace, the automatons ... everything is fishy. Forgive me for not trusting a southern deity, especially one that acts inexplicably friendly to mortals."

Hana folded her arms across her chest. "What makes you think that knowledge will help you, if I choose to share it?"

"I don't know if it will," said Malock. "But I do know enough about the southern gods not to blindly trust them."

Hana brushed her hair out of her eyes, sighed, and said, "All right. I suppose it wouldn't hurt. Besides, your food needs time to set. The fried octopus limbs in particular should be eaten at least an hour after being taken out of the oven."

Malock glanced over his shoulder at the table and said, "*That's* what those things are? I thought they were digger wings."

Hana walked around Malock, tossing him an annoyed glared as she did so. Then she stopped near the table and said, "Let's begin with the ice walls, then."

"Yeah," said Malock. "Tell us about them. We've been dying to know."

Hana leaned against the table, scratching her chin as she did so. "Those were constructed years and years ago by Xocion, the God of Ice. He originally ruled this island, mostly because it's little more than an icy wasteland. I wasn't there when he ruled it—wasn't even born yet—but I've heard stories about how Xocion created the ice walls as a way to shut out the rest of the world so he could rest."

"Ah," said Malock. "I wonder why Bifor never mentioned that."

Hana glanced at the window, so quickly that Malock dismissed the movement as being his imagination. "Probably because that was before the time of humans or at least before humans started worshiping the gods like you do now. Not everything that happens on this world is related to you humans, you know. Plenty goes on that you don't even know about and that you never will know about simply because it does not concern you."

"Nice dig at us humans," said Jenur, rolling her eyes. "Real subtle."

"Thank you, human," said Hana, her voice positively dripping with sarcasm now. "You have once again proven to me why I prefer to work with southern gods over northern gods—less humans and the few humans that do come down this far usually become dinner."

"Still not sure what the difference between northern and southern gods is, by the way," Jenur said.

"No time to explain," said Malock, waving off Jenur's question. "Now, Hana, you said Xocion designed this to keep others away? If so, then how did the Mechanical Goddess end up becoming its ruler?"

Hana yawned, like she was bored, but he saw her eyes flicker to the window again, almost as if she was waiting for something to happen. "The Godly War happened, as you very well know. The War ended with the Powers dividing Martir between the northern and southern gods. Since Stalf is in the southern seas, Xocion had to relocate. Wasn't very happy about it, from what I heard, but the Treaty is immutable and so he had to move out. The Mechanical Goddess took it very quickly, seeing it as the ideal spot for her domain."

Malock quirked an eyebrow. "I would think a mechanical deity would like an industrialized island, filled with factories, better than a mostly undisturbed natural island."

Hana scratched the back of her neck. "Sure, she would, but really, the Mechanical Goddess prefers her solitude. She's not a big fan of living beings, to be honest, and the only living beings on Stalf are the various wild animals you guys were hunting, animals that can't talk and aren't interested in bothering a goddess."

"So ... is the Mechanical Goddess an actual machine?" said Jenur.

"Hardly," said Hana. "She's a living being, like the rest of the gods, even though she sometimes doesn't act like it. She simply looks mechanical, although I admit that she's also a lot less prone to injury than the other gods are, due to her tougher-than-nails skin."

"What about the automatons?" said Malock. "Where did those come from?"

"They're the Mechanical Goddess's children, of course," said Hana. "Born from her womb, like any infant. They live here, under her protection, doing whatever she asks, living life. They're rather strange, but rarely get into trouble and are generally helpful so I never complain about them."

"That conveyor belt back there," said Malock, jerking his thumb over his shoulder. "Were those automatons building more of their siblings?"

"What they were building is not any of your business, prince," said Hana in her sweetest voice, tinged with just a hint of danger. "All I can tell you is that the Mechanical Goddess considers them her children and is very protective of them, like any good mother would be. It's a good thing you didn't harm any of them, otherwise you would have found yourself being shredded to pieces inside the Maw."

"The what?"

"Not important," said Hana. She clapped her hands together and said, "But what is important is that I have answered your questions, I believe. So why don't you sit down and have some dinner? You all look very hungry, starving even. Eat as much as you like. Hell, take some back to your ship with you, for your crew, when you leave."

Aseth and Kocas took a few steps forward, their expressions hungry, but Malock held up a hand.

"Hold on," said Malock, eying Hana suspiciously. "Something is still off."

"And what might that be?" said Hana.

"Everything," said Malock. "If we're just guests, then why is the door locked? Why are we not allowed to leave? And why do you keep glancing at the window like you're expecting it to rain?"

Hana pushed herself off the table and said, "Well, I guess you were going to find out eventually. They should be here any minute now."

"Who should be here?" Malock said. "More guests?"

"The true guests, of course," said Hana. "You probably haven't met them before, but rest assured that they will not treat you badly."

"Oh," said Malock, sighing with relief. "For a moment there I thought the other guests were going to kill us."

Hana smiled. "Oh, they will most definitely kill you. Just not in a painful way, you get me?"

Malock wanted to say that no, he didn't 'get' her, but he was interrupted by the sound of a lightning bolt striking somewhere nearby, causing him and his hunters to jump. The clap of thunder was followed by a lightning bolt flashing through the window, going over the table, and slamming against the wall on the other end of the room, leaving a burnt mark where it had struck. The lightning bolt immediately stopped, floating and flashing in the air as it turned toward them.

Not a second after that, a whirlwind of leaves, thick and sharp at the edges, also flew in through the window. The leaves floated above the table, taking the shape of a skull, the eyeholes focused firmly and dangerously on Malock and the others.

Before Malock could completely register that thing's appearance, a thick white cloud squeezed through the open window. Its shape constantly shifted, at times resembling a human, other times a goat, but generally retaining a shapeless form like most clouds.

Hana spread her arms again, gesturing at the guests. "Meet the Cloud God, God of Clouds; the Leaf Goddess, Goddess of Leaves; and the Lightning Goddess, Goddess of Lightning and Electricity. They all had a very long, very tiring journey to get here, so as you can imagine, they're quite hungry ... hungry, that is, for human flesh, which I see you have plenty of."

Malock took a step back, his heart failing him at the sight of the three deities. Jenur was visibly trembling, her hand automatically reaching for the knife that was no longer there. Aseth had actually fainted, while Kocas looked like she would rather be anywhere else than here.

Hana brought her hands together, her eyes glinting with glee. She turned to the deities and said, "Now, honored guests of the Mechanical Goddess, dinner is served."

"Kinker?"

The old man looked up and saw Deddio standing before him. The younger man was a mess, with a bloody gash running down his left arm and his hair ripped off completely in several places. Nonetheless, he was still alive, which Kinker silently thanked Kano for.

"Deddio?" said Kinker, pushing himself just high enough off the floor so he could get a good look at his fellow fisherman. "What are you doing down here? Shouldn't you be top deck fighting the baba raga?"

Deddio shook his head. "Was about to ask you the same question. The battle is getting worse. Another dozen baba raga showed up. Don't know how many people we've lost, but I figure the number is grim. I came down here to look for any weapons I could use."

"Is the Tusked God still there?" Kinker said.

"He is," said Deddio. "He's just watching us fight his followers like it's a play. He hasn't done much yet, but I'm thinking he's getting restless because he's taken to picking off random sailors whenever he feels like it."

"Not good," Kinker said. "But he won't be that way for long.

Help me up. We need to get to the cannons. Now."

Deddio looked at Kinker in confusion. "The cannons? What do you intend to do, blow the ship sky high?"

"No," said Kinker through gritted teeth. "Do you know how to work the cannons?"

"Sure," said Deddio. "It's what I was originally trained to do, in fact. Do you need my help?"

"Yes," said Kinker. "Because we're gonna blow that god straight to the bottom of the sea."

Deddio's face became even paler than before. "You're saying we should fire a cannon at a god."

"Preferably multiple, but yes," said Kinker. "It's the only way we can get him off our asses. You in or not?"

Deddio put his knuckle against his lips, as he always did whenever he was uncertain about something. "I don't know. That sounds awfully risky. What if it doesn't work?"

"Do you have any better ideas?" Kinker snapped, not even bothering to put up a pretense of civility anymore. "If we do nothing, he'll smash the ship into splinters and kill everyone on it. At least this has a chance of helping us survive, even if the odds are low."

"Fine," said Deddio, holding up his hands in defeat. "You're absolutely right. I don't know have any better ideas and honestly that sounds a hell of a lot better than getting mauled by a baba raga."

"Good man," said Kinker. "Now help me. Carefully, now, because my back hurts."

Deddio was by Kinker's side in an instant. He draped one of Kinker's arms around his shoulders and hefted the fisherman to his feet. Kinker let out a loud groan of pain, causing Deddio to say, "Kinker, you all right?"

"Doesn't matter," Kinker said. "We need to get to the cannon room as quickly as possible. No delays."

Fortunately, Deddio was a good listener. And despite being badly wounded himself, Deddio managed to keep them both upright, though their progress was inevitably slow thanks to Kinker's almost complete inability to stand on his own. Kinker tried his best to help, but he was so weak and tired and in pain from his climbing up and down the ladders that he could not do much except try to be less heavy.

The two fishermen made their way down the hall, Kinker's feet half-dragging across the floor. The sounds of battle coming from above were barely muffled by the boards above them. A small drop of blood fell on Kinker's head as they walked, but whether it was the blood of a friend or foe, he could not tell. He just hoped that his plan would work, that the cannons were still in one piece.

And, as it turned out, they were. They came upon the cannon room, which thankfully turned out to have not been destroyed. Unfortunately, the cannon windows were closed, probably due to how rarely the cannons were used, and the cannons themselves—about a dozen in all—were lined up against the opposite wall, with barrels of gunpowder and boxes of cannonballs stacked nearby. One box of cannonballs had fallen over, but the vast majority of them somehow seemed to have remained steady despite the relentless attacks by the Tusked God's followers.

Deddio let Kinker down near the door and said, "You stay here while I prepare a cannon."

"Can't you prepare multiple?" Kinker asked.

Deddio shook his head. "Not without ten other men. It will probably take me several minutes just to prepare one."

Kinker cursed. "Just do it as quickly as you can, then. Is there anything I can do in the meantime?"

Deddio pulled out the top drawer of a nearby chest of drawers and thrust it into Kinker's lap. "Look for the matches. We're going to need them if we're going to blow that damn god to hell."

Kinker nodded as he frantically searched through the drawer. It seemed like everything in the ship was in this drawer, from a piece of paper that appeared to be part of a map to a handful of gunpowder that got up his nose and made him sneeze. There was a little bit of everything except, it seemed, the matches themselves.

Nearby, Deddio had already filled one of the cannons with gunpowder. Now he was trying his best to move one of the cannonballs from the ones on the floor to the cannon itself, but they were clearly too heavy for him. He heaved and struggled, but he could only do it one-armed due to how wounded his other arm was. Kinker wanted to help, would have helped, but he doubted his back would have agreed to it.

Somehow, Deddio succeeded in lifting one of the cannonballs— which probably only weighed about eight pounds, by the look of it— and shoved it into the cannon's barrel. A loud clunk told Kinker that the cannonball was now sitting securely within the cannon; just in time, too, because Kinker found a small bland cardboard box with the word 'MATCHES' written on it.

"I found the matches," said Kinker, holding up the box. "Take it!"

Deddio ran over and took the box of matches from Kinker's hand. Unfortunately, Kinker had been gripping the box too tightly because it ripped apart and matches went everywhere, causing Deddio to drop to his hands and knees and start collecting as many of the little bastards as he could.

"You don't need them all, do you?" said Kinker in annoyance. "Just grab one and light the damn thing already."

Deddio had about four in his hands, but when he heard Kinker's order, he got unsteadily to his feet and ran back to the cannon. He got behind it and started to push it across the the floor, but the cannon was clearly too heavy for him to move on his own. He got maybe an inch before collapsing, panting hard and groaning as his arm continued to bleed.

"No use," Deddio gasped. "Can't do it. Can't push it."

"Yes, you can," said Kinker, feeling his temper rising. "Just do it, man. If you don't, then you can say good bye to ever seeing the Northern Isles again."

That little pep talk didn't seem to do Deddio much good. He just lay there, looking utterly defeated.

Kinker opened his mouth to yell again, but he didn't get a chance because an ominous creaking sound caused him to look at the wall where the cannon was supposed to fire from. A second later, the wall went flying off, letting in a blast of cold wind and revealing the Tusked God, who had apparently ripped off that part of the wall with his tongue.

The Tusked God pulled the chunk of wood into its mouth and crunched on it loudly enough for the sound to rise above the screams of people and the roars of baba raga, a sound which was amplified now that there was nothing between it and Kinker.

Deddio stared in shock, but Kinker yelled at him, "The match, Deddio, the match! Blow that motherfucker to hell!"

Deddio shook his head and immediately lit his match on the back end of the cannon. He grabbed the cannon's fuse, but before he could light it, the Tusked God's tongue shot out again and wrapped around Deddio. Kinker barely had time to yell out Deddio's name before the fisherman was yanked out of the room and into the open maw of the Tusked God, where he disappeared in a scream and flash of blood.

Kinker tried to scream, but he seemed to have lost his voice because he couldn't hear himself scream. He just sat there, with his mouth open, watching as the Tusked God munched contentedly on Deddio's bones. The deity didn't seem to notice Kinker, but that didn't make him feel better at all.

Deddio's dead, Kinker thought. *The ship is falling apart. Most of the crew is probably dead or about to die. Malock and the others are probably dead, too, I imagine. This must be how we all die.*

Then Kinker felt a few pieces of wood nearby. He wrapped his fingers around them and brought them up to his face.

They were matches, some of the ones that Deddio had failed to pick up. Kinker looked at the cannon and noticed how close the fuse was to him. It was just out of his reach, but if he crawled over to it ...

Kinker got on his hands and knees and crawled over to the fuse as quickly as he could. Every moment he remained aware of the Tusked

God, expecting any second now to be noticed and devoured just like Deddio. But he couldn't stop, not even with his back hurting as badly as it was, not until he reached the fuse and lit it.

Once he was close enough, he reached out with his free hand and wrapped his fingers around the end of the fuse. Hands trembling, Kinker tried to light the matches, but every time he did, a strong gust of gelid wind would blow it out and he'd have to try again. He went through three matches—far too many—before the fourth one lit and stay lit.

Then he brought the match to the fuse's tip and it caught fire. Kinker let out a hoarse whoop and looked up at the Tusked God, who was now looking at him with hungry eyes.

So Kinker shook his fist at the Tusked God and said, in a weak voice, "See you at the bottom of the sea, you son of a bitch."

The Tusked God opened its mouth, probably to snatch him up just like Deddio, but it didn't get the chance. The fuse reached the end and with an almighty *boom* a single cannonball flew out of the cannon's barrel directly into the Tusked God's gaping mouth.

The cannonball must have gone deep because the Tusked God gagged and coughed. A moment later, flames and smoke burst from the Tusked God's mouth, scorching its tongue and tusks. The Tusked God howled in pain, thrashing about in the icy waters, acting more like a wounded animal than a powerful god now.

Kinker figured that the Tusked God would kill them all now, but much to his surprise, the Tusked God sank back beneath the water instead. Its growls and moans of pain disappeared as it vanished beneath the waves of Stalf Bay and not a minute later the baba raga threw themselves over the side of the ship and into the water below. Kinker watched them fall, hoping against hope that they wouldn't notice him, but they seemed to be retreating now because they didn't even stop, not even when one landed on the floor in front of him. Soon they were all gone and the entire ship was silent.

Until now, Kinker hadn't realized just how tired he was. When he thought about this, his eyes drooped, his shoulders slumped, and he immediately drifted off into unconsciousness, unsure if he would ever awake again.

Chapter Seventeen

THE THREE DEITIES BEGAN to advance, eager to eat. Malock was too shocked to come up with a plan. Behind him he heard Aseth struggling to open the door, pounding at it, with Kocas yelling at him to pound at it faster. Jenur just stood nearby, perhaps having come to the same conclusion as Malock: that is, there was no point in trying to run because there was no place they could run to.

Then Malock got an idea. The same idea that he had used to make the Loner God spare his life, actually. He figured it would have to work; after all, these three gods were probably under the same Treaty as the Loner God, which meant that all he needed to do was announce his status as Kano's chosen and he'd be safe.

So Malock stepped forward, putting on his bravest expression, folded his arms over his chest, and said, "Halt, southern deities. I am Prince Malock, the Chosen One of Kano. You cannot harm me, as per the Treaty."

That actually worked. The three deities ceased moving and, although they all lacked eyeballs, Malock thought they were all looking at him now. Good.

"You can smell Kano on me, I'm sure," said Malock. "And you know that the Treaty prevents you from harming me, a mortal who is under her protection. I suggest you three go home now and get your dinner elsewhere. My crew is off-limits."

His smile quickly fell off his face, however, when the three deities scattered. The Leaf Goddess and the Cloud God flew past him toward Kocas and Aseth, who had failed to open the door and were now screaming their heads off. The Lightning Goddess made a move toward Jenur, but that girl was faster than lightning because she was now clinging to Malock like an octopus.

"Jenur?" said Malock, looking at her in surprise. "What are you doing?"

"You're Kano's Chosen One, right?" said Jenur. "I don't understand all this talk about this Treaty, but I do get that these guys can't hurt you. So I figure that I'll be okay as long as I stay close to you. Can't hurt me without hurting you."

Malock was not sure that it worked like that, but perhaps it did because the Lightning Goddess didn't try to attack them. She flashed this way and that, moved forward and backed off, but she didn't actually touch them. She succeeded in looking intimidating, but not much else.

Figuring they were safe for now, Malock glanced over his shoulder and felt his heart fail him again. The Cloud God and the Leaf Goddess had made short work of Kocas and Aseth. The two hunters didn't even have skin on their bones anymore. They just lay against the door, their white bones splattered with blood, bits of clothes hanging off their bones. The two deities were making strange munching noises, even though they lacked mouths.

Then Malock looked back at the Lightning Goddess, who was still thundering and flashing. Behind her, Hana was leaning against the table, looking amused.

"I think we're at a stalemate here, Hana," said Malock, raising his voice to be heard over the sounds of the gods. "I know your gods want Jenur, but I'm not going to give her up and they aren't going to attack her without harming me. Your only option now is to let us go."

Hana shrugged. "You'll have to barter for your freedom with them. They're reasonable deities. I'm sure they'll be willing to let their dinner go free."

Malock grit his teeth, but before he could respond, the Cloud God and the Leaf Goddess appeared, circling the two surviving hunters like hawks. The Lightning Goddess joined them, but like before she did not attack. Still, Malock had a feeling that eventually one of them would try something and he had a good feeling it would be the Lightning Goddess, even though he did not know her well enough to be sure about that.

How are we going to get out of this? Malock thought. *I can get out, of course, but Jenur can't. Unless I give her up, but I can't do that. I'm not going to betray her again.*

"Any ideas?" Malock muttered to Jenur, who was clinging even more closely to his body than before.

Jenur winced when the Lightning Goddess flashed again. "No. I'm pretty sure we're both gonna die."

"That's encouraging," said Malock. "You're just a barrel of

sunshine, aren't you?"

Jenur glared at him in annoyance, which looked more threatening than it should have when the Lightning God's light reflected off her eyes. "Hard to be a barrel of sunshine when there are three very hungry gods that want to eat you for dinner."

Malock shrugged. "Good point. Still, I would have thought you would have come up with something by now. You showed some quick-thinking when you defeated the Gray Pirates back there."

"This time, my mind's shot," said Jenur. "Sorry."

"We can't stay here forever," said Malock, looking at the circling gods. "We'll die of starvation or get tired or something else will happen. And you certainly can't cling to my arm forever."

"Yeah, I know," said Jenur with a gulp. "I really am starting to wish that I'd learned some magic back home. Or that Bifor was with us."

"Maybe I can bargain with them," said Malock. "Surely they must be reasonable beings who—"

Jenur put a hand over his mouth. "Don't."

Malock ripped her hand off his mouth and glared at her. "What?"

"They aren't reasonable," Jenur said, wincing as one of the Leaf Goddess's leaves scratched her cheek. "They're nothing more than forces of nature. You can't reason with a lightning bolt or a cloud."

Malock didn't want to admit it, but she did have a point. As far as he could tell, the three deities didn't even speak Divina. He could tell they were listening to their conversation, waiting for the right moment to strike. He was not going to let them find that opportunity, not if he could help it.

Beyond the circling gods, Hana continued to lean against the table, her arms folded across her chest and her face alight with the most arrogant smirk Malock had ever seen on another being. She seemed unlikely to aid them and her mistress, the Mechanical Goddess, probably wasn't going to do it, either, because it was obvious that the Mechanical Goddess had taken Malock and his party deep into her body so they couldn't escape.

She must feed them, Malock realized. *The Mechanical Goddess lures in mortals so her brothers and sisters can feast without having to hunt them down themselves. Very sly, that one is.*

Of course, that realization didn't help him. All it told him was that the Mechanical Goddess was a cold-hearted bitch whose only concern, perhaps, was how to clean up the bones and blood that the other gods left behind. Maybe they would be dumped into that 'Maw' that Hana mentioned earlier, though as far as Malock could see, the room only had two exits, the door behind him and the window above him, and both were out of his reach.

He glanced down at his feet and noticed something odd about the square of floor that he and Jenur stood on. Though it appeared perfectly flush with the rest of the floor, he noticed the tiniest of hairline cracks around it, like a square. It almost looked like a trapdoor, but why would the Mechanical Goddess have a trapdoor built in her dining room like this?

It's probably the trash compactor, Malock thought. *If it opens, Jenur and I will be shredded into pieces. Would that be better or worse than being eaten alive by a bunch of hungry gods, I wonder?*

Of course, Malock had no way of knowing whether that actually led to the Maw. What it if was actually an escape hatch? It might lead outside the palace, perhaps even outside the ice walls. If that was true, then he needed to figure out a way to open it. He couldn't open it, however, because he would have to move to open it and if he moved then the gods might try to attack Jenur. He saw no way out of it.

As it transpired, Malock didn't need to do anything because the panel fell out underneath them on its own. Malock and Jenur had only a brief moment to exchange a look before they fell screaming. The Lightning Goddess hurled a lightning bolt at them as they fell, but luckily it only skirted the top of Jenur's hair.

The fall quickly transformed into a slide, but it was narrow and reeked of blood and filth. It was also extremely dark, especially when the hole from which they fell covered itself again. The slide twisted and turned, Malock and Jenur clinging to each other to avoid being separated. Malock didn't know where this tunnel led or why it had opened. Nor did he think about the fact that they were in the bowels of a goddess, albeit a mechanical one.

At first, the slide was silent, save for their own screams and shouts. Then, the further they went, the louder certain sounds became. Even with the wind rushing by, Malock thought the noises sounded like the drums of Grinf, but the closer they got, the more he realized they were the sounds of machinery at work, pounding and beating against each other, but he couldn't see the machinery and frankly he wasn't sure that he wanted to.

Not that he had much of a choice in the matter. With the sounds came light, a dark, reddish light that made Malock feel woozy. The light revealed just how narrow the tunnel was; the ceiling couldn't have been more than a few feet above them. The light itself seemed to be coming from up ahead, causing Malock to raise his head just high enough to get a look at what it was.

Up ahead—steadily drawing nearer every second—was what looked like the maw of a giant monster. Huge metal teeth clanged open and closed so rapidly, Malock figured he and Jenur would be turned into little more than scraps of skin and bone if they passed through them. Even worse, there was no way to stop, no way to halt, no way even to slow down, no way to save themselves from their inevitably gruesome fate.

But at the last minute, another route opened right next to the compactor and the slide shifted abruptly so they went down that way instead. That miraculous bit of luck surprised Malock, but he quickly became worried that this route would take them to a worse place. He imagined a pit of molten lava, like the kind he had read about in history books back on Carnag, which in the past had been used to torture or kill prisoners.

Yet the tunnel slide simply went on and on, becoming narrower and bumpier, but otherwise not ending in death. They did pick up speed, but Malock felt no increase in temperature and saw nothing to indicate that death was just around the corner.

They rounded a corner and immediately a light appeared at the end of the tunnel. The next minute, he and Jenur went flying out of the tunnel, tumbling through the air, and landed in a shallow pit of water. The water was ice cold and made Malock gasp and shiver, but he quickly recovered and got to his feet, helping Jenur up as he did so. Then they looked around at their surroundings, trying to figure out exactly where they had ended up.

Much to Malock's surprise, it was the same cove where they had landed their rowboat several hours earlier. Not only that, but the rowboat itself was still there, causing Malock to actually hug the rowboat's prow, saying as he did so, "We're saved, we're saved, thank the gods we're saved!"

Jenur tapped Malock's shoulder. He looked up at her and saw that she was looking out at the sea. "What's the problem, Jenur? Aren't you happy that we miraculously escaped? Kano must have rescued us."

Jenur nodded, still not looking at him, perhaps not even listening to him. "The ship ..."

Frowning, Malock looked out over Stalf Bay, wondering what Jenur was talking about. But when he finally spotted the *Iron Wind* —saw that it was missing its mainmast and that its port had been ripped off entirely—any good or happy feelings he'd felt since escaping the Mechanical Goddess left him entirely, leaving a hollow, horrified emptiness in the pit of his stomach.

Chapter Eighteen

THE ROWBOATS WERE DESIGNED for four people to row, so it was supremely difficult to row it across Stalf Bay with only two people, even when Malock and Jenur put their backs into it. Nonetheless, Malock and Jenur rowed forth with all their might, although the *Iron Wind* was in such shabby condition that he wondered if anyone was still alive on the ship at all.

As it turned out, there were still people alive on the ship, but not nearly as many as when Malock first left. According to Banika, who had a makeshift bandaged wrapped around her head, a giant monster calling itself the Tusked God had attacked the ship with a small army of baba raga. The men had been on the losing end of the battle before Kinker fired a cannon at the Tusked God, forcing it to retreat, but not before they lost a staggering twenty sailors, about eleven humans and nine aquarians. The wounded were far greater, encompassing nearly every member of the crew that hadn't been killed in the battle.

Malock found out that Vashnas was not among the nine

aquarians who died in the assault (thankfully). Nonetheless, her limp was far more pronounced now and she shook when he hugged her. Still, she was alive and that was what mattered to Malock, who kept her in his stateroom to heal up.

As for the ship itself, it looked ready to fall apart at the slightest touch. Aside from the obvious missing mainmast and port, the foremast and mainmast had also taken significant damage. The deck had holes punched in it and several of the stays had been cut. The foremast's sail had even been cut down entirely, which had apparently crushed a sailor who had been unlucky enough to be standing below it at the time.

The enemy, according to Banika, lost maybe a dozen, possibly less. That seemed like a lot, until Banika informed Malock that the baba raga had numbered three or four dozen, meaning it wasn't quite as much as it could have been. Yet even that was not the best news because the dozen dead baba raga were credited with at least half of the crew deaths and more than half of the crew's injuries.

It was after this that Malock realized he needed to tell the crew about the true nature of the southern gods. He gathered those who were not dead and told them all that the Loner God had told him about the northern/southern divide, but most of the sailors did not appear to be paying attention or to care and those that did looked bitter, like they were wondering why Malock had failed to tell them this in the first place. When Malock thought about it, he realized that telling them this really didn't help them in any way. All it did was encourage a few sailors to toss their amulets overside, amulets that they had devoted to their gods, and among those few sailors, more than a few swore never to serve any god ever again.

From what Malock saw of the ship's damage, he did not think that they could repair the ship. Before the Tusked God's attack, they had already struggled to make basic repairs. With the mainmast at the bottom of the sea, the port in the Tusked God's stomach, and the rest of the ship in little better shape, Malock was convinced that there was absolutely nothing they could do to repair the *Iron Wind*. He was surprised it had not already fallen apart.

True, Stalf did have a lot of wood, but they did not have the tools necessary to chop down those trees or turn them into wood suitable for sailing. Even if they could chop down the trees, they had no way to haul the wood to the ship itself because almost the entire crew was in no shape to be doing intense physical labor of any sort.

For the first time on this voyage, Malock had to admit that they were defeated. He fully expected the Lightning Goddess, the Leaf Goddess, and the Cloud God to appear and finish them all off. He saw no reason for them not to; after all, the crew was in no position to fight back and even if they were there was no way they could defeat three gods. So when he awoke the next morning, he was surprised to find that none of those gods had attacked.

Another first for Malock was his taking a real part in the recovery efforts. Ranof and Bifor used their knowledge of medicine and magic to heal as many of the men as they could, but the two of them by themselves were incapable of making sure every sailor got the aid he or she needed. So Malock volunteered to help and put himself under Ranof's authority, doing whatever the doctor ordered him to.

That was how Malock found himself, not long after lunchtime on the first day after the Tusked God's attack, changing the dressings on an aquarian sailor named Vank. Vank had a squid-like head and had lost an entire arm to a particularly violent baba raga during the battle. His 'dressings'— really just a bunch of old dirty rags tied around his stump—needed to be changed every few hours, which wasn't a very fun task because every time Malock changed them, he got a good look at Vank's dried up stump, and its smell and appearance made his stomach lurch.

They were in the middle deck, in the hallway. The other rooms were full of resting wounded sailors, so more than a few were forced to rest in the hallway. The wounded had been moved below deck to keep them out of the snow that had started falling. Even then, though, it wasn't perfect. The big gaping hole, where the port had been, allowed the icy wind to blow through freely, even after they closed the door to the cannon room.

At that moment, a particularly strong gust of wind passed through the cracks in the door, making Malock shiver. That was nothing in comparison to Vank, who shivered so violently that he looked like he was about to die.

"Here," said Malock as he took off his coat and put it over Vank, like a blanket. "You need this far more than I do."

"Thank you, Captain," said Vank, whose voice was strained. He coughed up some blood on Malock's coat (which Malock didn't mind at all) and said, "Sir? Can I tell you something?"

Malock was just about to get up, as he had other patients to attend to, but he stopped before he could do so. "What is it, Vank? I'm all ears."

Vank looked extremely embarrassed, ashamed even, but he said, "Sir, I no longer ... I don't care about the gods anymore."

Malock blinked. "What do you mean?"

"I mean I don't worship any, don't pay homage to any, don't care about 'em at all anymore," said Vank. "I used to be a follower of Yaona, the Goddess of Music, because back home I was something of a musician and most musicians worship her. Now, though ... she can take that guitar of hers and shove it straight up her ass."

Malock bit his lower lip. "Why are you showing such disdain to the gods?"

"Sir, it's because of what's happened recently," said Vank, looking at Malock with a steely gaze. "A god tried to kill us and another three gods tried to kill you and Jenur. And then there's this whole northern/southern crap and I'm convinced that the gods are no longer worth worshiping at all. They're just like us mortals, except worse."

Malock had to admit that Vank had a point, but he said in a voice he no longer believed, "Not all of the gods are bad, Vank. Kano is good."

Vank snorted. "If Kano is so good, why has she not saved us? Why did she stand aside as the Tusked God ravaged our ship and killed or wounded our men? She is no better than any of the others. That is what I believe, sir, and if you think that makes me deserving of punishment or whatever, I'll take whatever you choose to do to me."

Under ordinary circumstances, Malock would have punished Vank. He did not tolerate heathens, those who refused to give the gods the honor and respect they deserved. Heathenism was a crime on

Carnag and most of the Northern Isles and it was a crime that he was always happy to see punished, as it was on his top ten list of worst crimes anyone can commit, right below murder and just above rape.

Yet Malock felt no rage at Vank's words. He felt nothing at all. All he did was nod and say, "I'm not going to punish you, Vank. After what we've all been through, punishment is the last thing we need."

Vank let out a long sigh of relief. "That's good. I thought you were actually going to punish me there for a moment."

"Just rest here," said Malock. "Don't move too much and try to drink as much water as you can. If your stump itches, don't scratch it because it should go away in a few hours."

Vank nodded as someone behind Malock said, "You're starting to sound more like a doctor than a captain now, Malock."

Malock turned around and saw that it was Kinker. Kinker was one of the few sailors to have avoided taking any life-threatening wounds, but he had not been helping in the recovery period because his back hurt him too badly for him to help.

Yet Kinker now stood before him, leaning on a chunk of wood like a walking stick, looking quite serious.

"Hello, Kinker," said Malock. "Is your back feeling better now?"

Kinker grunted and rubbed his back with his free hand. "Hardly. If anything, I'd say it's gotten worse. I just wanted to talk with you in private for a moment. Would that be fine?"

Malock rubbed his elbow. "I still have some patients to get to—"

"So?" said Kinker. "Not to be cruel, but there is little you can do for the majority of them. I have a feeling we'll be seeing more deaths in the coming days. Have you seen Bifor and Ranof? They both look like they're about to drop dead from exhaustion themselves."

"All right," said Malock. "I'll talk. Just for a few minutes, though."

"A few minutes is all I'll need of your time," said Kinker. "To make this private, how's about we go talk top deck?"

"All right," said Malock. "Lead the way."

It took them very little time to reach the top deck. Kinker walked over to the stump that was all that was left of the mainmast and sat stood beside it. There was no one else top deck besides them. It was snowing lightly, making Malock shiver. Off the port, the island of Stalf was still visible.

"All right," said Malock, hugging himself to keep warm. "We're here. What do you want to talk about?"

Kinker's eyes were looking out to the sea, like he was completely lost in the ocean's waves. "Everything."

Malock quirked an eyebrow. "That's a wide subject."

"I mean everything that has happened so far," said Kinker with a frustrated sigh. "Malock, I know you are young, but I didn't think you were dense."

"Excuse me, elder, for not knowing what you meant when you only spoke one word," said Malock. "Perhaps you're going senile in your old age. My grandfather started losing his mind when he got to your age, Kinker. I suspect the same may be happening to you."

Kinker raised his makeshift walking stick like he was going to pound Malock with it, but he let it down and said, "Fighting will do us no good. The only thing that will help us in this situation is to talk."

"About what?" said Malock. "Everything?"

"The voyage," said Kinker. "I am not the only member of the crew who suspects that this entire voyage is a fool's errand. Quite a few sailors just want to go home."

"But we can't," Malock said. "I've made that clear already. Besides the simple fact that I want to keep going, there is the fact that the ship is in no condition to be sailing and the sailors are in no condition to take it back north."

"Your naivety is so interesting, Malock," said Kinker, shaking his head. "Do you think that the crew really cares about any of that? They just want to go home and not have to deal with crazy gods and pirates and spies and other things like that. I agree with them and I don't even want to go back to Destan."

Malock's hands balled into fists, but he tried to keep his voice as level as he could. "Do you think I just woke up one day and decided I wanted to go on this voyage? That I wanted to explore the most dangerous, unexplored seas in the world for fun? I went on this voyage only because Kano summoned me. And you do *not* ignore the calls of a goddess, no matter how much you want to."

Kinker pursed his lips. "Then maybe that's the problem. Maybe you should have told Kano, 'Thanks, but no thanks.' Maybe people wouldn't have needed to die if you had shown more spine."

"Shown more spine?" Malock repeated in horror. "Kinker, I never thought I'd hear you say such a thing. Where I grew up, elders are the most pious, religious, and faithful of all. They regularly attend services, pray to the gods, and will answer their summons even in their old age. My own grandfather actually met Grinf once."

"Not everyone everywhere is like your elders," said Kinker. "I still follow Kano and yet ... as this voyage continues, I am starting to doubt that you were ever contacted by her at all. Perhaps you simply dreamed of Kano and mistook your dream of her for the real thing."

Malock walked up to Kinker, closing the distance between their faces to only a few inches. "You. Don't. Understand. Kano *did* contact me. I know it was her. It wasn't just a simple dream. It was an actual summons from the Goddess of the Sea herself."

Kinker leaned back, looking disgusted, and said, "Yet you offer no proof of that claim. The other sailors have noticed this complete lack of proof and it has done nothing to quell the mutiny that is boiling under your very nose."

Malock pulled back and turned away. "A mutiny certainly would be the most intelligent thing to do in this situation. After all, we all know the *real* reason we can't go anywhere is because I'm the problem. Not, you know, the fact that the ship is irreparably damaged or anything."

"All I'm saying is that you should address their concerns," said Kinker. "If you truly believe that this voyage is not pointless, that we will succeed, then show us why."

"Because ..." Malock struggled to think of a reason. "Because I don't think Kano would have summoned me if she didn't think I could make it."

Kinker let out a noise of disgust. "That is still not good enough. People have died on this voyage, Malock. Not just the ones we lost yesterday or even a few weeks ago back on Ikadori Island. I'm talking about the other ships, the ones that were part of the fleet. How many people were there per ship? I'm guessing a few hundred each. That's nearly a thousand lives lost because what, you thought a goddess summoned you?"

Malock turned back around to face Kinker. He could feel his face turning red, but there was nothing he could do to hide it. "Their deaths are regrettable, but that's what happens on these kinds of voyages and they all knew that going into it. I'm not responsible for whatever happened to them."

"You are the Captain of this ship," said Kinker, pointing at him with his stick. "The Captain is responsible for the wellbeing of every member of his crew. If you don't like that, then maybe you should step down from your position as Captain and give it to someone who actually gives a damn."

"Don't talk to me that way," said Malock. "I'm still your Captain; more than that, I am your prince."

Kinker laughed. "My prince? I am from Destan, not Carnag. You seem to have forgotten that your giant boot factory of an island isn't the entire world."

"Giant boot factory?" said Malock. "That is such a simple insult that I would be laughing at it right now if I wasn't so pissed off at you."

Kinker sighed. "Look, Malock, I am trying to help you. I am trying to make you aware of these problems. We have almost no edible food or drinkable water, the ship is basically a big floating piece of wood, we've lost so many sailors now that it doesn't even hurt anymore, and the rest of the crew is too injured to perform even the most basic of repairs on the ship. That's why I speak harshly and bluntly."

Malock didn't know what to do or say. All of those challenges Kinker mentioned were all very real and very true. He could not think of any way to fix them, no way to convince Kinker (or anyone else) that it was all going to work out in the end because as far as he could tell, it was not.

"Oh, and did I forget to mention that more and more sailors are starting to hate the gods?" Kinker said. "And not without reason, mind you. Those southern gods are absolutely vicious. And the northern gods have a mixed track record of being reliable and unreliable in equal measures. What say you to that?"

Malock put his head in his hands, not wanting Kinker to see his face. "I ... I don't know what to say to that."

Kinker's shoulder slumped. "And neither do I. None of us do. Perhaps none of us ever will."

Later that day, yet another collective funeral was held for the sailors who had died in the attack. As usual, they were dumped into the ocean. There was no eulogy given, mostly because the rest of the sailors were too wounded, tired, and defeated to think of any inspiring words to say. A few more precious amulets devoted to the gods went overside with the corpses, though Malock did not know who put them there.

Not only that, but they lost three more sailors to infection and cold shortly after the funeral. One of them would have been Arisha Frag, their cook, but luckily Bifor managed to cast a healing spell on her that kept her from dying. If they'd lost their cook, Malock was certain they would really be screwed.

Malock spent most of his free time looking at Stalf and the giant ice walls that protected the Mechanical Goddess. He kept wondering when those other gods were going to reappear, knowing as he did that they loved to eat humans. He didn't think that any of his men looked particularly tasty, but he doubted that those gods cared about that. He doubted they care about anything except filling their stomachs with mortal flesh and blood.

One thought that did stray across Malock's mind every now and then was Vashnas. Because he had volunteered to help take care of the sick and wounded sailors, he didn't get to see her nearly as much as he would have liked. She was recovering in his stateroom, which had somehow evaded destruction during the battle, and unlike the others didn't suffer from any terrible injuries, so Malock had little reason to spend much time with her.

But he did think about her. So far, her information about the southern seas had been spotty at best. Yes, Ikadori Island and Stalf did indeed exist and they were how she had described them, yet her information was clearly incomplete because she didn't know anything about the Loner God or the Mechanical Goddess or the automatons or anything. He didn't want to, but he was becoming more and more forced to conclude that Vashnas may have an agenda of her own, one that ran counter to his, but for the life of him he could not figure out what that agenda was.

He had no one to discuss these ideas with because he had always publicly displayed his support for Vashnas. The rest of the crew didn't like her as much as he did and if he tried to talk with any of them about it, it might somehow get to Vashnas's ears and that would get him into trouble. He couldn't even talk to Banika about it, mostly because of paranoia.

The sun set and the ship got even colder. Malock cuddled with Vashnas in his stateroom, but he remained all too aware of the moaning sailors, some of whom he allowed to stay in his stateroom until they were better. He wished there was something he could do to help, but for now he was utterly powerless.

In the morning, Malock was awoken early by Banika. He and Vashnas were cuddled together under his boat cloak, and all he wanted to do was sleep. So when Banika shook him slightly, muttering in a low voice, "Captain, wake up, there's something you have to see," Malock waved his hand at her and said, in a half-asleep voice, "No. I'm sleeping. Bother me later."

"It's urgent," said Banika. "She says she's not going to wait any longer if she can't see you."

Malock looked up at Banika and blinked. "She?"

Banika nodded. "A woman. Not just a woman, but ... well, I think you should see for yourself."

Malock got up when she said that, but carefully so that Vashnas wouldn't wake up. He pulled on his boat cloak, wrapped the blanket more tightly around Vashnas's sleeping form, and followed Banika out of the stateroom, stepping over or around the other sleeping sailors who had taken up residence in this place.

The morning air outside the stateroom was crisp and cold. He shook violently when he felt it, but he got over it quickly when he spotted the woman Banika had spoken of standing at the stump where the mainmast had stood. Though she wore furs now, Malock had no trouble recognizing her at all, her very appearance spiking his anger to new levels.

"Hanarova," said Malock as he and Banika stopped several feet from her. "Did the Mechanical Goddess send you to recapture me and Jenur?"

The katabans grinned. "Nah. The Mechanical Goddess has better things to do than kill a couple of disrespectful mortals with inflated egos."

Malock scowled. "Are you working for those other gods now? Because if you are—"

"Nope," said Hana, shaking her head. "Those three left when you guys escaped. They said the Mechanical Goddess let you free. Said they're not going to speak to her ever again, but they said that before. I imagine they'll be back in a couple hundred years when they fail to catch any mortals on their own and need something to sate their hunger."

Malock cocked his head to the side. "Then why are you here? Are you going to kick us while we're down? If so, you picked the perfect opportunity to do so."

Hana laughed. "Wrong again. The Mechanical Goddess didn't realize you were a Chosen One of Kano and feels rather awful for almost feeding you to her siblings. Though Kano is a northern goddess and she is a southern, she and Kano have generally gotten along pretty well. Therefore, the Mechanical Goddess has sent me to oversee a group of automatons who will repair your ship and make it better than new."

Malock's eyes widened and Banika actually gasped.

"No need to be so astonished," said Hana. "My mistress is a very generous goddess. She would rather that your boat not stink up the waters around her island anyway."

Malock shook his head. "No way. This has got to be a gigantic joke. You're going to reveal that you're actually going to kill us. Right?"

"If you're so skeptical, take a look over yonder," said Hana, gesturing with her head over to the starboard side. "Seeing is believing, isn't it?"

Malock, feeling as skeptical as Hana seemed to think he was, walked over to the starboard with Banika by his side and looked overside. He was surprised by what he saw.

Floating in the water by the *Iron Wind*'s side was a large platform that had a crane, several tons of wood, several large crates, and many other things resting upon its surface. Standing upon it were two or three dozen automatons, all identical in appearance. Around their waists were tied tool bags, with hammers, saws, and a variety of other tools Malock couldn't even name. They all stood at attention, like soldiers awaiting orders from their general.

"It's not a joke," said Malock, resting his hands on the railing. "I can't believe it."

Hana was by his side instantly, wisps of smoke rising from her hair like she had teleported. "As I said, my mistress is very generous. We also have food, water, clothes, and medical supplies for your entire crew."

Malock looked at Hana skeptically. "What's the catch?"

Hana leaned against the bulwarks, looking completely innocent. "What catch? Can't you accept that some people are just innately generous, expecting nothing in return for their kind deeds?"

"I've seen too much on my voyage to accept that," said Malock. "Gods usually expect something in return for any generous acts on their part. So what does your mistress want? Eternal servitude from me? Half of the crew so she can feed them to her friends or even eat them herself? Sexual favors of some kind?"

Hana grimaced. "That last one is kind of icky, but you're wrong on all fronts. All the Mechanical Goddess expects from you is that you make it to World's End. Unlike the other southern gods, she doesn't play politics and has no reason to attempt to thwart Kano's plan."

"Kano's plan?" said Malock. "What's that?"

"No idea," said Hana, shrugging. "She simply mentioned it in passing to me and didn't see fit to explain it. I'm used to it. She usually mentions things offhand like that and I've gotten used to not getting a straight answer from her or any answer at all when I ask."

Malock stroked his chin. "Well, if this truly is as you say it is, then tell your mistress thank you for her generosity. On these dark seas, I didn't think there existed beings who could be even half as generous as she is."

"She normally isn't this kind," said Hana. "The ship repair platform is usually reserved for her own ship, but she hasn't had any reason to travel recently so she is allowing you to use it. All that I ask is that you keep your crew from getting in the way while the automatons work."

"I suppose that is a reasonable request," said Malock. He looked over his shoulder and said, "Banika, go and tell the rest of the crew—"

But Banika was already gone.

He looked back at Hana and asked, "Have you had experience overseeing the repairing of a ship before?"

"Of course," said Hana. "These automatons aren't difficult to boss around, you know. If they had any sentience in them at all, I'd say they even enjoy it. Now you should probably go back to your stateroom so you don't get in the way, either."

But Malock didn't leave. He stayed out of the way, of course, but he believed it was pure insanity to assume that the Captain of the ship would simply let someone else work on it without him at least watching. He was especially concerned about the crane, which looked large enough to smash straight through the hull of the *Iron Wind* without much effort.

To his everlasting astonishment, however, Malock really didn't need to supervise them at all. Hana showed a surprising amount of leadership, ordering the automatons about like she did this sort of thing every day. She didn't speak Divina when she did this, but rather an odd language that the automatons had spoken earlier. All he knew was that he was happy that she actually seemed to be doing some good.

The automatons operated the crane and repaired the ship with expert precision. They installed a new mainmast, complete with sail, and repaired the sail on the foremast that had fallen off. It took them hours to repair the port, but when they did, it looked like it hadn't been ripped off at all. Malock would have sworn up and down that it was all magic, but when he thought about it, he couldn't recall seeing any spells cast.

They did all of that in just a few hours and after that they started to lift in the crates full of food. Malock personally inspected each one, just to make sure they weren't full of poison or hostile automatons or something even worse, but he discovered nothing but delicious food completely fit for consumption by both humans and aquarians. The medicine looked legitimate, too, but he was not a doctor so he couldn't be sure. The clothes all appeared to be fit for people to wear, too, and there was a variety for summer and winter times.

When the last crate was lowered onto the deck of the ship and the automatons began moving it down to the hold, Malock walked up to Hana and said, "Okay. Why do you have crates full of food and water and medicine and clothes for mortals? The automatons don't seem to need any of it and I can't see the Mechanical Goddess sitting down to eat a nice roast duck for dinner."

Hana smiled. "Remember the food we had laid out on the table back in the castle? Sometimes we actually let the mortals eat it. And as a katabans, I do need some of this stuff. Not all of it, obviously, but quite a bit of it is necessary for my physical form. I can only hope this is enough for your crew."

Malock shook his head. "It's more than enough. How can we ever repay your mistress?"

"Like I said, all the Mechanical Goddess expects of you is for you to reach World's End and see Kano," said Hana. "It's that simple."

Malock frowned. "It's never that simple with gods. You should know that, having served the Mechanical Goddess for as long as you have."

"I've found quite the opposite, actually," said Hana. "Sometimes, it is that simple. You forget that the southern gods in general tend to be less—how would I put this?—materialistic than their northern counterparts. They're a lot more simple, more in tune with nature. They rarely get involved in godly politics and generally have no patience for complicated plans that are designed only to get back at someone they don't like."

"Right," said Malock. "Unlike the northern gods, when these guys want someone dead, they just go and do it, rather than come up with some convoluted plan that may or may not work."

"Exactly," said Hana. "You seem to understand the southern gods very well despite having lived up north your whole life."

"You figure them out pretty quickly," said Malock. "Because if you don't, they'll kill you."

"Of course," said Hana. "Well, I do believe we have the entire ship repaired and your supplies restocked. I should be leaving now and I'll be taking the automatons with me."

Malock looked overside at the automatons standing on the repair float and said, "Are you sure we can't borrow a few? Just a few, you know. Not forever."

Hana put one foot on the bulwarks and threw him a smirk over her shoulder. "Sorry, but the Mechanical Goddess is very protective of her children. She would never let you have any of them, not even one. She's not *that* generous."

Malock sighed. "Okay. You may leave, then. We may have to stay in Stalf for a few more days, though, until most of the crew is feeling up to going south again. Is that all right?"

"Oh, I doubt my mistress would be very bothered by that," said Hana, brushing her hair out of her eyes. "Although, I'd suggest you leave as soon as you can. There's a pretty bad storm coming in a few days and if you can't leave now, well ..."

"I get it," said Malock. "We'll leave as soon as possible."

"All right," said Hana. "Then this is good bye, Prince Malock. May the final leg of your voyage give you more peace than the last leg did."

With that, Hana leaped off the bulwarks and landed on the crane with practiced ease. Half an hour later, the automatons who had taken the last crate below deck returned to the surface and joined their brethren on the repair float. The float then zoomed away from the *Iron Wind* to Stalf, skirting the ice ring and heading for the back of the island.

As the repair float zoomed away, Malock turned and looked back at the newly-repaired *Iron Wind* and smiled. Maybe things were going to get better for them after all.

Chapter Nineteen

To SAY THAT THE rest of the crew was ecstatic about this (and mournful that they couldn't take any of the automatons with them) was like saying Kano is the Goddess of the Sea. Those sailors who could still walk, ran around the ship, gaping at the new mainmast, testing the stability of the new port, and tasting the new food. Ranof in particular was pleased at the new supply of medicine they got, which turned out to be exactly what they needed.

But as Malock had predicted, the ship remained in Stalf Bay for another three days. The fact was, even with all of the new supplies, the crew still needed time to rest up and heal. This bothered Malock because the drive to reach World's End had reignited in his soul, stronger than ever, but he was patient.

Soon, however, most of the crew got well enough that Malock decided it was time to ship up and head out. This meant reassigning certain crew members to different tasks, especially the fishing crew, which he disbanded when he realized they had enough food that they no longer needed the trawl anymore. The surviving members of the fishing crew greeted that particular announcement with joy, which took Malock by surprise as he hadn't realized just how much they disliked that particular task. Even Kinker seemed happy about it and he was the only one who actually liked to fish.

When Malock learned that Deddio had been one of the sailors killed in the Tusked God's assault, however, he immediately understood why the other fishermen were glad they were no longer doing that task.

With slightly more than eighty crew members left, at least half of which were still recovering from the attack, the *Iron Wind* set sail south, in the direction that Malock could feel Kano pulling him. Rather than spend all of his time cooped up in his stateroom, however, Malock went around helping the crew in whatever ways he could, from helping Arisha Frag prepare breakfast in the morning to steering the ship with the coxswain in the afternoon and swabbing the poop with cleaning crew.

He did this for a couple of reasons. First, the lack of healed sailors meant that the crew needed every hand they could get if they were going to keep the ship in shape; that meant that Malock had to help. Besides, it allowed him to get to know his crew better, a fault of his he realized after his talk with Kinker. The crew was at first a little hesitant about letting him work alongside them, but they eventually relented and now no one found it strange when Malock was found throwing out uneaten food or helping to adjust the sails to the wind.

Furthermore, Malock needed some more time away from Vashnas. She was doing much better, well enough to go out and help around the ship herself. Nonetheless, Malock still had a hard time figuring out exactly how he felt about her. She was certainly a good aquarian, one whom he loved deeply, and yet ... he had the strangest feeling that there was more to her than met the eye.

In fact, he began to notice that the further south they went, the odder she acted. He at first thought that the change in weather—it was gradually getting warmer the further they sailed from Stalf—might explain her strange behavior, but when he noticed that the rest of the aquarians acted the same as they always had, he realized that something else was going on. She volunteered to be the new lookout, which he found worrying but which he could not dissuade her from doing.

Whenever she came down to eat, she spent a lot of time sitting by herself, muttering into her food, occasionally looking around at the rest of the crew like she couldn't trust them. Malock had no idea what that meant and the few times he tried to eat with her were so unpleasant that he eventually gave up, choosing instead to spend mealtimes in the stateroom, where he often ate alone, thanks to the wounded sailors who had stayed there now fully recovered from their injuries.

He had no idea what their next destination was, mostly because Vashnas hadn't told him yet. He didn't know how close they were to World's End, either; again because Vashnas refused to tell him. He had no idea why. After Stalf, surely they needed every bit of information they could get about possible future threats. Didn't she understand that?

Then again, when Malock remembered how well Ikadori Island

and Stalf had gone with Vashnas's advice, he wondered if maybe it was best that she didn't tell them what was coming up next. He figured they could take whatever it was. After all, if it was truly terrible, then Vashnas would undoubtedly have told him about it. Wouldn't she?

That was a question that haunted his mind as the days turned warm.

Though the fishing crew was disbanded, Kinker and Jenur still spent a lot of time together, if not at work then at mealtimes and whenever they had free time. Jenur told Kinker all about what happened on Stalf whenever they weren't working and he was absolutely astonished by what he heard. He was especially intrigued by how Jenur and Malock escaped.

It was just after lunch, before they had to go back to the galley to help Arisha (which was what most of the fishing crew was doing nowadays), that Jenur told Kinker about this. They stood near the new mainmast, having just finished a wonderful lunch of roast duck and green peas.

"So a trapdoor opened up underneath your feet and you guys went sliding down a tunnel that led you outside?" Kinker said, just to make sure he understood it correctly.

"Yep," said Jenur. "We have no idea how that happened or why. We didn't press any buttons or do anything to make it open. I think the Mechanical Goddess must have freed us."

"But why would she do that?" said Kinker. "I thought Malock said that the southern gods love to eat humans."

"Why would she repair our ship?" Jenur shot back. "I think she wants us to do something. She has her own agenda and she can't complete it if our ship is destroyed."

"What might that agenda be?" said Kinker. "Do you think she has a spy on board the ship, like Tinkar did?"

Jenur shrugged. "Who knows? Until a few days ago, I didn't even know that there *were* southern gods. I have no idea what's going to happen to us or what the Mechanical Goddess may or may not be planning. But you have a good point. We should keep an eye out for any unusual behavior among the crew, just in case."

That was the last conversation they had over the next week, as the ship suddenly got caught in a terrible storm that made everyone sick. At first, everyone believed the storm—with its whipping winds and torrential rain—was heralding the return of the Messenger or perhaps was the power of a god trying to kill them, but thankfully the storm passed, doing nothing more than making everything wetter than normal (although the tossing of the waves did cause the supplies in the ship's hold to fall over and spill out all over the floor).

That, and Kinker found himself playing doctor when he was not making food for the rest of the crew. While most of the crew had since recovered from the Tusked God's attack, there were still quite a few who were not even well enough to walk yet. All he really had to do was take food to the wounded, though, so he supposed he wasn't really playing doctor at all.

A day after the storm, Arisha gave Kinker the job of delivering Bifor his breakfast. Bifor had not been terribly injured during the Tusked God's attack; in fact, he had been one of the few to escape without any serious injuries. Instead, he had worked himself ragged using his limited knowledge of healing magic to help those who were injured and considering how many of them there were, it was no surprise when he collapsed one day and had to be taken to his room by some of the other sailors.

And yes, Bifor did indeed have his own cabin. Kinker didn't know that until Arisha told him. Apparently, as Bifor was the last mage on the ship, Malock had thought he needed to be kept safe from the hazards of sharing one tiny room with a dozen or so other sailors. That, and Bifor was unusually large and required more room than the others; hence why he got his own cabin.

The cabin itself was located below deck, near the bow, but just before the hold. Kinker carried the hot bowl of soup down the hatch as carefully as he could and walked down the hall, remembering Arisha's directions. He quickly found it, knocked on the door, and heard Bifor's voice on the other side say, "Come in," which he did.

He glanced around as he entered. Bifor's cabin was not fancy or particularly nice, like the rest of the ship, but there was an air about it that was very different from every other cabin Kinker had been in. He realized that it smelled better; not perfect, as Kinker was convinced that the stink of the sea was now an inherent part of the ship, but it didn't smell like shit, blood, sweat, and other bodily fluids like the rest of the ship did. Until he entered, he hadn't realized just how used he was to the horrible smells.

Bifor was lying in his too-small bed, his feet sticking over the end, a thick wool blanket covering his body. His face was drawn, his cheeks were hollow, and he looked more like a fallen tree than a human being. Nonetheless, he had a book open on his stomach, which he looked up from when Kinker entered the room. On the stand next to his bed lay his wand.

"Ah, Kinker," said Bifor, yawning. "I see you are my server today. What kind of soup have you brought me?"

Kinker placed the bowl of soup on the nightstand next to Bifor's bed, saying as he did so, "It's duck soup. Fresh from the stove top, made with the stuff we got from the Mechanical Goddess back on Stalf."

Bifor snapped his fingers and the bowl of soup levitated over to him. He grabbed the spoon out of the bowl and began eating the soup ravenously, like he hadn't eaten in days.

Kinker raised an eyebrow. "Looks like you're getting better already."

Bifor stopped eating briefly to look up at Kinker and say, "Oh, it's not as easy as it looks. Hence why I have my wand. Makes it easier to use magic."

Kinker nodded. "Yes, I've heard. I wonder if I could learn how to use magic without a wand. Sure would make my life easier."

"Not unless you undergo years of exhausting training," said Bifor before digging back into his soup. "As I said, it's not nearly as easy as it appears."

"Exhausting?" said Kinker. "What's so difficult about learning how to wave a wand or snap your fingers or say chants?"

Bifor almost dropped his bowl of soup as he looked up at Kinker in shock.

"Magic is tapping into the essence of the gods themselves," said

Bifor, stating that fact like it was something everyone knew. "It's not something you can just *do*. You need to be trained by competent teachers who have been practicing their art for years."

"Sorry," said Kinker. "I didn't know that."

Bifor sighed. "That's right. You're from Destan. I keep forgetting that. You fit in so well with the rest of the crew that I sometimes think you must be from Carnag or one of the other major islands up north."

"There's still a lot I don't know," said Kinker. "A lot. But I've been learning from all of you and I hope to improve as time goes on."

"It's not a problem," said Bifor. "It's just … very frustrating, you understand. With all of this shit that's been going on, I have more than enough on my plate already and I really don't want to educate my fellow crew on topics that are common knowledge to everyone over the age of six."

"I understand," said Kinker. He turned to leave, but then stopped and turned back around. "Just one more question. If magic is about tapping into the essence of the gods, then how do you get tired?"

Once more, Bifor sighed, although this time it seemed more like habit than anything. "The essence of the gods still has to be channeled through my body. That's another part of magic training; learning how to train your body so it can transfer magical energy through it without wearing down easily."

"You must be very well trained in that regard," said Kinker. "You managed to go for a long time without collapsing."

Bifor shrugged. "Larger people in general have an easier time channeling magic than smaller people. Body mass seems to affect how well one's body tolerates magic, but of course there are always exceptions, like Kargo the Short, who legend says used magic for a full month before collapsing."

"Sounds inspiring."

"It's just a story," said Bifor matter-of-factly. "Kargo the Short was probably a compilation of multiple mages from that time period. It's said that he lived a thousand years ago, so he probably didn't actually exist."

Kinker frowned. "Why did you feel the need to point that out?"

"Because myths and stories are often taken too seriously by people," said Bifor. "Now it's true that some of those myths are true and there are many we have not been able to verify. Still, I am always amused by some of the wilder stories out there, like the one about Hollech and the giant egg."

"Never head that one."

"You're lucky," said Bifor. "Anyway, I simply wish to make sure that no one takes these stories too seriously. Most of the myths and legends of the past were simply made up by people and then edited through various retellings throughout the years. They're very unreliable."

"Huh," said Kinker. "I never saw any reason to question them because the gods can do anything, can't they?"

Bifor looked out the lone window in his cabin, apparently lost in thought. "Before we got to the southern seas, I would have said the same thing. But if the Captain is telling the truth, then the gods do have certain limitations. When we get home, I will certainly have to write a paper on this to present to the Association of Mages. It will radically alter almost everything we know about the gods and how they operate."

"If we get home, that is," said Kinker.

Bifor looked at Kinker in surprise. "'If'? You sound pessimistic, Kinker. Chin up."

"That's difficult to do," said Kinker. "I mean, even with the *Iron Wind* repaired and the new supplies we have and all that, the southern seas are still dangerous, aren't they? Who knows what kind of dangers we'll run into between here and World's End?"

Bifor laughed. "Kinker, your concerns are understandable, but honestly I think you're worrying too much. I imagine we've already been through the worst; otherwise, I think Vashnas would have said something about it. It will probably be smooth sailing from here on out."

"If you say so," said Kinker. "Is there anything else I can get for you, Bifor?"

Bifor shook his head. "No, thank you. I'm going to take a nap now, I think. All of this talking is tiring me out."

"Okay," said Kinker. "If you need anything, you know how to contact us."

Bifor nodded. "Bye."

"Bye," said Kinker as he exited the room, closing the door behind him, his worries still not assuaged in the slightest.

Over the next week, the worst problem that the *Iron Wind* ran into was a leak that sprung open in the hull. That was an easy fix, however, due to the abundant nails and boards that the Mechanical

Goddess had provided them with. Bifor even helped, managing to gather just enough energy to seal the cracks around the boards so the water couldn't leak through.

Beyond that, Bifor's predictions seemed to come true. The seas were calm, the sky was bright and clear, and everyone on the ship seemed to be feeling better. Even those who had not yet recovered from the Tusked God's attack seemed more hopeful, as if the bright sun was shining down rays of hope rather than rays of light.

For his part, Kinker was glad his fears were unfounded. After all of the shit they'd been through, having a peaceful week was like a refreshing breath of fresh air. His back was getting better, he was sleeping more soundly than before, and he thought there was no way life could get worse.

It was just as the new week began that Vashnas, sitting in the crow's nest, reported seeing something on the horizon. She said it wasn't an island or any kind of land, but rather a tunnel that seemed to extend deep into the sea itself.

That odd description caused many sailors to go to the bow to try to see it themselves, but it wasn't until a few hours later that the so-called 'tunnel' Vashnas reported came into view. Even then, it was but a speck on the horizon for another day until they got close enough to see exactly what she had been talking about.

Her description was accurate. Directly ahead of them was a huge, open tunnel, easily tall enough and wide enough to allow the entirety of the *Iron Wind* to pass through with little problem. That itself was strange, but stranger still was the sound of a massive waterfall that could be heard just beyond the tunnel. Vashnas reported that the sea ended at the tunnel and began on the other side of a huge gap that they could not sail around even if they changed course.

It appeared that their only course of action was to go through the tunnel. This time, Vashnas didn't even tell them what they could expect. Kinker didn't know if it was because she honestly didn't know what was in the tunnel or if she simply did not trust her own memory or what. All he knew was that the peaceful, happy atmosphere that had been gradually building up over the past week was just as gradually fading the closer they got to the tunnel.

One thing they did know for sure about the tunnel was that it sloped. How far down it went, no one knew for sure, but Vashnas reported seeing the other end of the tunnel opening on the other side of the ocean, so they at least knew there was an exit. A lot of sailors tried to suggest alternative ways around it, but Vashnas confirmed that the gap in the sea stretched for miles in every direction with no end in sight, so it would simply be more practical to go through the tunnel. This did not reassure them much.

Nonetheless, the crew worked hard to secure the supplies. Because the tunnel sloped, they had to secure the supplies to make sure that nothing would fall over or break or spill out in the hold. Malock also gave them orders to stay below deck until the tunnel leveled out, as he didn't want to lose any members of his crew for no reason. As usual, Malock remained within his stateroom, along with Banika and Vashnas, while the rest of the crew went below deck.

The hold was far less crowded than it had been the first time the crew had been forced to stay below deck. Nonetheless, the hold still smelled of damp wood, the unwashed bodies of the human and aquarian sailors (the Mechanical Goddess, Kinker realized, had failed to supply them with any soap or personal cleaning supplies), and it was almost completely dark, save for the lamps that a few members of the crew had managed to light. Shadows cast by the lamps danced along the walls as the ship swayed.

Kinker and Jenur sat near the end of the hold, away from the door. They had just finished tying down the cargo and were now sitting among the rest of the crew who were all speculating about what was in the tunnel. Kinker listened to theories ranging from yet another god to some sort of sea monster that made the tunnel its den and everything in between. He personally wondered how they would defend the ship once they entered the tunnel, as the tunnel probably didn't have any light in it.

Without warning, the entire ship inclined down sharply. The ship's sudden movement threw Kinker and Jenur to the floor along with the others, including those who held the lamps. The lamps went out, too, plunging the entire hold into darkness.

Additionally, the ship was starting to pick up speed. Kinker heard the rushing of the water above the creaking of wood and the occasional shouts from the other sailors. All he knew was that they must be going down, down into the tunnel's depths, and he wasn't sure how to feel about that.

Luckily, however, they had tied down the cargo well because Kinker did not hear any of the crates fall over. They did lurch with the ship, however, and some of the sailors voiced their uncertainty about the ropes, but they thankfully held. Some of the sailors scrambled to find lights and in a minute a lamp was turned back on, held by Gino, although the light was too weak to illuminate the entire hold.

Just as Kinker was getting used to the downward trajectory of the *Iron Wind*, the ship jerked to a stop and he was thrown forward. He slammed into the wall of the hold and around him he could hear the other sailors cursing and yelling. Jenur nearby was cursing so badly that Kinker was surprised at her language, as her rather extensive knowledge of curse words included more than a few he had never heard before.

"Ow," said Kinker, rubbing his head as he turned around. "What stopped us?"

"We didn't stop," said Jenur's voice from somewhere within the darkness. "The ship is still in motion. Can you feel it?"

Kinker stopped talking and listened to the floor. Yes, now that Jenur mentioned it, he could feel the subtle movement of the ship beneath their feet. It was slow, almost imperceptible, but there was no denying that it was still in motion.

A sudden flash of light caused Kinker to raise his hands to cover his eyes. When his eyes adjusted, he lowered his hands and saw that it was Gino who held the lamp. In the weak light of the lamp, his unhappy expression looked like something straight from Kinker's nightmares.

"The tunnel has probably leveled out," said Gino. "But we still don't know what is on the outside."

"Someone should go and check," said Jenur, standing up and dusting off her shirt sleeves. "Anyone volunteered?"

"No," said Gino. "Remember the Captain's orders. We're to stay below deck for the entirety of the time spent in the tunnel, except in emergencies."

"That's bull," said Jenur. "I want to know what's out there and I'm going to take a look."

Kinker rested a hand on Jenur's shoulder. "Jenur, I think you should stay here. It might be too dangerous out there for a girl your age."

Jenur shrugged off Kinker's hand. "Kinks, I'm going to be fine. You know I can look after myself."

"Be that as it may, having more help is never a bad thing," said Kinker. "May I at least come with you? The more backup the better, if I do say so myself."

"Fine," said Jenur. "Gino, give me that lamp. I need to see where I am going if I'm going to go out there."

Gino didn't look like he agreed with that at all, but he nonetheless handed the lamp to Jenur. "Be careful out there. It could be dangerous."

Jenur smirked. "Gino, after almost getting eaten alive by three gods, danger doesn't frighten me anymore."

Gino shrugged and stepped aside. "As you wish."

Malock rubbed his belly as Banika mopped up the contents of his stomach that he had unfortunately hurled when the ship went downhill fast. He had had enough sense in his head to barf all over the floor, rather than on his desk, but it was still messy and Malock still felt rather sick. It didn't help that the stateroom was almost pitch black now, thanks to the tunnel's complete lack of light, although

Vashnas had been smart enough to bring a lamp with her before they entered the tunnel.

"I am so sorry," said Malock, contorting his mouth due to the taste of barf still in it. "I didn't realize I'd hurl like that when we'd start going down."

"Not a problem, sir," said Banika, swishing her mob back and forth across the floor. "Compared to what I've had to clean up before, this is nothing."

Malock nodded and glanced out the window, seeing only complete and utter darkness. He could hear the sound of running water outside, heard the creaking of the ship underneath his feet, but beyond that the tunnel was utterly silent, making him wonder if there was anything inside the tunnel at all.

He turned to Vashnas. She was sitting on the sofa, as usual, her hands folded behind her head and her legs crossed. She looked utterly bored at the proceedings and seemed to be on the verge of falling asleep.

Malock normally would have considered that cute, but right now she just looked insubordinate. "All right, Vash. Now that we're in the tunnel, what can we expect to run into?"

Vashnas yawned and said, "I don't know."

"Excuse me?" said Malock. "You're supposed to be the expert on the southern seas. Surely you must know what lives in this tunnel."

Vashnas yawned again, this time in a rather irritating fashion, and said, "I don't know every aspect of the southern seas, Mal. Last time I was here, I didn't even enter this tunnel. I thought it would be too dangerous, especially since I didn't have a ship."

"I thought you said you went to World's End," said Malock. "Didn't you tell me that at the beginning of the voyage?"

Vashnas shrugged. "I thought I said I *almost* got to World's End. Didn't I?"

Malock slapped his face. He didn't know why Vashnas was being so obstinate, but he decided that interrogating her about it would be a waste of time.

Instead, he said, "Then I suppose the next thing to do would be to go out to the deck and see what is out there myself."

To his satisfaction, Vashnas actually sat up and looked at him in alarm. "Mal, are you sure about that? I mean, of course as Captain of the ship you have every right to, but you don't know what's out there and—"

"And what?" said Malock. "It is true that there could be many hidden dangers out there, monsters waiting to attack, gods waiting to eat us, maybe another band of pirates. But remember, I have Kano's approval. I doubt anything can kill me, even if it wanted to. Logically, I am therefore the best choice to explore an unknown, potentially lethal place."

Vashnas put her hand on the back of her neck and glanced out the window. She was clearly trying to come up with a counterargument, but evidently could not come up with any. "Oh, all right. But it's just so dark ..."

"You don't need to come with me," said Malock, holding his hand out for the lamp. "You and Banika can wait here, if you wish, while I explore the tunnel or what little I will be able to see anyway."

Vashnas bit her lower lip, but nonetheless gave him the lamp.

"Just be careful out there, all right?"

"I will," said Malock. "I'll be back soon."

Emerging out of the ship's hatch, Kinker was struck by how immensely dark the tunnel was. True, Jenur carried a lamp with her, but somehow it seemed dim and insubstantial in comparison to the utter blackness of the tunnel. The light extended only a few feet in either direction, showing them nothing but darkness beyond their little circle.

The air was damp, much more so than normal. It was the kind of dampness that one experienced in caves that had water and it smelled that way, too. Yet it was a refreshing smell, far better than the stink of the *Iron Wind*, and Kinker breathed it in deeply, a refreshing change from the cramped hold.

Jenur raised her lamp and squinted, as if trying to develop night vision. "Can you see anything, Kinks? 'Cause all I see is darkness."

Kinker shook his head as he kicked the hatch closed. "My eyesight isn't as good as yours, so I see the same."

Just then, another light shone from the quarterdeck. They both jumped until the light was revealed to be Malock, carrying his own lamp. He walked over to them, looking both curious and annoyed. And though his light added to theirs, the darkness still felt overpowering.

"Kinker? Jenur?" said Malock, stopping a few feet from them. "What are you two doing out here? I ordered the *whole* crew to be below deck. Not just a few."

"We got bored," Jenur said. "We wanted to see what the tunnel was like."

"That is the worst excuse for disobeying my orders that I've ever heard," said Malock. "And believe me when I say that I've heard plenty of bad excuses on this voyage. So—"

A subtle shift in the atmosphere of the tunnel caused Kinker to raise his hand. Malock, frowning in annoyance, said, "What?"

"Don't you feel that?" said Kinker, speaking in a hush for reasons even he did not understand.

"Feel what?" said Jenur.

"Someone is watching us," said Kinker, his eyes darting back and forth. "I don't know who, but someone is."

Malock cocked his head. "Kinker, you're speaking nonsense. I sense nothing. We are alone in here."

"Alone indeed," said a voice that belonged to none of them, that seemed to come from the darkness itself. "Alone in the dark, alone in the world, alone on this very ship. Alone-ness, it would seem, is an inherent aspect of the mortal condition."

Malock, Jenur, and Kinker all looked around, waving their lamps this way and that, trying to spot the source of the voice, but it was impossible. The darkness was too absolute and their lamps were too weak. It was like sticking a light inside a thick layer of mud; in fact, Kinker wondered if the darkness was mud or solid in some way. It felt that way, at least.

"Who's there?" said Malock, his voice trembling with fear. "Show yourself."

"I don't think you would like that," said the voice. "I don't think you would like that at all. My appearance is not one you mortals would appreciate it; besides, isn't it funner to speculate about what I may look like? Use your imagination, use your creativity, or call on your history to tell you what I may look like."

"Sounds like someone is fond of spouting nonsense," said Jenur. "We're really not in the mood to solve riddles."

"Good point," said the voice. "I've never been a fan of my sister and her riddles, either. Nor have my other siblings, for that matter. Very well. I will show you who I am, how I look, but if you hate my appearance, then that is your prerogative."

A loud slapping sound echoed off the tunnel's walls, the sound of something soft and slimy landing on the deck. Yet nothing appeared in their circle of light, causing Kinker to think that the voice had lied to them when a bright light shone, near the mainmast, so bright and so sudden that it caused Kinker to cover his eyes again to avoid losing his vision.

When the light faded, Kinker lowered his hands and was astonished by what he saw.

Clinging to the mainmast was what appeared to be an octopus. Or, at least, it had the body of an octopus, eight slimy green tentacles, five of which were attached to the mainmast itself. Even stranger, the octopus had the head of a human. The human head was round and green, like the rest of its skin, and completely bald, but there was no mistaking the very human-like appearance of it.

Even weirder, the creature held a paintbrush in one tentacle and a palette in the other, a palette that seemed to have a dozen different colors ranging from red to blue. Its free tentacle floated in the air above its strange head, a light shining from its tip, the source of the light from before.

"What the heck is that?" said Jenur, her free hand immediately reaching for her knife.

The strange octopus-human-thing sighed. "See? I told you that you wouldn't like my appearance. Few do. Even my fellow gods shun me, which I suppose is why I don't get many visitors."

Malock shook his head and said, "So you are a god? Which god are you? The Paint God, the God of Paint? Or maybe the Octopus God, the God of Octopuses? Are you going to eat us?"

The god glared at Malock. "Your sarcasm is palpable. No, I am neither of those gods you mentioned. I am the Historic God, the God of History."

"History?" said Jenur. "Whenever I think of 'history,' I rarely think of octopus/human hybrid things that paint."

"My physical appearance is what it is, human," said the Historic God. "It is useful for what I use it for, the same as your frail bodies are good for what they are good for. Let's not make such low blows, yes?"

Kinker scratched his beard. "How can you speak Divina? Most of the southern gods we've run into couldn't."

"Because I record history," said the Historic God. "All of it, including the funny things you mortals get up to. Learning to speak your language is a hobby I took up after a certain mortal came through my tunnel one day. I caught her and tortured her for weeks until she agreed to teach me the language. Now I speak it quite proficiently, if I do say so myself."

Kinker's blood ran cold. "You tortured her? Why?"

"Because mortals are generally not allowed in here," said the

Historic God. "The name of this place is unpronounceable in your awkward human tongue, but I believe a rough translation is, 'Tunnel of History.' This is where the history of Martir is kept."

"So you write it all down?" said Malock. "Is that what the paintbrush and palette are for?"

The Historic God raised his painting utensils, as if making sure he had heard correctly. "These? No, I do not write. Instead, I draw paintings, paintings that depict the history of the world from the First Day to the present."

Malock looked around and said, "And where, may I ask, do you keep these paintings of yours? Do you happen to own an art studio or gallery where you keep all of these paintings on display for your fellow monsters—excuse me, I meant gods—can view them?"

The Historic God frowned. "You mortals are so disrespectful. What have I done to earn such hate?"

"It's not you in particular," said Jenur. "It's just the southern gods in general. Three of them tried to kill us and another one tried to sink our ship and kill everyone on it. So if we seem just a tad cynical about you, it's not your fault."

"Yes, my siblings can certainly be vicious," said the Historic God, nodding his head in agreement. "And no surprise. You humans smell delicious. It has been so long since I last tasted mortal flesh, perhaps a few decades. Very few mortals ever make it down this far south, you see, and unlike my siblings I rarely have time to scour the southern seas for any mortals who may have strayed from the north."

"Let me guess," said Malock. "You're going to eat us alive, aren't you?"

349

"Sadly, I am not," said the Historic God with a sigh. "I know you, Prince Tojas Malock. You are Kano's Chosen. And I can smell another Chosen One on this ship as well, though to be honest I do not know why she of all goddesses would put a spy on this ship."

"Um, hello?" said Malock. "We have already dealt with the spy. The Messenger came by a few weeks back and took Tinkar's spy away. Your sense of smell must be messing up or confused."

"No, I am sure it is not," said the Historic God. "It is as obvious to me as the scent of blood and shit that is inherent in this ship. I sometimes forget that you humans cannot smell the same things as we gods. If you could, perhaps you would treat the world around you much differently."

Kinker was starting to regret not bringing along a harpoon or some other kind of weapon. Though the Historic God had made no threatening moves yet, he was still a southern god and southern gods ate humans. Of course, not all southern gods did—the Mechanical Goddess being the notable exception—but the vast, vast majority of them did and so Kinker knew that he, Jenur, and Malock could not let their guard down around this deity for even a moment.

Then again, even if we do keep our guard up, is there anything we can do to stop a god that wants to kill us? Kinker thought. *A god is a god, even if he is a southern god. That means we are basically screwed unless he spares us.*

"Who is it, then?" said Malock. "Can you identify the other Chosen One for us?"

"No," said the Historic God. "I do not know the names of every member of your crew, so I couldn't identify them even if I wanted to.

Besides, like my brother the Loner God, I generally try to stay out of these silly and ultimately pointless conflicts my northern siblings often get into. Better to let them sort it out themselves, rather than get involved in a conflict that I have no personal stake in."

"That sounds very nice," said Malock. "But surely you are not going to simply let us go, are you?"

The Historic God shrugged. "There's little I can do to get in your way. Even simply speaking to you could draw me into a conflict in which I have no interest whatsoever. Still, I have been lonely these many years, observing history unfold like a flag, with visitors being few and far between."

"Then why don't you just leave?" said Jenur. "I mean, you're a god. You can do anything. No one is your boss, right?"

The Historic God chuckled, then burst into full on laughter. The laughter was gurgled and strained, almost demonic. "Oh, what a great sense of humor you mortals have. Just leave ... why, if I could do that, I would have done it eons ago. I hate this place with a burning passion, even though it has been my home since the end of the Godly War."

"Something's keeping you here, then?" said Malock. "What?"

"The Treaty," said the Historic God, his eyes downcast, his tone more than a little bitter. "Ah, the Treaty. That nasty little paper that tells us exactly what we gods, northern and southern alike, can and cannot do in this world. How I curse the Powers every day for it."

The Historic God's sudden change of tone—from a calm, leveled tone to one of pure bitterness and hate—took Kinker by surprise. The Historic God's tentacles constricted around the mainmast so tightly that Kinker was afraid he might break it.

"But why should I tell you my life story when you can see it visually?" said the Historic God. "Behold, my collection."

The Historic God waved his free tentacle and the bright light shot up into the top of the ship, all the way to the crow's nest. The bright light allowed Kinker, Malock, and Jenur to see the inside of the Tunnel now and what they saw silenced them in awe.

Along both sides of the Tunnel's walls and on its ceiling were paintings. Not just any old paintings, however. They were enormous paintings, depicting scenes and figures in such detail that they looked like the Historic God had simply taken them and put them on the walls. Even more amazing, the scenes all bled into one another, as if all of these smaller paintings were in fact part of a much larger whole that Kinker couldn't see.

One painting in particular caught Kinker's eye. It showed a large octopus-like creature that heavily resembled the Historic God rampaging through an island, uprooting trees, killing mortals, and smashing anything that got in its way. A handful of humans near its feet were trying to fight it off, but it was clear to Kinker that the humans could not stop it.

"Is that you?" said Jenur, pointing at the painting. She said this to the Historic God.

The deity nodded and said, "'Twas me."

"But you look so much larger in that picture," said Jenur. "Like, as big as a mountain."

"We gods can change size as well as shape," said the Historic God. "I took on the large form because it was so much easier to hunt and kill mortals than it was in a smaller size. I was actually the leader of the mortal hunters."

Malock looked at the Historic God in shock. "You mean you were the one who led your southern siblings in war against your northern siblings?"

The Historic God raised his brush and palette in a pacifying sort of way. "No need to get your pants in a twist, mortal. I didn't start the War, after all. And I technically wasn't a 'real' leader anyway. I was simply more vicious than the rest of my siblings, so I naturally killed more mortals than the others. I never took the life of another god, even though I clashed with my northern siblings several times."

"That doesn't make you very good," said Jenur. "Still doesn't explain what you're doing here, though."

"Watch," said the Historic God, gesturing at the paintings.

By now, the ship had floated a few more feet down the tunnel, revealing another painting. This one showed the open mouth of the Tunnel, with a much smaller version of the Historic God standing before it on the ocean. Though the painting version of the deity's back was to them, Malock could sense a feeling of dread from the painting, the kind of emotion that only the best painters knew how to invoke in their audience.

"The Powers were terribly angry with me when the War ended," said the Historic God. "They didn't like me, didn't like what I'd done at all. While the other southern gods were simply restricted to the southern seas, I was banished here, to this place, to cool down, so to speak. They gave me the task of recording all of history as it happened for the rest of my days."

"So you can't leave here, even if you wanted to?" said Malock.

"Yes," said the Historic God. "That may seem odd to you mortals, a god who cannot go where he wishes, but it is the truth. The Powers' might dwarfs that of all of the gods combined. There was nothing I could do to persuade them, nothing I could do to convince them to give me freedom. And so, I ended up here, where I have been painting every day for the past several thousand years."

Kinker shook his head in pure astonishment. "Surely you must have run out of room to paint after a while, didn't you? After all, this Tunnel doesn't go on forever, right?"

"That is true," said the Historic God. "But you assume I paint every minutiae of history. I do not. I try, to the best of my ability, to paint only the most important parts of history. That can be difficult, as I am not gifted with the ability to see the future like my brother Tinkar is, but so far most of the events I have captured in paint have indeed been important to future historic developments."

He sounded pleased with himself at the accuracy of his guesses.

"But I do wish I could be free," he sighed. "This Tunnel is deep and dark. All I ever do is paint day in and day out. If I could only get my freedom, get a taste of that fresh ocean air ... but alas, the Powers do not wish for me to be roaming the southern seas."

"With good reason," said Jenur. "You killed tons of people, I bet. I've never been a fan of the Powers, but this time I think they were right in locking you down here. You are insane."

The Historic God snorted. "Insane? I would suggest that your Captain is the insane one. A human, braving the southern seas, which are full of gods that would like nothing better than to devour human flesh, purely because he believes he was summoned by a goddess."

"It is not belief, Historic God, but truth," said Malock. "If it were not, then I never would have made it this far."

"Of course," said the Historic God. "Of course. Yet I suppose it has never occurred to you to wonder what my sister has summoned you for?"

Malock didn't see where this was going. "I have, but so what if I don't know? I trust Kano. She would never have summoned me without good reason."

The Historic God shook his head in amazement. "It has been so long since I last saw mortals that I forgot just how sycophantic you are. Then again, I suppose we southern gods do have a different view of our northern siblings that you mortals do."

"What do you mean?" said Malock. "Are you implying that Kano is untrustworthy?"

"It goes without saying that anyone who requires the worship of pathetic mortals such as yourselves is insecure," said the Historic God. "All I am saying is that what we gods want is not always what you mortals want. Surely you would have realized that by now."

"Yeah, we noticed," Jenur grumbled.

The Historic God licked his lips, like he was getting hungry. "All of this talking is making me quite famished. I have had to survive on the fish that swim into here over the years, but now a ship full of tasty mortals has ended up in my Tunnel. Lucky me."

"But you said you weren't going to eat us," said Malock, taking a step forward to protect Kinker and Jenur. "Right?"

"I did say that," said the Historic God. "I was merely trying to

355

make you uncomfortable. Just be warned that, when betrayal comes, it will be when you least expect it."

With that, the Historic God let go of the mainmast and crawled across the deck to the port. He climbed over the bulwarks and launched himself off, taking the light with him. When he disappeared from view, the darkness returned, held in check now only by Malock and Jenur's lamps.

"Well, that was weird," said Jenur, looking between Malock and Kinker. "Do you think he is really going to let us go?"

"I believe so," said Malock, his eyes focusing on the mainmast where the Historic God had been mere seconds ago. "He would have tried to kill us if he didn't mean it."

"Then why talk to us at all?" said Jenur.

"I don't know, Jenur," said Malock. "Perhaps he was lonely. Or maybe he just wanted to scare us. Either way, I have a bad feeling about this. A very bad feeling."

Chapter Twenty

THE REST OF THE voyage through the Tunnel was completed almost entirely in the dark. Due to the current in the Tunnel, there was no need to raise the sails or have any of the crew work. Therefore, before Malock returned to his stateroom, he gave Kinker and Jenur orders to tell the rest of the crew to stay below deck until they returned to the open seas.

When Malock returned to his stateroom, he found Vashnas and Banika waiting eagerly for him. They had apparently heard his, Kinker's, and Jenur's entire conversation with the Historic God through the window, which was open, but they didn't know all the details until Malock informed them. Banika took particular interest in the news that there was actually another spy on board the ship, while Vashnas seemed more than a bit disturbed by the idea that yet another southern god had spared them for dubious reasons.

Yet the Historic God kept his promise and soon the *Iron Wind* was heading upstream, because for some reason the water flowed upward in this place. It didn't flow up quite as fast as it flowed down, however, but they emerged onto the bright blue ocean soon enough, which was as beautiful as it always was and far less dank than the Tunnel was.

As soon as they exited the Tunnel, Malock could feel World's End drawing him towards it. He asked Vashnas if there were any more islands between them and World's End and Vashnas said that she doubted it, that it would probably be smooth sailing from here on out.

Somehow, that news spread quickly throughout the entire ship before Malock even told anyone else. The tense atmosphere that had been gradually building up over the last day immediately dissolved, replaced by nothing more than pure, unabashed joy at the thought that this mad voyage was finally near its end.

In fact, though Malock didn't order it, a handful of sailors started to celebrate a bit too early. Unbeknownst to most of the crew, the Mechanical Goddess had also given them a lot of wine—good wine, by the look of it—with the rest of their supplies and some of the crew had discovered it, brought it top deck, and were now drinking it and dancing and singing old shanties. It wasn't until Banika came to Malock's stateroom and informed him of the impromptu party that he went to see it for himself.

As Banika had described, about half a dozen sailors had started dancing. Half of them were human and the other half aquarian, but for once they seemed to have forgotten their xenophobic tendencies toward one another and simply danced liked there was no tomorrow. They were old sailor dances, not particularly elegant or well-choreographed, but that obviously didn't matter to them. For that matter, the shanties they sung were coarse and full of vulgarity and sexual innuendos of nearly every kind.

Despite that, more and more sailors were starting to join the party and for once Malock didn't tell them not to. He figured that after all of the crap they had been through over the past couple of months, they deserved a time to relax and let loose, at least for today. In fact, he even went and joined them, which surprised some of his men but no one actually objected to his presence.

The party went on for hours, well into the night. Even Bifor came up to watch, although due to still being weak he mostly just stood and watched, occasionally participating in a song or sipping some wine but otherwise observing. Malock paid little attention to the mage, instead dancing with some of his sailors (including Jenur at one point) and even partaking in a crude little ditty that Gino informed him was called 'The Sailor's Lust.' (It was actually similar in content to some of the songs sung in the Carnagian court, interestingly enough, even though the style was cruder.)

The sun crossed the sky as the party went on, until it soon became too dark to see. Luckily, some of the crew found torches to light (which had apparently been included with the supply crates that the Mechanical Goddess had given them) and so they continued to sing and dance by torchlight. More than a few sailors got drunk, but no one fell overboard, although a handful did pass out on the ship's deck.

Eventually, Malock got tired and had to take a break. He made his way to starboard, declining many invitations from his more drunken men to have 'just another sip' of wine, where no one was, and leaned against the bulwarks. His knees ached and his whole body shook with exhaustion, but it was the good kind of exhaustion, the kind that makes you feel like you did a good long day of work (or, in his case, play).

"Having a fun time?" said a familiar voice to his left.

Malock glanced to his left and saw Vashnas sitting not too far away, with her back against the bulwarks and her legs up to her chest. She didn't look very happy, nor did she appear to have partaken in any of the festivities. At least, Malock could not remember seeing her dancing or singing or drinking, though he supposed that he may have missed her somehow.

"I thought you were up in the crow's nest," said Malock, wiping some wine off his lips. "Why don't you join the party?"

Vashnas sighed. "I decided to come down and see what the rest of y'all were doing, considering how loud you guys are. I should go back up."

Vashnas stood up, but Malock grabbed her hand, prompting her to look at him in surprise.

"Yeah, back to the crow's nest with you," he said in jest. "In the darkness of the night, where you probably can't even see your hand in front of your face. Come on, Vash. There's no reason to spend the night cooped up there alone when you can be down here with us."

Vashnas didn't let go of his hand, but her hand did go slack in his. "I guess you have a point. It's just been so tense for such a long time that I'm having a hard time adjusting to this kind of happiness."

"True, it is rather different from what we're used to," said Malock. "But so what? I'd trade my crew of tense, possibly mutinous men for this crew of joyously drunk sailors any day of the week."

"Yeah, I guess so," said Vashnas, though her tone was distracted, like she wasn't listening.

Malock tried to look her in the eyes, but she kept averting her gaze. "Vash, what's on your mind? I can tell you're thinking about something. What is it?"

Nearby, some of the sailors had started to play a card game of sorts. Malock recognized the cards as belonging to his deck of divination cards, but for the moment he didn't care how they had gotten them or what game they were playing. All he wanted to do was listen to Vashnas's problem and find out how he could help.

She didn't look like she wanted to talk. Nonetheless, she did say, "I've been thinking about World's End. I've been thinking about this voyage in general."

"What about it?" said Malock.

This time, she actually did look at him. "I ... I'm sorry, Mal, but I can't keep this up. I'm tired of the secrecy between us, tired of how we've been growing apart ever since Stalf."

"You noticed?" said Malock.

"Of course I did," said Vashnas. "Before Stalf, you and I had such powerful, unbound love for each other. After Stalf ... well, I sensed you didn't quite trust me as you did before. You held me at a distance, maybe even hated me. That's why I took on the job of lookout. I didn't think you loved me anymore and I saw no reason to try to make you."

"Vash, that is simply untrue and you know it," said Malock. "I love you like the light of the sun."

"Then why have you not talked to me?" said Vashnas. "Why have you kept me at a distance? Why have you and I been chilly with each other?"

Malock bit his lower lip. "Well—"

"I think it's time we be straight with each other," said Vashnas. She turned to face him, no longer averting her eyes. "At least, I should be straight with you. After all the secrets I've kept from you, it's about time I tell you the truth."

Malock blinked as the rest of the crowd erupted into spontaneous applause, which a quick glanced told him was the result of Jenur performing a difficult dance move. "I knew it."

"What?" said Vashnas.

Malock pointed at her and said, "I knew you were keeping secrets from me. Ever since Stalf, I've been suspecting you of not being entirely honest with me."

Vashnas frowned. "That explains a lot. I suppose there is a lot about me that just doesn't add up."

"You're absolutely correct," said Malock. "Like why your knowledge of the southern seas seems to leave out the most important part: namely, the southern gods. I even began to suspect that you have never been to the southern seas at all and that you simply got your knowledge of the southern seas from the various rumors sailors spread about them."

Vashnas sighed again, this time more heavily, as if the weight of a thousand years were on her shoulders. "No, Mal, I knew about the southern gods the entire time. I just kept their existence a secret from you out of a misguided desire to keep you safe."

Malock looked at her incredulously. "Keep me safe? How is not telling a man wandering in the darkness about the cliff he's about to fall over safe?"

"As I said, it was misguided," said Vashnas. "Extremely misguided on my part. I was hoping that we could simply head straight down to World's End, never staying on one island for too long, and that maybe the gods would not bother us due to your status as a Chosen One. Evidently, I was wrong about that."

Malock balled his hands into fists, trying his best not to get angry but feeling the anger rise up in him like steam in a tea kettle anyway. "We could have avoided a lot of problems if you had simply been honest from the start. Maybe even saved some lives."

Vashnas looked down in shame. "I know, I know. I don't think there's any forgiveness for my keeping quiet. In the next life, maybe I will be punished for all of the blood on my hands."

Malock ran a hand through his hair. "Then what is the truth? Why did you really join my crew? It's not because you needed the money or because you have a thirst for adventure, is it?"

In the torchlight, half of Vashnas's face was covered in shadow, but the half that wasn't, revealed a grim expression that was out of place in the festive atmosphere. "I might as well get this out of the way right now. You see, Malock, I joined your crew for one reason and one reason only: To kill Tinkar, the God of Fate."

All of time seemed to come to a halt at that instant. The boisterous singing of the crew, the sound of their dancing boots beating against the deck of the ship, the jingling of coins as sailors traded what little money they had with each other over the card game ... all of that faded away, replaced by a faint buzzing sound in

Malock's brain that made it difficult to focus on anything except what he just heard.

He somehow managed a smile, a weak smile, a smile without any actual mirth behind it, but a smile nonetheless. "That's a great joke, Vash. Almost had me there for a second."

"I'm not joking," said Vashnas. "At all. I'm completely, one hundred percent serious."

That weak smile Malock managed? It immediately disappeared. "You ... are?"

"I know how that sounds and I know what you're going to say," said Vashnas, holding up her hands defensively. "Just hear me out, will you?"

Malock shook his head. "How can I hear you out when you are suggesting the impossible? I mean, I know some people dislike the gods, but deicide? That sounds like something only a madman would ever suggest."

"I'm not mad," said Vashnas. "I'm perfectly sane, thank you very much. Would you at least listen to my story, if nothing else?"

Malock staggered back against the bulwarks, feeling his body and mind grow sluggish with fear. "Oh dear ... now it all makes sense. Tinkar sent a spy on board this ship not to kill me, but to kill you. And I had no idea ... no idea at all that I was ferrying an assassin to World's End in order to kill him. By the gods."

Bile rose in Malock's throat at the very thought and he almost threw up, but Vashnas drew closer to him and patted him on the back, saying, "I know, I know, it sounds crazy. It might make more sense if you would listen to me first. Could you do that, at least?"

Malock rubbed his eyes and looked at her, hoping against hope that maybe this was all just a really weird dream he was having. Alas, he did not wake up in his bed, back in Carnag Hall, clutching his pillows like he sometimes did when he had a nightmare, so he had to conclude that this was in fact reality.

"Okay," said Malock, taking a big gulp of air. "You can tell me your story. I'll listen. If I seem zoned out, it's because ... you know, deicide."

Vashnas nodded. "I knew you probably wouldn't react well to my tale, but you seem absolutely sick. Do you really respect Tinkar *that* much?"

"It's nothing to do with Tinkar," said Malock, "and everything to do with the very idea of deicide. It is the ultimate act of treason against the gods. I cannot even imagine it."

"Then you have a very tiny imagination, Captain," said a familiar voice nearby. "After all, there was an entire war fought where deicide happened nearly every day."

Both Malock and Vashnas turned to see Bifor approaching them. With his back to the torchlight, his face was covered in shadow, which made him looked far more menacing than he was. There was also something in the way he walked, the way he held his wand, that put Malock on edge, although he couldn't place what it was.

"Bifor, what are you doing here?" said Malock in annoyance. "Vashnas and I were having a very private conversation that has nothing to do with you. Why don't you go back and party with everyone else?"

Bifor stopped, his face still shrouded in shadow, and waved his wand behind him. The air around Bifor, Malock, and Vashnas shimmered, like the air in a desert, but the shimmering quickly faded away, leaving the air looking normal. Malock wouldn't have given that gesture much thought if he hadn't noticed that the sounds from the rest of the ship were now entirely muted. He could still see, around Bifor's bulk, the sailors singing and dancing and playing cards, but he could not hear them, not even when Gino went dancing by, his eyes closed and his lips uttering the lyrics of a song he couldn't hear.

"I, too, wish to have a private conversation with you, Captain," said Bifor, his tone civil and even as he raised his wand, pointing it at them. "And with Vashnas as well. In fact, I've been waiting a long time for this moment, much longer than you would have supposed."

"What's going on, Bifor?" said Malock, his eyes on Bifor's wand. "If you wanted to talk with me and Vashnas, all you had to do was ask."

Bifor shook his head. "I forgot how terribly naïve you were, Captain. I suppose royalty in general is pretty naïve and childish. But then I suppose it doesn't matter because I'm afraid that neither of you will be living much longer."

"Is that a threat?" said Malock, trying to not panic. "Or a joke? Because if it's a joke, it's a pretty terrible one."

Bifor laughed. "Joke? I'm hardly a clown. No, it is a threat, just as Vashnas is a threat, and it is one I intend to go through with before this night is over."

Vashnas stepped forward, putting one arm out in front of Malock. "What do you mean? What do you want?"

"Isn't it obvious?" said Bifor, his wand arm never wavering. "I would have thought that you, out of all of the idiots on this ship, would have realized who I am and what I am trying to do. Especially considering your age. Perhaps the years have taken their toll on your brain."

"What is he talking about?" said Malock, looking at Vashnas. "Vash? What's going on?"

Her arm that was held up before him was as rigid as the mainmast. Her entire body, in fact, had gone rigid, like she had just realized a terrible truth that she did not want to accept.

"I see Vashnas is in too much shock to explain," said Bifor. "Very well, then. I suppose it won't hurt to tell you one more story before you die. There is nothing you can do to stop me, after all. Nothing at all."

"What did you do to the sound?" said Malock. "How come I can't hear anyone but you guys?"

"A simple barrier," said Bifor. "No one can pass through it, except for us. It drowns out all sound, except for whatever is inside the barrier. This is so we can keep this conversation private, as I wished."

Malock gulped. He had been hoping Banika or someone else would notice Bifor trying to kill them and try to stop him, but he now realized that was nothing but a pipe dream and that he and Vashnas were on their own now.

"But enough blabbering," said Bifor. "I might as well reveal to you who I truly am. I am not a Xocionian or a pagomancer. My knowledge and understanding of pagomancy is limited and elementary. And Xocion is a foolish god anyway, not worthy of the kind of worship and devotion I show to my true master."

"And who might that be, Bifor?" said Malock. "Who is your real master?"

Though his face was still covered in shadow, Malock imagined the mage was now smiling evilly. "I thought you would have put two and two together by now, but I suppose I shouldn't have expected such cleverness from a pathetic, small-brained royal like yourself. My true master, my true god—the only one worthy of worship—is Tinkar, the God of Fate. And he has chosen me to eliminate you both before you ever even see World's End."

Malock took a sharp intake of breath. "You ... are the spy? But that's impossible. The Messenger—"

"Was easily fooled," said Bifor with a snort. "It was not difficult for me to cast a spell that made Telka smell just like a Tinkarian. The Messenger relied on that smell and so naturally chose our poor doctor. Betraying Telka was not part of the plan, but it became necessary for me in order to continue to remain on this ship so that I might one day receive the opportunity to slay you both."

Vashnas gritted her teeth. "I knew there was a Tinkarian on this ship, but I never would have imagined it was you, Bifor. I should have seen this coming."

"I still don't understand," said Malock. "How can Bifor be a Tinkarian? What is Vashnas's conflict with Tinkar? And how do I fit into all of this? What's going on?"

"At last you show a semblance of intellectual prowess by asking the right questions," said Bifor. "I am not much in the mood to tell stories, however. I am here to kill, here to defend my god's life with my own. Perhaps Vashnas will be ready to tell you, even though I could relate her history at least well as my own."

"So you aren't going to kill us right away?" said Malock with a gulp.

"Under ordinary circumstances, I would," said Bifor. He glanced over his shoulder, however, and added, "But you know, I would like to buy myself enough time to come up with an escape plan. Admittedly, I did not plan to kill you tonight; I would have done it earlier, had I not been busy trying to survive."

Malock looked around Bifor and noticed that several sailors had gathered outside the barrier, Banika among them, pounding against the barrier with their fists and weapons. None of them had succeeded in making even one crack in the barrier's face, however, and Malock doubted they would, considering the magical nature of the barrier.

"Besides," said Bifor, "Vashnas's story ties into why I am here to kill her. And you, too, I suppose."

Malock looked at Vashnas. "So, Vash, what's your story?"

Vashnas never lowered her arm from in front of him. She kept her gaze on Bifor's wand, like it was a gun, as she said, "Malock, this may come as a surprise to you, but I am actually thousands of years old."

"What?" said Malock. "Okay, now that *has* to be a joke."

"It's no joke," said Bifor. "She is the oldest living mortal on Martir, almost as old as the gods themselves."

"Your interruption is not appreciated," said Vashnas. "But you do speak the truth. I lived even before the Godly War, before the Treaty was signed. That was before the gods became distant, before there was any difference between the northern and southern gods. It was a simpler time, but it did not last."

Malock had a hard time wrapping his mind around someone being thousands of years old. "But that's impossible. Thousands of years old ... no mortal can live that long. I know that aquarians have a longer lifespan than humans, of course, and some geromancers have succeeded in extending the natural lifespan of humans by a couple hundred years, but only the gods can live to be thousands of years old."

More sailors had gathered outside the barrier, perhaps half the crew now, but still none of them had any success in breaking open the barrier. One sailor, who looked drunk, was smacking his head against the barrier futilely.

"As true as that may be in general, it is not true specifically," said Vashnas. "You see, all those years ago, when the world was young and the gods were one, I was Tinkar's lover."

Now that caused Malock to do a double take. "You what? You were a lover of a god?"

"Indeed she was," said Bifor, the hatred in his voice surprising Malock. "She was Tinkar's one and only, the apple of his eye. He loved her above all other mortals, even had plans to ascend her into godhood so she may be his wife, but then she betrayed him, an event even he did not foresee."

"I did not betray him," Vashnas responded. In the torchlight, she really did look thousands of years old now. "His Cloak of Fate was stolen by someone else. I had nothing to do with it."

"That is what you said all those years ago, but you never offered any proof of your innocence," said Bifor with a chuckle. "Asserting your innocence is not a good way to clear your name, thief."

"What happened, exactly?" said Malock. "And how do you know all of this, Bifor?"

"Tinkar told me his side of the story," said Bifor. "When he first chose me all those months ago, he told me everything I needed to know about this voyage. Enough to know that I would be right in taking the life of this fish woman right here, right now."

Vashnas sighed. "What happened, Malock, was this: I used to live on World's End with Tinkar, before the southern seas became inhospitable to mortals. World's End is also known as the Throne of the Gods and was—and still is—where most of the gods live. At least, it is where they come to meet when they have to."

"But I thought the northern gods didn't live in the south," said Malock.

"It's basically neutral territory, even though it's located at the end of the world," said Vashnas. "Besides, the whole northern/southern divide is only really done for our sake. We mortals, humans and aquarians alike, are supposed to live in the north, which is why some of the gods live up there too. May I get on with my story?"

"Oh, sure," said Bifor in his most sarcastic voice. "You have all the time in the world."

"Shut up," said Vashnas. "Anyway, I used to live on World's End with Tinkar until one day his most precious material possession, the Cloak of Fate, went missing. No one knew where it was until it was discovered in my room, which led the rest of the gods into believing that I was the thief, even though I was not, even though I wasn't even there on the day it was stolen. They demanded retribution for my crimes, even though Tinkar tried to argue that I was innocent."

"Okay, I don't always understand the ways of the gods, but that seems a bit strange to me," said Malock. "If Tinkar was the one stolen from, then why wasn't he the one demanding justice? Shouldn't his opinion matter, considering that it was his Cloak that was stolen in the first place?"

"The other gods were worried that if I got away with my 'crime,' then other mortals might try to steal things from them," Vashnas explained. "They wanted to use me as an example of what happens to mortals who think they can steal from the gods without suffering the consequences. Most of them wanted me dead, but Tinkar managed to make a deal with them: I was banished from World's End forever and given the Curse of Senva, which is to say, I was granted immortality by the Goddess of Aging."

"How is immortality a curse?" Malock asked. "Never dying seems like a pretty good deal to me."

For the first time since Bifor had thrown up his barrier, Vashnas shot Malock an angry look. It was a deadly look, like she was daring Malock to say one more thing, just one more thing, if he felt confident in his abilities to defend himself.

"Consider what that means, Mal," said Vashnas, her chest heaving up and down like she had run a mile. "I can never die, true, but I can also never be with Tinkar again. Unless someone kills me, I will live forever apart from him. And he made that deal, knowing that he would never see me again. Would you do that to someone you loved, Mal? Grant them immortality, then banish them from your sight?"

"Is that why you want to kill him?" said Malock. "Because of

Senva's Curse?"

"Yes," said Vashnas. "When he did that, it became clear to me that Tinkar did not actually care about me. He only cared about appeasing his siblings. I have been stewing in my rage for years, waiting for the right opportunity to return to World's End, trying to find a loophole in the banishment. And I believe that I have, assuming all goes well."

"It won't," said Bifor. "Though you have gotten farther than I would have believed possible, much farther than I should have allowed, this is where you will end. You won't even get to see World's End on the horizon as a small speck of nothing."

"What did you do?" said Malock. "What is your plan, Vashnas? What loophole did you find?"

"The Mechanical Goddess," said Vashnas. "She has a long history with Tinkar, just as I do, and hates him as much as I do, if not more so. They were once lovers themselves, but they took different sides during the Godly War and as a result broke their relationship. I came to her servant, Hana, who was visiting in the north once, and through her made a deal with the Mechanical Goddess; that she, a southern goddess, would grant me, a mortal, her protection just long enough for me to slay Tinkar. Needless to say, she agreed immediately."

Bifor growled. "What this amounts to, of course, is two bitter, petty women trying to kill a man they both once loved. Sounds like a poor imitation of a Zarskian play, if you ask me."

"No one did," said Malock. He looked at Vashnas again and said, "But how can a mortal kill a god? I was told that only gods can kill other gods."

Vashnas reached into her coat with her free hand and withdrew a sharp disk from within. It reflected the light of the torches, causing it to shine like the moon. Malock had never seen anything quite like it before.

"It's another loophole," said Vashnas. "This disk was designed by the Mechanical Goddess. If I can lodge it in Tinkar's neck, it will cut his head off. She infused it with some of her godly energy; therefore, if I can hit Tinkar with it, it should kill him as easily as if he were a mortal."

Malock shook his head. "This is insane. Won't Tinkar see this coming? I mean, he is the God of Fate, after all. How do you know he hasn't already come up with a plan to stop you?"

"He hasn't," said Bifor, sounding disgruntled. "You see, whenever a mortal is under the protection of a specific god or goddess, that mortal is invisible to Tinkar's eye. Tinkar knows the fate of all of mortals, but he cannot know the fates of his fellow gods or his own fate. In essence, we chosen mortals are treated like gods. That is why he sent me."

"And you," said Malock, pointing at Bifor. "What's your story? I thought you were a follower of Xocion."

Bifor chuckled. "Oh, I never followed that god. Learning how to conjure ice cubes or make snowmen always seemed like a frivolous pastime to me. Why do that when you can learn what the future itself holds in store for you? When you can learn what your destiny is?"

"Why did you wait so long to strike?" said Malock. "You could have killed me at any point in this voyage. In fact, you could have sunk the entire ship without any of us ever knowing it was you, I'm sure."

"But I *did* try to kill you," said Bifor. "Several times, in fact. Did you ever wonder why you lost nearly all of the fleet on the first leg of this voyage?"

Malock took a step back in horror. "So you sunk those ships? All four of them?"

"I didn't sink them all personally," said Bifor. "The only one I really sunk was the ship I was originally on, *Our Beloved Lady*. I blew up the gunpowder in the hold. I miscalculated, however, and almost ended up drowning myself, but luckily I was rescued by the crew of this ship. I decided to wait after that, however, for a sign from Tinkar that would let me know when the time to strike was right."

"So you didn't sink the other ships, then?" said Malock.

"No," said Bifor. "But I imagine Tinkar must have manipulated fate in order to make sure that only your ship made it this far south. This way, it would be far easier for me to kill you and Vashnas. For that, I praise Tinkar. He is truly a glorious god."

Malock wished he had a weapon on hand to defend himself with, but he had not been expecting a fight tonight. He could only hope that he could keep Bifor talking long enough for him or Vashnas or someone outside the barrier to come up with a plan to save them, as unlikely as that was.

"I didn't want anyone to suspect that I was up to no good," said Bifor. "So I continued to pretend that I was a good, loyal sailor, one who would never think of betraying you. I worked hard every day to prove my loyalty and usefulness and I believe it must have worked because not even Vashnas suspected me of being anything other than what I pretended to be. Isn't that right, Vashnas?"

375

"Correct," said Vashnas. "If I had been smarter—"

"If you had been any smarter, Vashnas, you would have never tried to seek a vendetta against Tinkar at all," Bifor replied. "There were many close calls for a while there, but I knew in my heart of hearts that someday Tinkar would call me and tell me when to strike. And just earlier this evening, while I rested, I received a vision from him, telling me that the time to strike was now because of the party that the crew was going to throw, the party that would distract everyone from what I am about to do."

Malock couldn't believe his ears. "Even if you do kill us, you'll have to deal with the rest of the crew. They'll rip you limb from limb for your crimes. Just look behind you. They've already figured out what is going on."

Bifor glanced over his shoulder. By now, it looked like the entire crew had gathered. The low glow of the torches revealed that the crew was hitting the barrier with anything they could get their hands on, even though none of them were making even the slightest bit of progress whatsoever.

"You mean those uneducated bunch of sea rats?" said Bifor, returning his attention to Vashnas and Malock. "Yes, like the beasts they are, they would certainly rend me limb from limb if they got the chance. But I already have a contingency plan in place for just this occasion."

"What are you going to do, jump into the sea and swim away?" said Vashnas with a snort. "In your condition, I'm sure that would be loads of fun."

"Hardly," said Bifor. "You see, I've thought long and hard about this and have concluded that my time is at its end. I cannot teleport away, nor swim, and I certainly couldn't fight all of these sailors and hope to win even with magic. Death awaits me no matter what I do; therefore, I intend to go out in the way I want."

"And how may that be?" Malock asked.

Bifor gestured at the deck beneath his feet. "Right now, in this ship's hold, there is a ton of gunpowder ready for use in guns and cannons. Using my limited knowledge of pyromancy, I have set up a spell that will blow up the gunpowder when I command it to do so. Thus, once I finish both of your sorry lives, I will activate the spell and kill everyone on this ship, including me."

"You monster," said Malock. "That's what you are. A monster."

"Monsters do not graduate at the top of their class from North Academy," Bifor said. "Nor do monsters get chosen by gods to carry out their destiny. The real monster here is Vashnas, for daring to think that she could—that she should—kill the great Tinkar and get away with it."

Vashnas's arm tensed. "I know why you want to kill me, but what about Malock? What does Tinkar have against him?"

Bifor waved off her question like it was unimportant. "How should I know? All I know is that Tinkar and Kano have not gotten along well in recent years. It is not my place to question the dictates of my god and master. All I am to do is follow orders, no more, no less."

"That is a foolish way to live and you know it," said Vashnas. "But what am I saying? You are a Tinkarian. You idiots have always been the puppets of fate."

"You cannot fight fate," said Bifor. "Only live in accordance with it. That is the most important lesson that I as a Tinkarian have ever learned. If only the rest of the ignorant world would learn it, then maybe things would be better."

Then Bifor shook his head. Energy began crackling around the tip of his wand as he said, "In the end, it does not matter. I am done talking and telling stories. It is time for me to do what I came here to do, which is to say, fulfill my destiny. It is sad that neither of you will live long enough to fulfill your own."

Chapter Twenty-One

KINKER WAS NOT SURE what just happened. Then again, he wasn't alone in that regard. What had started as a happy party dedicated to celebrating the last leg of the voyage had quickly turned into a confused gathering of sailors around a barrier constructed by Bifor that separated the mage, Malock, and Vashnas from the rest of the crew. It had quickly became apparent that Bifor was trying to harm Malock and Vashnas in some way, but why he was doing it, no one knew, and how they could stop him was also a mystery.

It wasn't like they hadn't tried. Many sailors had hit the barrier with stools, chairs, metal pipes scrounged from the lower decks, swords, guns, and their good old-fashioned fists. Others had taken to charging the barrier in groups, but that had done nothing except give them headaches. Due to his old age, Kinker had done little to help, mostly doubting that the magical barrier could be breached through normal means.

Instead, he stood off near the mainmast, where one of the torches was burning low, watching as nearly the entire crew threw their weight into the barrier. It did nothing except cause the barrier to become visible for a moment, but no cracks appeared in its surface and it was obvious that it would only come down when Bifor wanted it to, not before.

Jenur staggered out of the crowd of sailors toward Kinker, rubbing her forehead with her hand. "Ow."

"What did you do?" said Kinker.

Jenur continued to rub her forehead as she said, "Hit my head against the barrier."

"I'm not sure that's what they mean when they say to use your head," said Kinker.

Jenur shot him an annoyed look. "Ha, ha. Very funny. Are you going to help or just sit there and snark?"

"I'm not sure there is much we can do," said Kinker. "Bifor's barrier is too strong. Maybe if we had another mage, we could break it, but as it is all we can do is wait it out."

Banika approached just then. For once, she appeared to have lost her cool entirely. Her short hair was disheveled, her eyes were wide with confusion and anger, and she looked just about ready to sock anyone she didn't like in the face. She actually looked a bit like Jenur, now that Kinker thought about it.

"Kinker," said Banika, her voice far harsher than it usually was. "Why aren't you helping the rest of the crew save Malock?"

Kinker shrugged. "I was sitting here trying to come up with an alternative way to break the barrier."

"I don't care what you were doing," said Banika, pointing at the barrier like a general commanding an army. "You get over there right now and help or the gods help me I will drag you over there myself."

"Hey," said Jenur. "Don't talk to Kinker that way. He has a good point, you know. That barrier really can't be breached by normal means."

Banika turned to face Jenur with the most terrifying eyes Kinker had ever seen in his life. "And why aren't *you* helping? I know you hate Malock, but that doesn't mean you have the right to abandon him to his death."

"I don't hate Malock," said Jenur, folding her arms. "And I *was* just helping, Miss Tight Pants. I just was taking a break to see what Kinker was up to and to rest my head, which is aching like hell right now."

"There is no time to rest when our Captain is in danger," Banika insisted. "We have no idea how much time we have left until Bifor kills Malock."

"How do you know that's what he's doing, anyway?" said Jenur. "What if Malock is actually—"

Banika slapped Jenur across the face so hard that Kinker was surprised the young woman's face didn't go flying off. Jenur staggered to the side, almost falling over, before she regained her balance and looked at Banika, rubbing the side of her face as she did so.

"The hell was that for?" said Jenur. "Almost knocked me out."

"For daring to imply that Malock is up to no good," said Banika, holding her hand high like she was going to slap Jenur again. "It's obvious that Bifor is holding him and Vashnas hostage. Don't you dare imply otherwise or I will toss you overside like the trash you are."

Jenur straightened up, still rubbing the side of her face, but

TIMOTHY L. CEREPAKA

Kinker noticed her other hand going for the knife at her belt. "I've always thought you never liked me, Banika, but until tonight I didn't know for sure. I wonder if an old bat like yourself could even do what you said you were going to do to me. Would be interesting to find out."

Banika took a step forward, but Kinker got between the two feuding women and said, "Hold on, ladies. This is no time to be fighting amongst ourselves. Our Captain and our lookout are currently being held hostage by someone who could kill them without even thinking about it. We need to work together."

For a moment, he was sure that the two were going to beat *him* up because they glared at him like they were trying to set him on fire with their eyes alone.

Then Banika's arms flopped to her sides and she said, in a half-defeated voice, "What are we supposed to do? None of us know any magic, so we can't pierce or break Bifor's barrier."

"And even if we could, I doubt any of us could stop him from killing Malock and Vashnas," said Jenur, glancing at the crew that was still gathered around the barrier. "Even with all of us working together, we might not be fast enough."

Kinker stroked his beard in thought. He had no ideas, either, until without warning he noticed exactly where Bifor, Malock, and Vashnas were standing. He had a terrible flashback just then, remembering how he shot a cannonball into the Tusked God's mouth. It was terrible because he recalled the exact look on Deddio's face when he was snatched up into the Tusked God's mouth, but he forced himself to ignore it because he had no time to break down and cry.

"I think I know how we can save them and defeat Bifor at the same time," said Kinker. "But it will undoubtedly be dangerous, might even not work depending on how strong the barrier is and how far it extends below deck."

"I don't care how dangerous your plan is," Banika said. "Tell me what to do and I'll order the others to do whatever you need them to do."

"All right," said Kinker. "Gather round, you two, because we will need to do this quickly. There's no telling how much time we have until Bifor decides to finish them off."

"They're running away," Vashnas said.

Her observation snapped Malock out of his concentration on Bifor's wand, which was still crackling with energy. He looked around the large mage and noticed that Vashnas was correct. The entire crew had backed off entirely by now; in fact, most of them seem to have disappeared entirely, like they had gone below deck. The only one left was Jenur, who was standing at a distance and doing all kinds of strange hand signals that Malock couldn't read.

Bifor didn't look over his shoulder, perhaps because he didn't want to give Malock and Vashnas the chance to escape. "I imagine they must have given up by now. They probably think that there's nothing they can do to save you or stop me. And they would be quite right in that regard. At last the unwashed masses show signs of intelligence."

Malock felt Vashnas slip her hand into his. He looked at her, but rather than seeing fear and resignation on her face, she looked focused, like she was mentally counting down to something.

"I would have liked to have an audience to see your deaths, but alas that is not to be," said Bifor. "No matter. Whether this is witnessed by a hundred or merely one, I will kill you just the same."

Jenur was shaking her head and jumping up and down, but Malock still didn't understand what she was trying to do. Was she trying to warn them of something? He couldn't be sure.

"Before you kill us, Bifor, may I ask for my last words?" said Malock. "Just a few words, that's all I ask."

"I am not the noble villain of Zarsk's plays, prince," said Bifor. "I do not offer my victims their last words. Too often, they—"

Bifor never got to finish that sentence because Vashnas immediately grabbed Malock's arm and dragged him to the bulwarks. She pulled, almost tossed, him overside, jumping down with him as she did so, even as a dozen or so bolts of energy shot over their heads. But Bifor's magic never hit them and soon they were falling down the starboard of the *Iron Wind*, the wind whipping Malock's hair and boat cloak until they hit the water with a splash.

Despite the warmth of the day, the ocean water was bitterly cold. It was also darker than the night itself and Malock struggled to find his way up. This was complicated by his boat cloak, which was beginning to weigh him down. Not only that, but it seemed like Vashnas herself was trying to keep him from surfacing, because she was holding him down with both hands and he could feel his air rapidly running out.

Yet even as he struggled for the surface, a loud *boom* from above echoed them, the sound slightly muffled by the water. Malock heard large things hitting the surface of the water above, but due to the darkness of the ocean he could not tell what was going on. Had Bifor blown up the ship after all? Were he and Vashnas stranded in the ocean, with no way of getting to World's End alive?

Then he felt himself ascending, courtesy of Vashnas, who was propelling them both through the water at an astonishing pace. His boat cloak weighed them both down, however, forcing Vashnas to actually rip it off him and let it descend into the ocean depths, much to his disappointment. On the other hand, he desperately needed air right away, so he didn't mourn its loss as much as he might have.

Then, without warning, the two broke the surface, Malock gasping as his wet face met the cold air of the night. He shivered violently, wiping his dripping hair out of his eyes and looked around at where they had emerged.

All around them, chunks of burning wood floated on the water. None of it was close enough to harm them or even warm them, but Malock and Vashnas would have to be careful when navigating it. Malock wondered where the burning wood chunks had come from before Vashnas pointed ahead of them and said, "Look at that."

Malock hadn't realized it, but they had somehow swam away from the *Iron Wind*, not just swimming underneath it. Or perhaps the ship had moved away from them when they jumped off it. Either way, Malock was still shocked and disappointed by what he saw.

The starboard side of the ship—the side that had been newly repaired thanks to the Mechanical Goddess's automaton shipwrights —was gone, replaced with a gaping hole in the side of the ship that reminded Malock all too much of how the *Iron Wind* had looked back on Stalf. He could see it because parts of the ship were now on fire, the flames illuminating the hole and the sailors who were working to put it out.

Malock looked at Vashnas in disbelief. "What ... was ... how did that happen?"

Vashnas began tugging Malock through the water toward the ship, carefully winding her way around the floating debris. "I don't know the exact details, but I think that the crew must have used one of the cannons below to blow a giant hole in the side of the ship."

"Why the hell would they do that?" said Malock. "And how did you know it was going to happen?"

"I recognized Jenur's hand signs," said Vashnas, stopping briefly to look at him. "She was trying to warn us that we needed to jump off the ship when the cannon was ready so we wouldn't be blown to kingdom come. I have to admit I wasn't entirely sure at first because of the darkness, but I'm glad I figured it out; otherwise, we'd both be in pieces."

Malock noticed a thin piece of wood floating by, which he snatched. It was Bifor's wand, burnt black, true, but still in one piece.

"So Bifor is dead?" said Malock.

"Looks like it," said Vashnas.

Malock stared at the wand for a moment and then threw it away in disgust. He heard it land in the water nearby, but he didn't bother to look for it. He was just glad that that bastard had been blasted to hell.

After being pulled out of the sea by the ship's remaining davit on the port, Malock immediately asked for the identity of the person who came up with the idea of destroying the starboard side. It was Kinker who came forward, his hands black with gunpowder, who seemed to think he was going to get punished, if the way he walked with his head down indicated anything.

Malock was shivering, still cold, even after Banika had fetched a blanket to drape around his shoulders. "So you were the one who decided to break the ship again."

"I'm sorry, Malock," said Kinker, not looking him in the face. "I didn't even know it would work. I was desperate and it was the only idea I thought would have a chance at succeeding."

Malock put one wet hand on Kinker's shoulder and said, "Kinker, I'm not angry at you at all. In fact, I am extremely happy with what you did."

Kinker looked up at him, disbelief etched in his face. "You are? But I damaged the ship, possibly beyond repair this time."

"Yeah, that sucks," said Malock, nodding. "But you saved my life and Vashnas's life as well. For that, I must thank you."

Jenur, who was standing nearby, patted Kinker on the back. "See? I knew you would have nothing to worry about. Even if you did blow up half the ship."

"What happened?" said Gino, who was also with them. "Why did Bifor try to kill you two? What's the story?"

Malock exchanged looks with Vashnas, who seemed to be as tired as he felt, and said, "That's a story for tomorrow morning, I'm afraid. For now, we all need to get some rest so we will be ready to face our next destination."

"And that is ... ?" said Banika.

Vashnas answered the question this time. "World's End, known also as the Throne of the Gods."

Chapter Twenty-Two

I N THE MORNING, MALOCK got to see the full extent of the cannon explosion and he had to cringe, despite not being angry with Kinker about it. Only one cannon had been used to blast a hole in the ship, but it looked like an entire arsenal of cannons had been unleashed on it. The fires had been put out, but the edges of the hole were still burnt black, crumbling anytime anyone got near them, and the cannon itself was little more than twisted, scraped metal. The other cannons had taken varying degrees of damage, from resembling the first cannon in almost every respect to being a little burnt but in good shape otherwise.

Unfortunately, it wasn't just the cannon room that had suffered from the explosion. The sails all had holes torn in them from flying shrapnel; not large enough to halt the ship entirely, but enough to worry him. Malock ordered several of the men to patch the sails up using some of the extra cloth they had in the hold, vividly reminding him of the day the old sails had to be patched, back when they first started this voyage so long ago. Thankfully, the ship was not in danger of sinking.

No one got hurt in the explosion, as Banika had made sure to get the entire crew out of the blast range. The only fatality the crew suffered from the explosion was Bifor and in Malock's opinion he couldn't quite call Bifor's death something that the crew 'suffered' from when it was clear that losing the mage was good for them all.

Speaking of Bifor, news of his betrayal quickly spread through the entire crew. The general reaction at first was shock. Most of the sailors couldn't believe how Bifor had been deceiving them the entire time. A few even insisted that that could not be true, but even fewer listened to them. The general consensus quickly became anger; anger at Bifor's betrayal, anger at how he had planned to kill them all, anger at his deceptions and lies. There was no funeral services held for him, although a handful of sailors did pray a vengeful prayer to their gods, asking for Bifor's soul to be tortured in the afterlife.

Malock sympathized with those prayers, but he prayed none himself, if only because he was taking the time over the next few days to think about everything he had learned last night.

He had no trouble believing in Vashnas's old age, at least not anymore. She was still insisting upon it, even the next day, and he saw no reason to argue when he thought about all of the other weird things he'd seen on the southern seas. He just wondered about the ethics of him, a thirty-year-old human, sleeping with a millenniums-old aquarian.

But that was nothing compared to the very idea of deicide. He at first thought that maybe Vashnas would give up the idea in the morning, after a good night's rest, but to his disbelief the first thing Vashnas told him, when she woke up on the couch in his stateroom (he had elected to sleep on the floor due to the aforementioned uncertainty about the ethical implications regarding his relationship with her) was, "I am still going to kill Tinkar."

Malock looked up at her from his spot on the floor, his blankets wrapped tightly around him in an effort to keep him warm. He propped himself up on one elbow and looked at her with complete disbelief. "Are you certain?"

"Of course," said Vashnas. "Now more than ever. With Bifor gone, I can do what I need to do without any interruptions. Unless you, of course, want to stand in my way."

Malock shook his head. "I wouldn't ... I mean, what you're suggesting is still insane. Killing a god is not what I went on this voyage for."

"You don't have to help," said Vashnas. "I can do it myself. Just take me there and I will do it myself."

"Yeah, but—"

"And this is Tinkar we're talking about," Vashnas pointed out. "The same god who sent one of his followers to kill you. Would you really care if he died?"

Malock pursed his lips, trying to think of a counter-argument. "Well, I guess I wouldn't cry about it or anything, but I don't think you understand the implications of what you're suggesting. Tinkar is a god. The gods are foundational to Martir. The Loner God back on Ikadori Island told me that during the War the deaths of so many gods completely messed up Martir's ecosystem and led to a lot of death and destruction."

"Are you saying it will be the apocalypse if I kill Tinkar?" said

Vashnas.

"No," said Malock. "But Tinkar *is* the God of Fate. What would happen if there was no one to control fate anymore?"

"I bet it would just shift to the Mechanical Goddess's control," said Vashnas. "She is, after all, the one who gave me part of her power. It's not my concern."

"It's still risky," Malock insisted. "And honestly I'm not sure it can work. Fate is such an all-powerful, all-guiding force in this world."

Vashnas sat up, the blankets falling off her chest. "Are you going to try to stop me?"

Malock almost said 'yes,' but he hesitated. He saw the light of irrationality in her eyes, saw the way in which her hands shook with rage, and realized that he had no idea what she would do to him if he stood against her. She might just leave him alone. Or she might kill him. Anyone who was willing to kill a god would have no trouble killing a prince, in his opinion; then again, Vashnas did love him, so perhaps he would be safe.

He needed to approach this issue from a different angle, so he sat up himself, took one of Vashnas's hands into his, looked her into the eyes, and said, "Vash, I still love you. I'm just worried what will happen if you try to kill Tinkar. What if you fail? What if the other gods try to stop you? You're immortal, true, but you're also a mortal. Tinkar could still kill you, couldn't he?"

"No," said Vashnas. "Remember the Treaty. Individual mortals under the direct protection of a god cannot be harmed by other gods. So I think I'm pretty safe."

"Oh," said Malock. That took out the 'I'm concerned about your life' angle he was using. "Well, how do you know Tinkar is on World's End at all? I know it's called the Throne of the Gods, but I doubt every god lives there all the time. He has no reason to be there, especially if he knows you're coming to kill him."

Vashnas cupped Malock's chin with her other hand. "That may be so. But I doubt it."

Malock raised an eyebrow, although he didn't tug his head out of her hand. "Why?"

"Because if Tinkar wanted Bifor to kill you, then that means he will probably be on World's End with Kano," said Vashnas. "He will be there to see you because I know Tinkar. He won't kill you, as you're still under Kano's protection, but he'll still be there anyway. To see you."

"I don't understand," said Malock. "What would Tinkar gain from remaining on World's End when he knows that you're coming to kill him? Even if he takes certain precautions to keep himself safe, it would still be more logical for him to be elsewhere, wouldn't it?"

"Perhaps it would," said Vashnas. "But no one ever said Tinkar was a logical god. It has been thousands of years since I last set foot on World's End, since I last saw Tinkar, and he will no doubt want to see me. It is only natural."

Malock let go of her hand, but still didn't push her webbed hand off his chin. "So there's nothing that I can say that will change your mind, is there?"

Vashnas nodded. "You are absolutely correct, Mal. Nothing at all."

TIMOTHY L. CEREPAKA

Despite the gaping hole where the starboard used to be, the *Iron Wind* managed to sail south smoothly and with little trouble. Quite a few of the sailors tried their hands at various makeshift fixes, such as putting a tarp over the hole (which was impossible to secure with the wind blowing and the constant movement of the ship) and even deconstructing some of the crates to use their wood to rebuild the starboard. All failed, however, so the hole was left as is, even though it caused many of the sailors sadness, especially those who were most proud of the *Iron Wind*'s beauty.

To say the least, the atmosphere on the *Iron Wind* was mixed. On one hand, everywhere Kinker went, he heard murmurs of hope and excitement at the idea that they were almost at World's End. A few sailors he even caught singing or at least humming a tune he didn't recognize, probably a song from somewhere up north. Most sailors were eager for this whole voyage to be done and over with.

On the other hand, mixed with this happiness and eagerness was a sadness and even anger at Bifor's betrayal. No one on the ship had suspected Bifor of being a traitor. He had worked so tirelessly to use his magic for the good of all that the idea that he was planning to kill them all in the end was almost too hard to believe.

Not to mention it caused some serious distrust among the various sailors. More than once, Kinker found himself being eyed warily by a fellow sailor, as if they thought he was going to try to pull a Bifor, too. He didn't see why, considering that he had done nothing to earn this suspicion, but he supposed that Bifor hadn't either and yet he had turned out to be the most dangerous traitor of them all.

Still, the air of distrust dissipated quickly when the water went from the deep blue of the ocean to the clearness of a creek stream in spring. This happened gradually, without anyone noticing until Jenur glanced over the side of the ship and said, "Hey, everyone! Look at the water! It's clear!"

This caused the sailors nearby—who happened to be Kinker and Gino, among six others—to run over to the port (the starboard was no longer good for looking over) and see what Jenur was talking about.

And indeed, she was correct in her description of the water. Kinker could see clear through to the bottom of the ocean. He saw the sand, a variety of colorful plants he couldn't even describe, and an even more dazzling variety of fish and undersea creatures. What particularly caught his attention were the strange, pink dolphin-like creatures that swam beside the *Iron Wind*, occasionally leaping out of the water to display their fantastic wing-like fins.

One such dolphin creature even managed to fly up to the port, getting so close to the sailors that Kinker could practically touch it. As it did so, a strange, melodious sound came from its mouth, which sounded like a song to Kinker, but it was a song he couldn't understand, a song he would probably never understand, and soon he didn't hear it at all because the creature dove back into the water to join its companions.

"What was that?" said Jenur in awe.

"A singing leaper," said Vashnas, walking up to them. "Sometimes called the divine fish. They're found only around the seas of World's End. Very beautiful."

"So that means we're almost there," said Jenur, clapping her hands together excitedly. "Right?"

"Yes," said Vashnas. "I imagine that World's End itself will be within view any minute now."

Kinker turned to look at Vashnas. While the others were all observing the beauty of the clear ocean, he wanted to keep an eye on Vashnas. He had heard that she wanted to kill Tinkar, a ludicrous idea if there ever was one, and so even when she joined them in peering over the side of the ship to look at the sea, he was not sure how he should treat her

Then again, is it really my place to judge her? Kinker thought, turning his eyes back to the sea, completely aware that she was still standing next to him. *And after everything the gods have put us through, maybe it's time we mortals fought back.*

The hours trickled by, or so it seemed, and eventually, in the distance, a speck of land appeared on the horizon. The speck grew larger, clearer, until soon the outline of what appeared to be a large city appeared in the distance. And beyond that city was a wall of blackness, the blueness of the sky gradually transitioning into an overwhelming darkness that made Kinker want to run and hide.

Vashnas pointed to the city and said, "That's World's End. Our destination."

Jenur frowned. She leaned over the bulwarks, squinting her eyes, and asked, "So what's that blackness behind the city? It looks weird."

"The edge of the world, of course," said Vashnas. "Beyond that blackness is the Void. Only the gods can pass through the Void."

"What would happen if we tried to sail past it?" said Kinker.

"Simple," said Vashnas. "The Void would annihilate us from

existence. Even those of us who are protected by the gods would not survive."

Jenur gulped. "Well, that's certainly an encouraging thought. Is there anything beyond the Void?"

Vashnas shrugged. "Perhaps the Powers. That's all I was told when I first came to World's End all those years ago."

"Well, I have no intention of getting annihilated," said Jenur, pulling back from over the bulwarks. She brushed her hair out of her eyes and said, "What is World's End like, anyway?"

"You will see soon enough," said Vashnas. "I would rather not describe it, except to say that it completely dwarfs any mortal-made city, whether those made by humans or those made by aquarians."

Kinker frowned. "That is hard to believe."

"Yet it is true," said Vashnas. She patted her jacket and said, "Not that it matters. I'll be killing Tinkar either way, whatever World's End is like nowadays."

That led to an awkward silence. Kinker bit his lower lip and looked away, while Jenur tried to pretend that she didn't hear that but clearly did. The other sailors had varying reactions to this little reminder of Vashnas's grim quest, including Gino actually walking away. Vashnas herself said nothing, but merely played with a strange little silver disk that she seemed to value highly.

As they drew closer to World's End, they saw even stranger things. The most notable were strange bird-like creatures that were vaguely humanoid in appearance. Their feathers were in every color imaginable, from the brightest of red to the darkest of black, and everything in between. They did not fly low enough for Kinker to see them in detail, but he admired their beauty nonetheless.

"They are the bird children," said Vashnas in response to an unasked question. "Children and followers of the gods. Like the singing leapers, they live only around World's End. They have no reason to go anywhere else."

"What are they like?" said Jenur, looking up at the bird children as they flew by overhead.

"Stinky, dirty, and not nearly as fabulous as they look," said Vashnas.

Kinker looked at her in surprise. "Did you have a bad experience with them or something?"

"They tossed me off World's End when I was banished," Vashnas said, her hands wrapped tightly around the ship's railing. "They did it rather gleefully, too."

The bird children kept their distance, although a few of the braver ones swooped in every now and then, like they had never seen mortals before. Sometimes they screeched or chirped like normal birds, but Kinker could not understand a word they said. He just watched in awe as one bird swooped down, plucked a fish out of the water, and flew back to join its companions that soared among the clouds.

They were not the only seagoing vessel on the waters around World's End, however. Scattered like pebbles in a park were dozens of small, one- or two-person fishing boats, lines cast, that reminded Kinker of the kind used by fisherman back on Destan. On these boats were what appeared to be men and women, but he could not tell for sure because they, like the bird children, kept their distance.

"Who are they?" said Jenur, pointing at the people on the fishing boats.

One of the people, a man in a blue shirt, waved at their ship as it passed as Vashnas said, "Katabans. Like Hanarova back on Stalf. "

"There are katabans here?" said Jenur. "Do they live on World's End?"

"Of course," said Vashnas. "All katabans live on World's End, except when summoned elsewhere by gods. It is their birthplace and their home. Last time I was here, the streets were full of them."

"They seem awfully friendly," said Kinker, waving back at the man, whose boat they quickly left behind. "Much friendlier than Hanarova ever was."

"Yes, and that's what disturbs me," said Vashnas, staring at a female katabans who was reeling in a large black fish with tentacles in place of eyes. "Kano must have told them to not attack us."

"That's good, isn't it?" said Jenur. "I mean, we're really in no shape to fight, considering ... you know."

"I know," said Vashnas. "Still, I would advise none of you to let your guard down around any of these katabans. They can be deceptive and tricky, even when they're friendly."

"So what, do you expect them to try to kill us or something all of a sudden?" said Jenur.

Vashnas shook her head. "I only expect the worst. That is all."

A few hours later, the island of World's End itself became close enough for Kinker to see it in some detail. And what he saw astonished him more than anything he had ever seen on this voyage.

World's End was not only known as the Throne of the Gods for nothing. The city literally appeared to be a giant throne. The buildings were arranged in such a way that the tallest of them scraped the sky and the smallest of them rivaled small mountains in size. Kinker had never seen such huge structures before and he was convinced at first that those were not buildings at all but rather strangely shaped mountains.

Then Jenur said, "Are those buildings?"

"Yes," said Vashnas. "Though they weren't quite so huge back when I was first here. They must have gotten a lot of construction done in the thousands of years since I was here last."

"But why would they arrange them to look like a gigantic throne?" said Jenur, scratching her chin. "That seems kind of impractical and unnecessary."

"Because the gods, I would think you would have realized by now, are really nothing more than giant show-offs," said Vashnas. "A giant throne on the edge of the world is quite dramatic, wouldn't you say?"

"But who are they trying to impress?" said Kinker. "Us?"

"Or each other," said Vashnas. "Or both. Even the southern gods tend to suffer from the kind of delusional pride that their northern siblings do."

"It's still amazing," said Kinker. "If I lived in such a city, I'd never leave it."

"The gods have to be out and about in the world," said Vashnas. "It's part of their job. If they never left the city, then the world would be worse off than it is now."

Kinker had no argument against that. He just watched as they drew closer to the island, as the buildings that made up the magnificent city grew even larger, towering above them so high that Kinker did not think he would be able to see their tops once he got close enough. Part of him was actually afraid. He wanted to run away. But he had nowhere to go, so he dismissed the feeling as the irrational impulse that it was.

This voyage is nearly at its end, Kinker thought. *Best to see it through, despite whatever may be waiting for us.*

The *Iron Wind* docked at the northern end in the island, which had a dock that seemed to have been designed with their ship in mind because they managed to lower the ramp down to it with no trouble. This surprised Malock, although he supposed that perhaps the gods or katabans used ships sometimes, which would explain the dock.

Malock gathered the entire crew onto the top deck, near the ramp, every surviving member of the original fleet that had set out from Carnag months ago. From his count, there were a little over eighty sailors left out of the hundreds that he'd started with. Standing in front of them on the top of the ramp, Malock grimaced at how small the crew was now and how weak and pathetic everyone looked, especially in contrast to the magnificence that was World's End.

Nonetheless, Malock gestured at the city and said, "My men, my sailors, my crew. Throughout this long, mad voyage, you have all struggled to survive, have been pushed to your limits and beyond. You have faced death, unimaginable pain and loss, dangers of the kind spoken of only in the legends of old, and suffered the loss of a good many friends and fellow sailors. That we made it this far at all, when by all rights we should have perished at some point during this long voyage, is a miracle in itself."

None of the crew responded to that little speech. Most of them seemed distracted by the Throne of the Gods, which shone lightly in the sun. Or perhaps they were so worn out from the voyage that even Malock's greatest praise meant nothing to them.

Either way, Malock had more to say: "I do not know what awaits us in the city itself. Kano has yet to reveal to me why she summoned me, but I do know this: I will not be going into the city alone. Instead, every one of you will get to come with me. There will be no one left behind on this ship, not even someone to act as ship guard. Everyone will come."

That got a reaction. Most of the crew began muttering in disbelief among themselves, while Jenur, who was one of the sailors closest to him, said, "You're kidding."

"I kid not," said Malock, shaking his head. "I've decided that all of you deserve a chance to walk upon a land spoken of only in legends. Besides, I would not feel comfortable ending this voyage by myself. I started it with all of you and will end it with all of you. Is that understood?"

"Yes, sir!" said the sailors in unison, their tone actually happy for once.

Malock smiled. "Then follow me and Vashnas. We will lead the way into the city."

Chapter Twenty-Three

As Malock and Vashnas, walking side by side, led the crew down the ramp and onto the large, well-polished wood dock, Malock glanced over his shoulder at his crew. Most of them were ragged and dirty, even those wearing the extra clothes provided by the Mechanical Goddess, hardly the kind of people you'd expect to see in a city meant for gods and spirits, but he knew he could trust each and every one of them if he ever found himself in danger.

That was why he was bringing them all along. He was not sure why, but ever since World's End came into view, Malock had the strangest feeling that he was never going to see Carnag or the rest of the Northern Isles ever again. While he was not afraid of World's End, he had no intention of staying or dying here. He had a throne to inherit back home, after all. All he wanted to do here was find out what Kano had summoned him for and nothing else.

So Malock brought along the entire crew because he hoped that maybe their numbers would keep him safe. He realized this was foolish. After all, any one of the gods could easily destroy them all without even trying. Only he and Vashnas were safe from harm, being as they were Chosen Ones, but the rest of the crew wasn't and if the gods did not want them entering their city ...

Malock chose not to dwell on that. He walked with a confident stride, his head held high, and his chest out. He did not want to make his men despair, especially when they were so close to finishing their voyage. As always, he would have to put on a brave face for them, even if he did not feel brave.

The path they took was a simple cobblestone path, which wound through a small jungle around the walls of the city. Overhead, the branches of the trees extended above them, like the trumpets of the royal trumpeters back home or perhaps more like miserable guards who were making sure no one escaped. Both images were appropriate.

It took them maybe ten minutes, if even that, to reach the outer walls of the city. The walls appeared to be made out of the purest iron, high and thick and shiny. The walls were not quite as tall as the buildings they protected (which made Malock wonder why they had been built at all), but they were nonetheless imposing, carved as they were with images of all of the gods of Martir. The images were carved so compactly that making out one god among the many was almost impossible, but Malock did see a tiny naked man with a leaf covering his penis among them, a spitting image of the Loner God. That did not improve his mood much.

The crew of the *Iron Wind* stood before a gigantic set of gates. The gates were too huge and thick for any of them to move. Even if the entire crew worked together, Malock doubted they could even so much as budge the gates.

Nonetheless, he confidently walked up to the gates and knocked on them like he would any door. That may have seemed a strange thing to do, but he had no idea how else to announce their presence, as he did not see any guards or gatekeepers who he could talk to.

Almost without warning, the gates began to open inwards. They made no creaking sounds, did not even appear to have hinges. They opened silently and gracefully and once they were opened wide enough, the crew began walking again, entering the massive city of the gods.

Stepping through the gates of the Throne was not at all like entering a mortal city. When Malock stepped over the threshold, a power unlike any he had ever known washed over him. It was almost enough to drive him to his knees, so unexpected and so powerful it was. He had never experienced anything quite like it before. It was like being frisked by a guard, but he saw no hands and there were no guards in his sight.

He looked at Vashnas, who didn't seem bothered by it, and said, "Did you feel—?"

Vashnas nodded. "Visitors to the Throne are always examined by the gods themselves. What you felt was the gods' collective presence washing over us. And unless I am highly mistaken, I do believe we have just passed."

Malock looked at his men. They had all passed over the threshold without trouble, but they looked disturbed. Many of them were scratching their bodies, like they had been bitten by bugs.

"What would have happened if the gods did not approve of us?" Malock asked.

Vashnas smiled grimly. "Oh, we would have all burst into flames. Or at least the others would have. You and me would probably have just been crippled for life."

Malock didn't quite know what to think of that, but the thought was driven from his mind when he got his first truly up close and personal look at the Throne of the Gods.

And what a marvelous city it was. All of the buildings appeared to be made out of crystal, rubies, emeralds, and other precious stones and metals that Malock could not even begin to name. The streets were paved with snow; at least, that's what it felt like underneath his feet. The stone was not hard, but soft and comfortable, yet capable of holding the entire weight of the city on top of it.

Crowds and crowds of katabans—that had to be who these people were—filled every street. There were young children, adults, and old people, much like you'd see on any street in any city, but these people looked different from the people Malock knew. Their hairstyles ranged from practical bowl cuts to extravagant flame-styles and those were the more conservative ones. Malock wondered if magic was what made those hairstyles possible, but he dismissed the thought instead to focus on his mission.

The katabans watched the sailors walk through the streets with varying expressions. Some of them looked on in disgust, because the dirty rags worn by the sailors contrasted so sharply with the beautiful streets of the city that even Malock felt embarrassed by it. Most simply watched with interest and wonder, as if they had never seen so many mortals before in one place. The children in particular looked on with big eyes, but whenever Malock looked at them, they turned and scurried away. Those few children who didn't look away had the eyes of elders, as if they had already lived a full, rich life and were ready to die happy.

Yet none of the katabans stopped them or asked who they were or what they were doing here. Actually, quite the opposite occurred. Wherever the crew of the *Iron Wind* went, the crowds of katabans parted. Even the big scary ones with rippling muscles did not stand in their way.

The crew themselves were utterly silent as they walked, aside from the sounds of their booted feet walking along the pavement or the occasional cough or sniffling. There were certainly a variety of interesting things on display in the city (such as a salesman hawking a potion that allegedly contained the healing tears of Atikos), but no one stopped to look at these things. For that matter, even the most oafish of salesmen went silent wherever the sailors passed, as if they were a funeral procession rather than a group of mortals about to meet their destiny.

Malock immediately understood the general silence and deference of the katabans. They had known that Malock and his crew were coming, most likely because Kano told them. He further speculated that Kano had ordered all katabans to allow the sailors to go to wherever the gods lived unmolested, although he was surprised that Tinkar had not ordered any to do otherwise. Perhaps the God of Fate hadn't expected them to make it this far.

Whatever the case, Malock wondered where they were going. He asked Vashnas this question.

"To the Temple of the Gods," Vashnas replied. "That is where the gods gather whenever they are visiting this island and it is where Kano likely is."

"So you know where this Temple is?" said Malock.

Vashnas nodded as the group turned down a street. "The Throne is different from how I remember it, but the basic layout appears unchanged, so I imagine we'll find it quickly."

'Quickly' was perhaps an understatement because not five minutes after she said that, the group turned down yet another street and found themselves in what appeared to be the center of the mighty city. It was a wide-open square, with a shallow, creek-like moat of water surrounding a magnificent building that put Carnag Hall to shame.

To call it a palace would be an insult to the building's greatness. It towered above their heads, not quite as big as some of the other buildings, but large enough to give off the impression of divine power. It had dozens of turrets and towers, each one individually crafted to reflect a different god, from the fiery flames of one tower to the flowing waves of another. Water poured out of the channels into the tiny creek-like moat surrounding it; pure water, even purer than the clear ocean around the island. Massive gates, made of the most brilliant marble and pearl, shone in the light of the streetlamps, carved with a symbol that resembled a sun radiating heat. A short bridge connected the Temple of the Gods—for that was what it had to be—with the rest of the street, but even that short bridge looked magnificent, as if the God of Sculpting himself had designed it.

Perhaps the most striking aspect of it all, however, was the raw energy radiating from it. There was no mistaking that energy for anything other than what it was: The very presence of the gods themselves, manifested so strongly that it was a wonder it didn't kill the entire crew of the *Iron Wind* right there and then. It was so powerful that even Malock feared for his life.

Vashnas fearlessly led the crew over the short bridge right up to the massive gates themselves. Up close, the gates were inscribed with writing in a language Malock could not read, yet which he understood to be the language of the gods. Every letter appeared to have been crafted with individual, exquisite care, so that even though it was impossible for Malock to read, he knew that it was above and beyond anything mortals could create with pen and ink.

Their journey was cut short, however, when something massive jumped down from one of the nearby towers and landed on the street in front of them, blocking their access to the gates. Even before the giant rose to its full height, Malock had no trouble recognizing the Verch or, as it was properly known, Messenger-and-Punisher.

Of course, the rest of the crew—barring Banika, Vashnas, and Jenur—had never seen it before. Most of them cowered in fear at the massive, tentacled giant, while the braver (or perhaps dumber) ones had drawn their weapons and looked prepared to battle.

Messenger made that strange sucking sound again and a moment later a familiar green blob of ooze shot from its obscured face. The blog splashed onto the street, its grime stopping just short of Malock's boots, and then a familiar upper humanoid body rose from it, looking exactly the same as it had on the day that Messenger had mistakenly taken Telka away.

"Messenger," said Malock, holding up his hand to signal to his crew not to attack it. "I did not expect to see you, of all entities, here. I thought you would be out running errands for the gods."

Messenger grunted. "Special request from Kano. Be gatekeeper for day. Boring as wood."

Malock had a hard time understanding how even a job as routine as gatekeeper could ever be boring in such a majestic city, but he nodded anyway and said, "Well, since Kano summoned me, I must ask you to step aside and let me inside. That is what I am here to do, after all."

"Fine," said Messenger. "But no crew. Stay out."

"What?" said Malock. "Why can't I bring them in with me?"

"Tinkar's orders," Messenger said.

"So he's here, too?" Vashnas said, her voice a mixture of dread and anticipation.

Messenger looked at her closely for a moment before saying, "Yes. Malock, Vashnas, and Kinker must go in alone."

Malock raised an eyebrow. "Did you say Kinker?"

"Yes," Messenger said, nodding. "No understand?"

"No, no, I do," said Malock. "But why Kinker?"

"Not understanding," said Messenger, in obvious reference to himself. "Messenger, not god. Ask them if you wish to know."

Malock looked over his shoulder at Kinker, who looked as shocked as anyone else at his being singled out. Nonetheless, the elderly man joined Malock and Vashnas at the front of the crowd, perhaps because he did not dare disobey the dictates of whichever god had summoned him inside.

"What about the rest of my crew?" said Malock to Messenger.

"You aren't going to harm them, are you?"

"No," said Messenger. "They stay. I watch."

"Ah," said Malock. "All right. As long as you don't harm them—"

"No reason to," said Messenger. "After doctor, no trust myself."

Malock was surprised to hear what sounded like regret in the Messenger's voice. True, it was always difficult to gauge the emotions of non-mortals, but the way the Messenger looked away—if only for the briefest of seconds—and its tone of voice told the prince that it was ashamed of having taken Telka mistakenly.

Then Messenger went back to its usual stoic demeanor and said, "Malock, Vashnas, and Kinker. Enter now."

The Messenger slid out of the way as the gates creaked open inward; not fully, but just enough that three mortals could slip through without trouble.

Malock looked between Vashnas on his left and Kinker on his right. "You two ready for this?"

"I have been ready for thousands of years," said Vashnas.

"I'm not," Kinker admitted. "But there's not much I can do about it, so I suppose I have to be."

Malock nodded. "Then let us enter. Today, my destiny will finally be fulfilled. This I know."

So the trio of mortals passed through the gates, Malock certain that whatever lay beyond them, whatever Kano was going to tell him, whatever Tinkar was going to try to do to them, they would be able to handle it.

The Temple of the Gods reminded Kinker of the Temple of

Kano back home on Destan. Of course, that temple was nowhere near as majestic or large as this one. The Temple of Kano was old and full of evil, not helped in the slightest by its decayed outer appearance. Unspeakable crimes had been committed there, once even by Kinker himself, and the place reflected the smallness of mortal minds (he was surprised to be thinking such things; perhaps it was the presence of the god affecting his thoughts).

The Temple's lobby was immense and wide-open, reminding Kinker more of the open seas than the inside of a building. The immense ceiling was supported by pillars made of marble and that same white stone that paved the streets, the pillars themselves carved with images of gods.

On either side of the path leading to the very end of the lobby were statues of the gods. It wasn't just a few statues either, but hundreds, maybe even thousands, of statues, each one representing a different god or goddess. It astonished Kinker, as he, Malock, and Vashnas made their way down the lobby, at how few gods he really knew of when he saw the dazzling variety of statues that took up almost the entirety of the massive lobby. He wondered who all of these gods were and exactly what roles they played in keeping the balance of Martir.

Of course, not all of the statues were in one piece. Quite a few appeared to have been smashed and not recently, either. Kinker vaguely recalled Malock mentioning something about some war between the gods that had occurred eons ago, near the beginning of time, and wondered if these smashed statues represented the fallen gods and goddesses from that conflict. He certainly felt no desire to pick through the smashed statues, although he wondered why they hadn't been cleaned up yet, considering that they took away from the lobby's magnificence.

Another striking feature of the lobby was its absolute silence. Outside of the footfalls of Kinker, Malock, and Vashnas, there was no sound to be heard. And this silence was not like the silence back outside, when the katabans were watching the crew make their way through the city. Rather, it was a kind of imposed silence, as if excessive noise was against the law here. This silence made Kinker feel very small, much smaller than he normally did.

Thus, he was glad when they reached the end of the lobby, where they found some human-sized double doors that were unlocked. Malock had no trouble pushing them open and he was the first to step through the threshold into whatever room awaited them. Even though no one had told them to enter, Kinker understood why Malock did; he could feel the presence of the gods drawing them to this room.

The 'room' they walked into was not a room at all. Even calling it a chamber was an insult to its size and majesty. It was like walking into a full-sized area stadium, complete with sand pit in the center, and stands rising up on all sides. The stands, however, were not quite stands, but rather thrones of varying heights and sizes. There seemed to be as many thrones as there were statues of the gods, except each throne was completely empty.

Moreover, the ceiling was a glass dome, so clear that Kinker at first thought there wasn't a ceiling at all, and light filtered in through the dome. Despite the bright light shining down on them all, it didn't make Kinker feel any happier. He instead felt tense.

The trio reached the center of the room, where they stopped and looked up at the hundreds of thrones that stood up all around them. As Kinker noted before, however, every throne was empty. There were no gods in the room, even though Kinker could still feel their energy and presence flowing through the room like a mighty wave of the ocean.

Malock scratched the back of his head as he looked around, frowning. "Where is everyone?"

Vashnas, too, was looking around, but she was scowling rather than frowning. "I imagine Tinkar, being the coward that he is, ran as fast as he could when he realized Bifor failed. He obviously didn't want to die today."

A powerful, aged voice swept through the room just then, saying, "I have always known of your low opinion of me, Vashnas, but I never realized just how lowly you think of me. Truly, the years have done nothing but make you bitter; bitter and arrogant."

When Kinker blinked, there was suddenly two other beings in the room besides himself, Malock, and Vashnas. The first was a young woman, perhaps in her thirties (although Kinker instinctively knew she was centuries older than that), sitting atop one of the thrones in the lists before them. He might otherwise not have noticed her if her hair had not been flowing—quite literally, like water—down her shoulders. In fact, her whole body was a clear blue and she herself was completely naked, which somehow didn't seem inappropriate on her.

The other was an old man, sitting on the throne a few thrones away from the young woman. Whereas the young woman sat up straight with the confidence of youth, the old man was bent over, his veined hands gripping a staff topped with a clock. He wore robes as white as the sand on Ikadori Island, which contrasted sharply with his dark-skinned face, etched as it was with lines.

Though Kinker had never seen either of them in person before, he immediately knew who those two were.

"Kano, Goddess of the Sea, Sand, and Art," said Malock, addressing the young woman. And to the old man he said, "And Tinkar, God of Fate."

The young woman smiled at Malock, folding her hands in her lap. "I am pleased to see that you have made it here alive, Prince Malock. I am equally pleased to see you, too, Kinker Dolan."

Kinker scratched his beard. "Really?"

"Really," said Kano. "In fact, I am more pleased to see you than I am to see Malock."

Malock looked like a shrunken jellyfish when she said that. "What?"

"It doesn't matter," said Tinkar. "I am not even sure why we are speaking to all three of you together like this. I would rather deal with Vashnas in private, by myself."

Kano shot Tinkar an annoyed look. "You know why we are doing this together, Tinkar. Or did you forget about the part where one of *your* followers tried to kill one of mine? I am certain that Malock would love to hear an explanation for that."

Tinkar didn't look at all cowed by Kano's sharp words. "I have not forgotten that. Nor have I forgotten how you stubbornly refused my requests to order your prince to kill Vashnas, even though he was sleeping with her every night. Do you value the life of one of your servants over the life of your older brother?"

Kano rolled her eyes. "Older, maybe, but not any wiser."

While the two gods bickered like children, Kinker noticed Vashnas reaching into her coat pocket. She pulled out that strange little disk from earlier, turned it over in her hand a few times, and quickly put it back in just as Kano and Tinkar returned their attention to the mortals.

"At any rate," said Kano, "the point is, you three are all here for a reason and we, too, are here for a reason. And that reason—or, I should say, reasons—are what we are here to discuss."

Malock raised a hand. "Excuse me, great and powerful Kano, but may I ask where the other gods are? Why are you two the only ones here?"

"Because we're the only two gods who have anything to do with this conflict, mortal," said Tinkar. "Of course, there is our younger sister, the Mechanical Goddess, but she has never been very fond of the Throne of the Gods and isn't likely to show up. Typical."

"She didn't come because she had me come instead," said Vashnas. "We're sick of the way you've treated us. I think it's about time that someone else got a say in fate, someone who isn't a jerk."

Tinkar didn't laugh. Instead, he looked a bit sad. "Vashnas, I am sorry for what happened all those years ago. It's just that I don't—"

"No excuses," said Vashnas, stepping forward, her hand reaching into her jacket again. "I've been waiting years for this moment. And I am not about to let it slip out of my grasp."

She pulled the shiny silver disk out of her jacket and hurled it at

Tinkar with amazing speed and accuracy. It sliced through the air and Tinkar didn't even try to dodge. He actually tilted his head to the side, allowing the disk to lodge itself directly into his neck, a move that shocked Kinker and Malock.

Smiling triumphantly, Vashnas pumped her right fist and shouted, "Yes! I did it! Your days are numbered, Tinkar, and there's nothing you can do to—"

Then Tinkar reached up and yanked the disk straight out of his neck. He looked at it in amusement as the wound in his neck rapidly closed up and then tossed the disk over his shoulder. A clatter of metal against stone was the last they heard of the disk.

Vashnas looked like someone had punched her upside the head. "What the hell? The Mechanical Goddess told me that would kill you. It was a direct hit. You shouldn't even have a head anymore."

Tinkar chuckled. "Indeed, that little trick might have worked if you actually had been chosen by the Mechanical Goddess. If she had actually bothered to grant you some of her power. If she actually cared about your little vendetta against me at all."

"What do you mean?" said Vashnas. "Of course she cares. She agreed to defend me so I could kill you."

"Oh, she didn't really mean it," said Tinkar. "Remember, the Mechanical Goddess is a southern goddess. She has little interest in mortals. She is also smart, smart enough to realize what would happen if I died. No, Vashnas, the Mechanical Goddess simply fooled you, just as I asked her to."

A stunned silence filled the room. The only one who didn't looked stunned by this particular revelation was Kano, perhaps because she already knew about it.

"What?" said Vashnas. "What do you mean ... asked her to?"

"Exactly what I mean," said Tinkar. "You see, Vashnas, I've always known that someday you would come back for me. Not because of my ability to see the fate of mortals—I cannot see yours, thanks to the Curse of Senva—but because you were so filled with rage and hate at me when you first left World's End so many years ago. I kept an eye on you as you made a life up north, waiting for the day when you would finally decide to strike back at me.

"Then you met Hanarova, that idiotic servant of the Mechanical Goddess. The Mechanical Goddess told me about you, about how you offered her a deal: that you would kill me in exchange for the Mechanical Goddess's protection."

"That's because I knew the Mechanical Goddess hated you," said Vashnas. "She wanted you dead as much as I do."

"And that, I am afraid, is where you are wrong, my pretty little fish," said Tinkar. "The Mechanical Goddess and I have had, ah, strained relations ever since the War, that's true, but she knows better than to risk another War via deicide. She decided to pretend to help you in order to give you over to me, thus circumventing the problem entirely."

"But ..." Vashnas struggled to come up with a response. "So you're saying, I was duped?"

"Of course," said Tinkar. "As old and long-lived as you are, Vashnas, you are nothing more than a mortal. You cannot out-think us, even if you tried to manipulate we gods into fighting each other. The only reason I let you get this far at all is because I wanted to see just how crushed you would look when I revealed the truth to you. And I must say it was worth every minute I waited."

Vashnas's hands shook, shook so bad that Kinker thought she was going to fall apart. "What now? Are you going to banish me from World's End again?"

"No," said Tinkar. "I am going to do what I should have done to you a long time ago: Kill you where you stand, so I no longer have to worry about you causing any trouble."

He raised his hand, but he never got to do whatever he planned to do because Malock stepped in front of Vashnas and said, "You aren't going to harm her. Or even touch her."

The throne room's atmosphere changed perceptibly. Tinkar looked enraged, while Kano seemed be trying hard not to smirk.

"Are you directly challenging me?" said Tinkar. "Me? A god?"

"Not challenging you," said Malock. "I'm simply protecting Vashnas. There are a lot of things she and I don't agree on, but I would die myself before I let anyone kill her. And that includes if the would-be killer in question is a god who controls fate."

Tinkar actually stood up. His back was still bent over, but that didn't stop him from looking like he was going to murder Malock where he stood. "Such insolence. It has been years since a mortal last stood up to me like that. I will not let you get away with this unpunished."

Kano held up a hand and said, "Remember the Treaty, Tinkar. Malock is still under my protection. You can fume at him all you want, but you can't kill him. I *will* intervene if you try anything against him."

Tinkar threw her an irritated glare, but he did sit down, his eyes full of anger and hate. "Yes. I almost forgot. I am so used to smiting insolent mortals that the terms of the Treaty almost crossed my mind. It does not change the fact, however, that I want to kill Vashnas."

"I care not what you choose to do to her," said Kano. "Insofar as harming her harms Malock, however, then I must step in."

Malock looked brave, standing there in front of Vashnas like that, but Kinker noticed the slightest tremble in the prince's demeanor. No wonder; if Kinker had stood up to any gods, he, too, would have been trembling in his boots. Vashnas looked both astonished and grateful at Malock's actions.

Kano turned away from Tinkar, who looked like he wanted to murder her, and said to Malock, "With that out of the way, I do believe it is time we discussed the reason I summoned you here in the first place."

Malock looked up her eagerly, though he still stood in front of Vashnas. "I am all ears, my goddess."

"Of course, the reason you are here has to do with why I asked Messenger-and-Punisher to allow Kinker inside, too," said Kano. "I am sure you were wondering about that."

Malock glanced at Kinker before saying, "Yes, I was."

Kano put her hands together, looking more than a bit excited. "You see, Malock, I summoned you here for a very specific reason: To deliver Kinker here, a task that I must say you completed admirably well."

It was amazing how quickly Malock's expression changed from excitement to disbelief. "Excuse me, Kano, I don't believe I heard you right. Did you say—"

"That you were supposed to deliver Kinker to me, yes," said Kano, nodding. "You heard right."

Malock and Vashnas looked at Kinker in disbelief as the old fisherman said, "Me? But why would you want me?"

"That's the same question I was going to ask," said Malock, before Kano could speak. "Forgive me for impudence, my goddess, but I was under the impression that you had summoned *me* for a reason, that you were going to reward me with something."

Kano tilted her head, as if puzzled. "Why would I ever reward you? You have done nothing to deserve any reward. Admittedly, you are the first mortal in many years to reach World's End alive, but that is mostly due to my protective aura and luck."

"But ..." Malock looked like he had just been told that his favorite kitten had died. "Why did you summon me at all? Couldn't you have ordered Messenger-and-Punisher to bring Kinker to you instead?"

Kano put the tips of her fingers together, as if deep in thought. "Messenger-and-Punisher is not really a very good transporter. Mortals who are taken by him to anywhere—even if it's only a very short trip—usually come out of it little more than gibbering lunatics. I wanted Kinker to be sane, so I decided that having you bring him to me would make more sense."

Malock looked like his brain was working overtime, as if trying to comprehend what he was hearing. "But ... I ... what ..."

Kano turned to Kinker and smiled at him. "The point is, you have made it here, alive and in one piece. And that, Kinker, my loyal follower, is an accomplishment."

"This is an honor, Kano," said Kinker, when he finally found his tongue. "To be chosen by you—"

"What makes Kinker so special?" Malock snapped, his voice higher than normal for some reason. "I am sorry for the tone, Kano, but Kinker is ... I mean, he's just a fisherman from a backwater island in the middle of nowhere. Why did I have to deliver him? Why did I have to risk life and limb just to play delivery boy?"

Tinkar smirked, probably enjoying the mental anguish that Malock was experiencing right now. Kano, on the other hand, looked amused at Malock's questions.

"Because of your nature," said Kano. "You are stubborn and driven. Considering the dangerous nature of the southern seas, I considered those values to be highly important. I believed that a man like you would reach World's End eventually, even if it you lost your ship, which as I recall nearly happened more than once."

Malock ran a hand through his hair in sheer agony. "You mean this entire time I ... I ... then why didn't you make Kinker a Chosen One?"

Kano raised an eyebrow. "You mean you failed to notice how he was one of the few members of your crew to survive my younger brother's misguided attack on your ship back on Stalf? I suppose I shouldn't have expected you mortals to know, considering how blind you are to the aura Chosen Ones give off, but I would have thought it obvious much the same. How else could he have survived murder season around the seas of Destan?"

Malock was briefly at a loss for words. He opened and closed his mouth several times, looked at Kinker helplessly, and then drooped his shoulders. He looked down at his feet as Vashnas placed a hand on his shoulder.

"But that doesn't explain why you wanted me, though," said Kinker. "I mean, I am honored to have been chosen by you, Kano, but why would you want me? Especially after what I did back on Destan. I would think you would have wanted to punish me for my crimes."

"You committed crimes?" said Vashnas, looking at him in surprise. "I always thought you were too good for that."

Kano regarded Kinker with confusion. "It was just a mortal boy, Kinker. Hardly a precious life. No, what you did or didn't do back on Destan is—"

"Just a mortal boy?" Kinker interrupted, despite himself. "My goddess, I was forced to murder the boy in cold blood. Surely that must mean I am deserving of some kind of punishment."

Again, Kano looked confused, almost as if Kinker was speaking a language she didn't understand. "But it's true. Who cares about the life of a puny mortal infant? He likely would not have gone on to do great things. Right, Tinkar?"

Tinkar grunted. "It's true. The boy was fated to die at your hands, Kinker, since his birth. Besides, we gods have killed far more mortals than just a boy. It's not like a forced murder disqualifies you from godhood."

Kinker blinked. "But I—wait, did you say godhood?"

Kano smiled and said, "Ah, I'm glad to see that you're catching on. Yes, Kinker, the reason—the whole reason—I summoned Prince Malock to deliver you here is to ascend you into godhood, as is your rightful destiny."

Kinker's heart stopped. He was sure of it. It had to. He looked into Kano's eyes, wondering if she was joking, but she looked completely serious. Tinkar looked just as serious, if a bit grumpy. Malock and Vashnas looked as shocked as he felt; in fact, Malock looked totally floored.

"Me?" said Kinker in a weak voice. "Ascend to ... godhood?"

"Yes," said Kano. "Lucky you. Very few mortals have ever been fated to join our ranks. The last one was my lovely wife Niham, who ascended six hundred years ago to this day."

Tinkar grunted. "I still hold that *that* particular ascension was a mistake."

"Only because you wanted to kill her for not groveling at your feet as a mortal," Kano pointed out. "But I digress."

Kinker raised a hand. "But ... why me? I am not special. I am not a prince, like Malock. I am not a priest or a rich man. I am actually quite poor. The only real skills I have are my fishing skills, but I don't think being a good fisherman means I am qualified for godhood."

Tinkar laughed. "You think we chose you? Hardly. We gods are so jealous of our status, we'd never choose any mortal to join our ranks if we could help it. Niham was a freak exception. No, when you were born, I saw in your future that you were going to become one of us someday."

"But that doesn't make any sense," said Kinker. "Someone had to choose me, right? I mean ... right?"

"Likely the Powers did," said Kano. "The Powers set the destiny of every mortal under the sun. I imagine that at the beginning of time, they set your destiny so that you would become a god one day. And that day, I am happy to say, has finally come."

"I still don't understand," said Kinker. "Don't you already have enough gods? I saw the statues back in the lobby. There are hundreds of you guys, maybe even thousands. What domain could I possibly control, were I to become a god?"

Kano smiled, a rather sad one. "A small one, I imagine. We don't have a God of Fishermen yet. Considering that that is what you specialize in, we speculate that that is supposed to be your domain."

"Wouldn't Tinkar know what I'm supposed to do as a god?" said Kinker, pointing at the God of Fate. "I mean, he knows the fates of all mortals, doesn't he?"

"I do," said Tinkar. "Except for yours. Before Kano chose you, I saw up to the moment of your ascension. Beyond that, my powers fail me because I cannot see the fates of my fellow gods."

He sounded sore about that particular limitation on his powers.

"This is all hard to take at once," said Kinker, putting his hands on his head. "I mean, all of it just seems so—"

"No!"

Everyone turned to look at Malock, who had shouted. His eyes bulged, his fingers twisted strangely in his hands, and he was breathing heavily.

"No, no, no, no!" Malock boomed, his voice so loud that even the two gods seemed to cringe at the noise. "This can't be true. Can't be. Just can't."

"What do you have your pants in a twist for?" said Tinkar in disgust. "Are you going insane? Because if you are, this Temple is no place for that."

Malock pointed one shaking finger at Kinker and said, "Him. That old fool."

"Fool?" said Kano, sounding genuinely surprised. "Malock, I thought you liked Kinker. Considered him a friend, even. Why do you insult him so?"

Malock pulled his hair, almost ripping it from their roots, looking utterly insane. "It just doesn't make any sense. It makes no sense at all. *I* was chosen. I am Prince Tojas Malock, Crown Prince of Carnag, Son of King Halock and Queen Markinia, Captain of the *Iron Wind*, Chosen One of Kano, and a thousand other titles that I could list. I should be the one ascending to godhood. I should."

Tinkar chuckled. "Sorry, mortal. We didn't make the rules. The Powers did. If you have a problem, bring up with them ... if you can survive the Void, that is."

"Shut up," Malock said, pointing at Tinkar. "Shut up, you evil, malicious, conniving son of a bitch. You've done nothing but make my voyage a living hell right from the start. You've killed off most of my crew, sunk my fleet, tried to have one of your followers kill me and Vash, all because of some grudge you have against Kano. Did you somehow manipulate fate so I wouldn't be chosen to become a god? Is that it, Tinkar? Is that it?"

Tinkar stood up from his throne again; this time, Kinker doubted he would return to his throne. "Did you just tell me, a god, to shut up? You mortals are truly arrogant. I always considered it amusing how you would give yourself 'royal' titles and prance around acting like that meant anything, but until now I never understood just how arrogant mortals like you really are."

"I am not arrogant," said Malock. "I am only pointing out the truth. I should be the one ascending to godhood. My family was chosen by Grinf himself to rule Carnag. Kinker is just an uneducated peasant from an island that doesn't even have a king. This is unacceptable."

"Oh, so you're pulling out the 'divine right of kings' card now?" said Tinkar with a smirk. "Right. Even we northern gods know better than to declare certain mortals rulers over others. Most likely, Grinf didn't do that sort of thing. It wouldn't be just and we all know just how obsessed my twin brother is with justice."

The way Malock looked now reminded Kinker of someone he had seen back on Destan some years back. It had been during murder season, when the seas around Destan were at their most dangerous. A certain rich man, not a priest but married to one, had left out his magnificent houseboat that he had bought from a northern company that built houseboats. When the morning came, the magnificent houseboat had been reduced to nothing more than scraps of wood on the water. The way the rich man had looked when he saw it reminded Kinker of how Malock looked now.

"So ..." Malock's hands shook. "You mean there's nothing special about me. Or my family."

"Nothing at all, mortal," said Tinkar in a gleeful voice. "The Powers love to mess with our expectations. 'The first will be last and the last will be first,' as the old saying goes."

Malock fell to his hands and knees. He looked like someone had punched him out.

"I am glad we have that out of the way," said Kano. "I am sorry, Malock, but it is true. Your destiny is not to become a god. You will simply remain a mortal."

Kinker felt sorry for Malock, but before he could go over and comfort the prince (despite Malock's rantings against him), Vashnas moved. She ran over to Kinker, moving much faster than Kinker could follow, and grabbed him with two powerful, slimy hands. She immediately pulled him in front of her, with his back to her, one hand twisting his right arm behind him, the other wrapped tightly around his neck, almost constricting his windpipes.

"Vashnas!" said Kano. Like Tinkar, she stood up, too. "What are you doing to Kinker? Let go of him now."

"No," said Vashnas behind Kinker. "I may be unable to kill Tinkar thanks to his godly nature, but Kinker isn't yet a god. Therefore, I am at perfect liberty to kill him."

Malock had gotten back to his feet now and was looking at Vashnas in horror. "Kill him? But why? Kinker didn't do anything to you."

Vashnas snorted. "Maybe not, but I saw how much anguish his destiny has caused you. The gods raised your expectations, making you think you would receive the most beautiful prize imaginable, and then pulled the carpet out from underneath your feet. Because I still love you, Malock, I can't stand by and let you suffer while Kinker gets an undeserved prize."

"But you don't need to kill him," said Malock. "I know I was ranting and raving earlier and yes I am still jealous, but I would never wish death upon Kinker. This isn't right."

"It is right, Malock, and you know it," said Vashnas. "Besides, I have nothing else to live for. I will die soon anyway, I am sure. I might as well go out with a bang, if you know what I mean."

Kinker wanted to say something, but his throat was being crushed under Vashnas's powerful grip and he was unable to hit her with his right arm due to the way she was positioned. He looked with panicked eyes up at Kano, but it was clear that the sea goddess could do nothing to help him in this situation.

"I am sorry, Kinker," Vashnas said in his left ear. "It's nothing personal. I really do like you as a person, despite what you did to that little boy. It's just revenge. You understand?"

No, Kinker did not, but he never got a chance to say that. Vashnas's grip tightened around his neck and a second later, all Kinker saw, heard, felt, tasted, and smelled ... was nothing.

"No!" Malock shouted as Vashnas pushed Kinker's corpse forward. "Vashnas, how could you—?"

He never got a chance to finish his sentence because Kano immediately leaped down from her throne. She landed with a splash right in front of Vashnas, where Kinker had stood, and thrust her watery arm into Vashnas's mouth. The aquarian writhed and struggled to get away, but she appeared rooted to the floor as Kano spoke.

"I know how much you like water, aquarian," Kano growled in a voice that was far more dangerous than the waves around Destan during murder season. "Let's see how you do without it."

Vashnas's eyes widened, but she never got the chance to respond.

Her entire body dried up, like a fish left out in the sun for too long, and Kano pushed it over. Vashnas's dried body smashed into pieces when it hit the floor, leaving behind only her clothes.

Malock stood still. He didn't know what to do. He wasn't even sure what to think. He just looked at Kinker's body and then at the remains of Vashnas's shattered corpse and his entire mind felt like it was going to implode, which given the circumstances did not seem entirely unreasonable.

Tinkar jumped down from the thrones, too, and landed not far from Malock. He looked at Vashnas's clothes with a sad expression. "I always suspected her fate would not be a good one. And it looks like I was right."

"What about Kinker?" Malock said. He said the words, but it felt like someone else was saying them. "Can you bring him back to life?"

Kano shook her head. "I am sorry, Malock, but we cannot. Even we gods are unable to revive the dead."

"We could get the God of Puppetry to reanimate his corpse," Tinkar offered. "Of course, that would make his body a puppet, but if you don't mind—"

Without thinking, Malock walked up to Tinkar, even as the god was speaking, and with all of his might slapped the God of Fate in the face.

That turned out to be a huge mistake. Tinkar's face felt like iron and when Malock's hand met it, he heard the bones in his hand *snap*, the sound echoing throughout the throne room like a gun shot. He cursed loudly and held his now-broken hand as Tinkar looked at him with astonishment and anger.

"Did you just slap me?" said Tinkar.

Malock looked up from his broken hand, met the god's eyes, and nodded. "I did."

"For what reason?" said Tinkar. "I didn't hurt you."

Malock could not believe what he was hearing. "Did you not hear the laundry list of crimes I accused you of earlier? Or are you just deaf and dumb?"

"Put that way, I do sound like a terrible being," said Tinkar. "But you should really be blaming Kano for all of this. She was the one who summoned you, after all, and it was Messenger-and-Punisher, working under her orders, who took the wrong guy. And she also, may I add, murdered Vashnas in cold blood."

Malock looked over at Kano. She was walking over to them, almost casually, as if she murdered aquarian women every day.

"I did what I had to do, Malock," said Kano, her tone cold. "Murdering a potential godling is a terrible offense. It is a slap in the face to the Powers themselves. Death was the only suitable punishment for such a crime."

Tears burned Malock's eyes as he said, "Was that so? You mean you couldn't have just locked her up or something?"

"Prisons can be broken out of," said Kano. "That is why we have none on World's End. I know how much you loved her, but—"

"But nothing," Malock said. "You gods ... I don't care how this sounds, but I think all of you—northern and southern—are nothing but sick psychos who aren't worthy of any form of worship or praise. Not a single one of you."

The tension in the room was so thick that Malock could feel it.

Both Kano and Tinkar looked equally enraged and for the first time he could understand how they were related. The way their mouths twisted, the way they stood ... the family resemblance was obvious. And Malock knew that every minute they wasted standing there was another minute he was allowed to live.

Finally, Kano said, "Get out."

"What?" said Malock.

Kano pointed at the double doors. "I said, get out."

"You mean you aren't going to smite me?" said Malock.

"Trust me, mortal, we would love to do that," said Tinkar. "But you are still under Kano's protection and for once your death would do nothing to help us. Just get out."

Malock glanced at Kinker's and Vashnas's bodies. "But Kinker and Vashnas—"

"Out," Kano said in her firmest voice.

This time, Malock didn't argue. Still gripping his broken hand, he made his way out of the room as quickly as he could. He didn't even look over his shoulder as he left, knowing as he did that the two gods might reconsider their decision if he showed any signs of hesitation or reluctance.

That was also why he kept his head down. He didn't want them to see the tears streaming down his face.

Chapter Twenty-Four

UPON EXITING THE TEMPLE, Malock was immediately greeted by Banika, Jenur, and the entire crew of the *Iron Wind*. He was almost taken by surprise at their appearance, having forgotten that they were awaiting him outside. Messenger was nowhere to be seen, although the putrid scent of his ooze hung in the air like a noxious gas.

"Captain," said Banika, stepping forward with Jenur by her side. "What happened to you hand? And where are Vashnas and Kinker?"

Malock didn't look them in the eyes as he said, "They're ... gone."

Jenur peered at him closely and said, "Gone? What do you mean? It's not like they won a free all-expenses paid tour of the city, right?"

Malock looked up at them both, not bothering to hide the tears running down the sad of his face, and said, "Dead. They're both dead."

Banika was as silent and still as usual, but somehow Malock

sensed that this was different from before. And he realized what was so different: She was in shock, expressing it in the only way she knew how.

Jenur, however, was far more expressive. She actually grabbed Malock by the collar of his shirt and said, "Impossible. You're joking."

"I wish I was, but I'm not," Malock said. "Both of them are dead."

Jenur let go of his collar and staggered back, like she had been slapped in the face. "But Kinker can't be dead. He's too tough for that."

"How did it happen?" Banika asked, her voice cracking through her usual calm tone. "Who killed them?"

Malock gave them a condensed version of the events that happened in the throne room. The rest of the crew was also listening and by the time he finished, he saw tears in the eyes of almost every sailor. He hadn't realized until today just how much the rest of the crew had valued Kinker and even Vashnas. It made him feel even worse about complaining about Kinker's destiny earlier.

Jenur glared at the Temple gates, which had shut when Malock exited, and said, "That damned bitch. If she was still alive, I'd take my knife and jab it straight up her—"

"Don't," said Malock. "Just ... don't."

Jenur sighed. "You're right. It's just ... how could she do that? How could she murder Kinker in cold blood? And where is Kinker's body? Why didn't you take it with you?"

"Kano and Tinkar didn't let me," said Malock. "They told me to leave. They gave me no choice."

Jenur looked up at the Temple. "I'm getting in and getting his body. I don't care if that means I have to fight a couple of gods to do it."

Malock had a brief mental vision of Jenur being drained of all of her fluids, just like Vashnas, and he said, "Wait, Jenur, don't—"

The gates cracked open again and Kinker's body was tossed out. It landed in an awkward position at Malock's feet, causing the prince to step back involuntarily. He did not see who had tossed out Kinker's body to them, but he understood that whoever it was, they cared little for the corpse of a mortal man.

Jenur immediately bent down over Kinker's corpse. It took Malock a moment to realize that she was crying, actually crying, which now that he thought about it was highly unusual for her. He had always thought of her as being tough, as being stronger than most people, but maybe she really was just like everyone else.

The rest of the crew gathered around to see Kinker's corpse. Despite the tears and sorrowful expressions on the face of every sailor, no one else went to touch Kinker's corpse, as Jenur was doing. And Malock understood. He understood that far too well, especially when he thought about Vashnas.

Because they couldn't stand there forever, the crew had to figure out a way to move Kinker's body out of the city and back onto the ship. Malock had made the decision that they would have to head back home now, because they had finally reached World's End and done what they had come here to do. No one protested, but a few sailors did seem to be a little reluctant to leave such a beautiful city so soon (although in Malock's eyes the city no longer looked as beautiful as it once did).

Banika, as cool and collected as she ever was, turned up with a stretcher that she claimed to have bought from a katabans salesman. How she had managed to buy it when they had no money and none of them could speak the language of the katabans, Malock didn't know, but he knew Banika had her ways of doing things and he didn't always know how she did it. At least no one was trying to get them, so he supposed that she didn't steal it at least.

However she got it, the stretcher allowed the crew to move Kinker's body with far less trouble than they ordinarily would have. Malock led the procession out of the city, remembering the exact route that they had used to find the Temple of the Gods. He remembered it only because Vashnas had shown him it when they were walking and he was trying to savor every last memory he had of her, now that she was gone.

As before, the katabans moved out of the way, making room for the crew to pass through with little difficulty. Also as before, most of the katabans watched the mortals hauling Kinker's corpse out of the city. Malock didn't know what the katabans were thinking or if they knew why Kinker was dead. All he knew was that he was glad they weren't bothering him and the others. Maybe they were still under orders by Kano or Tinkar not to.

Soon the procession reached the gates, which they passed through, and not long after that, the *Iron Wind* came into view again. It looked as battered and beaten as ever and Malock didn't think it would be able to make the journey back north, especially now that he was unsure if they had the protection of Kano anymore.

Yet the *Iron Wind* was not alone. Berthed next to it was a gigantic hulk of a ship, completely black and apparently made entirely of metal. It looked completely different from any ship Malock had seen; in fact, he wasn't even sure it could sail because it didn't have any sails, at least from what he could see. Amid the ship's smokestacks was a gray flag that fluttered in the wind, too high up for Malock to make out its precise design.

"Oh great," said Jenur as the procession stopped at the edge of the jungle. "What the hell is *that*?"

"Not sure," said Malock. "Could be a trap."

"Should we wait here, then, Captain?" said Banika.

Malock shook his head. "We have to go back to the ship eventually. I mean, it's not like we have very much left to lose, right? Let's just go down to the beach and see who it is."

So the procession started again, heading down to the dock. The gigantic metal ship was berthed on the other side of the dock, but it wasn't until they were on the dock themselves that a familiar female voice shouted, "Hey!"

Malock looked up in time to see Hanarova standing at the bulwarks of the other ship. On the ship's starboard were written the words *Clockwork Heart*, which he thought was the name of the ship. That didn't tell him what Hanarova was doing there, though.

She climbed onto the bulwarks of the *Clockwork Heart* and landed on the deck with ease. Malock gestured for the rest of his crew to take Kinker's corpse up to the ship even as she approached him with a smile on her face. It was an amused smile, though, and slightly incredulous, as if she could not believe that she was seeing them.

"I see you made it to World's End in one piece," said Hanarova in an overly sweet voice. "Good job. I thought for sure the Historic God would have killed you, but I guess he wasn't very hungry."

Malock regarded Hana with distaste. "Kinker's dead."

Hana didn't even blink at that. "Who?"

"A member of my crew," said Malock. "Vashnas is also dead."

"Oh, I know who *that* is," said Hana. "I am sorry to hear about that. Anything I can do for you?"

"Tell your mistress that she's an evil bitch who I hope suffers from rust on a regular basis," Malock said.

Hana quirked an eyebrow. "Tell her that yourself."

"How, pray tell, am I supposed to do that?" said Malock.

"She's right here," said Hana, gesturing at the *Clockwork Heart* with her head.

Malock looked at the giant ship. "She's inside the ship?"

"She *is* the ship," said Hana. "I told you about our ship, didn't I? She decided to come here in order to find out how successful your voyage was."

Smoke blew out of the *Clockwork Heart*'s massive smokestacks, which Malock could only assume was the Mechanical Goddess's way of confirming Hana's words.

"It was an absolute disaster," said Malock. "A mistake from the start. Not helped in the least by your conniving mistress, who lied to Vashnas and caused us great misery in the end. And I know that you knew all about it."

Hana shrugged. "So what if I did? You think I care? The Mechanical Goddess has had me do all kinds of horrible things over the years. Besides, based on the rumors *I* heard, it was Kano who killed Vashnas, not my mistress. So who are you really angry at?"

Malock wanted to say, 'Everyone,' which would have been the truth. He was angry at Kano, Tinkar, the Mechanical Goddess, Hana, and everyone else who had ever caused him or the rest of the crew grief on their voyage. He wished that he himself was a god so he could teach them a lesson for causing so much grief and sorrow.

Instead, Malock said, "It doesn't matter. We're going home now."

Hana glanced at the *Iron Wind*. "She doesn't look like a very good seagoing vessel."

"She will have to do," said Malock. "We don't have the time or money to get her fixed."

"You know," said Hana, looking at the *Clockwork Heart*, "we do have some repair equipment on board. If you want—"

"I want nothing to do with you or your mistress," said Malock. "And I mean *nothing*. Do you understand that?"

Hana raised her hands defensively. "Sorry. I was just being friendly."

Malock laughed hollowly. "After all I've been through, you have the audacity—the sheer *audacity*—to assume I give a damn about what you were trying to be. I don't. I really don't."

Hana shrugged. "Your loss. How do you plan to get home when your ship looks like she'll sink as soon as she gets too full of water?"

"I said we will manage," said Malock. He looked and noticed that most of his crew was now on board the ship. "I have to go. It was horrible seeing you."

"Same here," Hana muttered as Malock walked past her.

Malock made his way up the ramp with little trouble, where

Banika met him at the top.

"Kinker's corpse was placed inside the medical room," said Banika, following Malock to the door of his stateroom. "Ranof is currently preparing his body for burial."

Malock put his hand on the doorknob of his stateroom and looked at her in annoyance. "And? What do you want me to say?"

"We are currently awaiting your decision as to what should be done with Kinker's body," said Banika. "We can either take him home or dump his body into the sea."

Malock almost said, 'Dump him into the sea,' but then he remembered Kano killing Vashnas and he said instead, "We'll drop off his body on Destan on the way back. Maybe we'll even stop for repairs there."

Banika, as usual, showed no particular signs of emotion at his orders. "I shall inform Ranof and the rest of the crew about your decision."

Malock was already inside his stateroom before Banika finished speaking. He slammed the door shut behind himself and slouched over to his desk. He didn't dare look at the sofa, not wanting to spark all of the memories he had of sleeping with Vashnas on it.

He sat down in his chair behind the desk and lowered his face into his hands. And he cried once more.

Continued in:

The Return of Prince Malock

Book Two in the Prince Malock World

Now available wherever books are sold!

About the Author

Timothy L. Cerepaka writes fantasy stories as an indie author. He is the author of the Mages of Martir fantasy novels, the Tournament of the Gods fantasy novels, and The War-Torn Kingdom fantasy novels. He lives in Texas.

Find out more at his website: www.timothylcerepaka.com.

Other books by
Timothy L. Cerepaka

Prince Malock World:

The Mad Voyage of Prince Malock

The Return of Prince Malock

The New Era of Prince Malock

The Coronation of Prince Malock

Mages of Martir:

The Mage's Grave

The Mage's Limits

The Mage's Sea

The Mage's Ghost

Two Worlds:

Reunification

Alliance

Allegiance

Retaliation

Desinence

Tournament of the Gods:

Gathering of the Chosen

Betrayal of the Chosen

Invasion of the Chosen

Ascension of the Chosen

The War-Torn Kingdom:

Kingdom of Magicians

Kingdom of Heirs

Kingdom of Dragons

Kingdom of Gods

Kingdom of Demons

www.ingramcontent.com/pod-product-compliance
Lightning Source LLC
Chambersburg PA
CBHW020632020726
47494CB00001B/160